The Accidental American

Novels by Robert Upton:

The Big Tour

A Killing In Real Estate

The Faberge Egg

Dead On The Stick

Fade Out

A Golden Fleecing

Who'd Want To Kill Old George? (Société
Des Organisme Award winner)

Excerpts from previous reviews:

"Here Upton deserves a standing ovation for a turn-up that is, literally one for the books." *Publishers Weekly*

"... well drawn and realistic. The writing is breezy and irreverent." *The New York Times Sunday Book Review*

"Upton's knife-edge wit rivals Ben Johnson." *Publishers Weekly*

"Upton's style is fast, upbeat and funny." *Rocky Mountain News*

"Robert Upton is one of the keenest social satirists writing today." *Melvin Van Peebles*

"... the novel is extremely well-written." *Clarion Ledger/Jackson Daily News*

"Upton, a gifted and witty writer, has done a good job." *Minneapolis Star Tribune*

"A jem of a novel!" *Joliet Herald News*

"... well- worked-out, snappily written and often irreverent ..." *Newgate Callendar, The New York Times*

"... daring witty novel ... the story arrives at a socko finish." *Publishers Weekly*

The Accidental American

Robert Upton

To order additional copies of this book, contact:
Xlibris
844-714-8691
www.Xlibris.com
Orders@Xlibris.com
849194

CONTENTS

Affidavit of Christopher Rousby...xi

Chapter 1   Name as Destiny 1
Chapter 2   Bound for America 19
Chapter 3   Lost at Sea 41
Chapter 4   The New World..58
Chapter 5   Zeus doth not bring all Men's Plans to Fulfillment 72
Chapter 6   Running around with Cotton Mather........................ 144
Chapter 7   The Politics of New York 203
Chapter 8   Boys Night Out 214
Chapter 9   London..229
Chapter 10 Hockley-in-the-Hole 252
Chapter 11 Homecoming...267
Chapter 12 Letters Home...282
Chapter 13 Limping Home...296
Chapter 14 The Letter of the Law 302

Being a True Tale of His Sailings
with the Infamous and Notorious Pyrate
Captain Kidd

Including a Ribald Report on the Economic and Social Conditions
of America in the late 17th century, as well as a
Tasteful Account of the Villianies, Rapes,
Debaucheries, Mayhems, Murthers and
Plunderings along the way

Affidavit of Christopher Rousby

Having been commanded by the Honourable Lords of His Royal Majesty's Admiralty Court to render a full account of my recent voyage with Captain William Kidd, I hereby sweare that everything I write shall be the truth and nothing but the truth, so help me God.

Fully three days have passed since I thus began. I write slowly because I am not a writer but a sailor--or pyrate, as the Lords of Admiralty would have it. Also--and this is more than sufficient reason by itself--while I write I enjoy a private cell rather than the vomituous, disease-ridden, rat-infested pit to which I am otherwise confined with a hundred other vermin-laden inmates in this Godforsaken hole that is Newgate prison. The cell in which I presently and gratefully find myself is not much larger than a sail locker, and although it is full four floors above the dungeon, with an open, barred window at one end, there is still no relief from the stench that hangs over the prison like an invisible cloud. Still, here I can be comparably comfortable for the short time remaining me, while I attempt to write my confession.

It occurs to me--for the little chance the Captain and I have of coming out of this alive--that I might just as well slash my wrists and write my story quickly in my own blood. Yet unmerciful as is each waking moment in this hell, there is something within me that will not allow me to lop off even a minute of the precious but horrid time remaining to me. I also find, looking back at this last paragraph, that

I am rather better at this writing thing than I had supposed and, surprisingly, I find I'm rather enjoying it. Not the "affidavit" part--that is of necessity much too lacking in character, plot and atmosphere to be of interest to anyone other than the jurists who will hang me--but the introspective part about the will to live even in the face of utter despair. Also, the brief mention of jail conditions in 17th century England I think rather nicely imparts broader social meaning to the work, much in the manner of Mr. Defoe's writings. Pity there is no way to present an affidavit in the fine wrappings of literature, but to present such a document to my judges would be my death knell for certain, for the law requires that words be precise and capable of but one meaning, whereas the poet in me cries out for resonance and ambiguity.

The facts then--hew to the facts, damn you! Captain Kidd is accused of killing one of his crew and that is fact. He did strike Gunner Thomas Moore across the head with a bucket which did proximately cause the man's later demise, but only when the blackguard threatened to cause a mutiny and take the ship a-pyrating. And 'tis fact the Captain did later capture the Quedah Merchant and all its cargo (which was unfortunately the property of the powerful East India Company), but 'twas only to placate the mutinous crew and spare the lives of the God-fearing sailors amongst us.

But how am I to explain life aboard a pyrate ship to a group of Lord Justices whose nautical experiences consist of nothing more than an afternoon's punting on the Thames? And if I were to point out that Captain Kidd's so-called pyrating expedition was sponsored by none other than King William and six of the most powerful gentlemen in Parliament, I should find my head lopped off for treason long before I could be hanged for pyracy. Prithee, if my Lords will indulge me, I should like to begin at the beginning, confident that when all the extenuating facts and circumstances are known, ye just and Honourable Lords will see fit to release Captain Kidd and me.

"Gaoler, more ink!"

Chapter 1

Name as Destiny

Having been christened Christopher (after Christopher Columbus) at my birth in 1675, I suppose it was inevitable that I should one day go to America, although if I had known then what a cursed place it is, I'd as soon have shipped to the wilds of Ireland. But as I was a young man, more than full enough educated by my own reckoning, and destined for fame and fortune beyond the meager capacity of the seaside village in which I had been born and reared over the previous fifteen years, caution played little part in my decision. Doubtless, the reckless spirit of adventure resides in some measure in all boys, but in most it is checked by the wisdom of a cautious father, until that role can be assumed by a wife.

My father, however, the somewhat dreamy headmaster of the village school, rich in imagination if little else, was a fireside adventurer who filled my head with tales of ancient Greek travelers and modern day explorers such as Christopher Columbus, with never a thought for the consequences of his romantic tales. In other families a practical mother would have seen the danger and rushed in to correct it with a solid dose of reality. But alas, my mother had died only a few minutes after giving life to me, which I'm told was the cause of my father's dreamy mien. Also, while recounting the reasons for my destined departure for America, it is perhaps well that I mention Mr. Halburton, who offered me a handsome sum if I would but stand by to row him out to his ship when it might appear in Lyme Bay.

The arrival of Mr. Halburton and the veiled lady in our village on a warm day was, save the sardine run, the most exciting event of the season. I was just hauling my dinghy up onto the beach when I looked up to see the Southampton Coach pull to a halt in front of the Lyme Bay Inn where the owner, Mr. Hoghey, stood with his hat in hand. That a coach should stop at our village was unusual enough, but the two splendid people who stepped down from the coach were a vision such as none in our village had ever glimpsed. Indeed, had it not been for the sword at his side and the pistol in his belt, in these parts a man so dressed might risk being called a fop. His waistcoat, out of which a great scarf and collar bloomed like a spring lily, was of a scarlet material that glistened like the sea in the sunlight. And although the sun was already quite bright on that lovely afternoon, it seemed to grow in intensity at the moment the veiled lady followed him out from the cab.

It was impossible to see her face beneath the broad hat and veil she wore, yet the sight of her incredibly pinched waist alerted me instantly to a kind of beauty I had, until this moment, only sensed from my exotic imaginings of London or Paris. And the foot she extended from under the silvery skirt that billowed out like a wind-full sail, encased in pink satin of all things, was scarcely larger than a plover. But it was when she turned her profile to me in addressing Mr. Hoghey, showing her bosom perched unnaturally high and her rear thrust out like a rooster's tail, that I sensed myself not in the presence of a mere cosmopolitan lady, but of an ethereal being, floated down from the sky like an angel on brightly stained glass.

Lest the reader leap to the conclusion that I, already years beyond puberty, was experiencing nothing less than a sexual awakening, let me hasten to explain that I had recently experienced a dalliance with an older woman named Rebecca Hay, who had turned sixteen that summer. Rebecca was a green-eyed girl, although it was hard to tell as her eyes were always half closed, and one had a tendency to wink a lot, usually following a statement I only vaguely understood, or one that I understood but couldn't believe I had understood. To meet Rebecca

Hay, one might think she was so-called because hay seemed always to be sticking to her--in her hair, upon her blouse (which was always slipping from one shoulder or the other) or her skirt (which always seemed to be riding high on one bare leg or the other)--just as a man who tends graves is called Sexton, or a bricklayer Mason. But no, Rebecca Hay deserved her name solely because she was the daughter of Vicar Hay, who, beside my father, was the only other educated man in the village. Like me, she too was without maternal influence (her mother, if what the wags claimed was true, having run off with a tinker of grand proportions), which would explain Rebecca's wanton ways.

However, until a few weeks ago when I came upon Rebecca in the field where wildflowers grew, where I happened to be chasing butterflies for my collection, I did not know fully what was meant by "wanton ways". It was just something that was usually mentioned by the ladies in the market place whenever Rebecca's name came up, which was quite often--"Rebecca Hay and her wanton ways", much as "Schoolmaster Rousby, that poor dreamer" was heard round the square; or, "the Reverend Hay who was not of this world". It seemed to me at the time that men who were not entirely of this world had two things in common--they had both lost a spouse and gained an education. It was probably one more thing that determined my course for America, as I already knew education to be stifling, although I loved nothing more than a good read, and could see that women and marriage led only to tragedy.

Yet when I stumbled upon Rebecca Hay on that unusually warm summer day while chasing an exquisite Danaus plexippus--sprawled upon the trodden flowers and heather, skirts hiked up round her suntanned knees, blouse slipping this time from both shoulders, revealing two mounds of firm flesh and a dark cleft between, beyond which lay anatomic and erotic depths more mysterious and frightening than the deepest part of the sea--I felt a sudden inexplicable change stirring within me.

"Why, Miss Hay--!" I said, as I crashed through the tall sunflowers and halted just before her.

"Prithee, sir, what do you intend to do with that net--capture me?" she asked, aping a look of fear.

"No, no, not at all," I assured her. "I was in pursuit of Danaus plexippus and had no idea you were here."

"How very cruel you are, Christopher."

Although we had grown up nearby and I'm sure I'd heard her call my name many times, this was the first time it had set off sensations in parts other then my ears. Until this moment it had seemed she was always at a distance, even when passing close by. But now she was astonishingly close, peering at me with her drooped green eyes as if there were no more interesting fellow in the background, and the responsibility caused my heart to beat faster, making me feel bigger and bigger and bigger.

"Why cruel?" I asked, dopily.

"That you should prefer your Miss Plentipussy to me," she answered.

"Plexippus," I corrected. "A butterfly."

"Very well, pin me down," she said, throwing wide her arms and legs and falling back on the grass.

"Ha ha…." I laughed uncertainly. "I don't think you'd like to have pins stuck in your hands and feet and be mounted upon a sheet."

"I've been mounted every place but," she said, setting off a low laugh and a slithering in the grass that brought her skirt up farther and her blouse down still more, till there were very nearly two new rosebuds amongst the wildflowers. "But as for the pin pricks--umm, I might like that too."

Rebecca was causing me great confusion. For as it happened, I had recently come across a volume of Latin verses in my father's library having entirely to do with matters erotica, a term then as new to me as "wanton ways". It was only because the book was kept in the furthest corner of the highest shelf, laid flat behind Ogelthorpe's three volume study of *Agronomy in the New World*, that I chose to bring it out. The first poem, a particularly long though scarcely epic one entitled *Slave Boy*, was the tale of a poor Greek lad taken in battle by the forces of Julius Caesar and consigned to a mistress who used him horribly. He was an incredibly handsome young man but intelligent and resourceful nonetheless and, by dint of his most unusual imagination, did switch the mistress to slave and himself to master. I can't say that I fully understood the poem, as it was filled with expressions such as cunnilingus and fellatio, and other words that appeared not in my dictionary, but I was nevertheless able to understand that Rebecca and I were at that moment when that which is sensed is far more powerful than that which is understood.

"I have recently read a poem," I blurted.

Rebecca withdrew a piece of straw from between her lips and said, "Amazing."

"It's about a slave boy who must do everything his mistress commands."

"Everything?"

I nodded. "It's in Latin."

"Is it a love poem?"

"No. Well, perhaps, in a strange way."

"By Ovid?"

"I'm not sure. Could you recite a bit?"

"Gladly," she said, and began to recite:

> Do not be in too great a hurry
> to attain the limits of your pleasure.
> Learn, by skillful dallying,
> to reach the goal by gentle, pleasant stages.
> When you have found the sanctuary of bliss,
> Let no foolish modesty arrest your hand.
> Then will you see the love-light trembling in her eyes,
> even as the rays of the sun sparkle on the dancing waves,
> Then will follow gentle moanings
> mingled with the murmurings of love,
> soft groans and sighs and whispered words
> that sting and lash desire.
> But now beware!
> Take heed, lest, cramming on too much sail,
> you speed too swiftly for your mistress.

Now you should suffer her to outstrip you.
Speed on together towards the promised haven.
The height of bliss is reached when,
unable any longer to withstand the wave of pleasure,
lover and mistress, at one and the same moment,
are overcome.

She gasped as she finished, then looked up at me and asked, "Is that the one?"

"No," I replied. For my poem had nothing to do with sailboat racing. "In my poem, the mistress commands the slave to lie beside her."

"Then come, lie beside me," Rebecca said, patting the flattened grass beside her. When I hesitated she said, "Your mistress commands it."

So I went and lay beside her and stared up at the clouds. I was just making a duck when Rebecca interrupted. She put her lips close to my ear and whispered, "What did your mistress command her slave to do?"

Hesitantly I replied, "Take off all his clothes."

"Then take them off," she whispered. Then, in a firmer voice, "Your mistress commands it."

Concentrating on the duck, I slowly unbuttoned my shirt and wiggled out of it, one sleeve at a time.

"Now the interesting part," she said. "I command it."

Slowly, numbly, I unbuckled my belt and slid my breeches down.

"Well what a pleasant surprise," she said. "Now your mistress commands that you undress her."

"Yes, mistress," I said, and did as I was bade.

"Do not be in too great a hurry," she warned at one point. Then added, "But let no foolish modesty arrest your hand."

She led me then to the sanctuary of bliss and everything was suddenly clear. Or so it seemed. But I still had much to learn from my mistress, from whom soft groans and sighs and whispered words were now issuing.

"Beware!" she cried.

But too late. I lay very still and watched the duck waddle off while Rebecca instructed me in the meaning of one of those Latin words.

With my education completed, and ready once again, I mounted and drove my spur deeply into my courser's side.

"Whoa," Rebecca said. "Learn, by skillful dallying, to reach the goal by gentle, pleasant stages."

I obeyed my mistress: Then followed gentle moanings mingled with the murmurings of love that sting and lash desire.

"Take heed, lest, cramming on too much sail, you speed too swiftly for your mistress," Rebecca panted as we sped on together towards the promised haven. She writhed and heaved and bucked and cried out to heaven until at last, unable any longer to withstand the pleasure, lover and mistress, at one and the same moment, were overcome.

And that is why I say, my first glimpse of that lovely lady as she stepped from her carriage, was no mere sexual awakening. By this time Rebecca and I had passed enough afternoons together--in the meadow, in amongst the rocks on the beach, beside the river that runs into the sea, and in the hayloft--that by now our game of slave boy and mistress had proceeded firmly to one of slave girl and master.

Indeed, I had scarcely pulled my dinghy up onshore before Rebecca appeared in the square looking for me. Seeing the two women together, one looking more radiant than the sun, the other like something left out too long in it, I was filled with confused feelings of desire and loyalty. Just fifteen and already a fickle cad. But in fairness to myself I must point out that long after Mr. Hoghey had escorted the lady inside, Rebecca stood staring at the handsome gentleman with an expression very like the one she wore with me when I had found the sanctuary of bliss.

When the gentleman had seen to the unloading of their portmanteau, he, rather than follow his lovely wife inside, turned to the sea and stared out across her as if searching for something. His hair, black and smooth as a raven's feathers, got up a little in the wind, but everything else about the man remained unruffled. His eyes were but dark slits set wide above high sharp cheekbones from which two deep furrows, separated by a long straight nose, fell straight down to a broad lean jaw divided exactly in half by a deep cleft. He wore a moustache, black as his hair, and trimmed unnaturally thin in such a way as I had never seen before.

He had to be a Londoner, yet there was something foreign about him as well. Nor did the ambiguity stop there. For although he seemed every bit a powerful and sufficient man, there was a fugitive look in those slitted eyes that roved the horizon. When he saw me standing there by my boat, the eyes relaxed and opened a bit as he motioned me forward. I climbed directly up over the stones with my string of flounder and walked across the hard flat place to where the gentleman stood. As I approached I noticed the single flaw in his otherwise perfect face, a long scar running diagonally along the left cheek.

"Is that your boat?" he asked, in a voice that fit him perfectly, broad, flat and spare. It was an English voice all right, but it seemed to have been clipped and shorn of all its ornaments.

"Yes sir," I answered. She was a stout dinghy that had washed up on the rocks after last winter's storm. When no one came to claim her, I patched her up and she was now one of the best fishing boats on the beach.

"I have need of a good man with a boat," he said. "I'm expecting a ship sometime within the next one or two days. I have no objection to hiring a boy, but he must be dependable. He must be on the lookout each day at dawn and remain here until my ship comes. When it does he must come fetch me and my--wife, at the inn, and row us and our baggage out to the boat. And for that service," he said, pulling a small purse from his pocket, "I shall pay twenty shillings now and thirty more when we've been delivered to our ship. Can I depend on you?"

"You can, sir," I said, thrusting my hand eagerly forward. Fifty shillings was more than my father earned in a week, which convinced me that this stranger was either rich as Croesus or mad as a hatter. As I watched the coins tumbling from his hand to mine, glistening like waves dancing in the sun, it dawned on me that I was suddenly one of the richest young men in the village. And when I saw Rebecca out of the corner of my eye, I felt myself again growing bigger and bigger and bigger.

"What's your name, lad?" my employer asked, as I stuffed my unearned wages into a pocket.

"Christopher Rousby, sir."

"Mine is Halburton," he said, extending his hand. It was large and surprisingly rough for a gentleman. "I have one further request of you, Christopher."

"Yes sir...?"

"If you should see any strangers laying about, or if you should hear of anyone inquiring about me or my wife, I'd like you to come tell me immediately. Will you do that?"

"Yes sir," I answered, knowing now that I was surely right, he was a fugitive, hoping to make his ship before being arrested. I also knew, just as surely, that even the grand sum of fifty shillings was not nearly enough for the dangerous assignment to which I had just consented. But I was adventurous as well as mercenary at that young age, and so it never occurred to me to resign.

The only question I had was, who would be after Mr. Halburton and why? It would not be the King's soldiers come in their uniforms, for if so, Mr. Halburton would have so identified his pursuers, I reasoned. No, these would be anonymous men whom Mr. Halburton had never before seen, hired assassins. But hired by whom?

Then something occurred to me about the way Mr. Halburton had said: "my--wife" sort of hesitating, as if he were unused to the use of the word. This could mean that they were either newly married, or that Mr. Halburton was lying, they were not married at all. Certainly if I were married to such a woman I should state it proudly, not stammer it. Then if they were not married they were eloping, I reasoned. And they hoped to get away on a ship before her father's men caught up with them. Much as I wanted to test my deductive reasoning on Mr. Halburton, even if only to let him know what a clever boy he had hired, I was clever enough to keep my thoughts to myself. Instead I asked, "How will I recognize your boat, Mr. Halburton?"

"She's the bark Jan Kees, a merchantman of about two hundred tons. Do you have a good glass?"

"No, sir."

"I have one in my bag. You can come round for it later."

"Yes, sir."

"And Chris--"

"Yes, sir?"

"It isn't necessary to address me as sir."

"Yes--Mr. Halburton."

"Keep a sharp eye," he warned, then turned round and walked back to the inn. When he arrived at the door he paused to look down the road in the direction from which he had come, then stooped and went inside.

The moment he was gone, Rebecca gathered up her skirt and ran barefoot across the square as fast as she could, crying, "Who is he, what did he give you?"

"His name is Mr. Halburton, and he has hired me to be his lookout," I replied, in a dignified voice befitting my new station.

"How much?"

When I told her the amount, she repeated it loudly enough that Mr. Halburton could have heard it in his room.

"Quiet!" I ordered. "The man is a gentleman"

"I could see that plain enough," she replied. "And his wife is plainly a lady."

"She's not his wife," I said.

"Not his wife…! How do you know this?"

When I explained to Rebecca the theory I could not mention to Mr. Halburton, she was clearly impressed, though not so much by my keen wits as by the romance of the situation.

"The families must be sworn enemies," she decided. "If she marries a Halburton, her brothers will kill him, so they're fleeing to Europe to escape them."

"Not Europe, America," I said.

"America…! You don't think people like that go to America, do you?"

"I'm sure of it," I said. "For the ship they're sailing on is an American."

"He told you that?"

"He didn't have to. Their ship is the Jan Kees, the Dutchman after whom the Americans are called Yankees. They're sailing for America, Rebecca. And someday I'll do the same."

"You'll do no such thing," Rebecca said.

"I will."

"You won't," she said, with a quiet conviction that piqued my curiosity.

"Why do you say that?" I asked.

"Because I missed my monthly."

"Your monthly what?"

"You know--when it stops it means you've made a baby."

"You…" I said, pointing at her stomach.

"Us," she said pointing at me.

"But--you said it couldn't happen. You said you knew how to stop it."

"I was wrong," Rebecca said with a shrug. "And that's why you won't be going to America. You're going to be a father."

"But I'm only fifteen years old!"

"So…? I'm only seventeen."

"Seventeen…!" I gasped. "You told me you were sixteen."

"Approximately."

"You lied…!"

"That's not fair, Christopher. I only said it to spare your feelings."

"Well I wish you hadn't!" I blurted. "I wish you would have told me you were seventeen, and let me decide for myself if I wanted my feelings spared."

"You aren't sorry, are you Christopher?"

"Of course I'm sorry. Now I can't go to America."

"But you love me, don't you? You said you did. Remember the murmurings of love, soft groans and sighs and whispered words that sting and lash desire?"

"But now beware," I reminded her. "It's true, I said those things, but only after you had said them to me. I just thought that was the way it was done."

"Do you mean you were lying?"

"Not lying exactly. But they were just words we say when we want something, like prayer."

"Christopher Rousby, thou art profane!"

"Perhaps so. But thou wast no less profane than I."

"How dare you say such a thing to me! You know I only did it because I knew you wanted it!"

"You wanted it just as much as I did."

"I certainly did not! What a horrid thing to say to the woman who is about to become your wife and the mother of your child. I demand that you apologize, Christopher."

"I only spoke the truth," I protested weakly.

"Apologize!" she demanded.

"Very well, I'm sorry," I said.

"I accept your apology," she said, pulling up her blouse that had slipped off one shoulder during the argument. "Now we must go and see my father and tell him we wish to be married as soon as possible."

"But how can we be married when we have no money?" I protested.

"We have fifty shillings," she said, pointing to the pocket in which the first payment lay. "And," she said, opening her palm, "two pieces of gold."

I stared wide-eyed for a moment at the two coins in her hand, then looked up at her foxy grin and asked, "Are they real?" for I had never before seen a gold piece.

"Of course they're real. You can see where they've been bitten," she said.

"But--where did you get them?"

"They were a gift, a wedding gift."

"From whom?"

"A friend."

"What friend."

"Never mind. There is one for the bride and one for the groom," she said, taking one from her palm and trying to press it upon me.

"No," I protested. "It's yours. And anyway I should be afraid of losing so much money."

"Don't be silly, Christopher. After we're married everything I own will be yours. So you had better get used to handling it right now," she said, wrapping my fingers around the warm, gold coin.

I was terribly confused. Until today I never had more than several shillings at a time, and suddenly I had enough money to go to America. But with so much money I felt even less disposed to marriage than a moment before, and an even greater desire to sail for America. "This is a lot of money, Rebecca. But what will we do when it's gone?" I pleaded.

"Don't worry, there'll be more," she said.

"From where?" I asked, for it would surely not come from my fishing.

"The Lord will provide us a way," she said.

It seemed to me that along with a baby, Rebecca had also suddenly acquired a great respect for religion. Whereas I, on the other hand, had just cause to remain irreligious, because until Mr. Halburton had come along, the Lord had scarcely ever provided me with much more than a shilling.

Rebecca, however, seemed to have no doubts about the future as she took my arm and led me across the square, talking gaily of hearth and home. Near the front of the inn I stopped, halting her in mid-sentence.

"I can't go to see your father just now," I said.

"Why not?"

"I have duties to perform for Mr. Halburton."

"But surely they can wait for an hour over something so important as your engagement.

"I'm sorry, they cannot," I said, plucking her hand from my arm. "As a condition of my employment Mr. Halburton requires that I be on watch day and night." This was an exaggeration that would save me scant little time, but at that moment each hour of freedom was something to be grasped for dear life. "When my task is accomplished, I'll go with you to your father," I promised.

"Well, I suppose another day or so won't matter," she allowed. "But mind you, come the moment your ship has arrived."

"I will," I again assured her. "But if you'd care to come up the hill in the meantime, there's a snug place between the rocks…"

"Not now, Christopher. It wouldn't be proper," she said, backing away, then spinning and dashing off calling, "Come as soon as you've finished!"

"Yes, when I'm finished," I repeated as I watched her skip across the square.

My head, which only minutes before had been spilling over with romance, intrigue and danger, was now suddenly filled with visions of despairing domesticity. And America, which had until now figured so prominently in my plans, was but the vanished ambition of youth. That a life and career could so drastically change over nothing more than a moment's pleasure was both incomprehensible and dreadfully unfair. Yet, being an honorable young man, I was resigned to do my duty by Rebecca.

My despondency did not escape my employer's notice when I came round later that evening to collect his glass. He and his lady were going in to supper when I entered the inn. He had changed from his smooth and colorful finery to a plain black suit of a homespun quality. Yet, set against a white scarf and white hosiery that displayed a muscled leg, he seemed even more properly the gentleman this time than he had before. His lady, however, had changed to an even more elegant dress that revealed her shoulders and rustled like dried leaves when she walked towards me. She wore no hat this time, revealing a great pile of honey-colored hair held aloft by jeweled combs; neither did she wear her veil, revealing a face of such grace and serenity that not even her apprehension could cloud it.

"Is something the matter?" Mr. Halburton asked, as they both hurried to me.

Realizing that my absorption with my own problem had alerted Mr. Halburton to his, I quickly assured him that all was well. When he introduced the woman at his side as Mrs. Halburton, she smiled, whether at me or the unfamiliar appellation, I wasn't sure.

"You are most kind to help us," she said in a soft and furry voice, as different from the village women as ocean to mountain. "Have you had your supper?"

While I tried to explain that I both had and hadn't, she took my elbow and steered me into the dining room, where Mr. Hoghey waited smilingly with clasped hands. Seeing me, the smile disappeared, until Mr. Halburton informed him that we would be three for supper, Then he led us to the large round table in front of the hearth, where a rack of mutton and two great slabs of pork lay roasting on the spit.

Although I was quite nervous at having supper with Mr. Halburton and his lady, the prospect of meat after weeks of nothing but flounder and sole caused me to overcome my anxiety rather easily. So by the time Mr. Hoghey brought the meat to the table, I was more than ready to tear into it with fish knife and fingers--until I was arrested by something most curious. From her purse, Mrs. Halburton produced two rolled white scarves which she and Mr. Halburton proceeded to unwrap, revealing within each, a silver knife and another similar instrument having a three pronged head extruding from its handle. This latter instrument, I discovered as I watched them eat, was used in place of the fingers, to both hold the meat while cutting it into small bits, then to stab each bit and carry it to the mouth. It seemed at first a terribly cumbersome process, replete with many extra motions, whose only virtue I could see was to spare the fingers from the hot meat. Yet, after a bit of it, it seemed not at all unnatural, and whatever extra time was spent in the manipulation of the utensils was almost saved by not having to lick the fingers of fat and wipe them on one's breeches. Even though I had no *fork*, as I later learned it was so aptly named, its bare presence accounted for some changes in the way I devoured my own meat. I used my fingers as little as possible and cut each chunk into a size no bigger than an apple before bringing it to my mouth on my fish knife.

Something else I discovered about gentlefolk, as I watched them eat--they conversed at almost the same time. Mrs. Halburton would take a small bite, chew and swallow it, and then address a question to me. It required a few questions before I understood that I was expected to divide my attention equally between food and conversation, unlike the custom of the village which required that everything on the plate be devoured in haste and silence, and only then was it time to talk.

"I take it you live with your parents…?" Mrs. Halburton inquired.

I put down my meat for a moment, while I explained the sad circumstances that accounted for our reduced family. Mrs. Halburton seemed genuinely more distressed by the news than politely sympathetic, but seemed to take some solace in the knowledge that my father was a teacher.

"It's a sad thing to grow up without a mother, but all the same, you are a young man with prospects," she said.

"Once I had prospects, but no more," I said, causing Mrs. Halburton to stifle a laugh with her napkin.

Mr. Halburton, too, seemed amused as he asked, "All played out already, are you, lad?"

I said nothing, although I could have wiped the smiles from their faces easily enough. Too, my attention had been drawn to the door by the entrance of two men. In the dim light I thought at first they might be the assassins come for Mr. Halburton, but when they came further into the light I saw that it was Mr. Dunston and his son, Percy, dressed in his best suit and carrying a bag. The Dunstons lived in a great house several miles from the village and were one of the richest families for several counties around, and so I knew them even though they were hardly aware of my existence.

They walked across the room without a word to anyone and took the table next to ours. Mr. Dunston seemed annoyed, and Percy a bit sheepish, which wasn't unusual, as Percy was often in trouble with his father. Mr. Dunston had sent him away to school the year before, but Percy had returned in some sort of disgrace and promptly ran up some large gambling debts with Mr. Terlow, an itinerant horse dealer.

I didn't think Mr. Halburton had paid them any heed, until I leaned over to tell him who they were, and saw his hand resting on the pistol beneath his coat. Satisfied, he removed his hand and went back to his supper, without having interrupted his conversation with Mrs. Halburton. I couldn't be sure that she had noticed anything, but for the rest of the evening she was not so gay as she had been.

Whether her unease was prompted by fear for Mr. Halburton's life or annoyance with the Dunstons, who were quarrelling in angry whispers, I couldn't say. I tried not to overhear but instead concentrated solely on the beautiful woman who sat across the table from me, but it was impossible not to hear at least some of Mr. Dunston's angry admonishments. It seemed this time Percy had done something quite serious, and his father was sending him to work off his debt with Mr. Terlow, who would make a man of him, while Percy wished to remain a boy at home. Whatever the reason, before Mr. Halburton or I had finished supper, Mrs. Halburton asked to be excused. Mr. Halburton offered to take her up to their room, but she insisted he stay with me and finish supper, as she was capable of going to her room by herself.

"Mrs. Halburton seems a very independent woman," I dared to remark, after she had gone.

"She'd better be," Mr. Halburton replied, staring at the doorway through which she had just passed.

We ate the rest of the meal in silence, and when we'd finished, Mr. Halburton left me at the table while he went up to the room for his glass. Meanwhile, the heated argument at the next table had shifted to agriculture, hay in particular. Or so it seemed, until I realized it was my Rebecca they were discussing.

"When are you goin' to get it through your thick skull that it don't matter if Rebecca Hay has been with every man in England, unless you can prove it!" Mr. Dunston said, while knocking cruelly on poor Percy's head.

Realizing that this conversation was not about agriculture, but paternity, and perhaps my future as well, I immediately stopped trying to shut it out and pulled my chair closer. Percy complained that his father was hurting him, then grew sulky, so that I had to lean a bit to hear him. He claimed to understand the injustice of the law, but he failed to understand what he perceived to be his father's injustice.

"Why must *I* be the one to leave?" he whispered. "Why couldn't you have offered her a bit more money and sent *her* away?"

"I've agreed to pay her more than enough as it is!" Mr. Dunston replied angrily. "Today she agreed to pick another poor wretch to be her husband, but who can say she'll feel the same way tomorrow. Especially if you're around to tempt her. For as much as I've agreed to give the greedy bitch, the thought o'marryin' you and livin' in my house instead o' in a mud hut with some gypsy poacher, is goin' t' be a big temptation for the girl in the next few months. Besides which, I can't trust you to stay away from her either," he added.

"Father...!" Percy exclaimed. "How can you think for a moment that I could ever marry such a girl--a girl who wears no undergarments and behaves constantly like a cat in heat!"

At this Mr. Dunston stared quietly at his son and shook his head sadly.

When Mr. Halburton appeared in the doorway a moment later with his glass in hand, I jumped up from the table and hurried across the room. There was more to hear from poor Percy, but I had already heard quite enough for my purposes.

Chapter 2

Bound for America

My Dear Rebecca,

Your offer to marry me and furnish me a child is, I feel, an undeserved honor which I cannot accept, in that under the existing circumstances I feel Mr. Percy Dunston to be far more deserving of your generosity and you of his.

I realize the senior Mr. Dunston's enthusiasm for this union is not as great as my own, but be assured the law is on your side.

As to Mr. Percy Dunston, whom you will find in Mr. Terlow's employ at any horse show, I'm sure that whatever hesitancy that good gentleman has at present, can be easily overcome if you will but behave in such prim and proper manner as befits the wife of a gentleman--rather as you behaved with me at our last meeting. Also, be sure to wear undergarments.

With sincerest wishes for a happy marriage and a healthy baby, I remain,

Truly and affectionately yours,
Christopher Rousby

P.S. Would you please tell my father that I've gone to
America to seek my fortune and will write when I get
there, as well as return your gold piece with interest.

I was standing upon the deck of the Jan Kees, just past Land's End, at
the time Rebecca was opening this letter, assuming Mr. Hoghey had
carried out my instructions. Her gold piece was now in the hands of
Mr. Crump, master of the ship Jan Kees, and as fine a gentleman as Mr.
Halburton, whose kind intercession was ultimately responsible for my
presence among the ship's few passengers. Besides myself and Mr. and
Mrs. Halburton, there was Benjamin Franks, who was the first Jew I
had ever met outside the Bible, and a black giant called Chindomacuba,
who took great pleasure in telling everyone in his comically squeaky
voice, including Mr. Halburton, that he had no ballocks. They had been
sliced off, he said, by a sultan so that he might tend to his harem without
fear of performing any unwanted additional services. The sultan didn't
know, however, that the slicing only deprived Chindomacuba of the joys
of fatherhood, which the women of the harem weren't at all interested
in, while still allowing him to raise and lower his large staff whenever
the women were of a mind.

Poor Mr. Franks, who I was to learn had failed at a great many
enterprises in London, was on his way to Port Royale on the island
of Jamaica to establish himself in the jewelry business. Of all the
passengers and sailors aboard the Jan Kees, poor Mr. Franks, with his
droopy brown eyes and stringy gray beard, was the least suited for this
long and arduous voyage. He was seasick from the moment he stepped
onto the gangplank, and even the simplest of tasks proved to be so far
beyond his grasp that I was forced to help the poor man at every turn,
lest he do himself serious bodily harm.

We were forced to lay off Land's End for a day while we waited for
a naval escort, due to hostilities with France at that time. Everyone was
nervous while they waited, but once we were in among the squadron
our fear dissolved.

After Chindomacuba and poor Mr. Franks came two merchants
with goods they intended to sell in the Colonies, who fretted constantly

about water in the hold, and were subject to a good deal of teasing by our crew of fifteen. My first few days and nights aboard the big square-rigged vessel, running with the wind on a following sea, all her twenty sails filled to bursting, was as exciting as anything I'd ever experienced. But after a fortnight, monotony had already begun to set in, except with those who were still sick. By the time we reached the Isle of Madeira, I too was feeling sick, though not seasick, but rather homesick. So while Mr. and Mrs. Halburton and poor Mr. Franks poked about the waterfront, and the two merchants did a bit of trading among the natives, I remained aboard ship with Chindomacuba and wrote a letter to my distressed father.

My Dearest Father,

Leaving for America without saying goodbye is, I'm sure you believe, the cruelest thing I could have done to you. Yet please believe me, father, that it was the kindest, for I knew you would have begged me to stay, just as surely as I know I would have left, and in the end I would have only hurt you the more.

There is the possibility that I am wrong and you might have persuaded me to stay, and it is at this moment a possibility to have been devoutly wished, for I love you and miss you terribly, Father. It is only the thought that I will reach that place of which you had dreamed all your life and return soon, rich in money and experience which we will share for the remainder of our lives, that drives me on. My mission is your mission. It is a sacred mission. I go in your place to where you dreamed of going but could not go, because of the sacrifice you were forced to make for me.

Strangely enough, I also go because a similar sacrifice was asked of me. False rumors might reach you concerning my departure, which I'm sure you will know are just that. I go to America only for the noblest of reasons.

   With deepest and warmest love and gratitude for all you have done for me, I am, sir,

Your American son,
Christopher Rousby

It was the saddest letter I had ever written, so unlike the letter to Rebecca, which was the gayest I had ever written. When I had finished it, I went to the bow to fetch Chindomacuba as I had promised, and together we walked across the dock to the Black Porpoise Tavern, where my letter would be picked up by the next ship headed for England.

Mr. Crump had warned me that the Black Porpoise was a place of the most ill-repute, frequented by low women and brawling sailors, some of whom were often found dead in the alley the next morning, so I was eager to see the place. Unfortunately, we seemed to have arrived at a dull moment. To be sure there were a great many seamen in the place who looked the part of cutthroats, and several painted whores, but most were passed out on the filthy sawdust, or sprawled over the few unbroken tables scattered about the gloomy, low-ceilinged room and in no condition to play out the fantasies of a young boy.

So, with Chindomacuba close by my side, we ventured as far as the bar, where the barman took the letter from my hand without a word, and stashed it in a hole in the wall with a stack of others. It seemed a precarious system, but Mr. Crump had assured me that sailors' mail moved throughout the world in this manner and few letters were ever lost, as the brethren of the sea had a reverence for the custom born of a great need.

Our task completed, we left the foul-smelling tavern and stepped back out onto the dock for a much needed breath of fresh sea air. In England the sight of Chindomacuba bursting out of his English clothes would cause crowds to gape and horses to shy. But here in Madeira, where ships of all nations regularly put in for water, wine and provisions, the waterfront was awash with sailors of every size, shape and color, wearing everything from burnooses to caftans to pantaloons, and the sight of this black giant drew scarcely a sideways glance. Because many of these fierce-looking sailors were drunk and possibly dangerous, I was grateful to have Chindomacuba along, but puzzled as to why he had waited for me before going ashore. When I asked him about this, as we strolled back to the ship, he replied in broken English that he feared being taken as a slave should he venture forth alone.

"You mean they think I'm your--owner?" I asked.

"And master," Chindomacuba said, grinning at the joke we were playing on the unsuspecting white men around us, who would apparently sell a human being for a few bottles of rum.

"But how could they possibly think a small boy capable of controlling a man so big and strong as yourself?" I asked. Chindomacuba didn't understand my question, so using sign language and basic words, I indicated that he could crush me in his hands and run away whenever he chose.

"Run where?" Chindomacuba asked, sweeping his arm in a full circle.

I was of course aware of the practice of slavery, due to my readings of the Bible and the ancient Greeks, but I was not so sorely troubled by it in those days of old as I might have been, simply because there seemed to be at least some cruel justification for making a peaceful servant of an enemy taken in battle. Until this moment, however, it had never occurred to me that a man might be labeled slave only because he was black, and be fairly taken should he roam anywhere in the world but Africa. There was something so unnatural about it--as if God had colored grouse yellow so they might be better seen by hunters--that I was prompted to ask why he did not return to Africa rather than be abroad under such risky conditions.

"Dot where dey catch me up," he answered with a shrug and a laugh, as if enslavement and castration were a great joke.

"But you escaped," I said. "You're free."

"No escape," he said, shaking his great head. "Pirates take de ship. I defend de sultan number one lady, kill many pirates. But den dey catch me up and take de lady for dere pleasure. Take all de ladies, all day, all night. Good gosh, some big party."

"But how is it they didn't kill you?" I asked

"I kill many men, dey want me be pirate. I say no be pirate, dey tie me hands and feet, pull me under de boat--den I be pirate. Den de English catch us up, take us to London. Abolitionist man come help me. He say I no be pirate, be slave, and de judge set me free. Halleluja. Den abolitionist man give me money go home, but I no go home, I go America."

"Why America?"

"Man in jail tell me, in America, man be free."

"White men," I said, "not black men."

Chindomacuba smiled, as if sorry for my ignorance. "In America white men black men all de same. My American jail fran tell me dot."

I was aghast. Chindomacuba was sailing into the very depths of slavery, yet try as I would, he would hear nothing against America. To him it was the land of hope and promise, where even a black harem servant with no ballocks could become a prince. It was as if he had sat at his jail friend's feet, just as I had sat at my father's feet, listening to romantic tales of adventure and exploration--only his story-teller had gotten it all wrong. My father was at least aware that the Americans practiced slavery, but confident that they would soon cease such uncivilized behavior.

However, as I would later learn, my own narrator was only a little more reliable, in this and a great many other matters, than Chindomacuba's.

When I returned to the Jan Kees, I went immediately to Mr. Crump's cabin, where I found him in earnest conversation with Mr. and Mrs. Halburton. The three of them stood huddled together in the center of the cabin, Mr. Crump with his back to me, Mr. and Mrs. Halburton facing him and me. Mrs. Halburton looked so beautiful in a white gown, more appropriate for a ball than a ship, that for a moment I forgot why I had come. Even Mr. Halburton, standing beside her in his black suit and white stockings, appeared overly formal for these mean surroundings, until I realized, upon seeing a book in

Mr. Crump's hands, that I had stumbled in on a marriage. I quickly stammered an apology and attempted to back out--until I was halted by Mr. Halburton's kindly voice.

"Not at all, we shall need a witness," he called. "Come here, Christopher."

So there I stood beside Mr. and Mrs. Halburton while they, pursuant to the ancient right of sea captains, became truly Mr. and Mrs. Halburton. When the brief ceremony was done and all due compliments paid to the bride and groom, Mr. Crump turned to me and asked what had brought me running to his hatch like a banshee out of hell.

"It's Chindomacuba, sir," I said, and proceeded to tell him of the poor man's terrible misunderstanding of America.

"Indeed," Mr. Crump said, resting his hands on his protuberant belly. "I was of the impression the man had an established position awaiting him somewhere in the Caribee."

"And the Caribee is safe...?" Mrs. Halburton asked, with some relief.

"Parts of it is," Mr. Crump said. "And parts of it ain't. And it ain't always easy to tell which is which, what with the French and Spanish and Dutch and English and even the Danes takin' it back and forth from each other all the time. But it don't matter whose flag happens to be flyin' that day, it ain't ever a safe place for a man of Chindomacuba's hue."

"What will you do?" Mrs. Halburton asked, turning to her husband. "We can't deliver him into slavery."

"The man has a right to go where he chooses," Mr. Halburton answered.

"But he doesn't understand the danger," she said.

"It sounds to me as if Christopher has given him more than fair warning," Mr. Halburton said, clasping my shoulder.

It was meant as a comradely gesture but I shrunk from it nonetheless, as in this matter I was with Mrs. Halburton. If Chindomacuba didn't have enough sense to save himself then it was our duty to do it for him. Although Mrs. Halburton was as firmly convinced of this as I, Mr. Halburton couldn't understand her argument in the least, and it soon began to appear that their marriage of less than an hour might, over this question, extend not much longer than that.

"I don't see why we can't take him with us to Carolina where he'll be safe," Mrs. Halburton said.

When Mr. Halburton and Mr. Crump laughed at this, Mrs. Halburton's anger became such that Mr. Halburton was forced to capitulate, lest his wife return to England on the very next ship. After Mr. Halburton agreed that Chindomacuba would accompany them to Carolina, Mrs. Halburton grew immediately gay again, and Mr. Crump ordered the purser to serve up the wedding meal, to which I was invited by Mrs. Halburton.

Mrs. Halburton sat opposite me at the Captain's round table and smiled often at me, although Mr. Halburton neither smiled nor said much to me throughout the meal. We drank Madeira wine and Mr. Crump toasted the bride and groom time and time again, in increasingly sly innuendoes of the sort with which Rebecca Hay used to tease me, and which I now pretended not to understand. After the meal was finished and the plates taken away, Mr. Crump brought out a drink with which neither Mrs. Halburton nor I were familiar, called rum.

"It's a kind of American wine drunk at wedding feasts," Mr. Crump explained, while he filled our glasses.

Being as how it was American, I eagerly raised my glass. But when that American wine went down my gullet like a bolt of lightning, leaving me gasping and choking, I was suddenly filled with grave misgivings regarding my suitability for that raw country. And Mrs. Halburton, who sat frozen and wide-eyed like a pale marble statue, was plainly overcome by some of the same doubt as myself; while Mr. Crump, American to the core, sat grinning at us like a cat in the bird cage.

"And like love, it's hot at first, but the second will cool you down," Mr. Crump said, re-filling our glasses.

Neither Mrs. Halburton nor I could entirely believe this, but Mr. Halburton assured us that such was the peculiar property of American wine, and so we drank again. Which only taught me that the American sense of humor is as coarse as its national drink.

Immediately after this cruel joke, Mrs. Halburton had to be taken to the rail by Mr. Halburton, and from there to her cabin. Laughing in soft starts, Mr. Crump walked crookedly, and to me fuzzily, across the cabin to his mahogany desk, where he pulled a cigar from a burled wood case and lit it over the hanging oil lamp. I watched as he inhaled the smoke deeply, then blew it out with a satisfied sigh while staring intently at the cigar, as if unable to fully understand the pleasure that lay there. I had on rare occasions seen a traveler smoke a pipe or cigar at the Lyme Bay Inn, but knew it to be an expensive pleasure of London gentlemen--and an occasional daring lady if the rumor be true--so I was rather surprised by Mr. Crump's cache of cigars.

"Sure it's expensive," he said, after I'd made my information known. "But once a man's tasted the infernal sot-weed, there's nothin' 'e won't do to get the money for the stuff, even if it means killin' 'is poor mother. If you'd ever seen a poor wretch in the throes of withdrawin', writhin' about the deck and poundin' 'is head on the bulkhead, you'd surely never take up a habit so vile and dangerous as this."

"If you'll forgive my asking, sir, why is it then that you practice this habit?"

"Because an evil habit ain't evil to them what can afford to keep it up," he answered.

Nonetheless, I vowed then and there that no matter how rich I might become in the New World, I would never take up the sot-weed no matter how pleasurable, if only on the off chance I might some day find myself without the funds to serve my craving. I was worried, however, that the smoke in the cabin, which was contributing to my dizziness, might already be getting into my blood and setting off the terrible craving of which Mr. Crump warned, so I quickly paid my respects and staggered out onto the now dark deck.

After I'd heaved the last of the wedding feast over the rail, I felt a hand on my shoulder, and turned to see Mr. Halburton standing beside me.

"Feeling better now?" he asked, offering me a bucket.

"I think so," I said, after I'd scooped some water into my mouth, sluiced it about and spit it over the side, then splashed some on my face.

I did indeed feel a bit better, and thanked Mr. Halburton for it. "How is Mrs. Halburton?" I asked.

"Mrs. Halburton--I can at last truly call her that--will be fine," he answered.

"Now that you're married, Mrs. Halburton's father will call off his men, won't he?" I asked.

"Father...?" he repeated. "It's not her father's men who are after me, Chris, but her husband's. And when he learns that we've been married he'll only quicken the chase. For a man who would hang his tenant for snaring a hare is scarcely likely to forgive the theft of a wife."

The thought that Mr. Halburton had just married an already married woman and that I had played a role in it, however small, caused such confusion in me that Mr. Halburton felt constrained to assure me that I was not in any danger.

"'tis not the danger to myself that concerns me, sir," I informed him, "but the danger to your immortal soul. And poor Mrs. Halburton's," I added, for by now I was hopelessly smitten by the woman. And the thought that Mr. Halburton had compromised this dear angel filled me with a rage I was barely able to contain. Mr. Halburton must have sensed the fury building within me, for he wisely took me aside and made effort to calm me.

"Please, Christopher, hear me out," he said, as he led me away from the cabin door, behind which that troubled, doubly-married lady lay. "Even if you can't forgive us, I hope, when you've heard the full story, that you shall at least understand the gravity of the events that led us to risk our immortal souls."

When we'd arrived at the ladder leading to the aft deck, he stopped within the faint glow of the overhead lantern and leaned his elbows upon the rail, while I stopped a few feet distant and waited. I was desperate to find Mrs. Halburton blameless in this matter, but what mitigation could there be when a woman would knowingly commit a sacrilege. He stared silently across the dock at the yellow light glowing from within the Black Porpoise Tavern, from which a woman's high squeal suddenly issued, followed by the low rumble of male laughter.

"I first met Priscilla when I was just a few years younger than you," he began. "A couple of years later I became the stable boy on Lord Wallingford's estate, while Priscilla was the daughter of a village shopkeeper. My bed and board was either reward or conscience money, depending upon your point of view, as I was the orphaned son of the poacher whom Lord Wallingford had hanged for stealing one of his million hares."

My feeling for Mr. Halburton softened at hearing this shocking news, but I quickly reminded myself that this misfortune was distinct from, and no excuse for polygamy. Seeing that his disclosure had no noticeable effect upon me, he went on in his persuasive voice.

"Priscilla's earliest attentions to me were the result of sympathy over the loss of my father, who was a good friend of her father, as well as his occasional meat supplier. What began as kindness and the play of children, changed one hot summer's day to an intense, adult love. We made secret plans to be married just as soon as Priscilla should turn sixteen.

"Before that day came, however, Lord Wallingford's wife died suddenly and Priscilla was summoned to Wallingford Manor to help the family through their ordeal. When Priscilla stayed on, even after there was no further need for her services, I recognized that she had become enthralled by the opulence of Wallingford Manor and was finding it difficult to return to her former life.

"We continued to meet in our secret niche high on the cliff, and Priscilla claimed still to love me, but she would neither allow me to speak to her father, nor could she quit the manor house. "I was going mad," Mr. Halburton said, turning and looking into my eyes. "It was as if Lord Wallingford had cast a spell on her--one day she was mine, the next his. Then rumor reached me that Lord Wallingford had asked her to marry him, and I was no longer able to contain myself. I went to the manor house and pulled Priscilla out. I demanded to know what her intentions were, but she claimed not to know herself what she wanted. She loved me, not Lord Wallingford, but she loved that house. Oh, how she loved that evil house," he said, turning away once more to stare into the blackness.

"I demanded then that she make up her mind once and for all. Come away with me and never return to that cursed house, or I would leave and she would never see me again. She was distraught, but she agreed to leave with me. I had finally won.

"We were hurrying across the moor, on the way to our place on the cliff, when Lord Wallingford and his servants overtook us on horseback. He claimed I had abducted Priscilla, and although we both protested that this was not true, he slashed me with his crop." As he said this he brought his hand to his cheek and lightly stroked the old scar, as if to confirm for himself that the terrible event which he was about to recount had really happened.

"Without thinking of the terrible consequences, I pulled Lord Wallingford down from his horse, yanked the crop from his hand and slashed him several times across the face, before being pummeled to the ground by his servants. I was, of course, arrested and convicted of felonious assault upon a nobleman and sentenced to seven years at hard labor in Carolina. I served my term and, after a few more years, amassed a fortune in the tobacco business.

"In all my time in America, whether laboring in the fields in shackles, or finally reveling in my own plantation house, there was never a day I didn't think of Priscilla, even though I knew she was married to Lord Wallingford and could never be mine. I loved her and I always would, but I was resigned to never seeing her again. And even if we should somehow meet, I knew that nothing would come of it, as we both had too great a respect for the institution of marriage to in any way violate it. Also, by this time I no longer even bore Lord Wallingford any ill will for what he had done to me.

"Imagine then, Christopher," he said, opening his hands to me, "that in exactly this state of mind, I should find myself back in England--in London more precisely, purely on tobacco business, and without any intention of going up to Wallingford Manor to see Priscilla--when who should I run into at the opera, but Lord and Lady Wallingford!

"Oh, it was an awkward moment, I assure you, with the three of us posed like statues in the lobby. The strange thing is, I didn't know at whom I was looking, only that she was the most beautiful woman I had ever seen, and I wanted her more than anything else in the world. I knew this was impossible, as I was vaguely aware of a man standing next to her with a proprietary air, but I was nonetheless elated to find that I was finally able to desire a woman other than my beloved Priscilla.

I was about to move off, with a polite nod to her fortunate husband, when my eyes fell upon his terribly scarred face--and his upon my single scar--and I realized that this exquisite lady was none other than my own dear Priscilla! I stood there, unable to feel my own body, let alone make it do my bidding, when from somewhere, I heard my voice, speaking in the most calmly assured tone: 'Good evening, Lady Wallingford, Lord Wallingford,' it said."

"Clifton…!" Lady Wallingford gasped.

"Then, when it appeared she would collapse, I moved forward and caught her in my arms, and we stood that way for what seemed minutes but was of course scarcely seconds, while looking into each other's eyes, remembering everything, summoning up all the love that had lain deeply denied within us those many years. And in that moment we both knew that we were helpless in the face of it.

"'Well, Halburton--what brings you to England?' Lord Wallingford asked me, in a tight voice that was no longer any more familiar to me than his face."

"Then, as if we were best of friends, I proceeded to describe the business that had brought me to London, while mentioning the hotel where I was staying. But suddenly, while exchanging inane pleasantries with the passion of my life and the man who had made a convict of me, I was overcome by the absurdity of it all and began to laugh, uncontrollably, which in turn caused Priscilla to do the same, while poor old Wallingford could only splutter as he pulled her away."

At this moment Mr. Halburton stepped forward and gripped my shoulders fiercely in his two hands. "Believe me, Christopher, it was only at that moment, when I recognized the absurdity of our situation, all three of us--Priscilla and I deeply in love, and Wallingford the odd man out--that I realized the happiness of two people is too precious to be denied by the immutable constraints of any law of God or man. And I realized too, when Priscilla joined me in laughter, that she was no less aware of the absurdity than I, and we had decided, with that mocking chorus, to damn all convention and have each other again no matter the consequences!"

I was of course appalled by this sordid tale of adultery, and therefore required to know what happened next. "So you went to Wallingford Manor and took Lady Wallingford away with you," I said sternly.

"That was my intention, of course. However the next day I received a letter at my hotel, delivered to me by Priscilla's faithful maid. In it, she begged my forgiveness for marrying Lord Wallingford, and professed her undying love for me. She asked if she could come to me that evening, while Lord Wallingford would be at his club with friends, and I of course replied with a similar letter, urging her to come to me that night and thence to America. I then went in search of a ship and found good Mr. Crump, who would be willing to take us, but would not be ready to sail for a few days. As it was of course dangerous for us to remain in London, we agreed to rendezvous at Lyme Bay, where you, Master Rousby, became an unwitting part of my conspiracy, and for which I hope you will someday be able to forgive me."

Then, as if he had unburdened himself of a great weight, he released me and fell back against the rail. I was now more confused than ever. I could easily sympathize with Mr. and Mrs. Halburton or Mr. Halburton and Mrs. Wallingford, whichever it was--but did that make them free to decide for themselves which laws were absurd and therefore not be obeyed? For if Mrs. Halburton could leave her husband because she considered her condition absurd, couldn't a husband with ten children do the same?

It was too much for a fifteen year old with a dizzying headache, so I begged off making any decision that night, and bade Mr. Halburton goodnight.

I awoke next morning with Chindomacuba snoring on one side and poor Mr. Franks on the other, and a great heaving in my stomach, which I at first attributed to American wine, before finally realizing it was the American voyage. We were at sea again!

I was quite pleased when I stepped out on the deck and beheld Mr. and Mrs. Halburton standing arm in arm at the rail, watching Madeira disappear in our wake. For at that moment my decision was made clear as the sea air--they were as free of sin as any of God's cherubim and seraphim. It is said that men go to sea to free themselves of responsibility and that's true enough, for here no wife nor creditor can reach. But there is an even greater freedom at sea, the freedom to see things clearly and know what's important and what isn't. Mr. and Mrs. Halburton's happiness was more important than slavish obeisance to any law; and my American mission, which ashore was in danger of floundering on the rocks of homesickness, was once again as important as destiny itself; and the possibility of Chindomacuba's loss of liberty remained the most important problem of all.

Strangely, however, when I found Chindomacuba and Poor Mr. Franks in our quarters and informed him of Mr. and Mrs. Halburton's generous offer to be his protector, and take him with them to their home in Carolina, he was neither excited nor grateful at the prospect. In fact, if anything, it seemed he took my effort for interference in his affairs.

"Tanks but I got big business in Carribee," he replied.

"What business?" I asked.

"Big business."

"Believe me, business in the Vest Indies, it stinks," Poor Mr. Franks put in.

"I didn't know you had business in the West Indies," I said to Mr. Franks, although I had by now heard a great deal of his many failed ventures in London.

"Sure, sure, there too," he said, nodding sadly. "In '85 I am in the vool business in London--such a business, it stinks. So I close up and ship my inventory to the Vest Indies."

"But isn't it too hot for wool in the West Indies?" I interrupted.

"Such a kibitzer, why vasn't you there ven I needed you? All my stores, they rot on the dock. So I ship a cargo of rum to New York, but the crew gets drunk in a storm and they sink the ship. Oi vey, such a place the Carribee.... If the storm don't get you, the pirates will."

"Pirates!" Chindomacuba exclaimed.

"Hush!" I warned Mr. Franks, as it was apparent that just the mention of the word was still enough to alarm Chindomacuba.

During the long weeks at sea, while we sailed southwest on fair winds, I tried several more times to dissuade Chindomacuba from his suicidal plan, but it was like talking to the part-fish, part-lady that led our way to America. I would make one last attempt when we landed in Jamaica, I decided, but until then I would stop pestering the man.

Each day out it grew warmer and the sea calmer until, as we were approaching the Bahamas, it grew terribly hot, the sea flattened and our sails hung lifeless from the yards. Each day passengers and crew lay about the deck in whatever shade the limp sails provided, and prayed silently for the wind. It was terribly cruel to have come so far on a glorious, untroubled voyage, only to lay in irons just a few days off the islands where my namesake had landed in 1492.

"We're in the Horse Latitudes," the first mate, a roguish Irishman explained to the two merchants. "It's called that because when we must lighten the ship, it's the horses must first be thrown overboard. It's a sad thing to see," he said, removing his hat, "all them horses swimming after the ship until they tire and sink, or until the sharks get 'em."

"But we have no horses aboard this ship," one of the merchants pointed out.

"Aye," said the sailor, replacing his hat, "so 'tis the cargo will be first to go."

The merchants became apoplectic at this, but the mate assured them it was the unspoken law of the sea. "First the horses and cargo, then the lawyers."

The merchants seemed little disturbed and even pleased at this. But the cargo continued to bother them.

After a few days of sweltering heat and rolling swales that made some sick all over again, there was no more jocularity from the sailors, who took to drinking and quarreling among themselves more and more. Drinking was technically prohibited among sailors at sea, but it was tolerated by Mr. Crump and most other masters, so long as it didn't interfere with a sailor's chores. With few chores, however, the drinking became earnest and the fights increasingly violent, which caused Mr. Halburton to buckle on his sword and pistol as he walked about the deck with Mr. Crump, keeping the men in line. To spare Mrs. Halburton the sight of brawling drunken sailors, Mr. Halburton requested that she remain in their cabin, and enlisted me to keep her company much of the time, which rendered the doldrums a precious and delightful time for me. While Mrs. Halburton did her needlepoint, and I casually read a play called *The Tempest* by one William Shakespeare, our conversation drifted, aimless as our ship, sometimes pointing to America, sometimes England and often in the direction of the unknown.

"Aren't you at all frightened to be going off to a strange place?" she stopped to ask at one point, after lengthily reciting all the things Mr. Halburton said awaited her in Carolina. Whenever Mrs. Halburton put up her needlepoint when asking a question, I knew it to be a serious one.

"There is something about it that gives me pause, but it's not anything I recognize as fear," I began. "All I know is, I was more afraid of not going than going."

"Was your life at home so awful then?" she asked.

"It wasn't awful at all," I hastened to assure her. "There I had a loving father, good food, a warm hearth, enough books to last a lifetime, and ample time to dream of exciting adventures and faraway places. I didn't leave home because I disliked it--although there were some things I *didn't* like--but rather because of the things I *did* like. I thought, if things could be so wonderful just in Lyme Bay, just imagine all the more wonderful things that must be out there somewhere. It was only then that I became afraid, afraid I should never see those wonderful places."

"You are most fortunate," Mrs. Halburton said, smiling warmly, "to be in command of your own destiny. Perhaps, if I had made a single-minded decision to go to America, I should be as confident and fearless as you. But women lack that luxury, I'm afraid. I only chose to go with Mr. Halburton--whether to Russia, China or America made no difference. So while I have no doubts about Mr. Halburton, I must confess to some trepidation over this voyage."

"You're only feeling homesick," I said. "I experienced the same thing in Madeira, but it soon passed once we were under way."

"You're a dear, sweet boy," Mrs. Halburton said, and leaned over to kiss me upon the cheek.

At this I felt a warmth filling me from the flesh inwards, as if I'd been doused with rum. It occurred to me, as I sat staring at this wonderful woman, that she must also think me a dear sweet fool, yet I was unable to break my pose. Fortunately, at this moment we heard some commotion on deck, followed by the snap of a sail and a slight lurch of the ship that propelled us out onto the deck to see what was happening.

The wind came up as quickly as it had died, raising a cheer from the crew and filling the sheets, dipping the bow and pushing us off once more for America. When I watched Mrs. Halburton run across the deck and throw her arms around her husband, I was suddenly of two minds about the wind.

All that day we ran before an increasingly strong wind from abaft the beam, while all the time the waves reached slowly higher and higher, until it seemed we would very soon be riding a breaker directly into Jamaica Bay. The spirits of passengers and crew were greatly buoyed by the wind, yet Mr. Crump, I noticed, seemed preoccupied with some thing other than high spirits. When, a short while later he ordered some men aloft to shorten sail, I realized we might be in for a bit more blow than necessary, which in my ignorance I took for an exciting prospect. We landsmen stood in blissful awe, necks stretched back, watching men, like monkeys on vines, some fifty feet above the pitching deck, as they wrestled with the flapping canvas. It took the better part of an hour before the topsails were trimmed to Mr. Crump's satisfaction, and the men returned to the deck like falling cannonballs, but we passengers were quite pleased by their performance.

When the sun was low on our starboard side, the darkening waves became edged by a luminous white foam that blew over the stern and drove the passengers to their cabins. I elected to remain on deck, however, and huddled in the lee of the poop to watch the spray whip the deck in the last orange light of day. When, despite the soaking I was in for, I ventured to the rail for a closer look at the sunset, I saw the black cloud inching over the horizon behind us, and immediately understood Mr. Crump's preoccupation. We were running ahead of a storm, comfortably enough for now, but sooner or later it had to catch us.

Poor Mr. Franks slept fitfully that night, waking me several times with his loud moaning and dry heaving, while Chindomacuba lay in his bunk as if dead. I was vaguely aware of the rain that came sometime during the night, but I was not prepared for the deluge that greeted me when I stepped out onto the deck the next morning. I could barely make out the helmsman, shrouded in oilskin behind a gray sheet of water in front, and a great wall of black water behind. As I watched, the wall slid away and the ship climbed high on another wave, then slid down and struck her bow into the forward wall with a jolt that knocked me to the deck. As I tried to get to my feet, I was slammed back down by a tide from hell and rolled along the deck like a piece of cork, until I felt myself snatched up by a pair of strong hands.

"What d'ye think you're doin' out here ye dammed fool!" the first mate shouted while shaking me furiously. I tried to reply, but he cut me off: "Get below, damn you, and don't let me see you up here 'til the sun comes out!"

"Yes sir," I spluttered, as he dragged me along the deck and thrust me back through the hatchway from which I had just come.

I returned to my cabin and changed to dry clothes, while Poor Mr. Franks stared wanly at me, and Chindomacuba continued to snore.

"At least we're safe from pirates," the sick man said weakly.

"Where?" Chindomacuba shouted, bolting upright.

Later that day, a seaman come to my cabin with a most welcome invitation from Mrs. Halburton, to join her in her cabin. The sailor led me there by way of a series of mysterious passageways below the main deck that proved to be scarcely drier or safer than the deck itself. Water came spilling down everywhere as I was dashed from bulkhead to bulkhead in the darkened pitching ship, until by the time I arrived at Mrs. Halburton's cabin, I felt a wet bruised rat. She, however, was much too consumed with worry to notice my condition, though she professed to have summoned me out of concern for my well-being.

"I couldn't bear to think of you penned up with those two men while all this was going on," she said "But you mustn't be afraid. Mr.

Halburton tells me these squalls are quite common in the tropics. They blow fiercely for an hour or so, then disappear."

I assured her I was grateful to know that, choosing not to remind her that this storm had already been raging for almost twenty four hours and seemed to be growing worse by the minute. Instead, I politely inquired as to Mr. Halburton's present whereabouts, as it seemed most strange that he was not with her at such a time as this.

"He's gone out to help repair a pump," she said.

"Then that's where I should be," I said, jumping up from my bench.

"No!" she said, catching my hand. "Mr. Halburton requests that you stay here with me until he returns, which he assures me shan't be very long. There!" she said, pointing out the port. "I believe I saw the sun poking out just now."

I looked out the port but saw only a mountain of gray water that appeared about to engulf us, but instead fell away to reveal a plum-colored sky, seared by flashing bursts of lightning. I didn't know how many pumps the Jan Kees had, but if even one were down in a storm such as this, it had to be a serious loss. Until now I thought I was only imagining it, but now I knew--the ship was no longer riding as high on the leading wave as she had been earlier. The Jan Kees was taking on water faster then she could pump it out, and her master was reduced to calling on her passengers to keep her afloat.

It occurred to me that she had opened a leak, twisting and torquing on these abrupt waves as she was, until I realized that a few leaks in such a sea as this was beside the point. Each wave was more than sufficient to breach the gunwale, overwhelm the scuppers and slosh about the deck with nowhere to go but down the hatches. Although this was my first experience on a deep water sailor, the Jan Kees was strangely familiar as my own little dinghy in a rough sea. I was suddenly and instinctively aware of what each halting, straining movement of this behemoth meant, and how close each shudder and groan came to being her last. In the troughs, the moment of greatest danger, the waterlogged ship was momentarily becalmed, while on the crest of a wave the wind threatened to tear away her few storm sails or break away her mast. Yet Mr. Crump was powerless to trim her further, as she needed enough sail to outrun the following sea that threatened to engulf her.

I realized then that I must do nothing to betray this knowledge or fear, for convinced as I was that we might soon go down, I was determined to keep it from Mrs. Halburton until the last. It was nothing less than a sacred charge from Mr. Halburton, who had summoned me to be with his wife in his place during her last moments. I was of course honored to be chosen for so noble a mission, but at the same time it came to me that had I not been so honored, I'd be free to go to the launch.

When, in this confused state, I looked into Mrs. Halburton's eyes and saw that she was no less aware of our imminent demise than I, I grabbed her hand and pulled her after me.

"Where are we going?" she cried, as I pulled her aft through the same passageway I had just come.

"To the galley for provisions!"

Once there we gathered whatever food was in sight, a sausage, hardtack, and flask filled with grog. Then I grabbed her hand and pulled her out after me, up the ladder and out onto the main deck, where the wind screamed at us and the rain struck like pebbles. At the aft hatch, seamen were hauling up cargo and throwing it into the sea in a desperate attempt to keep the stern up, while the two anguished merchants pleaded with them to stop. Then I scrabbled along the rail to the double-lashed boat swinging wildly from the davits, deposited the provisions over the side, and made my way back to Mrs. Halburton.

"My husband!" she cried, followed by something I couldn't hear but nonetheless understood.

"We'll wait here" I shouted. "If the ship founders, he'll come to the boat!"

Mrs. Halburton knew as well as I that Mr. Halburton, laboring somewhere below the waterline on a pump, was the least likely of anyone to make it to the boats should the ship be suddenly swamped, but there was nothing for it but to hope for the best. In any event, someone must get to the boat, as it wouldn't be possible for Mrs. Halburton and me to get it away by ourselves.

At that moment, as the ship climbed the wave, I could fairly feel the braced mainmast straining against the deck, and as I looked up I heard a crack loud as thunder and saw the mast fall forward, taking spars and rigging down with it as the topsail kited out and dived into the sea like a shot albatross. The ship remained perched on the very crest of the wave for a silent, frozen space of time that would for me be forever, then slid down the other side in an exhilarating, death-defying dive. At that moment I looked at Mrs. Halburton and she looked at me, without fear or excitement or any visible emotion beyond resignation, and I remembered what she had said: "...I must confess to some trepidation over this voyage."

Chapter 3

Lost at Sea

It was the last thing I remember--until I found myself in the sea with no ship under me, nor anywhere else about. However this didn't mean Mrs. Halburton wasn't still somewhere nearby, as my vision was either blocked by twenty foot waves, or else I was racing down a giant breaker with little thought for sight-seeing. After the first of these, or the first I remember, I was amazed to find myself alive, even if half drowned. I managed to cough up a cup of saltwater and clear my eyes just in time to see the next wave high above my head, edged by a creamy froth, then collapsing on me with what seemed enough force to dash me clear to the ocean's floor. But again I somehow surfaced, coughing up a quart of water this time, and readied myself for the next slam. The next one, however, picked me up and carried me with it down a long gentle slope and set me down at the bottom while scarcely wetting my hair. Then no sooner than she'd given me some little hope, another wave fell on me with such force that I thought I'd found the ship.

And so it went, until darkness fell, and for what seemed a long time after that. I was no more rational than the sea, at times wildly hopeful, then suddenly suicidal. Once I put my face down in the water and tried to drown myself, but came up choking, resolved now to swim all the way to the Bahamas. It seemed that I slept while swimming, or dreamed anyway, of Mrs. Halburton sitting up in the bow of the longboat searching for me. Then I woke and saw that the rain had stopped, and when I lay back on the water I saw millions of stars blinking blearily at me, so close it seemed I could haul myself up on one and fly away. It was then I realized the mountainous waves, like the rain, had disappeared, leaving long gentle swells in their place, and I had a vision of one rolling me onto a soft Bahamian beach where Mrs. Halburton waited.

When the sun came up I saw no beach or longboat or Mrs. Halburton, and I knew, as surely as I'd known the Jan Kees was about to go down, that I was doomed. I tried one more time to drop my head under the water, but again I came up spluttering. Whether due to weakness or courage, I would have to wait until I became too exhausted to stay afloat, then sink slowly and peacefully to the bottom of the sea.

No sooner had I charted this peaceful course for myself, when I felt a firm bump against my shoulders. Shark! I thought, and knew my peaceful plan had been thwarted. That I, a young man made in the likeness of God should be torn asunder by such a vile, stupid beast, filled me with useless rage. That a man, who can build ships and cathedrals, compose symphonies and write epic poems, should be no more than a helpless meal for a voracious and worthless monster, is an injustice so cruel as would cause even a man in my perilous state to call into question God's wisdom. There are those people, I know, men of religion and science who would have it that all of God's creatures were put on this earth for some purpose, but I see no reason whatsoever for sharks. And very little for men of religion or science, as the former are intransigent as bulls, and the latter are constant as weather vanes. Even the most ignorant fisherman in Lyme Bay can see that the cod and the flounder serve a purpose, while the shark who would devour tons of them, as well as the fisherman too, requires the greatest leap of faith and science to justify its existence.

My greatest regret, when I was bumped for the second time, was that he hadn't come round sooner while I still had the strength to put up a good fight. Nonetheless I was determined to go down kicking and punching when I turned to meet him--and discovered my shark to be the aft hatch cover of the Jan Kees! Emitting a joyful croak, I threw my hands over the edge and found a finger hold. Saved! I thought. Until I realized I didn't have the strength to pull myself up onto the cover.

It was then that the real shark bumped me hard from below, thrusting me up out of the sea and flat out on the tarred planks, where I clung like a jellyfish for dear life. Each time my raft climbed high on a swell, I was in danger of overturning or being tossed off to the shark that awaited me, yet each time I managed somehow to stay aboard her. With my cheek pressed tightly against the deck, I could just make out his fin in the first light of day.

Despite the imminent peril, I must have fallen asleep for a time, for when I next remember anything the sun was high in the clear blue sky and the circling fins had increased to more than a dozen. And although my vision was blurred by salt water, it seemed they were passing within inches of my frail raft, sometimes scraping up against the sides and bumping it from beneath, so that any moment I expected to see those huge jaws open wide and a set of saber-sharp teeth clamp down on my raft and shake it to bits. Then I should find myself pitched in among those frenzied monsters who would instantly tear me into bite-sized portions, and fifteen year old Christopher Rousby would be no more. This was the time my life should have passed before my eyes in seconds, but nothing was happening. It had better start soon, I knew, as these voracious beasts would not wait much longer. What was the matter? Hadn't I lived a long or interesting enough life that it should pass before my eyes the instant before my death?

It was then that I heard a shout: "'e looks dead to me, Cap'n!" and realized that I might not die. I managed to lift my head slightly and there, just a few yards off, I saw a boat pulling for me.

"'e's alive!" came the cry, as the tiny boat pushed through the sharks.

Then I felt myself being slid across the tarred hatch cover and lifted into the boat. "Look out--sharks…" I warned in a croaking voice, to the black-bearded face above me.

"Sharks 'e said!" the black-bearded sailor shouted, followed by a laugh I feared would topple the boat. "Them ain't sharks, them's dolphins! And you're lucky they was, cuz if they wasn't, you'd be in some shark's belly long before this."

When we got back to the ship, I was passed up onto the deck and laid in the shade of a bulkhead. There were a great many voices then, some speaking a foreign tongue, and lots of bare feet standing round me. The black-bearded sailor who'd taken me from the hatch cover was among them now, amusing his mates with a tale of dolphins and sharks, while someone held a cup of water to my lips.

"Dolphins is good luck," a voice said.

"Aye, the boy is blessed," another said.

"'ere, make way for the Cap'n," someone said, as the bare feet separated and a pair of black boots stood in front of me.

My eyes traveled up his gray breeches, to the broad belt supporting a heavy cutlass and a pair of pistols, to a billowing white shirt open wide across a curly-haired chest. His brown hair was very long, pulled back and tied, falling down his back like a horse's tail. His face was square and stolid, with dark eyes set deeply under thick arching eyebrows. His nose was large, thickened and made even larger by a great many blows, and his lower lip, in contrast to the thin upper one, was a thick, blue, bulbous thing, framed by a pair of deeply etched lines flaring out from beside the nostrils and falling in a swooping curve almost to his broad jaw. It was neither a handsome face nor a graceful figure, but taken together I had the sense of a man competent in a great many situations.

"Let's hope 'e brings luck to this voyage," the Captain said.

"Yes sir," I replied.

"Talkin' are ye? How long were ye out there?"

"I'm not sure, sir. Two days perhaps."

"That's nothin'," the Captain said, raising some laughter from the crew. Studying them for the first time, they looked as if they might have been adrift at sea for a good long time at that. Their clothes, though crudely sewn, were of the richest silk and brocade, in colors more suitable for songbirds than sailors. Many of them wore great, broad-brimmed, salt-encrusted hats, while all wore their hair longer than any woman's and indeed, some wore it in the fashion of women, tied with bright ribbons and held up by jeweled combs. Some of their clothing, too, more resembled dresses than breeches, which I attributed to a lack of sewing skill rather than preference. It was only the beards, black, brown, red, yellow and gray, that somehow reassured me I was in the company of normal men, and not some unknown species that had sprung from the mysterious depths of the sea. Not even the sails, patched as they were with pieces of red, yellow, blue, and green silk, had escaped the embellishment of this ship's mad crew. Only the man before me in boots, breeches and flowing silk shirt, seemed, despite his long hair, to be conventional.

"I'm deeply grateful for my rescue, Captain ..."

"Kidd," he answered. "How did ye come to be in the sea without a proper boat?"

"I was bound for America on the ship Jan Kees when she went down in a storm. May I ask where you're bound, sir?"

"Wherever fortune beckons," Captain Kidd answered, setting off more laughter.

"Who's yer father?" the black-bearded sailor demanded, his voice suddenly harsh.

It was only then, as I looked round at the hard greedy faces of my *rescuers*, that I realized I was aboard a pirate ship! And it was the prospect of ransom, not human charity, that had occasioned my rescue by Captain Kidd and his gang of buccaneers. My poor tired brain began to whirl. If I admitted that my father was a penniless schoolmaster, these cutthroats might very well toss me back into the sea without another word; while if I claimed a wealthy father, I was at least assured of staying alive until my lie be discovered.

"My father is the owner of a great tobacco plantation in Carolina." It was a good answer, I saw, as the crew nodded and murmured their approval.

"What's 'is name?" black-beard demanded.

"Halburton, sir--Clifton Halburton. And my name is Christopher Halburton."

"What town in Carolina?" Captain Kidd asked.

"Town--?"

"What town lies nearest your father's plantation?"

"Why, no town lies anywhere near it, sir. My father's plantation is so large it's fairly a colony unto itself." This set off a great deal of nodding and shuffling of feet and even louder murmuring.

"But surely there's a town somewhere nearby. From where does he ship his tobacco--Boston?" Captain Kidd asked.

"Yes, Boston."

"So, we must get him home," the Captain said, smiling and stroking his broad jaw. Meanwhile, Mr. Mason, see that the boy is fed, then hang a hammock for him in the sickbay."

"Me, Cap'n?" black-beard said.

"Yes, you."

"I ain't much with children, Cap'n. Whereas Culliford and Burgess..." he said, which amused the men greatly.

"Just see to it," Captain Kidd said, turning and striding away.

I was greatly surprised at Mr. Mason's insolence to his Captain, which was something Mr. Crump wouldn't tolerate for a moment. But discipline aboard a pirate ship was a far cry from that aboard a merchantman, I was to discover.

For the moment, however, I was much too surprised by the appearance of Culliford and Burgess, both of whom at first appeared to be women, to give the matter further thought. Both men wore homemade silk shifts, one a bright red and one a deep blue, and their hair was arranged as carefully as ever Mrs. Halburton's was. The dresses were pinched tightly at the waist and cut so low in front that their nipples showed.

As they pulled me across the deck and down the ladder to the galley, they supported me in a most shocking way which I was powerless to discourage. Fortunately, Culliford, finding Burgess's hand where he thought his own should be, slapped Burgess's hand and, for the moment at least, I was spared their groping. Once in the galley they sat me at table and left me alone, busying themselves with finding food.

I felt vaguely hungry, but too weak and tired to manage, so while Burgess supported me and occasionally rubbed my stomach, Culliford cut up bits of cold meat and stuck them into my mouth, followed by sips of a familiar tasting grog.

"Rum and lime," Culliford explained, at my quizzical expression.

"And that?" I asked, as he came at me with another small bit of meat balanced on the tip of his finger.

"Turtle," he said.

I immediately pushed it away and a moment later heaved the modest contents of my stomach on the table.

"Now look what ye've done!" Burgess scolded.

"I'm sorry," I gasped, terrified at my imagined punishment at the hands of these cutthroats.

"Not ye, 'im," Burgess said. "I told ye 'is stomach's in no state for your turtle."

"It wasn't my turtle what done it, it was ye givin' grog to the boy!" Culliford charged.

"Keep still and fetch the bucket!" Burgess ordered, while continuing to rub my stomach. "There now, it'll be all right, don't ye cry."

"I don't cry, sir," I said.

"No, of course not. Ye're a nice big boy, ye are."

"No wonder 'e 's sick with you 'angin' round him so," Culliford grumbled, while he slid my puke across the table with his hand and into the bucket.

"We'll just tuck ye up into your hammock and let ye get some sleep," Burgess said, helping me to my feet. "Then when 'e wakes up 'e can have a bit of my hardtack. That won't upset yer stomach."

"Like as not it'll break 'is teeth if it won't kill 'im," Culliford said, as he followed us out of the galley.

They led me up and out along the deck, then down through the forward hatch to a narrow space in the forepeak, where a few sailcloth hammocks were hung. The two men picked me up and lay me gently down, then Burgess laced up the sides of the hammock until I was snug as a caterpillar. I thanked them both for their kindness as, despite my effort, my eyelids slid closed.

"We'll leave 'im get some sleep," Culliford said.

"Ye first," Burgess said.

I remember hearing both men starting out of the dark forepeak, followed by a quick kiss directly to my lips, followed by angry words, then nothing.

When I next awoke in the dark, pitching hold, it required several fearful moments before I realized I was not in the sea, but wound safely in my hammock aboard a pirate ship, safely for now at least. I must have cried out, for suddenly Culliford and Burgess were there, assuring me that everything was all right as they loosed me from my cocoon. Then they helped me up onto the main deck where I was able to walk unassisted.

"Look at 'im would ye, navigatin' all by 'isself," Culliford said.

"We'll have to find 'im some shoes," Burgess said.

"Where? These men are all healthy," Culliford said of the fifty or sixty men sprawled about the deck. All of them were barefoot but dressed in silks fit for a queen.

"This seems a most unusual ship," I said, glancing aloft at the brocade-patched sails.

"We took them goods off a Dutch merchantman right after we stole this ship from the French. Seems a waste, patchin' sails with brocade, but we didn't have much choice with the French navy chasin' us all over the Caribbean."

"Nor was I able to get to me tailor," Burgess said, holding his dress out for my inspection.

"It's--very pretty," I said. "But I thought only the nobility were allowed to wear colors."

Both men laughed. "If they caught us wearin' this in England, it ain't the color what'd get us hung!" Culliford said.

"If it come to that, we'd stand a damned better chance gettin' caught by the French than the English!" Burgess added.

"But we're at war with the French," I pointed out, lest the word had somehow not yet reached them.

'What war...? If King William wants to kill frogs, let ''im, it ain't got nothin' to do with us over here," Burgess said.

"Besides, I have a very good Friend who's French," Culliford added, poking at his hair.

"'e 's the friend o' every buccaneer in the West Indies," Burgess said.

"You don't even know 'im."

"Hah! I knew 'im in Hispaniola and again in Port Royale.

"Liar."

While they bickered, I managed to slip away, crossing over to the starboard rail and making my way aft, careful not to step on the dozing pirates who had already finished their daily grog. Burgess and Mason were not the only sailors of Greek persuasion aboard ship, I noticed. Two men, one in green pantaloons, the other in a blue dress, stood holding hands at the rail, looking every bit like Mr. and Mrs. Halburton on their wedding voyage. That these drunkards and sons of Sappho in their women's dress could fight and capture another ship seemed to me unlikely if not impossible. And I only prayed they wouldn't make the attempt while I was aboard. The only stalwart man I had so far observed was Captain Kidd, who was today nowhere about, as if perhaps the sight of his own men disgusted him. And even if the drunkenness and lechery were not enough to destroy his crew, the lack of discipline was more than sufficient by itself. The sailors went about without proper uniforms, holding hands and doing worse; the decks needed holystoning; weeds and barnacles sprouted from the hull; and the ship's sails looked like something to be found in a London fabric shop. If that black-beard Mason had spoken to Mr. Crump the way he spoke to Captain Kidd, he would have been tied to the mast and flayed alive, yet there he stood at that very mast, talking to Culliford and Burgess as if he hadn't a care. And what of those two, who could be hanged for saying King William's war against the French had nothing to do with English subjects who happen to be in America? Treason! It was a ship of drunks, deviates and traitors upon which I found myself. But it was, I had to remember, better than a hatch cover.

Later in the day, when the deck was too hot to tread upon and the crew had all but disappeared into their secret shaded niches, there came a cry of "Ship ho!" from the crow's nest. Then in what seemed no more than a few seconds, the decks were teeming with men, Captain Kidd was out on the quarterdeck with his glass, and Mason was hauling himself aloft with the speed and agility of a monkey, shouting, "Where? Where?"

"There! Just off the starboard bow!"

Mason threw his arms over the royal mast, pulled himself up onto the jacks and pulled a glass from under his blouse.

"Do ye see 'er?" Captain Kidd called.

"A three masted bark, layin' low in the water!" he shouted back.

"Make for 'er!" Captain Kidd ordered the helmsman.

The ship veered off on a starboard course and I moved up along the rail with the rest of the crew, all armed now with cutlasses and pistols, anxious for a look at our prey. I was amazed that these men, who only moments ago had seemed a drunken, degenerate lot, now stood poised and alert as hungry cats at the mouse-hole. And the Greek in a dress, who had earlier been standing hand-in-hand with his groom at the rail, stood now with a dagger between his teeth and an enormous broadsword in his hand, looking as fearsome as any maniac among them.

There was a grim silence aboard the ship as she tacked suspensefully after her prey, broken only by the shouted intelligence from Mason above, and an occasional quiet instruction from Captain Kidd to the helmsman, or to one of the mates who stood directly behind him. She was a merchantman in bad shape, showing some torn sheets but no colors as yet. She had seen her pursuer, Mason could make out her officers and crew at the rail. A moment before her masts became visible to us on deck, the bad news came down: "She's a slaver!"

The tension floated off on a sea of grumbling that seemed somehow more ominous than mere disappointment. Guns and swords came off and the pack dissolved as the ship pointed back to its original course. Yet we could not avoid eventually passing within several hundred feet of the slaver, now flying British colors to match our own. From her torn rigging and tattered sails, she looked as though she might have come through the same storm I had, yet her sides remained fouled with filth, and the smell of human waste was overpowering even as we passed a great distance downwind of her. I saw perhaps a dozen naked black bodies on the main deck, surrounded by a few blacks in tarred breeches wielding birch rods, which seemed hardly necessary as their charges looked near death.

The slaver's crew, nearly as naked and befouled as their charges, stood mutely at the rail as we slid past, while her Captain, in clean white breeches and proper naval jacket, exchanged a smart salute with our own Captain. Some of our crew stood silently at the rail with me, but just as many, it seemed, had chosen to be elsewhere until we were well past her. As for me, I was relieved there had been no battle, yet I felt no better than I might if I'd just come from a charnel house.

I was at first more than a little confused by the behavior of my shipmates, men forged on the cruel hard anvil of poverty who could slit a man's throat for a few shillings, but had yet somehow retained enough humanity to feel so obviously deeply for a passing boatload of black strangers. Nor did their silence, as they passed their fellow white seamen, even begin to convey the depth of loathing they felt for these sailors who would participate in such barbarity. All the men I later spoke to about this were of the same mind--they would rather sail the River Styx than ship on a slaver.

Oddly enough, their officers, many of whom are educated gentlemen, don't seem to share this aversion with their less privileged crewmen. They recognize that slavery is contrary to everything Christians hold dear, yet consider it necessary for the greater good of England. But I don't think money alone is the explanation for the difference between the attitude of officers and ordinary seamen, as even the lowliest hand is much better paid on a slaver than on any merchantman afloat. Rather, I think the common seaman sees the line between himself and the slave as thin indeed; while the officer and gentleman sees the line between himself and the slave as an uncrossable chasm. Fortunately, there is a movement afoot in England to bar this medieval barbarity, but as their members are presently thought to be just a handful of eccentrics, it's unlikely anything will be done about this cruel practice for at least several more years.

Late the next day I had my first glimpse of land since leaving Madeira more than a month before. It was a small island with the sort of broad sandy beach of which I'd dreamed while bobbing about in the sea, canopied by broad palm trees, of which I'd also dreamed while sitting before the fire in England. Excited though I was, this tropical paradise meant nothing to Captain Kidd's men, for whom such island paradises were either places to lie in wait for unsuspecting merchantmen, or friendly ports to trade their booty. While watching the island disappear over the taffrail, I had the feeling someone was staring at me, and turned to see Captain Kidd standing in the hatch that led to his cabin.

"Good afternoon, sir!" I called uncertainly, for in the few silent moments our eyes met, it seemed something was required of one or the other of us.

"Recovered, are ye?" he said.

"Aye, sir," I replied.

He looked at me and nodded, then motioned and said, "Come inside."

Fearfully--for if there were so many Greeks among the crew, might the captain not be one too?--I walked across the deck and followed Captain Kidd into his quarters below the poop deck. The cabin was a far cry from my wet black hole in the bow, wide as the ship, with a high ceiling and a bank of windows across the stern that lent a golden hue to the timbers and furnishings within. The Captain's bunk, a bed really, stood against the port bulkhead behind a curtain, while the opposite bulkhead was lined with muskets, and in the middle, two desks covered with charts had been pushed back to back. The impressiveness of the place, however, was marred greatly by the mess within--plates of half eaten food stood about, and discarded clothes hung everywhere except their proper place. It was plain that the expression of which Mr. Crump was so fond, shipshape, had little place in Captain Kidd's lexicon.

"Sit," he said, pointing to one of the chairs that stood beside the desks.

I sat stiffly, knees together, while Captain Kidd remained standing. He walked round behind me, stopped and suddenly demanded, "What's yer name?"

"Christopher Rous--Halburton," I answered.

"Yer real name. And don't lie to me again."

I twisted to look up at his stern visage and decided I'd best tell the truth, but no more than was necessary. "Christopher Rousby, sir."

The Captain came round to where I could see him, nodding, apparently satisfied. "And ye've never been to America in your life, or you'd know that Boston's not much closer to Carolina than London. Ye was travelin' to America with your parents and they went down with the ship, ain't that right."

"Yes sir," I said unthinkingly. "But I have uncles in England, and I'm heir to a large estate," I quickly amended.

The Captain smiled at this and I knew I was sunk. "No one with money goes to America," he said. "Ye have nothin' but the clothes on your back and not even a pair of shoes. But ye 'ave your wits," he added. "How old are ye?"

"Seventeen, sir--soon."

"Have ye any education?"

"Yes, sir. My father is--was, a schoolmaster who instructed me in the trivium and quadrivium."

"What's 'at?"

"Latin grammar, logic and rhetoric, arithmetic, geometry, astronomy and music."

"Sounds like a lot of cargo for so small a vessel," the Captain said. "Can ye read and write?"

"Of course."

He opened a desk drawer and came out with a book. "Read this," he instructed, dropping it in front of me. It was the Holy Bible.

"Which part?"

"Any part."

I let the Book fall open to where it would and began reading from the top of the page.

So they took up Jonah, and cast him forth into the sea and the sea ceased from her raging.

Then the men feared the Lord exceedingly, and offered a sacrifice unto the Lord, and made vows.

Now the Lord had prepared a great fish to swallow up Jonah. And Jonah was in the belly of the fish three days and three nights.

"'at'll be enough o' that," the sailor said, taking back the Holy Book. "Ye don't read like a Presbyterian," he said.

"I'm Episcopal."

"King William's religion." He seemed pleased. "My father raised me a Presbyterian. In Greencock--Scotland--on the Firth of Clyde. I ran away to sea when I was only a bit older than yerself. Be thankful ye didn't make that mistake."

"Yes, sir."

"Have ye thought about what ye'll do now yer parents are gone?"

"I intend to go to America and make my fortune," I replied.

The Captain frowned and shook his head. "I'm afraid the time is past for makin' fortunes in America. All the land from Canada to Florida has been carved up and doled out to those with powerful connections. In this world it's 'ard to make yer way without connections," he observed wistfully. "But 'ere in the West Indies there be plunder for the takin'. 'ere a man can grow richer in a single stroke than in a lifetime ashore and free of all the fetters as well. And what with the gov'nors of these islands pressin' every able-bodied seaman what walks to fight the French, ye can be sure of always findin' a berth. Not for the fightin' mind ye, you're still too green for that. But it's occurred to me," he said, glancing about the cabin, "that I could use a boy with your wits."

"You wish me to become a pirate?" I blurted.

"Pirate!" he shouted, making me jump. "There are no pirates 'ere, boy! We are all loyal subjects of King William engaged in lawful privateerin' against his enemies--the French and the Spanish. Although we're not at war with Spain just now, we no doubt will be soon enough again," he added. "And the infernal Dutch, of course. Even though we're not at war with them, we damned well ought to be. They already own half of Europe, and if we don't stop the crafty blighters they'll soon own all the West Indies as well. Besides, they trade with the French, and anybody what would trade with an enemy of England is an enemy as well. Do ye understand me, boy?" he said, aiming a blunt finger at my head.

"Yes, sir!" I snapped, although I didn't understand at all. Until now I'd thought piracy was stealing, when in truth it was service to the King, so long as a privateer obeyed the rules. But if Captain Kidd was free to attack anyone who was an enemy of England, or who would be, or who should be, it seemed he was free to attack almost anybody he chose.

"There's a great diff'rence 'tween a pirate and a privateer," he went on. "A pirate is interested only in plunder, he has no allegiance to king or country. But a privateer is a loyal subject, a militiaman, always ready to come to the service o' his king, to fight and destroy 'is enemies on the 'igh seas. Why if it wasn't for the likes o' men like me, the King would have to tax the people to the point o' starvation just to support a navy strong enough to defend the country. Either that or say the hell with defendin' the country, like the damned Dutch," he added. "And who do ye think keeps them and the frogs and the Iberians from grabbin' up all the islands in the West Indies but us privateers?"

"I'm sorry, sir, I had no idea what a noble occupation privateering is."

"Noble occupation--exactly," he said, stroking his broad jaw. "Then ye'll give some thought to my offer."

"Oh, I will, sir, yes, sir!"

"Good. Ye can hang a hammock in the sail locker. Let me know your decision when we dock in Nevis."

"May I ask when that will be, sir?"

"A ship is not a horse-cart," the Captain answered, showing me the hatch.

I was greatly confused when I left Captain Kidd's cabin. Could it be that my father was wrong, that there were no more fortunes to be made in America without proper connections? And if so, what choice did I have but to throw in with Captain Kidd and his privateers, or Pirates--for I was not entirely convinced that a brigand could become an honest man simply by calling it something else.

Nor was I reassured when I happened to overhear Mason, Culliford, and Burgess later that night. I was lying on the deck in the dark, taking the breeze through the hawsing, when the three of them came to the bow for a quiet talk. They had recently been on the French island of Mariegalante, where they'd raped, pillaged and plundered for five straight days, in what could scarcely be called a military victory. To Captain Kidd's credit, he apparently remained aloof of the proceedings, while at the same time claiming two thousand pounds as his share, which caused some grumbling amongst my informants.

"I tell ye, boys, our Captain's got a respectable streak runnin' down 'is back that's one day goin' to cause us a great harm," Mason whispered in his raspy voice. "If 'e wants t' be a gentl'man and a officer, let him join the British Navy. But if 'e wants t' be one o' us, 'e's goin' t' have t' get 'is hands dirty like the rest o' us."

"Aye, but 'es a damn fine cap'n, ye must admit," Culliford whispered.

"I don't say 'e ain't. But there's more'n a few think 'e ain't keepin' 'is mind on 'is proper business."

"Ye proposin' we call an election?" Burgess asked.

"I ain't proposin' nothin' damn it! And it better not get out what I'm sayin' or I'll cut yer foockin' tongue out!"

It occurred to me that I was in danger of having my own tongue cut out if Mason discovered I was privy to his mutiny, and so, on hands and knees, I attempted to back away unnoticed. But before I'd gone a foot, I bumped against the anchor chain and sent it clanking to the deck.

"Who's 'ere?" Mason whispered, and a moment later I felt his strong hands on my shoulder, pulling me to me feet. "Whadya hear?" he demanded.

Instead of answering I feigned a great yawn. "Why--Mr. Mason," I said, blinking in slow recognition. "I must have fallen asleep."

"Not bloody likely," he said, thrusting me hard against the rail.

It was apparent that he intended to throw me overboard, and I was about to cry out for the Captain, when Culliford and Burgess stepped in and tried to pull him off me.

"'e di'n't hear nothing,'" Culliford said.

"How d' ye know?" Mason grunted.

"Let 'im go!" Burgess said, while they both grappled with the bigger man.

Wedged between the three of them as I was, I would either be suffocated or drowned within the next few minutes. So I began kicking and biting and scratching like a cat in a sack, until suddenly, in an explosion of grunts and curses, I was free, stumbling down the deck, bouncing off unseen obstacles, arriving finally at the ladder to the quarterdeck where no one but the Captain and the helmsman dare go uninvited. I looked back to see Mason in the moonlight, coming for me, dragging Culliford and Burgess along, one on each arm. Faced with the prospect of a flogging for violating the quarterdeck, or drowning at the hands of Mason, I was about to climb the ladder--when Captain Kid burst out of his hatch shouting, "What the hell is--"

"I accept!" I cried.

Chapter 4

The New World

The next evening, after I had thoroughly cleaned the Captain's cabin and washed all his clothes (while Mason stood by glowering and wondering how much I knew and what I might do with my knowledge), we arrived at Nevis, a small steep-sided island with a broad wharf piled high with goods for shipment. The sweet smell of land after almost two months at sea was almost unbearable, but it would have to wait, I was saddened to hear, until Captain Hewetson of the Royal Navy had paid us a visit.

The prospect of his visit seemed to vex my Captain a good deal. I now wore a uniform of sorts, a plain white blouse, blue breeches and black shoes, and certainly made a smarter appearance than the rest of Captain Kidd's flamboyant crew. But still the Captain wasn't satisfied. He tied a blue scarf round my neck, then decided he didn't like it. When he was finally satisfied with my appearance he turned to my deportment.

"Captain Hewetson is a gentl'man," Captain Kidd warned me. "'e's been in some of the finest houses in England, so 'e's used to the best. Ye do me proud, Christopher, and I'll remember it."

"Aye, sir," I replied weakly, for it was obvious to me that my instructor knew little more about fine houses than I did.

Nonetheless, after a short course of instruction I began to feel accustomed to the role of servant, although not a little unhappy with the position. And when Captain Hewetson came aboard ship, wearing a familiar blue uniform such as I had often seen at home, I was suddenly filled with a homesickness such as I had not felt since Madeira. I stood just inside the Captain's cabin as instructed, ready to run to the cookroom or fetch a bottle of wine if requested, while Captains Hewetson and Kidd sat at the double desk in the center of the cabin.

"Have you done something to the place?" Captain Hewetson asked, after looking curiously about.

"I 'ave a new cabin boy," Captain Kidd explained.

"Well, I might have to press the lad," the British officer said.

"I would considered it an act of war." Kidd laughed when he said it, but Captain Hewetson didn't.

Then Captain Kidd sent me to his chest to fetch a bottle of wine, which I opened and poured just as he had instructed. While Hewetson watched me pour, Kidd watched Hewetson. When the glasses were filled I retreated to the corner near the bed and made myself inconspicuous, just as my Captain had instructed. They spoke briefly of the recent *campaign* at Mariegalante--both agreed it had been a great success--then Hewetson turned to the business that had brought him. A company of marines under the command of his friend, Sir Thomas Thornbill, had been sent to capture the island of St. Martins, but five French war ships had arrived unexpectedly and the marines were presently trapped on the beach. Hewetson did not like to ask, but those English lads had to be rescued, and only his own and one other navy ship was available.

"So with me it would be five against three," Captain Kidd calculated.

"Not very good odds, I'll admit--"

"Not very good for the French," Kidd said. "My ship and crew are at your disposal."

"By god you are one of us!" Captain Hewetson said, bolting to his feet.

Captain Kidd followed him up, and the two gripped hands so fiercely I worried that neither of them would be able to lift a sword when the time came.

When Captain Kidd assembled his crew on the main deck and announced our mission, leaving out the odds, there was some grumbling from the men, but Kidd quickly put a stop to it.

"Damn it, men, we're talking' about English lives! Do we just leave 'em? Sail away and leave St. Martins to the French? And if we do, what'll be next? Nevis, Antigua, Jamaica...? If we don't stop 'em now they'll soon have the whole West Indies! And one other thing," he added, "Captain Hewetson 'as promised that any goods we take from the Frenchies will be ours!"

This stirred some interest in the crew, but not much, for even I knew there was little chance of finding gold on a French warship. We were a sullen group when we set sail a short while later, threading our way northwest through the Leeward Islands, keeping the two ships of the Admiralty close by and arriving off St. Martins the following day. Slowly, with all gun-teams at their stations, the two ships of the Admiralty and the pirate ship Blessed William, tacked for the beach. After some fifteen or twenty minutes, a cry came back from the lead ship--the British marines were visible on the beach! From the quarterdeck where I stood, ready to carry messages to any part of the ship for Captain Kidd, I was soon able to make out the marines, about fifty or sixty of them it seemed, all running about like ants. When the Captain sent the boat-teams to the davits to ready the launches, it began to look as if we might rescue the marines without any interference from the French.

No sooner had that pleasant thought formed in my mind, however, when the French ships came round the point from our starboard side. Having the wind in our favor, we fell in line behind the two Admiralty ships and made for the line of Frenchmen bearing down on us. As the two lines approached, carefully remaining several hundred feet apart, the crew of the Blessed William began shouting, urging Captain Kidd to close with the French so they might board and engage them in hand-to-hand combat. These were pirates, not marines, and they neither wanted to sink their prize, nor risk the loss of their own ship in a gun battle. But this was to be a military battle, and Captain Kidd stood ramrod stiff on the quarter deck while the ship passed in a classic line encounter, cannons hammering at each other while sharpshooters fired from the rigging. The noise was deafening and rifle balls were plunking all around me, which was to be expected since I was standing close to

Captain Kidd, who had for some reason donned a blue naval jacket with gold braid for this encounter.

Still, we somehow went past five blazing warships amidst a scattering of white plumes where the cannon balls fell harmlessly into the sea, without receiving or inflicting any serious damage to any ship. Several men had been struck by musket fire, however, and were lying about the deck either dead or wounded, while the healthy continued to shout, urging the Captain to let them board the Frenchmen. But Captain Kidd was today sailing under Admiralty colors, not the skull and crossbones, and so once again we passed in a line, our hot guns blazing.

This time, however, we took a ball directly below the quarterdeck that shook us to the keel, knocked me to the deck and caused a great commotion. I felt someone pulling me to my feet and next saw Captain Kidd's large face in front of my own.

"Are ye all right?"

"I think so, sir."

"Then run down to the gun deck and tell me what's happened!"

The fear I had felt so keenly until now was suddenly gone, replaced by a strong and curious feeling of detachment. I could see and smell the acrid gunpowder smoke, hear the whiz of passing musket balls and the shrieks of wounded men, but I was only a spectator to whom nothing could happen. I descended the ladder and walked across the main deck, round and over wounded dying men, then down the hatchway to the gun deck. Here the air was blue with smoke, crammed with sixty, sweating, shirtless, sooty-faced gunners, four to each canon, as well as a score or so of others scurrying about in the haze, hauling bleeding men, putting out fires, or standing dazed and motionless, as if they too were just spectators like myself.

I turned to the light behind me and saw a gaping, torn hole in the side of the ship where the aft gun had stood, and through this hole, the French man o'war, poised to fire on us again. There was no sign of the big gun or stolid wooden carriage that had stood on this spot only minutes before, except for a great dagger of splintered timber that had entered the gunner's chest and exited through his back. I saw a leg lying by itself on the deck, and, propped up against the mizzen mast, another man sat staring at his innards, trailing out in front of him like giant blood sausages. While standing transfixed by this, I was jerked violently from behind, a split second before a great explosion, as the gun and wheeled carriage leaped back to the spot where I had been standing.

"Get out o' here before ye get yourself killed!" a blackened seaman shouted, while shaking me by the shoulders. It took a moment before I recognized this shirtless man with a black bandanna wrapped over his ears as Robert Culliford.

"Captain Kidd sent me," I replied. "What shall I tell him?"

"Tell, 'im 'e's a godamned butcher and a fool to risk us and the ship like this!"

"And when this is over we're votin' us a new captain!" a second blackened gunner shouted. I knew from his voice that it was Sam Burgess, but under all that blood and soot I couldn't have otherwise identified him.

I started to speak, but was interrupted by another fired gun before I could shout, "How many guns are out?"

"Ain't this enough?" Burgess said, pointing to the wrecked site where the gun had stood. "We lost four mates 'ere, and ye can tell 'im we'll lose plenty more before the day's done if he insists on fightin' like a gentl'man! Get up and tell 'im for God's sake!" he shouted, pushing me roughly.

I staggered back along the gun deck, stopping once as the sponger fired his gun. It leaped in front of me in a deafening explosion, spitting a muzzle-flash of crimson in the blue smoke. Then I was climbing out of the hatchway, bleary-eyed, gasping for air, then stumbling across the littered deck and pulling myself up the ladder. There was a last burst from us as the final French man o'war slid by, then silence. Captain Kidd was standing at the taffrail, affording the French sharpshooters a last chance, when I climbed onto the quarterdeck. At that moment I felt the tears break and run down my blackened cheeks and I was suddenly no longer a spectator. Keeping my head down, I advanced to Captain Kidd's side.

"Well?"

"Mr. Culliford and Mr. Burges said…

"Yes…?"

"It's hell down there." I tried to keep my head down to hide my tears, but Captain Kidd placed his hand under my chin and firmly lifted my face.

"There is no time for that on a man o' war," he said. "Now tell me, 'ow many guns are out?"

"The aft gun on the starboard side, sir. I think four men are dead and several more wounded. The men don't like it, sir."

"Did I ask that?"

"No, sir."

"Then stow it," he said. "And stand by for orders."

I expected the Captain would come about and pass by the French again, perhaps this time finishing us off for good. But I was mistaken. Instead, he turned to the signalman.

"Signal Captain Hewetson that I request a council o' war. Hold to your course."

The men were relieved when we sailed away from the French, rather than come about and have at them again. While we grouped at one end of the island and the French did the same at the opposite end, the marines waited in the middle for their fate to be determined. How strange, it seemed, that being intent on killing and maiming each other only a short while before, each should allow the other a peaceful time to plan the next deadly move, as if this were a sporting contest. Indeed, as I watched Captain Hewetson shaking hands with Captain Kidd aboard the Lion, they seemed pleased as any sportsmen about to embark upon a hunt. It was only the groan and cry of the dying that belied that pleasant image.

I was pleased that Captain Kidd should be gone from the ship for a while, as it allowed me time to recover after the mortification of tears. I was extremely angry with myself and at a loss to explain my behavior, as tears were never my wont. But I guessed that my ordeal at sea, the slave ship, and now all this carnage, was just too much in one week for a fifteen year old. At that moment I felt the greatest desire to be home with my father that I had felt since Madeira, but this time a hopeless desire, as I was certain we could not survive another line encounter against such odds.

When the ship's surgeon came up from the gun deck to see to the victims of the sharpshooters who lay about the deck, he was so black from smoke and soaked in blood that he might have been mistaken for a gunner, except that he wore a shirt and shoes. He moved from man to man, deciding quickly who should live and who should die, wrapping the limbs of the less seriously injured, while leaving the gut-shot for later. To cheer the men, the quartermaster went among them, ladling out a ration of grog to each. The healthy helped the wounded to drink, and that was good to see, while we all waited quietly to see what our Captain would do next. If his decision were to come back later for the marines, there wouldn't have been a single disappointed sailor among the men of the Blessed William. But I knew, when I had heard Captain Kidd call his privateer a man o' war, that he would never leave those marines on the beach. In just three days he had promoted himself from pirate to privateer to Captain of the Royal Navy.

When the Captain returned from the council of war, after more than an hour, he called all able hands to the main deck to announce his decision.

"After a council o' war with Captain Hewetson, we've come to the conclusion that we're badly out-gunned by the French, and our best advantage lies with our superior number. Therefore we will board the Frenchmen!" he said, followed by a great cheer.

This time there was no complaining among the men of the Blessed William as they bore down on the French. It was rumored that one of the French ships might be carrying Spanish gold, but even if she were carrying nothing save her ordnance, a French man o' war would make a fine pirate ship. For the French sailors, whose meager monthly earnings would not be augmented in the least by the taking of a prize, hand-to-hand combat was neither desirable nor rewarding, and so they could be counted on to offer little resistance to our pirates, who had a well-known fondness for the cutlass. Of course, it was also true that the seamen of the British Admiralty stood to gain nothing by boarding the Frenchmen, so by far the loudest and most enthusiastic cheers issued from the Blessed William as the squadron bore down upon the French. Our men hung from the rigging, waving cutlasses in the air and shrieking fiercely as we closed in on the reluctant French, while the men of the Admiralty stood in formation, bayonets fixed.

When the French men o' war began veering off, Captain Kidd tried to follow but lost the wind, and we once again passed in a line, our canons firing futilely. However, when we came about and picked up the breeze that had favored the French, it was plain to us that this time we would dictate the action.

It was apparently equally plain to the French commander too, who, instead of coming about to face us, chose instead to flee with the wind. This time a great cheer went up from the men of the Admiralty, who were about to rescue the marines with little injury to themselves; while the men of the Blessed William, watching their prey disappear, were left with a damaged ship and the loss of several precious hands.

It was not a happy crew that turned back to Nevis that evening, after boarding Sir Thomas Thornbill's marines. Yet Captain Kidd, who stood with his feet planted firmly on the quarterdeck, broad jaw jutting into the wind, looked every bit a gentlemen who had just won a great naval battle.

Governor Codrington was waiting on the dock to greet us when we sailed into Nevis. Our men stood at the rail watching as the Governor embraced Sir Thomas and shook hands with Hewetson and Kidd. Meanwhile, our wounded waited to be disembarked until the gangplank could be cleared of marines. When they'd finally been formed up and marched off to their barracks, the wounded were carried off our three ships and laid in a row on the dock. The Governor, who wore a dark coat over his spare frame despite the heat, glanced at the passing wounded and spoke an encouraging word from time to time, while all the time listening to Captain Hewetson's glowing account of the daring rescue. From what I could hear, Hewetson was convinced the French had fled to Anguilla as the result of superior military tactics, which he was describing fully with his hands, while to everyone aboard the Blessed William it was nothing less than the fear of having their throats slit. When Culliford and Burgess began to parrot the officer, in voices loud enough to be heard on the dock, Captain Kidd glanced reprovingly at the sailors but without any effect. The men were not pleased at having risked their ship and their lives for nothing, only to be treated as if they hadn't even been along.

Sensing this perhaps, Captain Hewetson turned to Kidd and said, "And Captain Kidd fought as well as any of us."

"His majesty is pleased," Governor Codrington said. "And I trust you too will have dinner with us."

"Thank ye, yer honor, I should be most pleased," Captain Kidd said, with a short bow.

"Will ye look at that now," Mason said in his hoarse whisper. "Our Cap'n 'avin' dinner with the Gov'nor, while leavin' us to pump the blood from the bilge."

Several others besides Culliford and Burgess nodded their agreement at this, I noticed.

That evening was my first ashore in almost two months, and how I reveled in it. There were so many amazing things I would discover in the New World over the next several years, many of them so ugly and brutal that I am still trying to forget them, while others, now scarcely remembered, were so beautiful I was sure at the time they'd stay with me forever. Oddly enough it was the lizards on the docks of Nevis that I remember most vividly to this day. They were tiny lizards, not as long as my hand, that I saw scurrying in and out of the cracks among the hot planks as I took my first steps ashore. I was aware of the danger from the many poisonous serpents and reptiles of the New World, yet I couldn't resist the urge to capture one of these miniature dragons and have a closer look. When I caught one by his tail, it broke off and he darted away, apparently unharmed. So I caught the next one amidship and hoisted him to my palm. He made no attempt to bite, just stood quietly staring at me with a friendly look that completely won me ever. But this wasn't all, for as I watched, a most amazing thing occurred-- the lizard changed color! He went from green to brown to blue, then back to green. It was a truly magical dragon I held in my hand, unlike anything else in nature, and I was sure it was an omen of good, or a symbol of power, or just something magnificent whose secret meaning would be later revealed.

Then a sailor, who had been watching me, spoke: "What are ye starin' at, boy, it's just a chameleon."

"Chameleon," I repeated, as I placed the magical dragon back on the dock. Even his name was beautiful.

Then, while the chameleon was looking up at me, the sailor brought his bare foot down on him and crushed the life from my magical dragon.

"Damned pests," he said, as he walked off.

I turned and ran away as the tears welled blearily in my eyes, then broke and ran down my face.

At dusk I climbed to the peak of the mountain and watched the sun set on the ships in the golden bay, and watched neighboring islands fade slowly in the darkness until they were indistinguishable from the sea. Yet I was more aware then of the great difference between the two, of all the land things I had until then taken for granted--my dear father, my warm dry room that neither pitched nor yawed, the shelves of books that provided more than enough adventure--than ever before, and I wanted desperately to be home. But all the wishing in the world would do me no good. I had made a terrible mistake and now it was up to me to somehow correct it.

Generous though Captain Kidd's offer of employment was, shipping with pirates was plainly no way back to England, and so I would tell him straightway that I could not accept. I would remain on Nevis-- she was an English colony after all--and wait for a ship returning to England. Yes, that's what I would do, I decided, as I rose and started down in the direction of the light at the bottom of the hill.

Part way down, a warm light rain began to fall, and I was suddenly besieged by doubt. Was it possible that Captain Kidd would refuse my resignation? If so I'd be forced to jump ship, and if caught I'd be lashed to ribbons. Or if he did let me go, where would I get the money to pay for my passage? I had assumed I would work my way back, but of course a boy with little experience at sea was scarcely as desirable as a paying passenger. It was terrible to think, after my recent experience aboard the Blessed William, that I might be compelled to remain with Captain Kidd, if only to acquire sufficient booty to pay my way back to England.

With this depressing prospect hanging heavily over me, I made my way slowly through the rain, along the dock in the direction of the Blessed William. A dim light glowed through the canvas that had been patched over the hole at the gun deck to keep the sea out, and as I approached I could make out several silhouetted figures huddled round a lantern, like players on a curtained stage waiting to perform. As I passed by this curtained glow, I heard the distinct raspy whisper of Mason and stopped to listen.

"We stole this ship once and we can steal 'er again!"

"We stole her from the French, not from Captain Kidd," an unfamiliar voice argued.

"Goddamnit stop callin' 'im Captain! We voted, 'im out di'n't we!" Culliford's voice this time.

"So why not just tell 'im?" another unfamiliar voice suggested. "The election was lawful, 'e's got to step down. Them's the rules."

"Why don't *ye* tell 'im," Burgess suggested, setting off a low rumble of laughter.

"Mason's captain, it's up to 'im. Ye ain't scared are ye?"

"Shut your foockin' hawse'ole!" Mason rasped. "I ain't scared o' any man, but I ain't a fool either. Kidd ain't a buccaneer no more. 'e thinks 'e's a foockin' gent and 'e' won't be bound by the rules o' the Brethren."

"And 'e don't have to neither, 'cuz 'e 's got the Gov'nor on his side," Culliford said.

"*We* might call it an election but the Admiralty calls it mutiny," someone cautioned.

"Then there's nothin' else for it" Burgess said.

I didn't stay around for the final decision, but it was plain enough they were going to steal the ship, and I wanted to be nowhere around when it happened. I would spend the night on the beach and pretend to be just as surprised as Captain Kidd when he discovered the ship gone in the morning, I decided, as I threaded my way among the casks and bales stored along the dock. But why would I sleep on the wet beach with the mosquitoes, rather than in my nice dry sail locker? No, Kidd would see through me in a minute, and I'd soon wish I was on the Blessed William with the mutineers. The only thing I could do was hie me off to the Governor's house and report to my Captain what I'd heard. That way he couldn't force me to sail with him, knowing the multineers would cut my throat the first chance they got, and he'd probably give me a reward sufficient to pay my way home. It was a great opportunity, I told myself, as I climbed the hill to the Governor's house.

Kidd and the Governor and several naval officers were seated at a long table, all quite drunk, when the black maid led me into the dining room. Governor Codrington sat at the head of the table, while Sir Thomas sat at the foot with Kidd, Hewetson and two other officers amidship.

"Eh--what's this?" Governor Codrington asked, peering at me through heavy-lidded eyes.

"My cabin boy," Captain Kidd announced. "What is it, Christopher?"

"It's just that--well, sir…"

"Speak, lad," Captain Hewetson urged.

"They're talking of stealing the ship, sir!"

"They're what…!" he roared, jumping to his feet, knocking his chair to the floor. "Those sons o' bitches!"

"Mutiny…?" Hewetson asked. "Flog 'em and hang 'em--!"

"Quickl…!" Captain Kidd said, coming round the table, grabbing and pushing me towards the door. Then, remembering himself, he stopped and turned to the Governor. "I'm sorry, sir--if you'll excuse me--wonderful dinner…!"

"Certainly," the Governor said, as Captain Kidd pushed me through the door.

The Captain hung heavily on me, firing questions as we staggered together down the dark hill in the tropical rain. "How did you hear? Which ones? When?" Whatever my answer, he seemed to have known it before I replied, saying, "I knew it, I knew it," to my every response. Mason was a scurvy sea-tramp whom he had known would do something like this the first chance he got. The captain reminded me that he was not a man given to harsh punishment, but he would nonetheless flog the sonofabitch half to death when he had him. "Culliford and Burgess too, those treacherous sodomites!"

Drunk though he was, his plans were well in his mind when he arrived at the dock, ready to charge up the gangplank and flog the mutineers to within an inch of their lives. However, when we arrived there was neither any sign of the gangplank or the Blessed William. Captain Kidd stared uncertainly at the empty berth for a moment, then turned to me and said in a fuzzy voice, weak with hope, "Wrong berth...."

"I fear not, sir," I said, as I hauled in the thick rope, still belayed to the bollard, and showed him the wet end, freshly cut and abandoned in their haste to get away.

"Sloppy, sloppy.... he mumbled shaking his head at such waste. "But they'll not make it without Cap'n Kidd, I promise ye that. How long do ye reckon they be gone?"

"Perhaps an hour."

"We'll go back to the Governor. I'll get Captain Hewetson and we'll go after 'em. Come along!" he said, grabbing and pulling me after, back up the hill to the Governor's house.

But Captain Hewetson proved not to be nearly so exercised by the villainy as was Captain Kidd. "The scum of the West Indies!" he proclaimed, as he filled his glass with wine. "You're well rid of the buggers, I say."

"Hear, hear!" Sir Thomas echoed, raising his glass.

"And that ship is no great loss either," Hewetson added.

"'tis true, they're an unsavory lot," Kidd, now quite sober, agreed. "And in some things I'd be the first to admit the Blessed William is sadly lackin'. But when it come to pullin' yer marines off the beach, Sir Thomas, both my men and my ship proved more than sufficient to the task, if I might remind ye."

"Hear hear," the marine commander repeated.

"With a modest contribution from the British navy--if I might remind you," Captain Hewetson said.

"I could no more forget yer contribution than you mine, sir," Captain Kidd replied with a short bow. "'owever there's one thing a gentl'man of the Royal Navy is like to forget: that is, when I lose my ship, the King don't provide me a new one."

"Quite right, quite right!" the Governor, whom I had thought asleep in his chair, piped up. "You've performed a great service for England, Mr. Kidd, and I intended to see that you have your ship."

"Thank you, Gov'nor," Captain Kidd said, uncertainly.

"Might I remind you, Governor, with all due respect, that I'm rather preoccupied with the French at the moment," Captain Hewetson interrupted.

"The very same preoccupation that caused Mr. Kidd the loss of his ship, if I remember correctly. But you needn't worry, I have no intention of sending you after the mutineers. I have a ship, Mr. Kidd, recently taken from the French. You may have her."

"Thank you, sir, thank you very much," Captain Kidd blurted.

"Unfortunately I can spare no men…."

"Oh I'll find 'em sir. I'll find 'em somewhere. And I'll find the men who stole my ship, and when I do I'll hang 'em from the yards," Kidd vowed.

"I do believe you will," the Governor said, teetering as he rose to shake Captain Kidd's hand.

Captain Hewetson also rose to shake Captain Kidd's hand when we took our leave a few minutes later, but this salutation was most cool. Kidd seemed not to notice, however, as his mind was filled with thoughts of vengeance.

Chapter 5

Zeus doth not bring all Men's Plans to Fulfillment

We, Captain Kidd and I, re-christened the French ship Antigua, although Vengeance would have better suited her, so intent was my Captain on revenge. Governor Codrington allowed us little more than a dozen men to sail the ship, old and enfeebled sailors unsuitable for combat against the French, yet Kidd seemed somehow to think them more than a match for his former comrades-in-arms. Mad as he was at this time, he was wily enough not to tell his infirm crew of their mission, informing them only that we are going on a *voyage of purchase* against the French, under a *no prey, no pay* contract, with a letter of commission signed by Governor Codrington. The old men assumed our commission extended only to the nearby waters of the Caribbean, and our prey would be no larger than a French fishing boat, and therefore did not share my great fear. That was why, during the few days spent outfitting the ship, I searched desperately for a means of escape.

I knew better than to ask Captain Kidd for permission to quit his ship, as disloyalty was much on his mind; and if I deserted on this small island, I would be quickly captured and returned. And although Captain Kidd had so far treated me no less kindly than my own father, I recognized that an act of mutiny, coming so soon after the treachery of his former crew, might very well test his goodwill beyond my endurance.

So while I toiled under my Captain's watchful eye, bringing supplies aboard the Antigua and seeing to their safe storage, I kept my own eyes alert to any ship that might be sailing out of Nevis, bound ideally for England, although I would have gone most anywhere to avoid Captain Kidd's insane quest for the Blessed William.

I have often wondered over the last several years, what changes my life would have taken had I managed to stow aboard a departing ship at that time, and had no further adventures with Captain Kidd. At first I assumed, so determined was I, that I would have returned home one way or another and become a schoolmaster like my father. But as I would soon learn, even the most rigid plans in life are oft but tissue in the stormy winds of fate. Sometimes the winds blow ill, but sometimes they push us to adventures of which we can neither conceive nor plan. I would not presume to advise others, but when you've heard my tale, I hope you'll appreciate as well as fear the wind.

It was Mr. Cleary, one of the old sailors in our new crew, who first made me aware of the unlikely surprises life holds for even the most settled of us. His family had been raising sheep on the same stretch of land on the southwest coast of Ireland for over two hundred years, and he had never given any thought to doing anything else for the rest of his life. Until that ominous day long ago, when he went for a walk along the beach with the lovely girl he intended to marry, and stumbled upon a group of drunken English seamen. The sailors tried to rape the girl, but Cleary managed to fight them off long enough for her to make her escape, which so angered the seamen that they tied him up and took him to their ship, a pirate ship.

The plan was to hold Cleary for ransom, but when a hundred enraged Irishmen came after them in fishing boats, they upped anchor and fled south, taking Cleary with them. Faced with little choice, Cleary joined the pirate crew, intending to get away at the first opportunity and return to Ireland, his sheep and his fiancée. However, after taking a Spanish merchantman in the Bay of Biscay and setting the Armada after them, they fled south with their prize. Near the Strait of Gibraltar a disagreement broke out among the crew, some of whom wished to enter the Mediterranean, where the plunder was good but the risk great; while others preferred to continue down and around the tip of Africa into the Indian Ocean, where the treasure might be less, but so too was the risk. Because Cleary's interest lay in a safe return home, not riches, he chose to switch to the lightly armed merchantman and sail to the Indian Ocean, while the majority chose to take the original pirate ship past the guns of Gibraltar and along the Barbary Coast to the Levantine.

By the time his ship reached the isle of Madagascar off the east coast of Africa, the unofficial headquarters for piracy in the Indian Ocean, Cleary found himself a wanted man, the result of having plundered a trading post, or *factory*, of the powerful English East India Company. So, at the first opportunity, he quit himself of his unsavory companions, changed his name to Riley, and jumped aboard the first ship he could find, an East India Company merchantman bound for London, its hold stuffed with silks and tapestries from Bombay. They proceeded from factory to factory along the west coast of Africa (where, at each landing, passenger Riley invariably became ill and remained inside his hot cabin), managing to avoid pirates all the way to the Canary Islands.

It was there that the pirates struck, although not on another ship, but rather on their own. It seemed that the sailors of the merchantman, realizing a single bolt of India silk was worth more than they could earn in a lifetime, decided to rectify this injustice by taking the ship and cargo for themselves. Just as passenger Riley was about to be pitched into the sea with the ship's captain and officers, he quickly let it be known that he was not an innocent traveler who might later testify against them, but a hardened pirate who could be of great help to them in their new career. Cleary apparently made an able spokesman on his own behalf, because when the vote was taken, only one man, the leader of the mutiny, opposed his inclusion. It proved to be a fateful vote, not only for Cleary, but for their former leader as well, who was promptly tossed overboard with the captain and his officers, one moment a rich and powerful man, the next shark food. Such are life's ironies and vicissitudes.

Their plan had been to slip into Tangier under Dutch colors and sell their goods, then return to the Indian Ocean on a voyage of purchase. Cleary decided he would accompany them as far as Tangier, then make one more attempt to get home. Unfortunately, they ran into a Royal Naval squadron off Casablanca, enroute south to protect the factories of the East India Company that had lately come under increasing attack, and they were forced to turn out to sea. Now the brigands began to have serious doubts about their new career, as they imagined the long arm of the British Navy everywhere, ready to pluck them from their ship and hang them from the gallows on Execution Dock. After another long discussion and a short vote, it was decided they would head for the Caribbean, where, it was rumored, a man could hide out on the islands of the French, the Spanish, the Dutch or the Danes, and be safe from English justice forever. Cleary was not happy to make his way back to Ireland by way of the Caribbean, but neither was he ready to swim for it, so he went along with the pirates.

Once in the Carribbean, they made their way successfully past the British navy to Port Royal on the island of Jamaica, a place notoriously hospitable to pirates, affording such pleasures as were beyond the ken of an Irish sheepherder. Like the thousands of other free booters already abroad in the Caribbean by then, Cleary was quickly taken by the tropics and, for the time being at least, put off his plan to return to Ireland. During the few days we worked together loading the ship, he filled my head with such tales of plunder and lust as caused my head to spin and my blood to boil, until at last I had to order him to stop so we might get our work done. But one might as easily silence a hurricane as an Irish storyteller.

When the time came for him to sign for the voyage, he replied, in answer to Captain Kidd's question, that he was about fifty and had been in the Caribbean for about thirty years. In all that time he had been privateering off and on throughout the Caribbean, Mexico, Central America, South America, and north along the American coast as far as New York, which he still called New Amsterdam, although it had been in the hands of the English since 1664.

"I'll sign for this one, but it must be my last," Cleary said, as he made his mark beside his name.

"Why is that?" Captain Kidd asked, fearing he might be ill and near death, as he surely looked it.

"I have a bride waitin' for me in Ireland," he answered.

And that was when I learned that Zeus doth not bring all men's plans to fulfillment.

To Captain Kidd, a bachelor of about forty years, Cleary's intention didn't seem unremarkable. Nor did it seem unremarkable to him that he and a dozen aged and crippled men, along with one fit though fearful cabin boy, would set out in pursuit of several times that many fit and hardened swashbucklers. Yet we did set sail on that February day in 1689, while Governor Codrington (whom I'd decided was either mad as Kidd or else wanted him dead), saluted confidently from the dock.

Immediately after Kidd's ship had been stolen, Codrington sent orders to the other British governors in the Caribbean to be on the lookout for the Blessed William, and when word came back that they had plundered a Spanish ship off the south coast of Puerto Rico, Kidd set sail for Ponce. When we arrived there we found the badly damaged Spanish ship lying on the beach, along with her badly damaged and demoralized crew. Cleary, who spoke Spanish, accompanied Captain Kidd and me and four rowers to the beach, where the wounded lay dying under the palm trees, while the survivors huddled helplessly nearby.

When Captain Kidd splashed out of the launch, dressed in his favorite blue coat, he saluted first the fallen ship, then the Spaniards on the beach, who regarded such formality with curious stares. When Captain Kidd told Cleary to inform them he wished to pay his respects to their captain, he said something that sounded like a mix of Spanish and French, to which none of the Spaniards made any reply.

"Say it louder," Kidd instructed.

But before Cleary could comply, a small dark man, wearing only bloodied breaches, rose to his feet. "I speak English a little," he said. "Captain dead. English kill Captain because we fight. Six more," he added, running a finger across his throat.

"Your Captain was a brave man," Kidd said, which was obviously true. Once a ship raises the red flag of piracy, a captain is faced with three choices: fight, flee or surrender. If he surrenders his ship and all its contents, he knows that custom requires his life be spared (although it's unlikely he will get another command from the British gentlemen of the East India Company); if he flees and is captured, it's likely he'll be killed; but if he fights and is captured, it's certain he'll be killed--and usually in a most unpleasant manner. Captain Kidd appraised the men on the beach with obvious admiration, then turned back to the wiry Spaniard. "What are your plans?"

The Spaniard shrugged. "We have no ship."

"I am Captain Kidd, and I have a letter of commission from the English government," Kidd informed him, removing a sealed paper from inside his coat. When he waved it in front of the Catholic sailors, it was as if he were a priest raising the monstrance, for they knew, even without benefit of the interpreter, that this was the talisman that allowed them to practice their *religion* without fear of interference by Protestant British gunboats. "We're off on a voyage of purchase, no prey no pay, eight shares to the crew, two to the ship," Kidd went on. "Tell them any man of courage is free to join us."

So while we repaired a discreet distance from the Spanish, they discussed Kidd's offer. It was plain that some were concerned about the wounded, while others were more concerned with the prospect of a new ship and the riches that awaited--for eight parts to them and only two to the Captain was a generous offer. When voices were suddenly raised, it seemed an impasse had been met. After a few minutes of this, the interpreter approached with a sheepish look on his face.

"The men, they want a paper," he said, making a signatory gesture. Apparently the eight-to-two split had sounded too good to be true.

"My secretary will draw up the articles once we're full aboard," Kidd said, with a nod to me to indicate I had been promoted from cabin boy to secretary.

The interpreter returned to his mates with this assurance, and a few minutes later our crew was enlarged by twenty-one men. We waited while the volunteers went among those who had chosen to stay, hugging each other in a way Englishmen never did, then ferried them out to the ship in two trips. Perhaps, I decided, if Mason and the others take a few more Spanish ships, we might yet assemble a crew sufficient to attack them.

When we returned to the ship with the first boatload of Spaniards, I was amazed to discover that several of them were familiar with some of our men. They embraced as they had on the beach, and fell into excited bilingual conversations about all that had happened since they last sailed together.

"Know 'im...?" Battersby, a grizzled old hand exploded, when I expressed my surprise. "Not only that, I sailed with his father before 'im!"

"Two generations of pirates?"

"Oh, more 'n 'at," Battersby replied thoughtfully. "Cuz I know 'is father's father was in the trade as well. And 'e claimed that his great great great great grandfather used to go piratin' in the Mediterranean with ol' Chris Columbus."

I of course believed no such thing of Christopher Columbus, but when I thought about it, it didn't seem at all unreasonable that there should by now be several generations of pirates in the Caribbean. After all, the business had begun shortly after Columbus's arrival in 1492, and had been expanding steadily for almost two hundred years. It was strange that while in England in 1688, America had seemed a new and primitive country with but a few thousand Europeans scattered in stockaded settlements among salvage Indians, when in every place I had been thus far, I was greeted by European civilization. True, it was not exactly English civilization, but neither could it be said to be Spanish, French or Dutch either, although it was certainly all of these too. It seemed that no matter how hard the English tried to make things like home, there always remained some foreign furnishings about. Yet when they all got mixed together, they didn't seem to be foreign anymore, just different, just American. On the beach the Spanish were Spanish and the English were English, while here on the ship with all of them together, they seemed to change before my eyes, like the chameleons of Nevis.

On the morning of the following day we arrived at the deserted side of the large island of Hispaniola.

"Here we'll find some *boucaniers*," Cleary said to me, as we watched the Captain ease the ship over the shoals that guarded the hidden cove.

"You mean buccaneers?" I asked.

"That's the modern word. About a hundred years ago, the Brethren of the coast left some cattle on these islands, so there'd always be food for a poor sailor to hunt and kill and cook over his *boucan*. These pups might call 'em buccaneers, but us old sea-dogs know they're boucaniers," the scholar said.

Just as Cleary predicted, we'd no sooner anchored in the boucanier's cove before the buccaneers, some with wives and children, rowed out in canoes to greet us. Once again everybody seemed to know everybody else, including Captain Kidd, with whom many of them had sailed in the past, and with whom they appeared eager to sail again. Had they known he was on a voyage of vengeance rather than one of purchase, they would not have been nearly so enthusiastic.

Then we all went ashore, where the boucans were fired up and the rum kegs cracked open, and the sides of wild beef brought out. Alerted by the scent of cooking meat perhaps, men and women and children continued to drift down to the beach from up in the hills. The men were all nationalities and colors, from bone white to coal black. Most were between twenty and forty, military deserters, runaway slaves, indentured servants, or simply common men unwilling to abide the constraints of society, but there were grandfathers and grandchildren among them as well. The women varied from black to tan, except for a few white Europeans, and the children, some twenty or thirty of them, from babes in arms to boys and girls my age or a bit older, were mostly the hue of golden honey. Most of the girls were quite pretty, while the wives divided about equally in two camps. As if to compensate, some of the men, whose wives were not so attractive, had taken two or even three, but the prettier women were rationed more sparingly. There were men like Burgess and Culliford among them as well, holding hands and clinging to each other just like the husbands and wives, and no one taking any notice at all.

Their clothes were as varied as the bodies they adorned. Many women and men wore crudely sewn dresses or trousers from purloined silk of unlawful colors, while others wore fancy gowns or breeches that might have been taken off the backs of their owners at sword-point. While the men drank and regaled one another with their exploits of the past, several wives got up and walked to the edge of the water where they removed all their clothes. This of course drew some enthusiastic whistling and cheering from the men. Then, with three or four on each side, they pulled a canoe into the water to about waist depth and stood very still. I couldn't imagine what this was all about, but as no one followed, I saw it was not to be a big naked frolic in the sea. When the women had remained motionless and quiet in the water for a minute or so, two of them suddenly raised their hands out of the water and a large glistening fish splashed into the canoe. Then another and another and another, until soon the canoe was filled to the gunnel with flopping fish.

After they brought the fish in they came and stood by the fires while the men jostled one another to rub·them dry. Because these men were not their husbands (who preferred to lie on the sand with a cup of rum), I expected to see cutlasses flashing at any moment, but their husbands didn't mind in the least, and the wives enjoyed it fully. In fact when one of our men proposed going off into the bush with one of the women, her husband was quick to assent.

"Just don't come back with 'arry's baby like the last time!" he shouted after them.

"Is 'at so?" Harry asked.

"That one right there," the husband said, pointing to a boy of about four who did indeed look like Harry.

"Well I'll be flogged," Harry said, coming forward to tousle the boy's hair. Then he quickly remembered the press of things more urgent and ran off to perhaps present his son with a sibling.

That was just the beginning. Later in the evening, after the fish and wild beef had been eaten and the rum devoured, all the men who were up to it went off with a woman or two. Being a Christian, I could of course not condone such behavior, yet I could understand how the life of the buccaneer might appeal to a great many men of lesser fortitude. For what man could object to living in a tropical paradise where fishes jumped into the boat, fruit fell from the trees, cattle were free for the taking, and a man could have as many wives as he wished?

I must admit, that in a moment of weakness, I too went off with a woman that night, a girl really, a bronze girl about my age, with a face that danced and glowed like the sun setting on the cove. Nearly everyone else was drunk (except for Captain Kidd who had presided over the revel like a stone statue) and I was a bit tipsy myself, when the beautiful girl, whom I'd not noticed before, came and sat beside me.

"What is your name?" she asked.

"Chris'opher," I slurred.

"Like the island," she said. "I am Roxanne."

"Roxanne," I breathed. I had never heard such a beautiful name, except for chameleon, in all my life. At home the girls had names like Prudence or Faith--except for Rebecca--of whom Roxanne rather reminded me, especially her eyes when they caught the last light of the sun.

"Would you like to come with me?" she asked.

"Where?"

"To my secret cove."

"Well, all right. But I mustn't miss my ship," I warned, as she pulled me up after.

She promised she would have me back in time, then took my hand and led me along the beach and around the point to her secret cove. It was a broad pool encircled almost entirely by sugar-white sand and arching palms and, across the opening to the sea, a coral gate to keep out sharks. At the back of the cove a waterfall dropped from a cliff in front of a cave and trickled down the beach into the cove. I stopped at the water's edge and peered down. It was almost dark, but a full moon had risen and I could see the clean white sand through the clear water, and hundreds of fishes flitting like particles of rainbow

"Does anyone else know about this place?" I asked, for it was too beautiful for any but us.

"Only my friend."

"Your boy friend?"

"You will see," she replied, as she pulled what appeared to be two tiny speckled eggs from her dress. "When you have eaten the flower."

"Flower…?" I said, as she raised it to my lips. When she placed it on my tongue I realized it was not an egg but something heavy and solid. And when I followed her lead and bit down on her *flower*, I discovered that it tasted more like ground weeds.

"Swallow," she ordered, when it appeared I was about to spit it out. Again I obeyed.

Then, some time later--I don't know how long but it was dark--I felt Roxanne's warm breath tickling the hair at the back of my neck and her breasts pressing against my back as her hands went round my waist to my belt. I stood motionless while she undressed me--she had already removed her dress--and together we walked into the water. The water was warm and soft as a pillow, and there was no need to swim as it was impossible to sink. Unless I wanted to dive down to the white sand bottom, then push myself up and break the surface like a--"Shark!" I spurted.

For a brief nightmarish second I was back at sea, floating on the hatch cover, while dolphins that appeared to be sharks, glided and circled around me. However, when a moment later I heard Roxanne's sweet voice, I was immediately calm. I was swimming in Roxanne's secret cove, guarded by coral gates, safe from sharks and drowning, suspended in bliss.

"It's my friend," she said, as a dolphin appeared before us. The dolphin dived and rose out of the water, stood on its tail and spoke her name—"Roxanne."

"He talks," I said, not at all surprised.

"Only to me."

"Your friend is a dolphin," I said, greatly relieved.

"My dear dear friend."

Then the dolphin rose under Roxanne and she was astride him like a horse, both of them gleaming and gliding round and round the pool, up and down, up and down, smooth as combers on a clear summer day. Suddenly the dolphin turned and made directly for me in the center of the pool. I felt his smooth skin as he slid past me, then turned back and nudged me gently with his bottle-nose.

"He wants you to get up," Roxanne said, extending her hand.

I took her hand, threw one leg over the dolphin, then wrapped one arm around Roxanne's waist, and we were off. I had marveled at how Roxanne stayed atop the plunging dolphin, but now I saw there was nothing to it. The dolphin dived to the bottom and leaped high in the air, and I remained firmly astride him all the while, unable to fall off unless I willed it. Sometimes we remained under the water for several minutes, yet I felt no need for air, and sometimes we exploded out of the water on a wake of phosphorescent froth, and rose high into the night sky, up among the fiery stars, soaring, soaring, then settling back down, plunging into the water, clean as an arrow.

Then, as suddenly as he had come, the dolphin was gone and I found myself alone in the center of the pool. "Roxanne...?" I called.

"I'm here, Christopher," I heard, though I didn't see her.

Then in a moment she appeared at my side, quick as a dolphin, being one moment here then another there, until I thought she might be an apparition. Or a mermaid luring me to a watery grave. But then I felt her hand on my tiller, and I let her steer me where she would, and we swam about like a pair of dolphins intent on mating. But we weren't dolphins, we were a boy and a girl in deep water with nowhere to stand or lie down. I was about to suggest that we swim for shore where we could lie on the warm sand and make love like humans, when Roxanne turned her back on me, and I worried that our tryst was done. Until she pressed her stern against my tiller and skillfully steered me to her port of pleasure. Now with me upon her back, we sped together towards the promised haven, round and round the cove, accompanied by the groans and sighs and whispered words that sting and lash desire, until, unable any longer to withstand the wave of pleasure, Roxanne and I, at one and the same moment, were overcome with bliss.

When I awoke on the beach at dawn with a throbbing head, not far from last night's party, I was surprised to find that I was alone. And when I inquired of the bleary-eyed revelers where I might find Roxanne, there were none who knew of her. No matter, on an island so small I would surely find her--if given the time. But time was precious, the debauch was done, and Captain Kidd was anxious to sail. I never again saw my beautiful swimmer.

With the addition of twenty-six bleary-eyed buccaneers to our crew, we began to resemble a formidable pirate ship, with almost sixty men now under arms. Now I understood why Captain Kidd had been so unworried about finding a crew--pirates were as numerous among these islands as sea turtles. All a privateer had to do was put into an island, red flag flying, and wait for the pirates to report for work, each carrying the tools of his trade--a musket, a pistol, a cartridge box and a cutlass. Nor were their great numbers hard to understand. Being an Episcopalian I could of course not condone the life of the pirate. Yet the freedom it afforded, where no man was master to another and all shared equally in the enterprise of the group, had its appeal, as any civilized man who would answer honestly must admit. Here a man might have a wife or a harem--or a boy if such were his taste; he might dress in the bright colors of a gentleman and not be put in the stocks for it; or he might go about naked. If he crave gold or excitement he might catch a passing pirate ship, or he might just lie all day in the shade and watch his children grow.

Yet, for all the freedom, there was an order among pirates, something of which I learned when Captain Kidd called me into his cabin soon after we'd sailed off with our new crew. Word had somehow surfaced from among the new men (the way messages flew and paths crossed throughout the vast community of pirates was something akin to alchemy) that the Blessed William was bound for the island of Blanquilla, and so we threaded our way southward through the Lesser Antilles, picking up a few more buccaneers along the way.

Cleary and our Spanish interpreter--his name was Francisco but aboard the Antigua he quickly became Frank--along with several other members of the new crew, were assembled in the Captain's cabin when I arrived. I didn't know why I'd been summoned, but I knew it must be an important occasion when I saw the Captain sweating profusely under his blue coat.

"Do you write as well as you read, Master Rousby?" he asked as I stepped inside.

"That depends upon what I am reading," I answered.

"Quite right, quite right," he said. He placed an arm on my shoulder and led me to the table where paper, quill and ink awaited me. I sat at the table, dipped my quill and waited Captain Kidd's dictation. "This is to be a contract between me and the crew of the Antigua."

"Yes sir …?"

"Well, write," he ordered.

So across the top of the page I wrote in large hand, CONTRACT--which gave rise to some pleased murmuring among the crew, whether at my skill or their prospects I knew not. Then after appending the parties to the contract, Captain Kidd got quickly to the terms. The voyage of purchase, as the Captain termed it, was no prey no pay, and of course the pirates would have it no other way. They had not fled the penurious wages of the merchant seaman, nor the harsh discipline of the man o' war, only to settle for an assured though modest wage. At the end of the voyage, after the value of the booty had been calculated and expenses deducted, Captain Kidd would receive twenty shares and the crew would divide the remaining eighty shares between them.

"I trust ye know there's no ship's master alive what makes a fairer offer than that," the Captain said.

Knowing most captains took thirty or forty shares--but only with the blessing of crew--the men murmured in agreement. This group, having been elected officers by their mates, would each receive an extra half share, but anyone caught *holding back* or otherwise stealing from the plunder, would forfeit his share. The same held true if any man was cowardly in battle or too drunk to perform satisfactorily. It was understood that a buccaneer might take a good draught of courage before the attack, but it was up to him to draw his own line.

"What about the boy?" a buccaneer with a horribly burned face asked.

"'e gets a full share," the Captain replied.

"Beggin' your pardon, Cap'n," the burnt-faced buccaneer said, "but on whatever ship what I ever sailed, lubbers 'n boys gets no more'n a half."

The others nodded and murmured in agreement, but Captain Kidd was firm. "The boy shares full."

"Aye, Cap'n" the burnt-faced one said, but not without a glance at his mates that implied the matter might be open to later discussion.

I wished there was some way to tell him not to worry, as I would be gone at the first opportunity, but I could of course say nothing or do anything, except keep out of his way until then.

Next came a provision most important to pirates, in that most of them were either burned, scarred or missing some body part as the result of previous campaigns--the disability clause. If anyone were to lose a limb or any eye, he would be paid five hundred pieces of eight or its equivalent, but only fifty pieces per finger or toe. If killed in battle, his heirs would share fifteen pounds or its equivalent, even if the voyage brought no purchase. If in the opinion of the Captain, corporal punishment were required to discipline any sailor, approval by a majority of the crew was required.

"What about the handlin' of the ship, Cap'n?" Tom Cleary asked.

"Where we go is my decision," Captain Kidd said, setting off some discontent among his officers.

"Surely not without consultin' us," the burnt-face one said. "'at ain't the way it's done on no ship what I ever sailed."

"Nor 'ave ye ever received eighty shares, but that's the way it's done on my ship," the Captain replied, laying a hand on the butt of his pistol "And any man objects is free to take the longboat and go."

There was some grumbling over this but the men eventually assented and made their mark at the bottom of the paper. Then Cleary and Francisco went out onto the main deck and brought the crew in, one at a time, to sign the ship's articles I had just drawn. A few proudly wrote their name, even if it was only a meaningless design they had memorized, while others drew a design next to the name I phonetically transcribed, such as a bird or a dagger, but most were content to inscribe a crude X somewhere in the vicinity of their name. In the end there were fifty-six tightly drawn names appended to this legal document.

"Now ye, Christopher," Captain Kidd instructed as the last sailor left the cabin.

I signed my name, Christopher Rousby, in the cramped space at the bottom of the page and we were fifty-seven, still no match for the more than eighty hardened pirates aboard the Blessed William.

"Ye write as well as ye read," the Captain said, peering over my shoulder.

"Thank you, sir, Will there be anything else?"

It was apparent there was when the Captain walked across the cabin and pulled the hatch closed. He returned to the table, picked up the contract and rolled it into a tight baton, "Ye been a most loyal boy, Christopher."

"Thank you, sir."

"And valuable. Although I can write as well as the next man, ye know," he added.

"I know," I assured him.

"Hold this." While I held the scroll, Captain Kidd tied a short length of ribbon round it. "Loyalty, true loyalty, is a hard thing to come by. Lately I've come to appreciate it perhaps more than anything else in a man. In short, Christopher, ye will be rewarded for your service."

"Thank you, sir," I said. I watched as he placed the ship's articles in a cabinet on the port bulkhead.

"I suppose ye wonder what I'll reward ye with, as there can't be much profit in takin' the Blessed William. But there is booty aboard that ship, I promise ye. Besides what they took from the Spanish, I have almost a thousand pounds hidden in my cabin, and if nothin' else ye'll get a piece o' that once we've taken the scoundrels. Ye have that on my honor as a gentl'man," he pledged.

"Yes, sir," I replied, unconvinced. For a pirate who fancied himself a gentleman was hardly a man to be trusted.

"Durin' the weeks ahead, while we search for the Blessed William, there's likely to be some dissatisfaction amongst the crew. They might insist we go in search of easy prey, when as ye know, my mission is to retake my ship. Money's important, as I'd be the last to deny, but so too is honor. Honor is of little value to the likes of them," he said, thrusting his broad jaw towards the main deck where the crew would be lying about. "But amongst gentl'men 'tis a trait both revered and rewarded. 'tis because I behaved honorably towards Governor Codrington--goin' to the aid o' his marines--that I was rewarded with this ship. And 'tis because ye behaved honorably towards me that ye shall be rewarded. Do ye begin to see how 'tis between gentl'men, Christopher?"

"I do, sir," I replied dutifully. Although on balance it seemed to me the loss of ship, crew and life's savings was a dear price for honor and a leaky French tub for which the Governor had no use anyway.

"From yer perspective the world must seem a terribly complicated place--and 'tis. But the simple wind that drives it is patronage. Always remember this, Christopher."

"I will, sir."

"Find a powerful patron and ye'll sail far and fast in this world. In other words, Chris, I want ye to think of me as your patron. I want ye to be my eyes and ears on this voyage. If there be even a hint o' mutiny aboard this ship, I want ye to come to me. Will ye promise to do that?"

"You can count on me, sir," I answered.

"Good lad," he said, patting my head.

I certainly didn't feel like a good lad, nor an honorable one. For while agreeing to report any mutiny aboard ship, I myself was planning to desert at the first opportunity. Aside from the lesson of patronage, I learned another valuable lesson on that day--that discretion is the better part of honor.

Rumors that the Blessed William was headed for the island of Blanquilla proved, unfortunately for the Taino Indians living there, to be true. Seeing no ship in the harbor where the village lay, Captain Kidd was hopeful we had arrived before they had. But as he scanned the shoreline with his glass it became painfully clear that someone had been there and had visited a terrible destruction on the island. The Tanio huts had been burned, their canoes lay in broken pieces on the beach, and all the villagers had apparently fled. Nonetheless the Captain dropped anchor and ordered that the launch be lowered.

There was some grumbling from the officers when he ordered them to accompany him, as there was no raping and plundering to be done in this place. But Kidd had already lost one ship when he left his officers alone with her, and he would not again make that mistake. I stood conspicuously at the davit until, at the last moment, the Captain signaled me into the launch and I bounded forward.

I sat beside him in the bow while our officers rowed us over the flat green sea and up onto the sand among the broken canoes. They were huge boats, carved from thick, silk-cotton trees, some more than fifty feet long, with an outrigger along one side. Although most of the huts had been burned, several survivors remained among the tall palm trees that dotted the gentle slope beyond the beach. They were circular, quite large and airy, set on poles a few feet above the ground, with a broad porch across the front. The walls were constructed of strong bamboo lashed tightly together, and the conical roofs were covered by palm leaves. In front of each hut was a small garden, all of them trampled and picked clean by whoever had plundered the place. Although I had been in the West Indies for months and seen great numbers of Africans as well as Europeans, this was the first Indian village I had seen--even if I hadn't yet glimpsed a single Taino. Columbus had reported millions of them living in the West Indies less than two hundred years ago, and now there were only a handful left on a few remote islands such as this, so I was naturally eager to meet some.

The first hut, however, proved to be empty of all but a few hammocks and benches strewn over the woven grass mat that covered the whole floor. There was a statue of what appeared to be a winged fish carved in stone, several necklaces and bracelets of bone and polished coral, wooden bowls and shells, and some brightly colored pottery of intricate design, but scarcely anything more. The Tainos, it seemed, required very little.

It was much the same in all the standing huts we visited, but in the clearing behind we discovered the bodies, perhaps thirty or forty naked men, women and children, all lying in a bloody heap. Some, the fortunate ones, had been slashed the length or width of their bodies, while others, except for missing hands--or in the womens' case breasts--were unmarked. Some remained in a sitting position, as if still alive, searching in wide-eyed terror for missing hands and breasts while their blood had pulsed through these ghastly rents. Several heads lay loose around the edges of the pile of bodies, as if carelessly mislaid by their decapitated owners. It was then that I became dizzy and felt myself mercifully fainting from this carnage.

When I came to, I found myself over Tom Cleary's shoulder, bouncing back to the launch. He lay me down in the bow and Captain Kidd splashed sea water on my face. But it wasn't necessary, I was fully conscious. I lay stiff and silent in the bottom of the launch, listening to the grunted comments of the oarsmen as they pulled for the ship. They seemed at first sufficiently appalled at what they had seen, yet by the time we reached the ship they were certain the Tainos must have done or failed to do something that contributed to their horrible end.

"They should've give 'em the gold," the burnt-face one said.

What gold? I wondered, thinking of the bone and coral jewelry I had seen among those few poor artifacts in the Taino huts.

We beat north along the southern coast of North America, keeping well off from the Spanish fortress of St. Augustine. Even though the Spaniards had been thoroughly thrashed by Sir Francis Drake in the last century, and again by Captain John Davis only twenty-five years ago, they remained determined to keep a foothold in North America and would dispatch their dreaded barca-longas after any Englishman who ventured too close. Too, Captain Kidd had no wish to test the loyalty of his largely Spanish crew in a battle with their countrymen, especially against a Spanish man o' war carrying no wealth save guns and powder.

It wasn't just the Spaniards who were growing impatient with our Captain as we sailed north, but the English, French and Dutch as well. We had been at sea for almost a year, seeking the Blessed William in every quarter of the Caribbean, with never so much as a glimpse of her, and in all that time we had not taken a single worthwhile prize. Whenever we put into a port known to be friendly to the Brethren of the Coast, Port Royal or Hispaniola or one of the many others that dotted the Indies, it seemed that Captain Mason and his brigands had just left, usually after trading a ship full of goods for a fortune in hard currency. And although the tradesmen we met were eager to tell Kidd where more prizes were to be found, so that he might trade with them, he was only interested in learning where Mason was headed. Then after allowing his men just a single night of drinking and whoring ashore, the Captain weighed anchor and set off again on his obsessive quest.

I had several opportunities to jump ship while we were still in the Caribbean, but having witnessed Kidd's single-minded determination to find and punish the men who had wronged him, I was loath to bring such wrath down upon myself and managed at each opportunity to find a reason not to flee. The rest of the crew, however, suffered no such constraints and each day the threat of mutiny grew greater. Until, when we reached Charleston, an infamous pirate's den second only to New York, the Captain refused to allow anyone save me and Tom Cleary to go ashore.

We anchored just past the Charleston bar, close enough to see the lamplight from the taverns that lined the town wharves, but too far to swim. Then under the malevolent glare of the assembled crew, Tom and I lowered the small boat and rowed ashore. Our instructions were to poke about the taverns and inns for any word of the Blessed William, then get back to the ship just as soon as we had news. In addition I had one further responsibility--I was keeper of the purse, a precaution intended by Kidd to assure that Cleary remained sober. On its face it was a sound tactic. However had Captain Kidd known that I intended to desert once safely ashore in Charleston, he certainly wouldn't have provided me a purse-full of American money to aid my endeavor.

As we rowed closer to the lights of Charleston, sounds of gaiety began drifting out to us--a woman's laugh, the sound of a door slamming, a flurry of shouts--and Cleary suddenly stopped rowing. The way he sat very still with his oars dripping, I was sure he had heard something more than I had.

"What is it?" I whispered.

"The sweet smell of ale," he breathed, then thrust his oars deep in the water and pulled hard.

We wended our way by moonlight through the many ships lying at anchor in Charleston Harbor and made for the brightest, loudest spot on the wharf. It turned out to be a corner tavern with much coming and going, and each time the door swung open I was assailed by a dreadful chorus of male voices singing a madrigal. And if that wasn't enough, Cleary suddenly added his own reedy tenor to the chorus:

> My love in her attire doth show her wit,
> It doth so well become her;
> For every season she hath dressings fit,
> For winter, spring and summer.
> No beauty she doth miss
> When all her robes are on;
> But beauty's self she is
> When all her robes are gone,

he sang as I rowed. "By God it's been an age since I've sung that song!"

"And let's hope it'll be another before you do it again," I said, for Tom Cleary was the first Irishman I'd met who couldn't carry a tune in a sail bag.

We eased our boat in among the others, tied her bow to the wharf and pulled ourselves up. After stamping about a bit as sailors do upon landing, we proceeded to the well-lighted place at the corner, the Planter's Tavern.

"The place should be a font of information," Cleary said, rubbing his hands as we approached. "Give us a few pounds and I'll go in and question the barman."

"Where you go I go, and where I go the money goes," I reminded him.

"But I can't be seen takin' a mere lad into a den of thieves and whores and English Protestants."

"Then I'll go alone," I said, thinking I might slip out the back and be away without the expense of so much as a shilling.

"Aw, have a heart, lad," he pleaded. "Spyin' is dangerous and dry work and should be worth a pound at the least."

"I'll stand you to an ale while we make our inquiries," I allowed as I pushed the door open.

"I'm afraid I'll not be able to get a question out of my mouth until I've first oiled my tongue a bit," he warned as we made our way to the bar.

The place appeared to be filled to the gunnels with sailors and old whores and a sprinkling of gentlemen, but it was hard to tell as the tavern was so filled with smoke that the deeper dark recesses of the room couldn't be clearly seen. The dreadful singing was coming from a group of drunken sailors at the bar in front of the windows overlooking Charleston Harbor. Those sailors who had goods to trade or money to spend were seated at tables with crafty looking merchants or half-dressed whores, while those without sat about on empty wine casks or on the floor. Most of the whores were white, some with the mark of the servant burned upon their arm, but there were also a few younger ones of a darker hue mixed among them. The sailors too were a great mix, but pirates to the man, judging by the lopped limbs and fierce, scarred faces. It was a place, in short, of which I wished to acquit myself as soon as possible.

But Tom Cleary was of another mind. Quick as a skylark he'd flitted to the bar where he stood already with a tankard of ale in one hand and a cup of rum in the other.

"Pay the man," he ordered.

I dug into my purse and came out with one copper which I placed on the bar. But the barman shook his head and gestured for more. A second copper and a third elicited the same response, and not until I'd dropped four coppers on the bar was he satisfied. If things were this expensive in the New World, I would soon be out of money and must give serious re-consideration regarding my plans to desert, I decided as I returned my lightened purse to its place on my hip.

"A fine establishment," Cleary said, wiping the foam from his lips with the back of his hand. "I'd like to have a place like this myself someday."

"Let's be about our business," I said.

"Go easy, lad. There's plenty more coppers in the purse and a good deal more of this fine ale to be drunk, and the sooner we have our information the sooner we must go back."

"Not necessarily," I said.

"What do you mean?"

"I could go back with the information and leave you here to gather more."

"Aye, now that's a sound idea! And our Captain would surely approve if he were but here. Barman!" he called, sliding his empty vessels across the bar. "Fill 'em up! And we would have a word with you."

While the barman replenished Cleary's drinks, I fished four more coppers from my purse and placed them on the bar. When the barman reached for them, after placing Cleary's drinks on the bar, I covered them with my hand. "If you wouldn't mind, sir, we have a question..."

"Then ask it and release my money."

"We're looking for a ship, the Blessed William--although it's possible she's changed her name. She's captained by William Mason, and his mates are Robert Culliford and Sam Burgess. Is it possible you might have seen them or that you might know anything about them?"

"It's possible," he said, motioning again for more money.

He continued to motion until I had placed ten more coppers on the bar. "That's all you'll get," I said.

He swept the coins off the bar and slid them into his pocket. "Never heard of 'em," he said, then turned and walked away.

"Damn...!" I'd spent eighteen coppers already and knew no more than if I'd never left the ship. "That will have to be your last drink, Tom," I said.

I fully expected this to set off an alarm in my mate, but he said nothing. He was staring, transfixed, at the several young women who, with an older woman, had just entered the tavern, setting off a great stir among the patrons. And no wonder, for these girls were certainly prettier and fresher than any other in the room, although their trade was plainly the same. But while the older and less pretty women wore bright paint and thin, low-cut gowns through which everything showed, these girls were scrubbed and wore their blouses buttoned up somewhat, and still the men clamored for these primmer young ladies over their more experienced sisters. The older women seemed not so much dismayed by, as resigned to the competition, as they turned easily to conversation among themselves.

As the young girls navigated among the tables, the older woman followed, sparing her charges free caresses as best she could, while at the same time negotiating for their services in a most charming manner. Indeed, it seemed the older woman, who was still rather pretty, was every bit as popular with the men as her young employees. Such was certainly the case with Tom, who fixed his eyes on the older woman and never took them off her as she moved about the room. After watching for a good while, he turned to the man standing beside him and asked who she was.

"Madame Lafavre," the man answered. "But we call her Madame Le Fever."

"Then she's French…?"

"Course she's French," his informant replied, which seemed to disappoint Tom Cleary.

"Tom," I said, pulling at his sleeve, "I think we'd better try another place."

"Yes, yes," he said, "in a minute."

Tom continued to watch Madame Lafavre as she moved about the room, negotiating on behalf of her girls, rejecting some offers with an amused laugh that served to neither embarrass nor abuse the failed bidder, while accepting others with such dignity and grace that one would think she had arranged a marriage with a prince. When all the contracts had been made and most of the girls had gone upstairs with their clients, Madam Lafavre came to the bar for a drink--just like a man!

"Give me the purse," Tom said softly.

"No."

"If Kidd's men were by, she'll know. Give me the purse!" he demanded thrusting his hand into my pocket.

I struggled but he was too strong for me. He came away with the purse and pushed me off as I tried vainly to take it back.

He turned to the woman, bowed from the waist and said, "Madame Lafavre…"

"Yes…?" she said, turning and looking him up and down. When she smiled, her cheeks grew full and crinkled up at the corners, leaving lines such as chickens leave in the dust. Her lips too were full and soft, and despite her age her teeth were straight and fairly white. The only blemish to her beauty, most men would say, was a black mole on her left cheek and another on her right breast just to the side of the deep cleft, but which I found intriguing.

"You speak English?" he asked.

"Een my poor way," she answered, with a helpless flutter of hands.

"Would you have this drink with me, Madame?"

"Certainement, monsieur--"

"Captain--Captain William Kidd, master of the Antigua," he said with a bow.

"Oh my God…." I breathed.

"Avec plaisir, Capitaine," she said, extending her dainty hand to be kissed.

Tom was briefly confused before taking her hand and kissing it. "And what would you like to drink?"

"Zee barman know," she said, raising her hand. "Paul…?"

But Paul had disappeared. A minute later another barman appeared and went off to get Madame Lafavre's drink, which turned out to be a large glass of Whiskey. I watched Tom stuff the purse deep down in his pocket after paying for the drink and calculated my chances of getting it. As long as he held the purse, escape was impossible, while the longer he held it and the drunker he became, the better my chance of filching it. However with each passing hour my fortune would grow alarmingly smaller, so I would watch closely and when the time was ripe, grab the purse and dash to freedom.

Meanwhile, the two of them prattled on like old friends while I stood by like a knot on the bar, until finally I poked Tom in the ribs to remind him of our business.

"Terribly sorry," Tom said. "This is my cabin boy, Christopher Rousby."

"I am most 'apee to know you," she said, smiling so sweetly that I almost forgot how annoyed I was with Tom.

"My Captain has a question to ask you," I said

"Oh yes…" Tom remembered.

He asked the same question I had asked the barman, with the same result, although I sensed a flicker of recognition in Madame Lafavre's eyes when Tom mentioned the names of our quarry.

"It's not important," Tom said, turning his back to me and his full attention to Madame Lafavre.

How frustrating it was to have to stand there and listen to Tom go on when, if only I had the purse, I could have slipped away unnoticed and disappeared into America forever. I needed a drink.

I was well into my first pint of ale and Madame Lafavre was well into her third or fourth whiskey when I noticed that her accent was slipping. At first I blamed the ale but after listening a bit more I realized it was the whiskey was causing it--Madame Lafavre was beginning to sound much like Tom Cleary! If Tom didn't notice, it was no wonder, as he had drunk more than any of us and was blathering about a song from his youth.

"The sailors at the bar were singin' it when I came in…"

"My love in her attire doth show her wit…?"

"You know it!"

"And who'd you think taught it them."

"But it's an Irish song--my fiancè' used to sing it to me."

Madame Lafavre stared wide-eyed at Tom for a moment, then gasped, "Tom Cleary…?"

"Mary Boylan!"

Then the two fell upon each other, hugging and rocking and keening and wailing in a strange tongue like wild heathens, until at last they settled down a bit and lapsed into a sort of English.

"They tried to convince me you were dead so I'd marry Flynn, but I told them you'd come for me one day!" she cried as the tears fell from her face and coursed between her bosom.

"Flynn…! The undertaker's son?"

"He was the only young man left in the village after the potato famine."

"Potato…? There are no potatoes in Ireland."

"There are now," Mary said. "They brought them in from the New World and they grew so well we got rid of the sheep. But then the blight struck and we had no crop for two years and all the young men fled the village. As did I, for it was that or starve."

"How terrible," Tom said

"My life has not been easy," she replied, wiping her eyes. "Nor will I burden you with it. But tell me, why is it you go by Captain William Kidd and not your proper Tom Cleary?"

"Hush!" he warned, bringing his finger to his lips. "For it's a secret mission I'm on, with which I'll not burden you, as it could be dangerous for you to know."

"You're most considerate."

"Thank you."

"And you are a ship's captain…?"

"Oh yes, very much so," the varlet lied. "But tell me, Mary, how is it you found your way to Charleston?"

"Oh that's a most dreadful story, Tom Cleary, and I'm sure you'll not be wantin' me to tell it."

"No, of course not, Mary Boylan. Not if it pains you to tell it. I can well understand, as my own life has been no smooth sail either."

"I'm sure it hasn't, Tom. But for a woman it's worse, far worse."

"I'm sure."

"The things that happened to me-- it causes me to shudder just to think of them--"

"You mean you were forced to—to…"

"No, Tom, it didn't come to that. Although they tried, you can be sure. They stripped me naked and tied me to a tree and flogged me half to death, and all the time I kept cryin' out: 'I will not! I will not!' while all the time thinkin' of my dear betrothed."

"Mary…." Tom breathed, as he grasped her hand in his.

Judging by the large expanse of smooth bare back and shoulders revealed by Mary's gown, it was either a most gentle flogging to which she had been subjected or else it took place in nether regions.

"But them with their whip weren't half so evil as that fine gentleman came round the village, tellin' us poor girls of the land of milk and honey that lay across the sea. He told us that if we'd agree to come to work in the house of a decent, God-fearin' gentleman in the Carolina

Colony for just seven years, teaching hymns to Christian children and reading the gospel to the elderly, then at the end of that time we'd each get ten fertile acres for our own."

"It sounds too good to be true," Tom said.

"Pity you were not there at the time to advise me," she said, looking up at him and doing something with her eyes.

"I am truly sorry, Mary, for I know what an ordeal it must have been. However, them pirates that took me was most insistent that…"

"For it was not the house of a decent, God-fearing gentleman to which we were sent in a leaking, rat-infested barge, but a sporting house!"

"No!"

"Yes!"

"But you didn't…"

"I already told you I didn't," she responded, somewhat sharply. "When my master finally realized he could kill me but I would not bend to his evil will, he relented and put me in charge of those who would."

"Ah, I see. And that's the reason you're in this business today…"

"Sadly, it is all I know," she said, heaving her great bosom helplessly. "I tried to escape this vile business at every opportunity, but each time it resulted in something far worse. Once, after I'd wandered lost and alone in the forest for several days, living on roots and berries and little else, I was captured by Indian salvages and held for many months. Oh it was terrible."

"You needn't talk about it if you don't wish," Tom said.

"But I was finally rescued by a company of British soldiers."

"Thank God…"

"Which was not a whole lot better than the salvages, I might add. And when they returned me to my master I was beaten most horribly and given an additional seven years of servitude."

"The monster!"

"But you don't want to hear all that."

"Not if it pains you to tell it, Mary dearest," Tom replied soothingly. "It puts me in mind of my own time with the pirates, those blackguards."

"It's not the same thing."

"I'm sure. But that's all over with now, Mary."

"True."

"And you must try to forget it."

"Don't you think I've tried?"

"I'm sure you have."

"I'm livin' a comfortable and prosperous life at last, but still there's not a night I don't wake up screamin' for all the things I've seen."

"Prosperous did you say...?"

"The debaucheries and the treacheries, the mayhems and the murthers... I, a good Irish Catholic lass, raised to believe that man was made in the image of God, have had my faith sorely tested by this infernal America, I can tell you that, Tom Cleary."

"I'm sure you can..."

"But I shan't. For I can see the glow of innocence still shining in that angelic face," she said, lifting her hand to his mottled cheek.

"And I see the same in you, Mary Boylan. For in spite of all you've been through and the many ways you've been cruelly used, you're still to me as pure as a newborn lamb on the Irish hillside in spring. And it's no matter if you're forced to make your livin' off the wages of sin, prosperous though they may be. I take it you work on a percentage...?"

"The whore gets thirty per cent, I keep seventy."

"Seventy...!"

"But I allow her to keep the gratuity."

"Plus the gratuity...! Tis far too generous of you, Mary!"

"Do you think so?"

"I know so. And being a sailor, it's not a profession with which I'm unfamiliar--albeit in an academic way. Which I hope you will allow..."

Mary tossed her bosom in the air and replied, "Not to worry, I'm a woman of the world, Tom Cleary."

"As am I--a man of the world. And as such I can assure you that your portion of the whole is much less than is customary throughout the Indies, where the whore gets ten or no more than fifteen per cent of the total, including the gratuity."

"You're right, Tom, of course. But you know me--a heart as big as the Blarney stone. How good it must be to have a man to rely on in matters of business."

"And for other purposes as well, eh, Mary?"

"Tom, you rogue!" she yelped, as she jumped at the same time.

"Forgive me, dear, I forgot myself. I'm just so excited to see you."

"Well, it has been more than twenty years," Mary said, smoothing her gown in back.

"A lifetime. And in all that time, Mary, you've never once married?"

"Never. Within the Church, that is."

"But outside the Church...?"

"Not even that--hardly."

"Might I ask what you mean by *hardly*?"

"I'm sure you'd not like me to tell it, Tom."

"Not if it pains you too much, Mary dear. But if it don't, I wouldn't mind."

"It still hurts me to talk about it, Tom dear. Even though I was entirely without fault in the affair," she added. "After all, you could hardly call a salvage wedding a consensual wedding now, could you."

"You were married to a salvage...?"

"The big chief."

"How big?"

"Huge. However it wasn't anything I desired, you understand. When I was captured by these salvages I feared they were all going to have me and there was nothing I could do about it. But then this one big black one, who was obviously in charge, took a liking to me and --"

"Black one...! I thought they were *Indian* salvages."

"All but the chief--Chindomabu."

"Chindomabu!" I exclaimed, startling both of them. "You don't mean Chindomacuba...? A great black man with no ballocks...?"

"No ballocks...!" she laughed. "Like great purple plums they was! If Chindomabu had no ballocks I'd hate to see the black salvage that does. Night after night after night, the great beast swivved me near to swooning. Oh it was a terrible ordeal, Tom," she said, grasping his arm. "And I'd just as soon not talk about it if you don't mind."

"But I sailed with a Chindomacuba," I put in. "And he claimed to have been a eunuch in a Turkish harem."

Mary laughed again. "That would be just like the old cocker! But either there are two Chindomabus, or else yours is a magician who can be two places at once, with or without his ballocks!"

I had many more questions about my old friend, but Tom, fueled by the twin fires of love and commerce, would brook no interference from anyone.

"I won't press you further about the salvage because I can see what a painful subject it is," Tom interrupted. "But were there any other husbands--outside the Church?"

"Nary a one, Tom. You have my word on that," she said, crossing her bosom. "I'm as free to marry today as I was on the day of our last meeting."

"Then will you at long last be my wife, Mary Boylan?"

"How sweet it is to hear those words I'd just about given up ever hearin'. Of course I'll marry you, Tom Cleary!"

"You've made me the happiest man in the world, Mary Boylan!" Tom said, seizing and kissing her.

"Just think of it, I'll at last be free of all this shame and degradation," Mary said, smoothing the front of her dress.

"Let's not be too hasty, Mary dear. After all, we're both people of the world. And there's some would say that what you're doin' is a noble service to mankind."

"But, Tom, it's sinful."

"So's swivvin' a great black salvage--about which I've agreed to say nothin'. So it seems only fair that you should be willin' to do something for me in return."

"Tom, you do have a ship, don't you?" she asked.

"Only a very small one."

"You mean you lied..."

Tom nodded. "But so did you. After all, the line between whore-master and whore is rather a fine one, isn't it?"

"Bastard!" she shouted, raising a fist.

"But one I'm willing to recognize!" he said, catching her wrist as she swung.

While they cursed and struggled, the barman suddenly re-appeared--this time accompanied by three familiar faces--Mason, Burgess and Culliford.

"It's them!" I cried, seizing Tom's arm.

But Tom was busy with his own struggle. He pushed me off with a powerful thrust that propelled me in the direction of the door, while at the same time I heard Mason's gravelly command to, "Come back 'ere!"

There was no chance of that as I plunged headlong through the crowd and out the door onto the wharf. I started for the boat but quickly thought better of that and ran on down the wharf as fast as I could. I would have to find some place to hide until those cutthroats grew tired of looking for me, then slip back to the boat later.

I could hear shouting from behind that gradually lessened as I sped along the wharf. I was satisfied that I had almost sufficiently distanced myself from them and in just a few more minutes would be safely beyond their reach--when I came up against a high wall that ran shoreward from the water's edge. Afraid the splash would alert them if I jumped into the water, I turned away from the shore and continued along the wall, deeper into Charleston, expecting at any moment to come to the end of it and break out into the fores, or whatever lay beyond. In the faint light I stumbled over a sleeping man who awoke with a fearful cry that would surely alert my pursuers. Becoming reckless, I stumbled into an empty cask, sending it jouncing like a drum in the night. From somewhere in the distance I could hear Culliford urging his mates on, and I thought I heard Mason's angry snarl as they came for me.

It seemed the wall had to come to an end at any moment, yet it continued on and on, until suddenly it jutted off at a right angle, running back along the west end of the town. The whole damned town was walled against Indian attack, I realized. When I came upon a tree growing beside the wall I shinnied up as quickly as I could, just as I heard Culliford call, "'ere 'e is!" I could fairly hear the hounds baying as I climbed out on a limb as far as I could, then dived headlong over the wall with no idea what, be it sharpened stakes or pit vipers, lay beneath me.

Thankfully it turned out to be nothing more than solid earth that reached up to welcome me in a hard embrace that knocked the wind from my lungs. While I lay on the ground breathing hoarsely, trying to suck air back into my lungs, I heard Culliford's shouts from behind the wall. "'e went over! Get a lantern!" Then I heard grunting and the rattle of leaves as Culliford hauled himself up in the tree. "'e's 'ere, I c'n 'ear 'im breathin'!" he shouted, just above the wall now.

Afraid to stand lest I be seen in the faint moonlight, I began to crawl silently along the forest floor, startling unseen creatures that thrashed off ahead of me as I made my serpentine way forward. Or was it sideways or backwards? For I soon had no idea which way was which. Until I saw the light poking through the tops of the trees and heard Mason's angry voice rolling through the forest. They had appropriated lanterns from somewhere and were coming over the wall after me.

Damn them! Why don't they stop? Why am I so damned important? I asked myself as I plunged through the underbrush. For if they thought taking me hostage would improve their chances with Captain Kidd, then they very much underestimated him, as he would sacrifice his own mother before he would allow their theft to go unpunished. I kept hoping they'd realize this and turn back as I thrashed my way through the dense thicket, but each time I stopped and looked back I saw the lanterns coming after me. Damn, damn, damn!

Suddenly I felt myself snatched up from the forest floor as if by a hurricane and a hand clamped over my mouth before I could even think of crying out. My first thought was that I had been captured by one of my pursuers but I quickly realized, as I was borne swiftly and silently through the forest, that I was in the hands of someone bigger and stronger, someone able to move familiarly through these woods even in the dark. Now I was confused as well as frightened. Was I in the hands of a savior, or was I in even greater danger than before?

After bouncing through the forest for several minutes, we emerged on the shore of a smooth tidal basin, where I was quickly thrust into the bottom of a dugout canoe. I felt the canoe being slid into the water, then gliding buoyantly and rapidly across the smooth surface. When I looked up I saw the broad, bare back of the man who had rescued me, lunging forward and back with each powerful stroke of the paddle. In a moment I saw that it was not just his back that was bare--the man was naked. Except for a scrap of cloth hanging down in front.

Oh my God! I thought. I've been abducted by a naked Indian salvage! For what fiendish purpose? As a hostage to be traded back to the white settlers for some beads and trinkets? Or am I to be initiated into his tribe by some heathen, salvage rite and never again see a white European face? Or am I to be roasted and eaten by cannibals? Oh why did I run from those civilized pirates from whom I would have received nothing worse than a flogging or keelhauling? While thus considering my fate and wishing ardently for another, and while lying in the bottom of the canoe watching my abductor rise and fall back on his haunches with each paddle stroke, I could not help but notice the salvage's large member hanging down from between his legs, but--no ballocks!

"Chindomacuba!" I gasped.

He hissed me quiet but said nothing more and I was suddenly uncertain. Could this be Chindomacuba, plucked miraculously from the sea as had been my good fortune, or was this just another slave who had been coincidentally so disfigured by still another possessive sultan?

My ruminations were cut short by another hissing sound as we glided through the tall grasses that closed in on us where the estuary narrowed. I thought briefly of going over the side and trying to make my escape in the marsh grasses, but decided it would be futile. Too, there was still the chance my abductor was Chindomacuba, in which case I was probably safer in the canoe with him, in spite of whatever he'd become since I last saw him, than in the swamp with alligators big as boats. So I lay still and silent in the canoe while Chindomacuba, or whoever he was, took us ever deeper in among the mysterious estuaries of the tidal marsh.

Finally, in the gray light that comes just before the dawn, we arrived at our destination, marked by several canoes pulled up onto an island. My abductor, his back still to me, rose and stepped out of the canoe. Then, as he pulled the boat up onto the island, the top of the sun poked

up and shined directly on his face, and there could no longer be any
doubt.

"Chindomacuba…!"

"Christopher…! I t'ought you be dead!"

"And I thought you were dead!"

"Some joke, huh?" Then his face broke into a great grin, followed
by the high-pitched laughter I thought I should never hear again.

"What about the others--Mrs. Halburton…?" I asked, scrambling
out of the canoe to grasp his hand.

"Don't know 'bout no odders. I t'ink dey all go down. How
'bout you?"

So I proceeded to tell Chindomacuba all about my ordeal on the
raft and my rescue by Captain Kidd, and of all the later events that led
to my being chased through the wilds of Carolina by pirates.

"By God, dot some story," Chindomacuba said when I'd finished.
"Me I float on de basket like de baby Moses maybe tree four days, den
de slaver pick me up."

"No!"

"Yep. He take me to Charleston wid all dem odder poor Africans
and sell me to de plantation boss. Terible cruel man, dot boss. You
be right, Christopher, America no place for de black man. Or for de
red man neider," he added, as suddenly a dozen or so of the subject
race appeared, silently and mysteriously as the sun--men, women and
children, wearing only waistcloths like Chindomacuba's

"Doan be 'fraid, you be safe here wid us," my friend assured me.
"Dese be my people now, de Stono people. When I escape from de
plantation boss dey take me in."

They seemed a docile, even pathetic group, these Stono people,
nothing at all like the blood-thirsty salvages I had heard the North
American Indians to be. I followed Chindomacuba up onto the high
ground where the tall grass was trampled down to make a big soft
bed. He introduced me to each of the Indians, speaking easily in their
tongue, and they responded politely if unintelligibly.

"Once dey be t'ousands, now just dis many," he said, pointing to the sad remnants of the Stono nation. "But sit, we have a good Stono breakfast."

So we all sat in a circle on the soft grass, the black man, the white boy and the Stono Indians. Two old women, with alligator skin and dry paps, passed out large clam shells, which I took to be serving plates for the good Stono breakfast to come. Chindomacuba traded comments with the men, which were obviously about me and which evoked some smiles, even a little laughter. When there was a lull in their conversation I asked Chindomacuba how he happened to be in the forest outside Charleston when I needed him.

"I go to kill white men," he answered.

"But why?"

"Because dey kill red men!" he laughed. "And women and children. My fran in de jail say in America all men be de same, but him full of shit for sure. Here de black man free to be de slave, nottin' else. And de red man free to be dead, nottin' else. So we make a great nation of de black and de red and drive de white man back to Europe."

"But that's not possible," I said. "There are too many Europeans and more coming every day."

"Dere are many more Indians to de west," Chindomacuba said with a careless sweep of one arm. "Dey will join us."

"Then you'll all be killed," I said.

"Prob'ly," he agreed. "But if we doan do nottin' we still be killed," he said, followed by a great hoot of laughter in which the Stono Indians joined uncomprehendingly.

"But you needn't stay here and die. You can come with me, you can sail with Captain Kidd," I implored. "It's true the pirate's life is hard but there everyone is treated the same."

"Doan like boats."

"Nor do I. But life is fairer there than on land. When I came ashore last night I intended to stay here in America forever. But after what I've seen so far, I intend to join Captain Kidd and get back to England just as soon as I can. There are no slaves aboard a pirate ship or indentured servants. And if we don't like our captain we're free to throw him out and elect another. It's not perfect, but I fear it's as near to it as anything you or I will ever know."

Chindomacuba shook his head. "I must stay wid dem."

The two old women re-appeared, accompanied this time by two pretty girls about my age, wearing only a piece of cloth that hung down in front and flapped freely about as they moved around the circle, ladling out a yellow mush. The way they looked at me and giggled as they flounced about, I had the feeling they were flapping their waistcloth more than was necessary, which was causing me some discomfort. I will only say that I was greatly relieved not to be wearing one of those loincloths myself.

The cold mush, which was firm to the bite but without much taste, was corn, Chindomacuba explained. After this came peas and wild rice, and finally some strips of roasted deer, all of it cold but tasty.

"Too close to Charleston for de fire," Chindomacuba said by way of apology for the cold food. "We can't stay in one place too long, dey be always lookin' to kill us."

"That's no way to live," I said.

"Dot's de only way!" he laughed. "But it doan be so bad. Got enough to eat and nobody floggin' me back. Got a pretty wife too," he said, nodding at the beautiful woman next to him, who lowered her eyes and smiled.

"But no children."

"None of dem, none of dese!" he laughed, grabbing at where his ballocks should have been and coming up empty-handed.

"That reminds me, do you know a woman named Mary Boylan, who also calls herself Madame Lafavre?"

"Le Fever! Sure, I know her. She de one bring de poor girls over from Ireland, tell dem dey marry de rich planter. But dey ain't no rich planter, just de scurvy sailors wid de French pox. Soon de girls die, but Le Fever brings more over. Not a nice lady."

"Were you ever married to her?"

"What...!"

"She says she was married to a black man with ballocks big as plums who used to swiv her all night."

"She say dot…?"

"She did."

"Hmm--funny t'ing 'bout white women--lots of 'em have dot dream."

"She said his name was Chindomabu. Do you know who that might be?"

"Oh sure--dot be my cousin."

"You have a cousin in America?"

"Hundreds of 'em. My whole village ober here. De planters need Africans so de slavers bring 'em ober by de t'ousands. Just like Le Fever."

"I think you're pulling my leg," I said.

"What's dot…?"

"I don't think you were lurking outside Charleston to kill white men at all. I think you were on your way to visit Mary Boylan."

"You must t'ink I be very brave or very dumb, 'cuz no black man wid any sense gonna visit no white woman in Carolina. And you know I ain't got no ballocks."

"You could have tricked her."

"How I do dot?"

Maybe they were real plums you had somehow attached to your body," I tried. The coincidence was too great to fail for the want of ballocks.

Chindomacuba's cackle at this was even higher than usual. "Or maybe I suck 'em up in my body when I doan be needin' 'em, let 'em back down when I need 'em!"

"Then how do you know so much about her?"

"Everybody know 'bout her--she be Seth Sothel's mistress."

"Who is Seth Sothel?"

Chindomacuba repeated my question to the stono people in their language, provoking a rumble of laughter from the Indians. "He de governor of Carolina and de most evil man what ever set foot in dis colony. He tax de people til dey starvin' and he keep all de money for hisself. He run de gamblin' houses and de whore houses, and Mary Boylan be de one bring him de whores. He give whiskey to de Indians, get dem drunk and steal dere goods, den send de settlers to kill 'em cuz dey goin' on de warpath."

"The blackguard! Why don't the people throw him out of office?"

"Dey did. Dey t'row him out. He go away, come back, promise to be good and dey believe him. Dey make him governor all over again and he go right on doin' de same t'ing. Seth Sothel jus' like de snake--cut him in half he doan die, dey just be two of him."

I was aghast. In England I had heard tales of political corruption but nothing to match this. I resolved then and there to re-double my efforts to acquit myself of this accursed country and get back to England before I should become as corrupt as these Americans. Too, I had no wish to run up against a terrestrial devil so evil as Seth Sothel.

Later, after finishing my breakfast, and after I'd made known my intention to de-camp as soon as possible, Chindomacuba gave me the bad news.

"Too dangerous to move in de daylight," he said. "For now we must live like de deer, sleep all day, move at night. When de sun go down I take you back to de ship. But now you sleep wid Orsa and Unca, dey be nice girls to you."

I didn't have to ask who Orsa and Unca were, when the two giggling girls with the floppy waistcloths leaped to my side. Each of them took a hand and began pulling me towards an opening in the tall grass, as I tried to pull in the opposite direction. I attempted to explain that I could sleep alone, but of course they didn't understand a word I said, and if they did it wouldn't matter.

Chindomacuba's high laugh followed me through the twisting labyrinth as the two girls pulled me past the series of "bedrooms" of matted grass. Their room was at the end of the tunnel, a hollowed out cave about the size of a master's cabin, with deerskin rugs on the ground. They stood me in the center of the grass room and circled me in a slow appraising dance. They touched my hair and rubbed my cheeks, exchanging serious comments as they examined me. Then Orsa, the tall one with the long black braid that trailed down to the cleft of her rounded buttocks, pulled my shirt off, while Unca, the shorter, shapelier one, began unbuttoning my trousers, and in a moment we were all naked. They were salvages of course, and no match for civilized women, but they were still very handsome in an earthy sort of way. They were red as smoldering embers and lithe and smooth as cats, and although they seemed gentle, there was a wildness in their dark eyes. They were of course simpler than their civilized sisters, yet there was a mystery about them that fairer women had long ago abandoned, it seemed to me, as I watched these two naked women circling me like lusty animals.

I was to be a part of some kind of salvage rite, it seemed, when they brought out an earthen jar and began rubbing a pleasant smelling oil all over my body, even up my bumb! I was shocked, but being part of the ritual, I was careful not to offend. And when the oil was offered to me and I was invited to rub it all over them, I was sure to get it well up both their bums as well, which pleased them very much indeed. At first I was only able to finger one bum at a time, until they bent over side by side and I stood behind with a finger in each of them, like a charioteer driving a team, while they whinnied and neighed like a pair of very happy mares. When I felt another hand next to each of mine, I realized that Orsa had her hand in Unca's other passage and Unca was doing the same for Orsa, and both girls were bucking and heaving so hard that I feared they might break their stays and plunge through the grass wall and out into the swamp.

But it never came to that. For after a race that raised a lather on all of us, they crossed the finish line at the same time and collapsed on the grass for the moment, leaving me in a decidedly unfinished state. After catching her breath, Orsa climbed to her hands and knees, slapped her ass a couple of times and looked back at me with a come hither swing of her pony tail. Realizing that the Jesuits had not yet been here, I got down and prepared to guide my dinghy to the port of bliss. But this was not what Orsa had in mind, I discovered, when she squirmed away and attempted to steer my dinghy to a much smaller port. At first I resisted, certain that there was no room in that port for this dinghy. But as I pushed gently, the cove opened and I slid in as Orsa sighed deeply and pushed her buttocks firmly against me, again and again and again. The rhythmic thwack of flesh and bone grew louder and quicker, accompanied by Orsa'a cries of encouragement, until suddenly she stiffened and went silent. Then she squeezed me so tightly that when I burst I heard a great explosion and saw fiery stars falling from the skies.

Exhausted, I crawled across the grass and collapsed on a deerskin rug. It was time for all of us to rest, I thought, as I closed my eyes. But I was wrong. Within a few minutes I heard soft moans of pleasure and opened my eyes to see the two salvage maidens locked together in a Gordian knot, their bodies sleek and shining with sweat and oil. Watching as they went on without me, transporting one another to a level of bliss that I fear was greater than any which I had inspired, was a humbling experience. Lusty and demanding though Rebecca Hay had been, I had always acquitted myself well enough to come away with a vague sense of superiority, a feeling that no matter how much she had enjoyed herself, I had enjoyed myself more; a feeling that although God (a man of course) had given the gift of sex to both men and women, he clearly meant for my sex to enjoy it more. Women, after all, were given babies to enjoy, which was surely meant as compensation for this inequality. But now as I watched Orsa and Unca, sweating and writhing, grunting and groaning with each powerful shudder of pleasure that racked their oiled bodies, like Amazonian wrestlers in the agonizing throes of combat, I suddenly became fearfully aware that the lust of women was a boundless thing.

Heathen Indian women that is. For despite the effect upon me of this awesome exhibition, with all its frightening implications, there was some solace to be had in the thought of the pure, civilized Englishwoman, like Mrs. Halburton, who could never be reduced to the spectacle before me. And knowing that such civilized English innocence would soon enough be mine, I plunged back into the fray with all the heedless pagan passion at my command.

"Whooee!"

After several hours, when I decided I'd had enough of this heathen excess, I pushed through the wall of grass, despite Orsa and Unca tugging at my slippery feet, and promptly fell asleep, wrapped like an innocent babe in a blanket of grass. After perhaps an hour, I was startled into wakefulness by the sounds of musket fire and the screaming and crying of women and children. From the sounds of the muskets, they seemed to be firing from all directions at once, except from behind me, deeper into the grass. With no clear plan in mind, except to get away from the musket balls slicing through the grass above my head, I called to Orsa and Unca, then slithered through the grass, naked as a salvage.

After crawling some distance the firing fell off, only to be replaced by shrieks and cries more horrible than before. Rather than thrash on blindly through the grass and risk stumbling upon the attackers, I carefully peeked my head up to get my bearings. There on the water surrounding my tiny island, a boatload of armed Europeans stood watching as a circle of ferocious salvages waded through the water and up onto the island of the Stone people.

"There's one!" a European shouted.

I dropped to the ground as a musket ball whizzed through the grass at approximately the place my head had been just a second before. I hugged the ground and listened to the tortured shrieks, interspersed by shouted orders and an occasional musket shot. The men behind me were calling across the island to the others to stop firing, as they were all coming ashore--to search for me!

"There's still a salvage in the grass!" an Englishman shouted.

"Nay, I got 'im," another replied.

"Spread out and look!"

I could hear them thrashing through the grass, getting closer, as I started back to where I had left Orsa and Unca. I backed my way along the path I had just made, pulling the grass back up behind me as I went, so that my pursuers should not be led directly to me. When I had nearly reached the end of the trail, I could make out Orsa and Unca sitting in the clearing, their arms wrapped tightly around each other. I was about to call softly to them, when suddenly a salvage with a hideously painted face burst into the clearing, followed quickly by another. I had to retreat farther into the grass to keep from being seen as the two Indians maneuvered around the seated girls. Both the salvages were naked, except for loincloths and European hats. Unlike the Stono people, their bodies were covered with strange tatoos from head to foot, and their painted faces, separated from mine by scarcely more than a few feet of grass, were of a most ferocious mien. With the salvages in front and the Europeans behind, I was hardly in a position to move one way or the other, although I'm not sure I could have anyway, so frozen with fear was I. Contributing to this was the hysterical shrieking of Orsa and Unca joining with the chorus of women's cries that issued from throughout the camp. The women were being raped, I supposed, conditioned as I was by my time with pirates, a fate that was about to befall Orsa and Unca, about which I was helpless to do anything.

But it was not the prospect of rape that occasioned such shrieking, I saw, as one of the men grabbed Orsa's hair, placed a knee between her shoulders and jerked her head back with such force it seemed he might have broken her neck. From the girdle at his waist he produced a bone knife, with which he made a quick incision entirely around her head, then with a violent tug, ripped the scalp from its mooring. Despite the screaming, I could hear the sound of flesh tearing away from the skull. Then before the incredulous horror of this event fully impressed itself on my wide eyes and stunned brain, there came a second tearing sound, followed by a great whoop and cry as the salvages danced about, waving their grotesque prizes in the air.

I wanted to be sick, even if it meant discovery and death, but I could summon nothing, not even vomit. Just as it began to sink in that I had witnessed two ghastly murders, the salvages pulled the two girls to their feet, and I realized, with ever-mounting horror, that they were still alive. Blood poured down over their faces and over the hair that remained in back, but they were able to stand, like living corpses, while I stared numbly at this incomprehensible cruelty. As one of the salvages spun Orsa around before pushing her out into the tunnel, I caught her blood-filled eyes in mine and I was sure she had seen me. Then they were gone, pushed and dragged through the tunnel, back to the main clearing.

When I was able to move, I crawled a little way off and stopped. There was no reason to go farther, escape was impossible. I could hear the salvages thrashing through the grass towards me. It occurred to me that I might stand, show myself to be a white man and possibly escape this cruel, salvage fate, but I had no desire to do so. Instead I began to dig purposelessly in the soft ground with my hands.

I was thus engaged when two Europeans passed by a few minutes later. Each man looked directly at me as he passed, but neither saw me. I was invisible. I continued to dig and pile the dirt to the side of the hole as the screams played in the back of my brain. A fire was struck. I could smell the smoke curling through the grass. And hear the shrieking of women and children. And the shouted curses of the Stono men. And the high-pitched laughter of Chindomacuba. Who, with or without ballocks, would not live to swiv another day.

The screams and curses continued through the rest of the day and throughout the night, dying finally with the coming of the sun. Only then did the Europeans and Indians depart in their boats. By now my hole was deep enough that I might crawl in and cover myself with the earth. But I didn't. Instead, after the sun had risen well above the eastern grasses, I made my way slowly through the bloody tunnel to the clearing where, twenty-four hours earlier, I had enjoyed my first and last Stono breakfast. What I saw now was breakfast for vultures.

The scalped, bloody bodies of the Stono men lay strewn over the burned ground, while those of the women and children hung suspended from a mounted pole over a dying fire, their lower torsos burned to the bone. The fires had been carefully controlled so the torture of the flames should last for hours before death should mercifully come. The men had been tied head and foot to stakes in the ground, then flayed alive from head to foot. Cooked strips of their flesh lay about on roasting sticks, some sticking out of the mouths of the dead who had been forced to eat their own flesh. Some of the younger, stronger men, had first had their feet and legs burned to the bone before being taken down and flayed. These, I knew, were the brave men who had cursed and laughed at their tormentors, urging them on to greater and greater atrocities, spitting their own flesh back in the face of the beast.

I looked among the charred and flayed bodies of these brave men for the remains of Chindomacuba, but without his black skin he looked the same as the others. Nor could I identify him by his unusual omission, as more than a few of these brave men had either lost these parts in the fire, or the salvages had cut them off.

Finally I was able to be sick.

While vomiting near the water's edge I imagined I heard my name, it was a faint, high-pitched voice calling, "Chris, Chris…"

"Chindomacuba!" I gasped, jumping to my feet.

But I saw no one. Only the stillness of death. The bodies twisting on the pole. Or anchored to the earth by stakes. I looked about. Whatever crude tools the Stono people had were now gone. It would be impossible for me to bury the dead. Indeed, everything they owned had been either taken or thrown on the fire. The canoes had been burned, their scanty waistcloths…. My own clothes had probably been taken by those salvages with a fondness for European hats. Everything was gone. Soon all that would be left of the Stono people would be a pile of bleached bones. I couldn't bury them, but I would at least take down the women and children.

While I was untying the rope that held the first child, I heard my name again. I looked down the line, past Unca and the old women, and then I saw the faint movement in Orsa's blood-encrusted eye.

"Orsa!" I cried, plunging barefoot through the coals, kicking them away.

Over and over I repeated her name as I untied her and lowered her to the ground. It was the only thing I could say--a prayer becoming a sob. And the tears pouring from my eyes. I held her bloody, burned, scalpless body next to mine and cried and cried until I thought I should never stop. Until Orsa smiled. Smiled! It was only a faint smile, hardly a smile at all. But a smile. Then she died.

Naked as the day I entered this barbaric world, and little more conscious of it now than then, I walked down to the water's edge and waded blindly out until I was forced to either sink or swim. The decision was made as much for me as by me as, instinctively as a dog, I began to paddle for I knew not where. I swam heedlessly among the tall grasses, touching bottom at times, then losing it and finding it again. I passed hours this way, until eventually I came to a broad bay separated from the ocean by a low-lying reef stretching northward away from hellish Charleston for as far as I could see. I realized I might not make it, but after resting in the shallows for a bit I plunged into the bay and began stroking for the island.

About half-way across I began to tire. Suddenly life seemed more desirable than it had when I'd heedlessly--perhaps suicidally--struck out across this wide bay. God grant me the strength and the time to repent of my folly, I prayed, as I stroked weakly for the island. When I finally came close enough to clearly make out the broad smooth beach, crested by a crown of sea grass and palms but still a long way out, I could feel the last of my strength leaving my body. I could no longer move my arms or hold my head above water. There was a moment of fear, a weak flurry of hands, then I calmly let go. It was a terrible injustice to come so close to shore only to drown, but one I was able to quietly abide, so I began to sink.

But not very far. Far as I was from shore, the smooth, sandy bottom was scarcely five feet beneath the water's surface. After crawling up onto the warm sand, I collapsed and fell almost immediately unconscious.

When I awoke some time later, I was immediately alert and fairly bursting with energy. I leaped to my feet and began to run along the hard-packed sand, faster and faster, hearing only the wind whispering in my ears. I was running, naked and alone on a desolate island, with no idea what I was running to, driven only by a clear idea of what I was running from. I angled off to the right, up over a wind-sculpted dune, stopping finally when the ocean came into view. I threw my head back and pranced about, drawing in great gasps of sweet air seasoned by the white combers rising and falling lazily on the broad beach. After walking down to the water's edge, where I stood facing England for a few quiet moments, I turned and resumed my northern run.

Alternately running and trotting, I passed thousands of green turtles basking on the sand and raised flocks of sea birds so thick they blocked the sun, without ever seeing another human being all day. I allowed my tortured mind to wander, pretending to be Adam alone in paradise, searching for Eve. When I began to feel the sun burning my back, I dashed into the surf, came out and rolled about on the beach until I was covered from head to foot with sand, then resumed running.

I was no longer Adam, but a naked running salvage, not yet the red hue of the Indian, but no longer a white European either.

At the end of the day, while the sun stood just above the dunes and waving grass, it occurred to me that I hadn't eaten since the good Stono breakfast the morning of the previous day. So I cut back across the barrier reef to the bay in search of a seafood supper. Before I'd waded in beyond my ankles, I could see that the clear water was teeming with fish of all sizes and species. Merely by cupping my hands under the water for a few seconds, then raising them, I came up with half a dozen tiny, wiggling fish. These I was able to eat, though I vowed to stay away from anything larger until I had the benefit of a fire.

As I waded along the edge of the bay, scooping up minnows and popping them into my mouth like an efficient heron, I noticed I was preceded by tiny spurts of sand, like thousands of miniature explosions on the bay floor. When I stuck my fingers into the sand, I came out with a small mollusk with a wavy-edged shell, quite unlike any clam or oyster I had ever seen. With the aid of a sharp-edged bone I was able to easily pry the shell apart and scrape away the white muscle.

"Zounds!" I exclaimed after carefully sampling it. It tasted good as an oyster.

So, I wouldn't starve in this paradise, except for loneliness, I decided, as I plunged my hands into the sand for more of these tasty clams. I hunted and ate like a salvage pig until, finally sated, I climbed back up over the dunes, found a deep hollow out of the breeze, and lay down for a short nap.

The next morning I was awakened by the sun rising over the east wall of my snug sand castle, accompanied by the soft crash of rolling combers. After a piss, I ran down to the bay for more of those wavy-edged clams, then resumed my northerly run to nowhere. After running for about an hour, startling all manner of wildlife but nary a human, a great flock of ducks rose into the air, then another and another until the whole sky was black with quacking ducks. It occurred to me as I stopped to watch these ducks flying towards the mainland, that I too would have to eventually make for the mainland, if only long enough to locate a ship bound for England. Of course in my present naked state

I was in no condition to take an ocean voyage let alone disembark in England, and this too was a problem I would have to address sooner or later. Preferably before the weather took a turn for the worse. So for the next hour or so I swam from island to island in the direction of the mainland.

After making my way fearfully (for although I'd heard alligators were not usually found in salt water, neither were naked English lads) along and over several links of the chain to the mainland, I discovered a ship lying at anchor near the mouth of a narrow river. She was more boat than ship, being a flat-bottomed, two-masted, gaff-rigged vessel of a kind the Americans called shallop. What she was doing here I couldn't imagine, as there was not a sign of habitation anywhere onshore, nor did there seem to be anyone about the ship. Keeping the islands between me and the boat as much as possible, I circled around, almost to the heavily-treed shore, then moved towards the ship from under the water, surfacing quietly from time to time for air.

When I reached the anchor cable, visible all the way down to the anchor that lay partly buried in the white sand, I pulled myself up slowly, hand over hand, and broke the surface with scarcely a sound. The name of the ship, *Yankee Peddler*, carved on the name board above the hawsehole, seemed a friendly enough one, so I hauled myself up onto the deck. There I stood dripping, when suddenly the aft cabin hatch burst open, revealing a stolid burgher clutching a blunderbuss.

"Stand still ye bare-assed thief afore I blow your arse off!" he shouted.

"Please--I'm not a thief!" I pleaded.

"And why else might ye be swimmin' out here naked and climbin' up on my ship without makin' so much as a sound?"

"Indians stole my clothes! I was fleeing them when I came across your ship! The only reason I didn't make any noise is because I was as much afraid of you as you are of me!" I stammered as he advanced.

"Afraid...! Why should I be afraid of a naked boy?" he demanded, thrusting the gun at me.

"There's no reason you should, sir. For I assure you I mean no harm to you or any man. I only boarded you to see if I might have a pair of breeches--or just a piece of cloth to cover my nakedness."

"I've got breeches and cloth enough to clothe an army, that's no problem. The problem is, what've ye got to trade for' em? Or are ye carryin' yer purse up your bunghole?"

"It's true I have no money with me, but I have some on my ship, a great fortune."

"Do ye now--and what ship would that be?"

"The Antigua."

"The Antigua!" he shouted, loud as his blunderbuss. "Those be the dastardly pirates what chased me in here! And if the tide 'ad been a foot higher the thievin' blackguards would've followed me in and robbed me of all my stores!"

"I'm sorry about that, sir, I truly am. And I had nothing to do with it, as I was in the clutches of wild salvages while it was happening. But if I had been there, I assure you I would've done everything in my power to stop them. But I'm not there, I'm here--and very much in need of a pair of breeches, if you please, sir."

"And I very much need to see yer money. For if ye think I'm goin' to deliver ye to yer thievin' brethren to collect my due bill, then I should shoot ye just for insultin' my intelligence," he threatened, raising his blunderbuss to his shoulder.

"Oh no, sir, I wouldn't ask that of you!" I assured him. "Just a bit of credit is all. If you'll give me a pair of breeches and your address, I'll mail the money just as soon as I get back to England."

"Ye're insultin' my intelligence," he warned, lifting the gun.

"All right, no credit! I'll work for you--I'll clean the ship!"

"Why should I hire somebody to do somethin' I can do by myself?"

"So you'll have more free time."

"I don't want more free time, I hate free time! I don't even like the name *free time*. What I crave is more market time."

"Then you'll have it! Every hour I save you will be an extra hour of market time."

"Hour...? ye expect me to trade ye a pair of breeches for one hour's work!"

"Oh no, sir, not at all. Much more than that."

"How much?"

"Four hours…?"

"Four!"

"Eight…?"

"More like eighty I should say."

"Eighty!" I howled.

"Which still doesn't get around the fact I don't need anybody to work for me and take my money. But--I could sell ye as an indentured servant…"

"For one pair of breeches! On second thought I don't think I'd like to work for you at all," I said, and moved towards the rail, preferring to take my chances with the salvages rather than this skinflint.

"Stay where ye are!" he ordered. "There's some money to be made here, I just have to figure out how." I held my place while the merchant considered his problem. "I have a proposition for ye," he said finally, "I'll give ye an entire suit o' clothes, includin' shoes. Then I'll take ye to New York and sell ye and we'll split fifty-fifty."

"Never!"

"All right, make it sixty-forty."

"No!"

"I'll throw in an extra pair of breeches…"

"I don't care if you throw in your whole ship, I'll not be any man's servant!"

"It'll just be for four years," he coaxed.

"Not for four days!"

"Ye drive a hard bargain," the merchant lamented.

"I'm not bargaining. My freedom means too much for me for that."

"That word again," he said with a grimace. "Believe me, anything that's free is worth just what ye pay for it. I'd rather be a servant with a good suit o' clothes, two pair of breeches and a few shillin's in my purse, than a free, naked, penniless boy."

"Well I wouldn't and that's an end to it."

"We'll make it two years."

"I said no!"

"To a decent master who won't work ye too hard. Ye don't happen to read and write do ye?"

"Of coure," I replied.

"Excellent! Ye should fetch a damned fine price. And I have just the position--clerk to a merchant on Wall street, a fine gentleman. Ye'll work just six and a half days a week, not more than fourteen hours a day, and for that we should split no less than ten pounds."

"Ten pounds…?"

"Five for ye, five for me."

"You said sixty-forty."

"That was four years. Two is fifty-fifty."

"I'm not interested," I said. Although to be in New York with five pounds in my pocket, presented an opportunity for escape that was quite interesting. "And you said sixty-forty."

"All right, sixty-forty," he said. "For that kind o' money it's not worth my time, but I'll do it just as one human bein' to another and take my reward in heaven."

While he grumbled about the bargain he thought he had made, I became suddenly terrified by what I had almost done. There were severe sanctions regarding indenture. If I were caught trying to escape, my sentence could be doubled or trebled. And what assurance did I have that this money-grubbing skinflint would keep his word and not sell me for more than two years? No, it was entirely too risky.

"I won't do it," I said.

"What…! We have a deal!"

"I didn't sign anything," I pointed out.

"Honorable business men don't require a written contract."

"But how do I know the man you intend to sell me to is an honorable man?" I argued, meaning of course, how did I know he himself was an honorable man?

"Not honorable!" he exclaimed. "The man I intend to sell ye to is one of the most prosperous merchants in New York and a close personal friend of the gov'nor himself. Until the poor man, like me, was chased from New York by that scalawag Leisler, who now claims to be governor. But never mind, the usurper will be tried and hanged by the time we get back. Ye can trust me on this, lad, the man I propose sellin' ye to has one of the finest houses in New York. He's married to the most beautiful young woman in all the colonies and he has two lovely little daughters. But no son, which is another reason ye would be wise to become his servant. How, I ask ye, could such a fine gentl'man be anything other than honorable?"

"May I know the gentleman's name, sir?" I asked.

"Ye may. His name is Mr. John Oort."

"He's Dutch?"

"He was, but now he's English. Though he can be Dutch when he wishes. Like myself."

"I see," I said, in spite of my confusion. "With all due respect, sir, might I know with whom I am negotiating?"

"Mr. Livingston--Robert Livingston Esquire, of New York City," he announced, throwing back his rounded shoulders and jutting both chins out. "Victualer to His Majesty's troops, Town Clerk, Clerk of the Peace, Clerk of the court of Common Pleas, Secretary for Indian Affairs and Sub-Collector of the Excise, as well as Proprietor of the Manor of Livingston, consistin' o' some one hundred and sixty thousand acres lyin' hard beside the Hudson River."

"Zounds!" I said, for he certainly sounded an impressive man. "How is it that such an important man from New York happens to be way down here?"

"That's the doin' of that German scoundrel Jacob Leisler who has taken upon himself the office of gov'nor and driven all the upstandin' English gentl'men from the colony. He's the most dangerous man in all America, fillin' the heads of the Irish and the Jews with the dangerous idea they're the equal of an Englishman."

"You mean he made himself governor without an election?"

"Election be damned!" Mr. Livingston shouted. "What use is an election if *everybody* is allowed to vote! But King William has dispatched a new gov'nor from London, and when he arrives in New York I intend to be there to see Jacob Leisler hanged, drawn and quartered! Then I shall have my offices returned to me and my past due victualling fees. If the King thinks my bill is inflated now, let's see if he ain't willin' to loosen up on the purse strings now that I've let the army go hungry for a couple 'o months. Nothin' like a little mutiny to teach a king the error o' his ways," he said with a chuckle.

"Zounds!" I said, for this merchant played a dangerous game. But reckless though he was, I could not believe he had sailed alone from New York to Carolina.

"I had an assistant," he explained when I asked. "But the ingrate jumped ship in Virginia--after a labor dispute."

Then you'll require an experienced seaman to get you back to New York!" I said, seeing my way out of a hard bargain. "Just give me a pair of breeches and I'll be your man!"

"Ye heard my offer," the hard man replied. "Take it or leave it."

"First I want to see the suit," I, no fool, demanded.

"Ye'll see the clothes when we get to New York."

"What...! You expect me to sail naked all the way to New York?"

"How else can I be sure ye won't jump ship on me like that other scalawag."

"Sir, I find your offer unfair, unreasonable and outrageous!"

"Ye're free to take yer business elsewhere," he answered.

So in the end, Mr. Livingston drew up a contract of indenture subjecting me to two years of servitude, and I reluctantly signed it.

On the next high tide I was made busy sailing the shallop out of the bay and up the Carolina coast, naked. At first I worried that Mr. Livingston might be keeping me in this natural state because it afforded him some lecherous pleasure, but I soon learned he had no interest in me other than financial. And when he told me he was a married man I began to relax and was soon scarcely aware of my nudity as I climbed about the ship's rigging. I found it hard to believe that so selfish a man as Mr. Livingston could even share his life with another person--until I learned his wife was a rich woman in her own right and it all became clear.

He was a Scotsman, like Kidd, even about the same age, but there the similarity ended. For although Kidd was a thief and pirate, he would never sell a helpless English lad into slavery; while to Mr. Livingston, helplessness was simply a negotiating tool insuring an unconscionable bargain. When he was twenty years old he went from England to Amsterdam, staying long enough to learn Dutch, then went on to Albany, a Dutch fur trading post in New York, intending to try his hand at that lucrative business. He soon learned, however, that the fur trade was very much a Dutch business and most uncordial to the British, whom the shrewd Dutch traders deemed good for soldiering but little else. To rectify this injustice Mr. Livingston went looking for a Dutch wife. And promptly found one.

Her name was Alida van Rensselaer, the unattractive daughter of the patron of Rensselaerwyck, and a relative of nearly all the important Dutch families down the Hudson River as far as New York. Although her relatives were not pleased with the aggressive Scotsman she brought home, he was nevertheless reluctantly allowed into the family of fur *handlaers*, and soon proved himself to be even more Dutch than they. Through his wife's Dutch connections and his British birth, he was able to make his way nicely in the cosmopolitan entrepot that was New York city, where he could be either an English politician or a Dutch merchant, depending on what the occasion demanded. Although Mr. Livingston had so far hardly impressed me as a generous, civic-spirited gentleman, I had to assume that any citizen who served his government in so many offices--while at the same time acting as confidant to Governor Nicholson (who had been run off by Jacob Leisler)--was at the very least a patriot. But not so.

"Patriotism is a mug's game," he scoffed, as we sailed up the American coast. "In England ye can be a loyal Englishman, in France a loyal Frenchman and in Germany a loyal German, and so on and so forth. But in America we be all those things, so what've ye to be loyal to? Money, I say. For money's the only thing we all have in common. The Englishman might hate the Dutchman and vicey versey, but pounds or guilders, it's all the same to both of 'em."

I had to agree that might be true of an international place like New York, but surely the rest of the colonies were as English as tea and crumpets. But Mr. Livingston didn't agree.

"They might've been the same once, but they ain't any more. These Englishmen in Virginia are too busy pretendin' to be gentlemen to do a lick o' work, while them New England egalitarians don't do nothin' else but. The Southerner likes nothin' better than to dress like a French fop, pinch snuff, drink, play cards, race 'orses and prattle like women; while the New Englanders don't drink, smoke blaspheme or say ten words all day. But the New Yorkers, God bless 'em, talk business all day in eighteen languages, and everybody knows what the other's talkin' about. Money!" he exclaimed, throwing his hands in the air. "Religion and race and nationality don't mean a thing to the New Yorker, and he's a damned sight better off for it. The business of America is trade and all else be damned! Take the wheel, I gotta piss," he instructed.

I was at the wheel and Mr. Livingston was pissing over the stern when we were smacked athwart the starboard beam by an errant wave that lurched us into a trough, followed by a whoop and a splash. After steadying the ship, I looked aft to see Mr. Livingston floundering in the wake of the Yankee Peddler and, although it shames me now, I must admit it occurred to me at that moment that the quickest way out of my onerous contract, was to leave my master to his own devices while I sailed on alone to New York. Nevertheless I came quickly about and a short while later managed to haul a spluttering though extremely grateful Mr. Livingston up on deck.

"I'm much obliged to ye for savin me life." he gasped. "Much obliged. And if there's anythin' I can do for ye, anythin', ye've just to ask it."

"You can give me my clothes and relieve me of the obligation to sell myself in bondage," I suggested.

Mr. Livingston regarded me with some confusion. "But--we have a contract," he said.

I tried to make him understand that some things, like saving his life, ought to prevail over the customs of law, but to no avail. So, after protracted negotiations, I settled on a comb and hairbrush as my reward for saving his life. I should have liked a mirror to go along with them, but they were in great demand by the Indians, he explained.

It was late afternoon when I made my way carefully through the channel at Cape Fear, while Mr. Livingston stood in the bow with the hand lead and line, calling back the few precious fathoms of water between the keel and the bottom of the sea.

"If we're going to have visitors, might I have my breeches?" I asked, after we'd anchored at the mouth of the Cape Fear River.

"So ye can flee the moment my back is turned? Ye can stay below while they're here if ye're so damned modest."

Rather than protest, for I'd learned by now that Mr. Livingston was moveable as Olympus, I foraged about and came up with a scrap of sailcloth which I fastened about my middle.

"That's fifty shillin's out of yer share," he said, when he saw me so attired. "Now start bringin' them muskets and rum up on deck."

Grumbling, for I could buy a proper pair of breeches for that much, I went below for the goods. By God! I said to myself as I looked about the hold. If Captain Kidd had caught the Yankee Peddler he'd be a rich man today. The hold was stuffed with bales of sot-weed, piles of furs, casks of rum, and enough muskets and powder to outfit a continental expedition.

"Who are you trading these guns and rum to?" I asked, as I passed the stuff up to Mr. Livingston.

"Governor Sothel," he grunted. "Not that it's any of yer business."

"Seth Sothel…!"

"That's right."

"But he's the most evil man in all of Carolina! He taxes the people unconscionably and steals their money; he's a white slaver who operates whore houses and gambling dens; and he sets Indians on settlers and settlers on Indians just so he can sell them both guns and rum! You're going to trade with a villian like that?" I cried.

"I don't see why not," Mr. Livingston answered.

I was aghast. Mr. Livingston's trade in arms would soak the earth with the blood of Englishmen, women and children, as well as thousands of Indians, but try as I would, I could not make him understand that it was wrong.

"It ain't the gun what kills, it's the man behind it," he insisted. "And if I don't provide 'em, somebody else will." Once he had winnowed the choices down to a loss of life versus a loss of profit, the answer to this moral dilemma was quite clear.

"Shut up and pass the muskets," he ordered.

The sun had almost disappeared behind the moss-draped trees that lined the shore when several Indian canoes emerged from the river and made directly for us.

"It's Seth Sothel," Mr. Livingston said, peering through his glass. "Go below and don't make a sound till he's gone."

I went below and made my way to the sail locker at the stern, always a comfortable place I'd learned during my days aboard the Blessed William and the Antigua. I lifted a corner of canvas and crawled under, then curled my knees up against my body and tried to think of home. I thought of my father seated in front of the fire in the library, reading an exciting tale of America aloud to me, and I cursed silently. I heard muffled voices from the deck and listened while the pelts were hauled aboard. When the guns and rum were loaded into the canoes, Mr. Livingston and Seth Sothel entered the cabin just above my head, while from outside came the splash of paddles and the deep guttural sounds of salvage tongues as the Indians pushed off.

One Indian had remained behind in a canoe for Seth Sothel, I saw when I looked through the small port. While I was watching, his painted face drifted into the lamplight from the cabin, setting off an involuntary cry from me. It was the same salvage who had scalped Orsa. A few moments later the hatch was thrown open and I was pulled to my feet by Seth Sothel. Except that it wasn't Seth Sothel.

"Mr. Halburton!" I exclaimed, then passed out.

"Christopher—Christopher..."

"Mr. Halburton--?" I asked, opening my eyes to a dead man.

"Yes, Christopher, it's me."

"I thought you were drowned. Mrs. Halburton too."

"No, we're both very much alive. And I'm pleased to see that you are too. Until now I thought we were the only ones who had survived."

"Chindomacuba too was saved," I informed him. "If only to be lost again to Indians."

"I'm sorry..."

"You know this boy?" Mr. Livingston, standing behind Mr. Halburton with a lamp, asked.

"I'm pleased to say that I do," Mr. Halburton replied, and proceeded to tell him of the circumstances.

"But why does he call ye Halburton when yer name's Sothel?" Mr. Livingston asked suspiciously.

"He's not Seth Sothel!" I replied firmly. "Seth Sothel is a man of the most ill-repute, and Mr. Halburton is a fine gentleman!"

Mr. Halburton smiled. "Thank you, Christopher. But how is it you know so much about Seth Sothel?"

So I told him everything Chindomacuba had told me before he and the Stono people were so cruelly murdered by salvages. His eyes tightened as I described my own close call at the hands of the demonic Indians who scalped, burned and flayed their victims.

Suddenly I screamed. There in the hatchway stood the very salvage who had torn the scalp from Orsa's skull.

"It's all right!" Mr. Halburton said, grasping me firmly by both shoulders. "This is my friend, Tonabucka. He looks fierce, as do all salvages to whites, but he's a church Indian."

"How do you do?" Tonabucka said in stilted English.

When he smiled, all the fierceness in his painted face disappeared, and it was suddenly impossible for me to believe what I had been certain of but a moment before, that he was a murderous, heathen salvage.

"I don't understand one bit of this," Mr. Livingston said. "Am I dealing with Governor Sothel or Mr. Halburton? Not that it matters one way or the other to me, just so long as the trade's a good one, and I got no complaint there."

"Nor shall you," Mr. Halburton assured him. "And if we might all repair to your cabin, I shall be happy to enlighten you as to my need for disguise."

So with Mr. Livingston in the lead, Mr. Halburton, Tonabucka and I followed him up to the cabin where we sat ourselves at table and listened to Mr. Halburton's tale.

"It's true I am Clifton Halburton, tobacco planter, not Seth Sothel, governor of Carolina. Had I known you make no distinction between a villian and an honorable man where business is concerned, I should not have bothered with my deception," he said, with a nod for Mr. Livingston.

"Thank you--"

"But as I have, I now owe you an explanation. And you, Christopher. For everything Chindomacuba told you about this infamous villain is true--and more. Much more. Seth Sothel is the embodiment of a peculiarly American evil which I call the bent politician. He is a master criminal of a sort with which the European mind is totally unfamiliar and therefore unable to detect and bring to justice. He is a man who takes money from under the table, never over it; a merchant whose stock in trade is neither the product of honest labor nor a decent mind, but rather improper influence and unconscionable graft."

"No inventory...?" Mr. Livingston mused.

"Nor scruples nor honor nor decency. And because there is neither man nor agency in all of Carolina capable of destroying this Machiavellian excrescence, I am forced to take on that duty myself. But the man is a veritable hydra and I no Hercules. No sooner do I chop off his head before another sprouts in its place. So to destroy the demon I am forced to play the devil's game. When I learned that Seth Sothel had an appointment to trade furs for muskets and rum to incite the Indians, I arranged for the Governor to be in Hatteras rather than here when Mr. Livingston arrived."

"How'd ye manage that?" Mr. Livingston asked.

"By disguising myself as your Dutch messenger," Mr. Halburton answered in a broad Dutch accent. "Knowing he would leave his furs here with Tonabucka--who is incidentally a spy in my service--I told him he was to rendezvous with you at Cape Hatteras, then sail down the coast with you to Cape Fear where the trade would take place. At this very moment Seth Sothel should be pacing irritably up and down the beach at Cape Hatteras while waiting anxiously for the Yankee Peddler."

"By God ain't he a one!" Mr. Livingston whooped as he pounded the table. "All the time I thought I was givin' him a good rogerin', he was tradin' somebody else's goods!"

"Profit is not my aim," Mr. Halburton answered with quiet dignity. "I only intercepted these arms to be sure they would not get into the hands of those who would use them in furtherance of Seth Sothel's perfidious designs."

"Still and all, I admire your skill, Mr. Halburton."

"But what will you do with the guns?" I asked.

"Trade them for plowshares," Mr. Halburton answered. "But what of you, Christopher? How is it you're running about this ship like a naked salvage?"

"Mr. Livingston refuses to give me any clothes lest I run away before he can indenture me," I replied quickly.

"I gave ye that piece o' sailcloth, didn't I!"

"For fifty shillings!"

"Fifty shillings!" Mr. Halburton exclaimed.

"I never intended to hold the lad to it."

"He did so!"

"I did not!"

"What about selling him into servitude?" Mr. Halburton asked.

"Oh I intend to do that."

"I think not," Mr. Halburton said, iron in his voice.

"I have a contract…"

"What choice did I have!"

"How much will you take for him?"

"Well, I could get twenty five pounds for him in New York."

"He told me ten!"

"I lied."

"I'll give you five pounds and save you transporting him," Mr. Halburton said, pulling a roll of notes from his breeches.

"I couldn't take less than ten."

"You could take considerably less," Mr. Halburton said, revealing the pistol at his waist.

"Five will be fine," Mr. Livingston said.

A few minutes later, seated in the canoe between Mr. Halburton and Tonabucka, I was a free man, off on a new adventure.

We paddled up the Cape Fear River for most of the night and arrived at the Wilmington settlement shortly before dawn, where one

of Mr. Halburton's church Indians awaited us with a wagon and team.
After loading the muskets into the wagon, we piled in and started up
the hard clay road that led to a broad two-story house at the top of the
hill. Mr. Halburton had required silence on the canoe trip, as Seth
Sothel's men, as well as murderous salvages, were everywhere about, and
it wasn't until we were almost at the house before the silence was broken.
Although Mr. Halburton and Tonabucka had previously conversed in
English, they now lapsed into the Indian tongue as our carman pulled
the wagon into the front yard, where several saddled horses stood tied to
a long rail. Lamps glowed from the downstairs windows and the sound
of drunken voices carried out into the first gray light of dawn. What
I had until now assumed to be Mr. and Mrs. Halburton's plantation
house, appeared now to be some sort of crude tavern or inn.

After some instruction to Tonabucka, Mr. Halburton told me to
get down and follow him inside. What I encountered when I stepped
into the low, timbered room looked much like the Planters Tavern in
Charleston, although the smoke was thicker and of a strange, sweet
smell, and all the men and whores who sat at the tables smoking Indian
pipes had drunk themselves into a trance. They sat like wax dolls at
the several tables scattered over the stone floor. A few oil lamps hung
from the timbered ceiling, their yellow glow pale and fuzzy in the
dense smoke. I felt awkward trailing Mr. Halburton through the tavern
while wearing nothing but a scrap of sailcloth, but there was no reason
I should, as nary a one of the patrons looked up at me as I passed, and
some of the whores were wearing little more than I. Although I hadn't
yet seen enough to fairly judge, it seemed the further north I went in
America the more depraved it became.

By the time I'd walked nearly the length of the room I was
beginning to feel dizzy from the smoke, which did little to clear up my
already confused mind. For this was certainly not Mr. Halburton's fine
plantation house, nor even a respectable inn, and hence I was unable to
understand why we had come here. Of course it was entirely possible,
I had to remind myself, that when a gentleman chooses to fight an
enemy so vile as Seth Sothel, he cannot expect to meet him on the high
duelling ground, but rather must seek him out in even the most fetid

swamp. And this was surely the most fetid place in which I had ever been, and certainly the last place in the world I expected to find the virtuous Mrs. Halburton.

Yet for a moment I thought I saw her, sitting alone at a table, smoking a pipe.

"Mrs. Halburton!" I cried.

However when the woman lifted her face and looked dopily at me, I saw my mistake. Although she resembled Mrs. Halburton in broad outline, it was a portrait bereft of color, tone and texture. Nor would the saintly Mrs. Halburton be sitting in a place such as this, wearing only an undergarment that fell so low from her shoulders as to reveal the red bud of one breast. Mr. Halburton, understandably annoyed that I should mistake this harlot for his wife, even in the dim light and thick smoke, jerked open the door at the end of the room and pushed me into a small chamber, empty of all but a bed and nightstand, then pulled the door closed after him. I began to apologize, but Mr. Halburton cut me off.

"You'll stay here until I get back," he said. "The innkeeper will bring your meals, but you're not to leave the room or speak to anyone until I return. Do you understand?"

"No, sir, I don't," I replied, looking about the small room with its single barred window. "I feel as if I'm being held prisoner here--if you don't mind my saying it, sir."

"It's only protective custody," he assured me. "No friend of mine is safe so long as Seth Sothel remains a free man--which won't be much longer if my plan goes as intended." He walked to the door and opened it. "Be patient and you'll soon know everything," he promised. Then he was gone.

Patience, unfortunately, is not the strength of a sixteen year old boy. And trust, which sixteen year olds usually have in abundance, was with me a scarce commodity after my experience with Mr. Livingston--as well as the cruel, murderous salvages; and Mason, Burgess and Culliford; and the slave ship; and the massacre at Blanquilla, and all the other terrible things I had witnessed in this violent land. Prior to coming to America I would have trusted just about anyone, but now

I approached each new acquaintance with the wariness of a feral dog. This damned country was robbing me of my youth.

One look at the crusted blanket that covered the bed of this barred chamber revealed that, although it was for me a jail cell, it's primary use was otherwise--which nonetheless reassured me little. I threw the blanket to the floor, turned the straw mattress, fell upon it and went promptly to sleep for the rest of the day, in spite of my loss of faith in mankind. Such is the resilience of sixteen year olds.

I was awakened in the early evening by a joweled man in a soiled apron bearing a tray of food, which I dived into with scarcely a word. The last meal I'd had, as guest of Mr. Livingston, had been so carefully weighed and measured that I left the table hungrier than when I'd sat down. This by comparison was food enough for a small party--peas and hominy, a great slab of boar, fried potatoes, a fuzzy fruit that proved to be delicious despite the nap, and a great tankard of cider to wash it all down. When I'd eaten everything except the *grits*, the innkeeper removed the tray, then returned a short while later with a bucket of water. If my imprisonment was not to be a long one, it would be bearable, I decided as I washed from head to foot while the innkeeper watched.

"May I ask when Mr. Halburton is expected to return?" I inquired of the taciturn innkeeper.

When he replied, "Who--?" to my question, I knew I could expect no information from him.

"Do you think you might find me a pair of breeches and a shirt?" I tried next.

"No," he answered, then turned and left the room.

Still naked, but sated, I lay back down on the bed and stared at the ceiling timbers in the fading light and tried to think of home. I pictured my cozy room, the dormer above the garden where I sat so often watching the seasons change. I tried to remember the sketches of ships and landscapes I had made and pinned to the walls, but found I had forgotten many of them. Then a tear broke and ran down my cheek, and I rolled over and tried to think of something other than home. I thought of Mrs. Halburton, the only purely decent memory

I had since my voyage began, and wondered if I should ever sit beside her again and listen to her sweet voice as I had in her cabin aboard the Jan Kees. When I closed my eyes I found I was able to picture Mrs. Halburton even more clearly than my dear father, and I was filled with a bewildering mix of pain and pleasure. A woman like Mrs. Halburton had a powerful effect on a man.

But more than that, the *absence* of women like Mrs. Halburton had a terrible effect on men. Left to ourselves we were like beasts, capable of such wickedness and depravity as we would not even dare recite in the presence of such women. It shamed me, but from what I had so far observed of my sex, without women like Mrs. Halburton, we were irredeemable.

While musing thus over the sad state of men, I was alerted by a squeaking sound from above and looked up to see Mrs. Halburton gazing down at me from the shadowed ceiling. Before I could utter my amazement, she brought her finger to her lips and, as quickly as she had appeared, disappeared. I had about decided my mind was playing tricks on me when a ladder began to descend from the ceiling and Mrs. Halburton appeared again in the opening of a trap door I had not previously noticed.

"Hurry!" she whispered, motioning me up the ladder.

Forgetting I was naked, I bounded off the bed and up the ladder and into Mrs. Halburton's arms. How shall I describe the warmth and sweet-smelling softness that engulfed me, the taste of lips that sought blindly with unthinking passion. And when I stripped away her undergarment, the only garment she wore, her body burst forth like a voluptuous flower, a rapturous sunrise and a swelling chorus of heavenly voices.

When I had finally recovered from this dizzying passion, I found myself in a clean soft bed in a large and pleasant room, with flowing curtained windows open to the warm breeze.

"Then it *was* you I saw downstairs."

"Sadly, yes," she answered. When I reached across her to turn up the lantern that rested on the table beside the bed, she stopped my hand. "No!"

"But I want to look at you," I said.

She shook her head and turned her face away. "I'm not the woman you knew," she said in a choked voice.

When I turned her face to me and kissed her, her cheeks were wet with tears. "You'll always be the same to me," I vowed.

"No, Christopher. I can never be that woman again,"

"Why? What has happened to you?" I asked.

"Things too shameful to say. You mustn't ask me to speak of them, for if I did I should surely die. Or so I wish."

"Very well, I shan't ask you a thing. But I must see you," I said, reaching again for the lamp.

"I've let you fook me, Isn't that enough!" she exclaimed in a pinched harsh voice such as I had never before heard from her, while slapping viciously at my arm. I pulled back, stung, unable to believe it was Mrs. Halburton I had heard.

"I'm sorry, Christopher," she said, her old self. "It's the drug."

"The drug...? You mean the sot-weed?"

She laughed, not the delighted laugh that had so buoyed me at sea, but a laugh that suggested a cynical conversation with herself. "Nothing so innocent. I speak of laudanum. Your--*Mr. Halburton* would give it to you just as he has all the others. He'll tell you it's medicine but it cures nothing except the very desire to live. He used to put a drop of it in my wine--to entertain his friends. Entertainments so vile I can't bear to think of them. So I take more laudanum."

"But you mustn't!" I blurted. "Not if this strange drug causes you to do things you'd rather not!"

"Rather not...!" she laughed. "Have no fear, dear boy, I don't take laudanum in my wine anymore. I smoke it. It's called opium. And I'm willing to participate in the most degrading entertainments Mr. Halburton can devise so that I can continue to smoke it."

"I can't believe it--Mr. Halburton," I said.

"*Mr. Halburton* is not a tobacco merchant as he claimed--or at least it's not his principal business--but he is the proprietor of this opium den, as well as a great many others throughout Carolina. He is a merchant of opium, prostitution, gambling and corruption in any shape he can devise. Nor is he Mr. Halburton, as he claimed, but Mr. Seth Sothel."

"No!"

"Yes. Everything about Clifton Halburton is a lie. He assumed that name when he was forced to flee from Carolina to avoid execution for his heinous crimes while governor of the colony."

"But what of all the things he told me--that he was condemned to Carolina for attacking Lord Wallingford, whom you later married--?"

"What...!" she exclaimed. "Do you think I married my own father!"

"Father! Mr. Halburton said your father was a shopkeeper!"

"Indeed--! My father is Lord Wallingford. Seth Sothel was sentenced to Carolina because he raped me."

"The monster! How could he!"

"One day, after returning from a ride on my pony, Seth surprised me in the stable, where he worked for my father. When my father learned of it, after I was taken home bleeding from the internal damage he had done me, he found Seth and gave him a terrible beating, which is the cause of the scar to his face which he still bears."

"Then Seth Sothel's father wasn't hanged by your father for poaching?"

"Hardly. Seth's father was hanged for murder. My father took Seth in when no one else in the village would have him because of the evil that had run in his blood for generations. His grandfather had been hanged for arson and his grandmother was burned as a witch. But my dear father was a rational man--he believed villains were made not born, so he took Seth in and treated him like a son."

"And he re-paid your father by raping you..."

"Which doesn't prove my father's theory wrong, only that he got Seth too late to change his nature."

To hear Priscilla say this, to think that she could still have such faith in mankind after all she had been through, filled me with shame over my own recent loss of faith, as well as a new hope for the future. Then I went on to repeat Seth Sothel's lurid tale of how she had been called to the manor after the death of the mistress and had stayed on to marry the elderly lord after the stable boy, whom she truly loved, had been sentenced to Carolina for assault.

"How absurd!" she said.

And when I finished with the happy ending, telling her how the stable boy had returned a rich man to take her back from her elderly husband and return with her to America, Priscilla broke into that delightful laugh of former, happier days.

"And you believed such rot...? Really, Christopher, it sounds like nothing so much as a dreadful, woman's novel. How could you...."

"I was younger then," I replied stiffly, as I did not enjoy being laughed at by the woman I adored.

"Still, I thought you were old in too many ways to be taken in by a story such as that."

"I believed him, Priscilla, I didn't marry him," I cooly reminded her.

"Touchè," she replied. "But believe me when I tell you, I had no other choice. My father had been tricked in business by a London merchant who held a mortgage on Wallingford Manor, as well as another large note which my father was unable to pay. He was in the process of foreclosing on Wallingford Manor and sending my father to debtor's prison, when suddenly Mr. Sothel returned to our village."

"The audacity...!"

"His debt to society had been paid, there was nothing anyone could do about it. Though naturally I did everything in my power to avoid him. I was unmarried--the injuries Mr. Sothel had caused me left me unable to conceive--as well as unreceptive to the process."

"I can understand."

"Don't be too understanding, Christopher," she chided. "For a woman can despair as much over one as the other. And by now it no longer matters to me if I'm fooked by man or beast, they're all the same."

"If you're trying to tell me not to make too much of this, you're too late for that too," I said. "I love you more than all the world, Priscilla Wallingford. And I intend to take you back to England with me."

"Hush your bosh and let me finish my story before the need comes over me again," she said, pressing her hand over my mouth. "On the eve before my father was to begin his sentence, Mr. Sothel appeared at

Wallingford Manor and asked to see me privately, on a matter of the greatest urgency, affecting my father's fortunes. I had no choice but to receive the rapist into my house. The rest you can guess."

"I'm afraid I don't know much about commerce," I said, though I could sense where she was going with her story.

She turned her head and looked at me with some impatience. My eyes had grown accustomed to the dark, and I could now see the toll of drug and depravity she had wanted to keep from me. She was certainly not as fresh as she had been, but it made no difference to me. I loved her and I was going to stay with her for the rest of my life, no matter what Seth Sothel tried to do about it. Meanwhile, the sordid festivities had begun downstairs and the din of men and whores was reaching up through the floor.

"We met in the library, appropriately enough, where Mr. Sothel began by apologizing for what he had earlier done to me. I listened impassively, but when I saw the tears in his eyes when he was finished, I felt myself strangely and uncomfortably moved. Had I been more experienced with such men, I would have seen him for the artful deceiver he was. But as I wasn't, I began to feel sorry for what had happened to him as the result of a youthful urge that had briefly overwhelmed and robbed him of reason. And although he didn't say it directly, he even somehow managed to convey the impression that his violation of me was a declaration, however crude and savage, of his love; and his deranged state of mind was but a tribute to my allure."

"By m' faith, 'tis no wonder he managed to get himself elected governor," I opined.

"Part of the reason he was in England was because the voters had thrown him out of office, and he had been forced to flee for his life. The other was to settle an old score with father and me. But of course I was unaware at the time of either his fugitive state, or his insanely vengeful and evil nature. He claimed he had come only to make amends for the grave injury he had done me and my father, and to prove it he offered to purchase my father's debts from the merchant who would put him in debtor's prison. He said he was now a rich man and could afford to return Wallingford Manor to my father and tear up his note. My father would have his house and not have to go to jail."

"But only if you would marry him…"

She looked away and nodded. "He had an uncanny way of seducing me into a pact with the devil, while causing me to feel grateful."

"So you did what you had to do to save your father," I concluded, to save her further pain.

"But I didn't save him," she said.

"What…?"

"From the beginning he was a loving husband and perfect gentleman, but once we were in Carolina the villain revealed his true nature. No matter how successful he had become here, he never forgave me for what he imagined I had done to him, and until he avenged himself his life was incomplete. It was he who had employed the London merchant to bankrupt my father, and he never had any intention of saving Wallingford Manor or sparing my father debtor's prison. By the time we arrived here the house had been foreclosed by Seth's lawyer and my father was in debtor's prison--where he died a short while later."

"My God…" I breathed. "Does the evil of the man know no limit?"

"'twas only the half of it. He had managed to destroy my father while I, by his depraved reckoning, was still intact. To be forced to lie in bed with the man who had raped me and then killed my father seemed to me more than enough punishment for one lifetime. But for Seth it was only the beginning. Next he made me an opium addict, without my even knowing what was happening. Then he turned me into a whore."

"No!" I shouted, bolting up in bed.

"His sole purpose in marrying me was to debase and destroy me in the most depraved manner his diseased mind could concoct. Do you know what an *exhibition* is?" she asked, giving it the French pronunciation.

I said I didn't, and she proceeded to describe in lurid detail the depraved public spectacles in which she was forced to participate, while I covered my ears and begged her to stop. At the same time I was assailed by the whistling and cheering and stomping of her lecherous customers from downstairs where the first act had begun.

"Do you still wish to take me home to England to live with you in a rose-covered cottage among the good people of Lyme Bay?" she asked.

"Yes! Yes, yes, yes!" I shouted.

"Well I won't," she said, quiet but firm.

"But I love you, Priscilla. It doesn't matter what he's made of you," I assured her.

"Oh, but it does," she said. She suddenly sat up and snatched a leather pouch from under the table beside the bed. "Can you give me this?" she asked, waving the pouch in front of my eyes.

"Opium...?"

"Opium."

"You won't need that."

"I will," she said, "Seth has seen to that. I'll always need it and I'll always do whatever I must to get it. Seth knows he can go away for days and I'll be here when he returns, just as sure as if he had locked me in the cell downstairs. But you won't be, Christopher. I at least have the power to deny him you. There are clothes and money for you atop the chest. Get dressed and go."

"Never," I said. "Not without you."

"Then we'll both be here when he returns, decide for yourself," she said, turning her head wearily from side to side. "It's taken all my strength to do this much. Soon I must have my pipe, then we shall no more be together than if I were on the moon."

"I won't let you!" I insisted. "Come with me and together we'll overcome this accursed drug."

"Christopher, don't you understand? I don't wish to overcome it. I love opium more than anything."

"More than me?"

"More than anything, especially a man."

"I don't believe you."

"Believe me, Christopher. I once thought all men were like my father, but of course they're not. They're like Seth Sothel. And I can't live in such a world without my pipe. I love it above all else, even you. So get dressed and go!"

"You don't mean that," I said. When I reached for the hand that held the opium, she pulled it away and turned her back to me, once more urging me to go. But I was determined to stay and see her through this, for I didn't believe God had put any evil temptation on earth that we were not capable of overcoming, even tobacco. However, I was then but sixteen years old.

"Where has Seth Sothel gone?" I asked.

"To stir up the Indians. Now go."

"But why would he stir up the Indians?"

"Oh God… The people are fed up, they want to throw him out of office again, this time for good. But if the Indians are on the warpath they won't be so inclined to change governors. And when Seth ends the hostilities, which he can order whenever he chooses, the people of Carolina will forget their complaints for a time, and allow him to go on plundering and stealing some more."

"And when they become fed up again, he'll start another Indian uprising?"

"Until there are no Indians left."

"The man is a Machiavelli."

"And that's why you must go while you can. Quickly, Christopher, for I'm growing needful of my pipe."

"I'm staying with you," I said.

"You'll stay with me while I smoke?"

"Yes."

"And while I perform with the hound?"

"Yes…"

She shook her head. "No you won't. You'll break before then. You'll either break or take up the pipe with me, which is the same in the end. You'll become an opium eater and stay here with me for the rest of your life--which shouldn't be too long. Would you like to do that?"

"No, I…"

"Then go!"

"But I love you!"

She laughed weakly. "So there must be a way…?"

"Yes…"

"You're a young fool, Christopher. And I could never love a fool so much as my pipe. Now get away from me!" she demanded, kicking at me, driving me from the bed. "Take one of the horses outside and ride north to Virginia. And for God's sake, spare me any more of your moony drivel."

While I dresed, Priscilla filled and lit her pipe, and soon the sweet smell of opium made its insidious way into my lungs and heart and brain. I stood beside the bed and looked down at the beautiful woman I loved, stretched out naked, her eyes closed, receding further and further from me. While I watched, thinking of the perilous journey that lay ahead, I longed to take the pipe into my own mouth, deep into my lungs, and float off forever with Mrs. Halburton. I knew that if I waited a moment more it would be too late, and yet I stayed.

I was reaching for the pipe when there came a knock on the door that startled me and arrested my hand.

"Five minutes, Mrs. Sothel," the innkeeper called.

"Thank you," she replied drowsily.

I took my last look at Mrs. Halburton as she struggled to rise, then turned and went through the window into the perilous night.

Chapter 6

Running around with Cotton Mather

In matters of commerce
The fault of the Dutch
Is giving too little
And asking too much

17th century couplet

My flight north through America on my purloined stallion, through swamp and forest, rain sleet and snow, over high mountains and deep valleys, shallow streams and turbulent rivers, chased by howling salvages and menaced by Highwaymen, wolves, bears and rattlesnakes, did little to prepare me for New York. There were almost three thousand souls living there in 1691, of every race, religion and nation the world could provide, speaking eighteen different languages, while crawling all over each other like bees in a hive, without one somehow ever stinging the other. There were Dutch, English, French, Jews, Germans, Irish, Scots, Swedes, Norwegians, Negroes, Indians, Walloons, Huguenots, Catholics, Quakers, Presbyterians, Baptists, Anabaptists--all united solely in the pursuit of money, and too busy to give any thought to the differences that elsewhere set men against men in the cruelest ways. What a contrast these business men were—willing to behave civilly with each other so that business might thrive—as compared to their backwoods brethren who seemed to me to be united only in their hatred of everyone but themselves.

The pirates of my unlamented past had spoken fondly of New York, an open city where "anything goes," notoriously friendly to all the thieves and cutthroats the sea could cast up, just so long as they brought money or goods to trade, and there wasn't a man or woman who couldn't be bought for the right price. But worse than any crime the pirate might commit on the high seas, was the crime the Dutch merchant would surely commit when he sat down to trade with that unfortunate sailor. For although there seemed an unspoken code of conduct among these men of business, for his customer it was *caveat emptor.*

It was even rumored that one of these Dutch sharpers, a wily agent of the Dutch West India Company named, Minuit (but called *Minute* for the time it took him to fleece a poor man naked) had bought the whole island from the Manhattan Indians for just twenty-four dollars--which I find hard to believe even of a Dutchman. Fortunately, King Charles had the good sense to take the island away from them in 1664, so I had reason to hope these cunning Dutchmen weren't yet running about unrestrained. For if the damned Dutch could buy Manhattan Island for twenty-four dollars, what was to keep them from buying the rest of America for a few hundred dollars more?

One of the first things I noticed upon setting foot in the city was the deplorable condition of the congested streets. They were a mess, ankle deep in mud and pig shit, deposited by the garbage-eating hogs that freely roamed the city and could be had for the taking by any hungry citizen. The wealth of some, the English, French and Dutch especially, was sufficient to cause Croesus envy; while the poverty of others would cause Christ to blush. Yet they all had food and clothing and a small room at least, and it seemed there were none save me trying to get back home. And what clothing! Unlike the Americans I'd seen in dour Philadelphia who went about in dark homespuns, these New Yorkers dressed like pirates, in silks and satins and linens and woolens from every corner of the world. Oddly enough the women, dressed otherwise like fine London ladies, went everywhere except church, barefoot, even on chilly days, as the mud and pig shit was too great a foe for fine bootery. And they were a comely and gay lot in their shortened dresses that showed a goodly expanse of ankle, coming and going as freely as men, even mingling with them in the coffee houses and taverns that were so plentiful in this busy city.

It seemed scarcely believable, no more than a bad dream as I stood on the waterfront, my valiant stallion at my side, gazing at the broad avenues and tall buildings of New York, that scarcely a day's ride behind me lay a primordial wilderness where men reveled in debauchery and mayhem; yet here in this bounteous city, the prospect of America set a spark in my cold heart that stirred a wild flutter of hope in my breast. But not enough to keep me here.

"Come along, Seth," I said, pulling at the reins of my great, dappled, gray horse. He had been the biggest one at the rail in front of Seth Sothel's opium den and, it turned out, wonderfully fit for the arduous journey that lay ahead for both of us. I had named him Seth after being called upon to whip him mercilessly when attacked by Cherokee salvages on the very first day of my dangerous passage. However, compared to the mean, base and abject treacheries of my fellow Europeans encountered along the way, these salvages were at least frank and honest as to their harmful intentions. For it soon became apparent to me that those rheumy-eyed, rickety-limbed, foul-smelling Americans who called themselves *pioneer* and retreated to the wilderness out of a claimed hatred of civilization, really hated all men and animals alike, and themselves most of all. They would steal the pennies off a dead man's eyes and rape his widow o'er the grave. They lied and cheated me every league along the way, until it was all I could do to get to New York with the clothes on my back and the horse under me. These treacherous vipers were proud of their ignorance, enjoyed cruelty, and were intent on raping and destroying everything in their path, be it man, woman or land. And yet for reasons I could not understand, these homely misanthropes were much celebrated by Americans who had never met them and who understood them not at all. These rapacious gypsies who would plunder each other, the land and all that lived upon it for their own selfish wants, were in truth no different from the Robert

Livingstons, but fortunately lacking in their wit for grand schemes. It is to be devoutly wished that the King of England not wash his hands of this America, as such men as these are surely unfit to govern themselves.

While considering this, my thoughts turned to Captain Kidd, who, for all his rapacious ways, was still the most admirable gentleman I had yet met in these Americas. For while the Captain loved gold as much as Mr. Livingston or any other man, there was in him an urge to be an honorable, respectable man that these others lacked, and so their ship of greed sailed without any rudder at all. For men like these, the mere *appearance* of respectability was sufficient, while men like Kidd held themselves to a private, though more demanding standard. It pained me greatly that I should never again see him so that I might explain my *mutiny*, and that good man, who was so kind and generous to me, should go to his grave thinking I'd betrayed him. But I was young and I'd soon get over it, as my good father was wont to say. However, in view of the mistaken portrait of America he had thus far painted for me, it was entirely possible that I should remember poor Captain Kidd every day for the rest of my life.

As Seth and I approached Fort George, whose steeply-pitched armory roof was the first thing I'd seen from the deck of the Sandyhook packet, I saw a contingent of British soldiers assembled for a parade. Or so it seemed, until the soldiers let go a volley of musket-fire at the fort.

"Whoa, whoa…!" I urged my frightened horse, reining him tightly in. After all we'd been through I thought him beyond fear in this civilized place, yet even in New York it seemed a man might get shot in the street. When Seth was calmed, I edged over to a group of well-dressed burghers who stood watching the action from a safe distance.

"Prithee, sir, could you tell me what is happening?" I asked.

"What's 'appenin'…?" one repeated, looking me up and down most suspiciously. "Leisler's 'oled up in there and refuses t' come out, 'at's what's happenin'."

"Jacob Leisler, the governor?" I asked.

"So ye calls 'im gov'nor, does ye?" he asked, scowling menacingly.

"Not I sir," I quickly appended. "'twas Mr. Livingston called him that."

"Robert Livingston...?"

"Aye."

"Where'd ye see 'im?"

"In Carolina"

"So 'at's where the pusillanimous poltroon's run off to," the gentleman said, provoking some mirth among his fellows. "Well if ye see our faint-hearted friend ag'in, ye c'n tell 'im it's safe t' return t' New Yawk, as Major Ingoldsby'll soon 'ave the traitor 'angin' from the gallows at Beekman's Swamp."

I was about to say that I did not expect to ever see Mr. Livingston again, when a voice from another group went up: "Jake Leisler's no traitor!"

"Long live Gov'n'r Leisler!" a second cried, craftsmen by the look of them.

When they moved towards me and the merchants, the merchants moved off in the direction of Major Ingoldsby's soldiers, while I moved off in the opposite direction. There were two opinions about Jacob Liesler, I learned. But more important, I learned that Mr. Livingston was still out of town. Not that I thought he would seek to enforce his contract of indenture after selling me to Seth Sothel for five pounds, yet I should be glad to be away when he arrived and spare him that test.

With escape in mind, I hurried off to the horse trader on Wall Street--who proved to be as eager to cheat me as any Carolina pioneer, but infinitely more able. He and Seth eyed each other suspiciously while the trader circled round him, felt his legs and looked into his mouth.

"This horse has been rid hard," he observed, after finishing his mysterious appraisal.

"Aye, it's a long ride to the church," I said.

The dealer regarded me with one eye closed, as if to say that in spite of my Christian aspect I was an abject liar, then inquired, "How far'd ye come?"

"New Jersey."

"Ah," he said, nodding, "harsh country, Jersey. I c'n give ye five pounds for the poor animal, if only to spare him any further cruelty."

I knew nothing of horse trading, but a bit about fish mongering, and so replied, "I couldn't sell him for less than twelve pounds."

"Done," he said, and I realized quickly that a Lyme Bay fishmonger was no match for a Yankee horse trader.

"I was about to add," I tried desperately, "that neither could I sell him for twelve."

"This is New York, lad, not Jersey," he said, handing me my money.

Nor was it Lyme Bay. I took my money, bade a sad "God be with ye," to my gallant horse, then, tears welling in my eyes, turned and hurried down to the docks to seek passage home.

The first ship I came upon was the Mercury, a merchantman of the East India Company, taking on a cargo of beaver pelts. I found the *skipper*, as these New Yorkers called their ship's master, standing at the rail.

"Sir—sir…?" I called a few times before getting his attention. "I'm a seaman, sir, with little money but a willing spirit, looking for a ship to England."

"How much money?" the skipper asked.

"Ten pounds…?" Between Priscilla's charity and the twelve pounds Seth had brought, I could go to fifteen and expected to do so. But until then I was ready with a lengthy brief of my nautical qualifications. "I've served as foretopman aboard…"

"Done," the skipper said.

Wondering if I'd been had again, I went aboard the Mercury, paid my ten pounds and signed on as an able seaman. We were to sail for London on Saturday morning and, as I had an unexpected five pounds remaining me, I elected to spend my last few nights in New York, at an inn rather than aboard ship.

Walking back uptown, I passed by the Kings Armes Tavern with its beckoning fire glowing from the hearth and a company of fine gentlemen seated at the tables, but did not go in, as it looked too dear. I found Mr. Clapp's, "A Kinde of Pleasure Garden" to be most inviting, though perhaps still too expensive, and settled finally on Madame Smith's Lodging House, where the mix of clientele, from bewigged gentlemen in fine clothes to itinerant peddlers in muddied breeches, promised a decent bed at a reasonable cost.

And such proved to be the case when Madame Smith--neither French nor English as I had supposed, but the plump, pink-cheeked, Dutch widow of an Englishman--informed me that a room was available for just twenty shillings, with supper.

"How long do ye stay?" she asked, after I'd pronounced the room satisfactory.

"I sail for England on Saturday," I replied.

"Ye iss sailor?" she asked, regarding Seth Sothel's clothes curiously.

"Not exactly," I said, then told her how I'd nevertheless talked my way onto a ship with the promise of labor and just ten pounds.

"Ten pounds!" she exclaimed. "De vay de Royal Navy iss pressin' seamen, dey should gif *ye* ten pounds!"

So I'd been in New York less than a day, executed two business transactions and been roundly cheated both times. I was doing no better than the Manhattan Indians.

That evening at dinner, I sat next to a stern-faced Puritan at the single table that ran the length of the dining room. Everyone at the table was a bit tipsy, except for me who had only just arrived, and the disapproving man at my side who had no tankard before him. They were raucous as pirates, these New Yorkers, full of ambition and a strange drink served by a pretty maid who rushed about the table keeping the tankards filled.

"Will ye have some lemonado?" she asked, with a flirtatious smile that drew some response from the table.

I thanked her and took a wary sip. But it was only rum, sorely diluted by lemon juice and sugar, and as nothing to an old Caribee sea-rat like myself. So I quaffed it down and extended my tankard for another, while the Puritan beside me glowered.

"Me name's Fiona," she said.

"Christopher," I said, as she danced away, smiling over her shoulder at me.

Had I made a conquest--so short a time after Priscilla? It was hard to believe at that moment, but when Priscilla had driven me off I was certain I would never again desire another woman, and already I wanted the lovely Fiona. So perhaps my father was right after all, time heals all wounds, including the cut I'd accidentally made to Captain Kidd.

The unrestrained talk that went round the table with the lemonado jug was of business and politics, all entwined in a three-stranded Turk's head that defied separation. They argued over a *charter of liberties* that sounded like nothing less than treason to me, and showed no fear in speaking openly of political independence and of the refusal to pay taxes! Even the sober traveler sitting beside me expressed some satisfaction with these inflammatory opinions, which until now I'd never heard outside a pirate ship. The main topic of conversation, however, was Jacob Leisler who refused to give up the governor's chair and surrender to Major Ingoldsby's soldiers.

"Id was de people make him governor and de people vant him stay!" a diner shouted.

"He'll surrender to the governor when the governor gets here," the young man sitting across from me said.

"Then let him surrender to Major Ingoldsby!" the merchant next to him argued.

"Ingoldsby represents no one--except the Van Courtlandts and Philipses and Livingstons," the young man replied.

"A den of t'ieves!" the first diner shouted.

"Does he mean Robert Livingston?" I asked the Puritan sitting next to me, as the Swede ranted on.

"He doth," he answered. "Though I be only a Boston clergyman and not a New York man, I believe the Swede speaks truth. Those men have used their office only to enrich themselves."

"How is that?" I asked, which was a mistake.

From this out-of-town preacher, for whom words were like drink, I learned more of Robert Livingston and Jacob Leisler--as well as the part this Puritan claimed to have played in the drama--than I ever could have wished. After King William took the throne from James, in what this protestant clergyman called the Glorious Revolution, this frail cleric claimed he had driven the Catholic governor of Massachusetts from office almost single-handedly--and the governor of New York as well! At this I of course realized that my dinner companion, man of the cloth though he be, was a fanciful liar from whom there was no immediate escape.

"When Governor Nicholson fled, ye people of New York drove Livingston and ye other patrons from ye city and fairly installed Jacob Leisler ye governor, a good protestant man," the cleric informed me. "Governor Leisler has said he will surrender his office when ye new governor arrives from England, a good and fair Irish army officer named Henry Sloughter. But Livingston and ye others want him out now, so they can resume their treacherous offices before Sloughter hears of their crimes against ye people of New York and removes them. And to that end they have persuaded Major Ingoldsby to drive Leisler from Fort George. But I have come from Boston to see if I can persuade Ingoldsby that he is being used by the forces of evil, and get him to withdraw until Governor Sloughter arrives."

"And I wish you well in that, Reverend…?"

"Mather. Reverend Cotton Mather," he replied.

"Christopher Rousby," I said, graciously shaking the hand of the artful deceiver.

At about that time, Fiona entered with the first course, a soup more thick in meat chunks and vegetables than any pirate stew I'd ever tasted, along with loaves of hot bread and still more lemonado. While poor Reverend Mather called for water, but to no avail, the rest of us noisily finished our soup. In a pinch this might have been quite enough, but this was soon followed by beans and bacon, roasted lamb, salad, peas, roasted chicken, tarts, curds and cream, cherries, mulberries and currants. It was only when this enormous meal was done that these sated New Yorkers were finally quiet.

However, when the Reverend Mather took this opportunity to offer a prayer of thanks for this good and generous meal, there came a grumbling from the table and a few calls for more lemonado. Still thinking myself something of a Christian, although a fornicator, horse thief and pirate, I alone at table bowed my head and joined the Reverend Mather in prayer and, when finished, commented as to the excellence of the meal.

"'twas passing good," he allowed, "but at ye Kings Armes, ye portions are much larger."

Some at table were dozing when Fiona began clearing away the dishes and uneaten food, of which there remained but a few peas and some salad. As Fiona took my empty plate she leaned over, affording me a good look at her full bosom, and whispered in my ear, "I shall be a coopl'a hours, but then I'm free if ye'd like t' meet me in the shed in the garden."

When I said I would, she rubbed her bare foot against my leg, tossed her hair over her shoulders and pranced off to the kitchen. I thought no one had noticed this exchange, but I was wrong.

"That girl could use a dunking," Reverend Mather said, which surprised me as she was quite clean. "I subscribe to a brisk walk after a meal," he added, pressing a cloth to his thin lips. "Wouldst thou care to join me, Master Rousby?"

"I should be pleased, sir," I replied, as I had two hours to pass before my eagerly anticipated appointment with the feverish Fiona.

Leaving the others to doze at table, Reverend Mather and I want outdoors for a brisk walk. Instead of setting directly off however, as I was ready to do, the Reverend first put himself through a series of unusual contortions, bending from the waist, touching his fingers to his toes, then resting each foot atop Madame Smith's fence and stretching out to reach his hands around his foot. I stared, I'm afraid, thinking it some sort of religious exercise, until suddenly the Reverend straightened up and started off, not at the brisk walk I had expected, but rather a brisk jog.

We would run down to the docks, then turn round and return by a different route, the cleric informed me as we ran--which at this rapid pace would leave me with still more than an hour to kill before my date with Fiona. I was surprised to learn, before we had gone very far, that Fiona was as much on Reverend Mather's mind as my own.

"Art thou virgin, Master Rousby?" he asked.

"Not exactly, sir," I replied.

"An inexact virgin…?"

"I have in a weak moment lain with a woman," I admitted.

"A whore?"

"No, sir, an angel."

"Indeed. Do'st thou knowest fornication is a sin against God for which ye might rightly roast in ye fires of hell for eternity?"

"I do, yes," I replied

"And yet thou woulds't call the harlot that woulds't tempt ye to lie with her, an angel?"

"'twas but a weak moment for both of us, sir," I pleaded.

"Exactly!" he exclaimed, pointing to heaven as we jogged briskly along the eponymous Broad Way. "'tis that very weakness destroys ye soul of ye man and ye spirit of ye nation. Discipline, work, frugality and self-reliance--'tis these will make ye selfe and ye nation great; while fornication, blasphemy, drunkenness, gambling and ye theatre woulds't destroy thyself and thy nation."

"'tis true," I puffed.

"Still thou woulds't meet Fiona this night. Who 'tis true is most comely, with voluptuous haunches and great breasts as woulds't fairly bounce out of her blouse. Such women, Master Rousby, are temptations of ye devil and are to be avoided at all cost."

That he said this all in one breath amazed me, as he had now begun to jog at a furious pace, as if religious fervor fueled his legs, while I, a sinner, had little breath left over for talk. His face, however, had become suddenly quite flushed.

"But is she not," I gasped, "a creation of God?"

"'tis true, she is creation of God. But she can also be ye instrument of ye devil," he replied easily.

"Sir, I am frugal. Self-reliant. A hard worker. I do not blaspheme. Get drunk. Gamble. Or attend--ye theatre. Coulds't I then--not be permitted--one weakness--and allowed to meet--Fiona tonight?"

"Nay nay nay!" he cried, all in one breath. "Fail this test, ye fail thyself; fail thyself, ye fail thy nation!"

I understood. But as I was about to leave this nation within a few days, I saw no reason I shouldn't meet Fiona in the shed that night. Yet my chest was heaving, my lungs and throat were burning, and my legs were trembling, so rather than argue I said nothing--which the

Reverend correctly took to be a rejection of his religious principles. As we ran, he continued to urge me to put away all thoughts of Fiona's body, while describing it in such sensuous detail as to make it impossible for me to think of anything else, even if I'd wished.

The sermon continued as we passed Fort George, where a small contingent of Major Ingoldsby's army rested on their muskets, while from within the Fort came shouts and laughter, as if this stalemate were not a serious thing at all. I had the feeling that although Reverend Mather could never persuade me to miss my rendezvous with Fiona, Major Ingoldsby would tomorrow prove to be no match for him. How little I understood American politics.

When we reached the dock, Reverend Mather was immediately ready to turn round and run back, but I had to stop, hands on knees, and gasp for time. While I tried to catch my breath, Reverend Mather ran around in little circles while continuing to exhort me to abandon my sinful plan. It occurred to me that if I ran back to Madame Smith's at the same pace we had come, the Reverend would get his wish despite my intentions.

While bent over, gasping and coughing, I felt myself suddenly seized from two sides, followed by a shouted, "Got 'im!"

It was Battersby and the burnt-faced buccaneer, I saw as I struggled to get free.

"Won't Cap'n Kidd be 'appy t' see this deserter!" Battersby exclaimed triumphantly.

"I'm not a deserter!" I cried. I tried to explain what had happened, but they pinched and pulled with such force that I could scarcely talk for the pain. "Please, let me go!" I begged, as they wrestled me to the edge of the dock.

"And miss collectin' the reward for ye? Not very likely," the burnt-faced one said.

"Reverend Mather, do something!" I called. "They're kidnapping me! Call the soldiers!"

"Nay! I see the hand of God in this, Master Rousby!" the cleric called. "If it takes such men as these to save thy immortal soul from that strumpet Fiona, then may'st God's will be done!"

"Nay, nay!" I cried, as the pirates wrestled me into their press smack. They bound my hands and feet and threw me violently to the bottom of the boat, then quickly pushed off.

"God be with ye!" Cotton Mather called after me from the dock as the pirates rowed for the Antigua.

The last I saw of the Reverend Mather, he was sprinting pell-mell up Broad way, coat-tails flapping, bound directly--if I'm any judge of horseflesh--for ye same instrument of ye devil of which he had warned me.

I was rowed out to the Antigua, hauled roughly aboard and dragged up the ladder to the captain's quarters, then dropped to the deck like a shot.

"'ere 'e is, Cap'n, the mutineer hi'self," Battersby announced.

"Slip 'is 'awser," the Captain ordered, from somewhere deep in the shadowed cabin.

"I dunno, Cap'n, 'e put up a fair fight..." the burnt one began.

"Untie 'im," Captain Kidd repeated, in an ominous voice that bode no good for me.

The burnt one produced a knife sharp as a Madagascar rock and slashed my bonds with little care. Then the two pulled me to my feet and I had my first good look at Captain Kidd since leaving the ship at Charleston. He stood framed in the leaded stern glass with New York in the background, wearing a new, bottle-green coat with shiny brass buttons and a white shirt with a high stiff collar and frilled front, such as Mr. Livingston's friends at the Front had worn.

"Thank ye, ye can go now," the Captain said.

"What about the reward?" the burnt one said.

"Later," he said, motioning them out.

They backed out grudgingly, leaving the Captain to regard me with a look of the gravest concern.

"So--the deserter has returned," he said.

"Pardon, sir, but I did not desert. Cleary stole the purse and I was chased by Mason, Burgess and Clifford, then by bloodthirsty salvages until I was taken by Seth Sotel and --"

"Luff off!" he shouted, immediately silencing me. "Now, from the time ye left the ship, slowly…»

"Aye, sir," I said, and began to recount the fearful tale of my flight from Charleston, including the massacre of the Stono people; my brief indenture to Mr. Livingston; my "rescue" by Seth Sothel; and my escape with the help of Priscilla (leaving out our romantic interlude); followed by my flight on horseback through the wilds of America while being chased by salvages and harassed by pioneers; my stop in Philadelphia, and my arrival in New York just the day before; right up until my capture by Battersby and the burnt one, following my exhausting run with that crazy cleric.

"Is that all?" he asked, when I'd finished.

"All but for my solemn oath that I at no time had any wish to be away from my ship, and I've devoted every day since then trying to find her. God bless Captain Kidd!" I concluded.

The captain studied me closely, which made me worry that I'd gone too far with that blessing. Then he raised his arm and lunged across the cabin with a great cry of, "Dear, dear boy! Has any man had ever a friend so loyal and true?" he asked, clutching me tightly, pressing his wet cheek to mine.

"I'm happy to be home, sir," I replied.

"And I'm glad you're back," he said, going to the liquor cabinet. "Mason and the rest o' them trait'rous scum was hidin' out 'ere in New York and I didn't know it," he grumbled, as he poured the rum. "Enjoyin' the protection o' that damned German--"

"Jacob Leisler?"

"Ye know 'im?"

"I've heard of him."

"Another damned traitor."

"There are some say he's a good man."

"Who?"

"Reverend Mather."

"Cotton Mather?"

"The same."

"That man's no less a traitor than Jake Leisler, preachin' rebellion to the people o' Boston. Where in hell'd ye meet that scoundrel?"

"I was running with him when…"

"Who was chasin' ye?"

"No one. He's of the opinion it's a kind of physic."

Captain Kidd shook his head at this, then walked across the cabin and handed me a cup. "Welcome home!"

"Thank you, sir." I lifted my cup and drank.

"Sit," he said, indicating the chair beside his desk.

The desk was covered, not with charts but pamphlets, both for and against Leisler, it seemed at a glance. Captain Kidd picked one up and stared absently at it. In large letters across the top it read: *Jacob Leisler, Governor of the People, for the People, and by the People.*

"I've never met this Leisler, as 'e's been 'oled up in Fort George since I arrived," the Captain said, dropping the pamphlet on the desk. "'e might be a good man, or 'e might be a bad man, it don't matter. But I 'ave met Major Ingoldsby and 'e's introduced me to some powerful members o' the court party--men like Mr. Philipse and Mr. Van Courtlandt. And they might be good men or they might be bad, but that don't matter neither. What matters, lad--and this is the lesson I learned in Nevis--is ye gotta be on the side what wins. And that's goin' to be the aristocrats. And I've joined 'em!" he said, raising his cup

"You mean--we're not going after the Blessed William…?" I asked, my heart suddenly filled with joy.

"Hardly. The Blessed William is now sittin' at Hunt's Ship Yard and 'tis as sorry a hulk as ever I did see--just as I expected from them sea-rats."

"And the man who stole her…?"

"Gone. That scoundrel Leisler gave Mason an illegal commission and 'e took six French prizes up the Gulf o' St. Lawrence, and is right now sailin' for the Indian Ocean on one of 'em."

"No…!"

"Aye. I know it pains ye as much as it does me, lad, but I want ye to forget about those scoundrels. Do ye think ye can do that?"

"I'll try, sir."

"Good boy. For as the Good Book says, there be a time to cast away stones, and a time to gather. I sense a great opportunity here in this New York. Somethin' tells me we be 'ere at an 'istoric moment, and if we but keep our eyes open and grasp fortune by the neck, we'll come out o' this honorable gentl'men."

"Aye, sir," I said. Coming from the man who had advised me there were no more opportunities to be had in America, this change of heart puzzled me.

Battersby and the burnt one were not pleased when I retired to my old cabin that evening, apparently a free man. Neither was I, but I made a great show of happiness at being reunited with my fellow brethren of the coast, while at the same time planning my escape to the Mercury at the first chance. I passed a restless night in my hammock and was awakened early the next morning by Captain Kidd's urgent summons. I found him in his cabin in a state of disarray.

"Major Ingoldsby's comin' aboard, get the place stowed away!" he ordered. "Then stand by as ye did with Hewetson--gentl'man's gentl'man, ye know the drill."

"Aye, sir," I said, then quickly set about cleaning up the place.

When Major Ingoldsby arrived an hour later, the place was neat as any officer's mess, and I as proper as any gentleman's gentleman. I opened the hatch to the tall soldier in his bright red coat, then melted into the corner, ready to run to the galley for whatever he might desire. But the Major was too preoccupied for food or drink.

"No, nothing--I must get back to the Fort," he said, pacing about the cabin. "A couple of my men were killed and a few wounded by Leisler, that damned traitor...!"

"I heard, I heard," Kidd murmured sympathetically. "...damned murtherin' dog."

"For which he'll pay dearly...!"

"'ear, 'ear...!"

The Major didn't mention that his soldiers had been firing on the Fort since shortly after he arrived. He and Governor Sloughter had sailed together from England in separate ships, but the Governor's ship had run aground off Bermuda. Then when Ingoldsby arrived with the army (but without the Governor) the aristocrats came out of hiding and urged him not to wait for Sloughter, but to get rid of Leisler immediately, which he attempted to do. When Leisler said he would surrender, but only to the new governor, Ingoldsby took offense and opened fire on the fort, and now several men were dead.

"I wanted to wait for the Governor but they wouldn't hear of it," the Major lamented as he circled about the small cabin. "But I did nothing wrong."

"Of course not," Kidd agreed.

"You were there--you ferried ammunition for me--you heard them."

"I was witness to it all."

"Exactly! And I want you to make that clear to the Governor."

"Me...?"

"You're an impartial witness. He'll have to believe you. I'm sending you as my official delegate to meet the Archangel."

"To meet the Gov'nor...?" Kidd asked, scarcely able to believe his luck.

"This is important."

"It is indeed."

"You do well by me, William, and I'll do well by you."

My Captain smiled. "I'll not disappoint ye, Richard."

Nor did he. I didn't go aboard the Archangel with Captain Kidd when we sailed down to Sandyhook to meet the Governor the next day, but when he returned to the Antigua, after both ships had docked in New York that night, he was in a bonny mood. In fact he was quite drunk. As was "'enry", as the Captain now called his new friend.

"By m'faith, that Irishman can drink," Captain Kidd slurred as I aided him to his bunk. As I was carrying both the Captain and a great jug of Irish whiskey--a gift from 'enry--it had taken a great effort to navigate thus far. "But I matched 'im drink for drink, so 'tis unlikey 'e'll be assumin' 'is duties for a coopl'o' days at least."

I left him sitting on the bunk while I, after finding the key in its usual hiding place, stowed the jug in the liquor cabinet, then returned to undress him. But by the time I got back he was already asleep in a sitting position, and when I lightly touched a button, he fell over in a swoon from which he didn't move all night.

When he finally summoned me late the next morning, he was in a most wretched condition. Nor were his spirits lifted when he learned that Governor Sloughter had risen at dawn and effected Leisler's surrender before breakfast--without so much as a shot being fired.

"No…" he said to the messenger who had brought the news.

"Yes indeed," the messenger, Mr. Pecksniff, replied. He was secretary to an organization of merchants and their go-between with Ingoldsby. "Needless to say, Major Ingoldsby should not have minded had it taken a while longer. However my employers are most happy to see the usurper in jail, along with his villainous son-in-law and the rest of his treasonous council. Oh, we have the wretches on the run now, and soon all the decent gentlemen of New York will be back--thanks in no small measure to you, Captain Kidd," Pecksniff said with a bow.

"'twas but my duty," Kidd replied. He was seated at his desk, eager to get back to the cup of Irish whiskey he had hastily stowed in the drawer upon Pecksniff's arrival.

"Nonetheless, I am bound to say you will find my employers to be not ungrateful."

"The esteem of such fine gentl'men is more than reward enough, Mr. Pecksniff."

"I shall make known to them that fine sentiment."

"Thank ye, Mr. Pecksniff. And whils't ye're about it, would ye please be so kind as to make it known to yer distinguished employers that I'm most eager to continue to serve their good cause in any way they deem fit."

"I shall be pleased to make this too known to them," Pecksniff said, rising.

"Bein' a naval man," the Captain went on, rising quickly but painfully after him, "and 'avin' some little familiarity with the law, I might be of some use to the Admiralty Court."

"I didn't know you had experience at the bar, Captain."

"I've had experience at the awardin' o' prizes," Kidd said.

"I see. I shall mention it to my employers."

"Most grateful, Mr. Pecksniff."

"And I shall tell them you'll be available to testify against Leisler…?"

"I know nothin' about the man, but I'll be pleased to do my duty."

"For which we are pleased," Pecksniff said, with another bow.

I opened the hatch and Mr. Pecksniff stepped out, followed by the Captain.

"By the way," Kidd said, as they started down the passageway, "'ow was the Gov'nor feelin' this mornin'?"

"'Fit as a fiddle."

"'e was…?"

With the Captain preoccupied by political ambition, I concentrated on making my escape to the Mercury before she sailed the next day. Although I had won Kidd over completely, Battersby and the burnt one remained less than convinced of my devotion to the pirate's trade, and to add insult to injury, the Captain had refused to pay the promised reward for my capture.

"The reward was for the return of Rousby the deserter, but Christopher is no deserter, ergo no reward is due," the Captain, rehearsing perhaps for the Admiralty Court, judiciously explained.

Although my captors might have understood and appreciated the Captain's fine legal reasoning, they disagreed strongly with the decision and would not rest easily until I proved them right. Which I resolved to do that very day.

At first I thought escape would be fairly easy, what with the launch coming and going most of the day, carrying able seamen to shore, then returning with supplies and extremely disabled seamen. But each time the boat put off, Battersby and the burnt one were there to see I did not go with her. I knew that they, watching their mates pushing off for a good time ashore, would soon grow thirsty and join them; but as the day wore on and they remained at their post, I saw that I had underestimated their resolve. They could not keep it up forever, nor even more than a day, but that was sufficient to cause me to miss my ship, and so something had to be done very soon.

If I could get them drunk I could then slip away, but the only spirits Captain Kidd allowed aboard his ship were those he kept in this cabin for entertaining notables, and the sailor that stole it was not long for the Antigua. But what would that mean to me who would be safely on his way back to England by the time the theft was discovered.

So with gift in hand I made my way to the rail where Battersby and the burnt one stood guard.

"What's 'is?" Battersby asked, taking the jug.

"A gift," I answered.

"O' what?" the burnt one questioned, thinking perhaps I meant to poison them.

"Irish Whiskey."

"Where'd ye get Irish whiskey?"

"Captain Kidd gave it to me--to welcome me home. But because I owe my reunion to you both, I thought you should be the ones to have it."

"Aye, 'at's right enough," Battersby agreed.

"But it don't mean we ain't gonna 'ave yer 'ide," the burnt one said, snatching the jug from his mate.

Leaving the two sailors to enjoy their gift, I returned to the Captain's cabin with a deck-scraper, and with it broke the lock off the already open door of the liquor cabinet. By the time I returned to the deck a short while later, both men were quite drunk on the Captain's fine Irish whiskey, and by the time the next launch left for shore, they were unable to see it--let alone see that I was hauling one of its oars.

The moment the boat struck the pilings, I clambered out and made my way quickly along the crowded dock to the Mercury's berth. The aristocrats, in all their finery, were out in force, strolling insouciantly about the waterfront now that Jacob Leisler was safely in jail, while the Leislerians skulked ruefully about, beaten but unbowed. There was an unmistakable tension in the air that afforded me one more reason to get home as quickly as possible.

I found the skipper on the Mercury's only gangplank, locked in a heated argument with a ship's chandler when I arrived, and quite blocking my way. I waited nervously at the foot of the gangplank while they argued--apparently over some stores of flour that contained more maggots than the skipper found acceptable. I tried a few times to slip around the combatants but found them unyielding, so I waited. And waited.

Finally the problem was solved, not when the chandler agreed to take back the spoilt flour, but when he agreed to reduce his price by several American dollars. Resolved now to stay away from the biscuits during the trip, I asked permission to come aboard.

"What's the hurry, someone after ye?" the Captain barked.

"No, sir."

"Where's yer bag?"

"My things are being delivered," I replied.

"Well now, ain't 'e the lord."

He was about to wave me aboard when we were distracted by a commotion on the dock. A cutpurse apparently, with a pair of Redcoats in pursuit, followed by his howling victim.

"'at's 'im!" Get 'im!" the victim shouted, as the soldiers continued in our direction.

A second later I saw the pursuing victim--Mr. Livingston!

I tried running forward but ran into the stalwart skipper, then back down the gangplank and into the hands of the soldiers. Hard as I tried to break their grip, I knew escape was impossible.

"'old 'im! 'old 'im right there!" Mr. Livingston shouted. "'e 's the one! 'e 's the one run off on me in Carolina! I got 'is indenture bond right 'ere!"

"I'm not his servant!" I cried. "Mr. Sothel purchased my bond!"

"'e's lyin'! Where's 'is master now if 'e bought 'is bond?"

"He set me free!"

"Hah!" Mr. Livingston cried, waving his bond to heaven. "Deliver 'im to Mr. Oort! And if ye try to run away again, I'll give ye such stripes ye'll never straighten up again!" he shouted, pushing me off.

"Hold the ship, I'll be back as soon as I've straightened this out!" I called to the skipper as they hauled me away.

"Aye, yer lordship," he replied.

So instead of sailing for England a free man, I found myself indentured to Mr. John Oort for two years. The work, keeping Mr.

Oort's accounts, was dull but not unwelcome after the many hazards of my previous occupation, and the living conditions were everything a young man could wish. My room beneath the crenellated eaves of Mr. Oort's fine Dutch house on Hanover Square was so serenely comfortable that I was even able to enjoy the view of ships sailing for England, even though I was not on one of them.

Nor was I confined to my snug quarters, as Mr. Oort kindly allowed me the run of the house during my free time, including the use of his handsome library on the parlor floor. Although Mr. Oort read little besides his ledger books and the inflammatory broadsides of those rebellious Leislerians (who had only become more strident following the jailing of their leader), his shelves were well-stocked with modern authors with whom I was only slightly familiar, owing to my father's prejudice. So after a satisfying supper in the downstairs kitchen with the servants, I was free to repair to my room with a volume of Milton, Jonson, Bacon, Donne or Shakespeare, to enjoy an evening of light reading, if I chose. Or I might remain in the library to read aloud to Mr. or Mrs. Oort.

Comfortable though I would be in my new position, I of course had no hint of it when I was dragged there by Mr. Livingston's soldiers on the day of my capture, just when my escape lay so near at hand, and so I was too miserable and angry to take any notice of the magnificent dwelling to which I was taken, or of the fine Dutch and English furnishings within. And even though Mr. Oort, a middle-aged man of weak appearance, seemed unusually kind and solicitous at our interview, I was still not ready to rejoice at being the slave of any man, nor would I ever be. And no matter how that decent gentleman wouldst inveigle me with his assurances of ease and comfort, I remained quietly but stubbornly resolved to burst my velvet bonds at the very first opportunity, even at the risk of jail.

Until, on the day Mr. Livingston first delivered me to my would-be-owner, Mrs. Oort entered the room.

My clenched jaw dropped and my pinched eyes widened as this American goddess floated round the table and came towards me. Her enchanted smile filled my head with light and silence as I felt my spirit leave my body and join with hers--Sarah--! Sarah, Sarah, Sarah--'twas the only sound I heard, like muffled thunder echoing from a place deep in my brain. She was plainly an English woman, or perhaps Dutch--Northern European anyway--yet one who suggested sun and fruit and merrily gusting winds, more than mere humankind.

"I'm pleased to meet you, Mr. Rousby," she said, with a conspiratorial smile--conspiratorial because she was so very young, much closer to my age than her husband's, who seemed more than twice her age--and her smile was an acknowledgement of this and all the other things youth holds in common.

While I was listing in my mind all the pleasures this divine young woman and I would share, I became aware of Mr. Livingston listing my attributes for his potential customer. Having exhausted my intellectual abilities (I could read, write and add a column of numbers), he was now listing my physical attributes--clean, strong, healthy and mild-mannered--which led me to expect they would next open my mouth and feel my legs. Nor would I object, for they could do with me what they would, just so long as they did not remove me from the woman who stood across from me, glowing like the Bruekelen sunrise.

"I'm sure de boy iss able and vell vert de price" Mr. Oort said when Mr. Livingston had finished. "But I fear he iss not pleased vit de arrangement."

"He was pleased enough to put his signature to my indenture bond," Mr. Livingston said.

Aye, when it was either that or be thrown naked to the salvages! I would have cried out, but for the American beauty in whose glow I basked. Instead I replied, "Pardon, sir, but if I appeared displeased at first, it was owing to something quite other than your kind offer, and you may be assured that I am most eager to assume whatever duties you--or Mrs. Oort might prescribe me." I then bowed in the direction of that glorious lady.

"How delightful and refined he speaks!" Mrs. Oort cried, clapping her small hands together. "Oh, do take him, dearest. For whatever time you can spare him his commercial duties, I know the girls would be that much enriched by the company of so gracious a young man."

Although Mr. Oort did not seem to be entirely convinced, he apparently relied heavily on his wife where the children were concerned. "Den ve haf a deal," he said, shaking Mr. Livingston's hand.

Thus began my two year's of indentured servitude to Mr. John Oort and a lifetime of impassioned servitude to Sarah.

Despite Mr. Livingston's assurances, Mr. Oort soon learned that I had no head for business, and was quite willing to spare me to Mrs. Oort whenever she requested, which to my great pleasure was most often, while still not often enough. I longed to be with her at every moment of the day and the night, but knowing my servitude would be abruptly terminated should Mr. Oort become aware of my passion, I did my best to feign at least a modest interest in his affairs. Mr. Oort's principle duty, as well as that of all the merchants who frequented the uptown coffee houses in the Wall Street area, seemed to be avoiding the Port Collector who taxed all goods coming in or going out of New York Harbor, at an "unconscionable rate!" However I must say that when I was shown these rates and duties by Mr. Oort, I did not find the taxes to be nearly so onerous as those men complained. The tax on a gallon of distilled liqor imported from England was a mere four pence; and for a whole pipe of wine, a trifling forty shillings.

Yet how they did complain. And contrive diabolical schemes to slip their goods past the Collector. The most common method was to off-load an incoming ship at Sandy Hook and smuggle the goods into Manhattan by wagon. Unfortunately, local privateers often took a greater toll on these shipments than did the Port Collector. Some went so far as to hire Indians to row out and meet their ships offshore in the middle of the night, then sneak back into Manhattan with pots, pans, guns, crockery and a host of other items of European manufacture that had little place in an Indian canoe.

Of one tax, however, every English merchant in New York was in agreement--the tax on anything Dutch. Yet no matter what customs duties or trade barriers the King and his loyal American subjects could erect, the Dutch somehow managed to out-trade the English and the Americans at every turn, and Dutch-damning remained one of the favorite topics of conversation in all the coffee houses of New

York. Fortunately for the merchants, because commerce was severely interrupted due to the war with France, much of their trading was done with pirates, to whom levies and tariffs meant nothing. Knowing the cutthroats would kill him if they couldn't bribe him, the Port collector wisely chose the latter every time, allowing the buccaneers to trade their stolen goods more freely than any honestly owned goods ever were. Some claimed that Leisler only lost favor with the merchants when he attempted to close the port of New York to pirates, but the merchants denied this vehemently. They insisted they were unalterably opposed to piracy, even while trading guns and swords for Oriental silks and Spanish doubloons, which had somehow floated to the pirate ships through lawful channels.

However, even more than taxes and Dutch-damning and the pirate trade, the subject most discussed in the coffee houses and taverns of New York at the time, was Jacob Leisler. All the propertied Englishmen (or the court party as they called themselves) favored his hasty execution; while the "foreigners", which apparently included any Englishman without sufficient wealth, angrily demanded that he be released immediately. And in the middle of it all, importuned from all sides, sat that newest American, Governor Sloughter, whose first important decision in his new post would be the life or death of Jacob Leisler.

Taking counsel from the aristocrats Leisler had run out of New York, Mr. Livingston chiefest among them, Sloughter had no difficulty with the decision of their hastily drawn court that the defendant and his son-in-law were both guilty of treason. Yet something occurred during the trial--whether a paucity of evidence presented by the prosecution or an abundance of character exhibited by the accused--that caused the Governor grave misgivings about the death sentence. Each morning the order was placed on the Governor's desk, and at the end of each day it remained still unsigned. And each evening the aristocrats, led by Mr. Livingston, met at Mr. Oort's house to complain about the Governor's indecisiveness and search for the means to remedy it. Mr. Dudley, the prosecutor, and Mr. Bayard, whom Mr. Leisler had once confined to the goal at Fort William Henry, were most insistent that the prisoners be hanged, drawn and quartered immediately, as an example to the rabble who would threaten the established order, while Mr. Oort cautioned prudence.

"Vy such a hurry to kill de man?" Mr. Oort inquired.

"Because people are saying the trial was unfair," the prosecutor replied. "And for each day the Governor delays carrying out the sentence, he is throwing another log on the fire."

"And a threat to business!" my former bondholder cried.

"And as long as the man is alive, we are faced with the threat of insurrection," Mr. Bayard added.

All the men sitting round the table were in agreement, except their host who replied solemnly, "I fear Jacob Leisler vill prove a bigger threat in de grave dan in de jail."

Day after day the rumors went round--one day the Governor was going to set Leisler free, the next he was going to execute him--and each rumor sent either the Leislerians or the anti-Leislerians on a rampage. It amazed me that these Americans took such political matters to be their business, while in England government was left to the governors, and if any citizen dare complain he had best do so in private. However I must say I found the idea an exciting one.

Despite the turbulence all around me, I passed some of the most tranquil days of my life in the company of Sarah Oort at 119-21 Pearl Street. Although she was just several years older than I (and in some ways younger), I was surprised to learn that she had already been once widowed before marrying Mr. Oort.

"I know what you're thinking, Christopher," she said, teasingly.

"What am I thinking?" I asked. We were seated in the library where I had been reading aloud from a volume of William Shakespeare's sonnets, some of them rather suggestive.

"You're thinking that Mr. Oort is an unusual choice for a woman so young as I.

"I would not presume to think any such thing," I replied.

She laughed softly at my polite lie. "But you do. You must understand, Christopher, that when a girl barely twenty doth lose her husband and is left with two babes, she daren't sit long in the Fore-seat."

"The Fore-seat…?"

"The front church pew, where marriageable women sit for inspection," she explained. "And when such a poor girl is selected by one of the wealthiest and most important men in New York, she is apt to overlook so small a thing as age. For a while," she added, dropping her chin. Then she quickly lifted it and smiled bravely. "That is why I'm so happy you've come, Christopher. I need some one my own age to talk to--or almost my own age. For even though you're just a boy, unsullied in the ways of men, you are finer and better educated than men twice your age, and in spirit you are very near my own."

I thanked her. I longed to tell her I was not unsullied and I was perfect for her in *every* way, but least of all spiritual. I wanted to tell her I loved her with the ardor of youth, while yet possessed of the patience of age. I wished only a sign from her and I would wait, unsullied, until she was once more a widow, but this time she would not take so much as one step towards the Fore-seat. I wanted to tell her all these things, but wisely kept my mouth closed. For I recognized that my beloved Sarah had taken a great step in saying this much to me, and if I showed myself to be young and anxious she would go no further. Her words were an admission and a test. She loved me as I loved her, I was now sure of that. But we were bound to pretend we were innocent, unsullied children, playing children's games together, but nothing more. Until the time we should be free to openly declare our love. At the realization of this, I felt an exhileration as if we had declared and consummated our love at that very moment!

"I trust we shall always be close--in spirit," I began slowly, so that she might know I had listened closely to her carefully crafted words and fully understood their meaning. "And until the time we're able to speak freely, I'm honored to be your spiritual friend and dutiful servant."

"Oh, but you must never think that!" she cried. "For I didn't take you to be my servant, but to be my young companion."

"I understand," I replied knowingly.

Young Companion. The expression quivered with all the erotic intensity of Mr. Shakespeare's most salacious sonnets.

During the next several days I was seldom away from Sarah's side. We played at children's games all the day long, until it seemed to me she was growing younger each day. Either that or she had always been something of a woman-child, practical but playful, but I hadn't noticed. I worried that Mr. Oort might either grow tired of our play together or suspect something more, but due to his preoccupation with the Leisler affair, he paid little attention to either of us while at home. So while he tried to preserve order in the dining room or parlor among his increasingly impatient friends, Sarah and I were off playing and laughing together in some other part of the house.

It was during one of these meetings, a particularly raucous one when I was summoned to the library, that I thought the axe was about to fall on my neck. But no, it had nothing to do with me or Sarah--Mr. Oort simply wanted me to deliver a letter to Governor Sloughter. Somewhat reluctantly, it seemed.

"You'll find him at de kings Armes," Mr. Oort said wearily, handing me a folded and sealed piece of paper. From his wan pallor, as contrasted with the flushed faces of his guests hovering over him, it seemed that Mr. Oort had finally acquiesced in the political feud that had been raging over the past several evenings in his home. "Gif him dis and request his reply."

I assured the assembled gentlemen that I could be relied upon, tucked the letter in my pocket and departed for the Kings Armes Tavern which was situated uptown, a block beyond Wall Street. Due to the recent spring rains, the streets were even muddier than usual, and it was some time after ten when I arrived, just the shank of the evening, judging from the look of the place.

All the tables were filled with well-dressed gentlemen and quite a few women as well, while a great many others were crowded around the bar, hoisting tankards and chattering as only New Yorkers do. At home a tavern was primarily a place for travelers away from home, while here they seemed to be a place where people gathered in place of going home following the day's business. This New York was a public place where nothing was held secret for long, and its citizen the most public-spirited I'd ever seen or heard of--except possibly the ancient Greeks. Indeed, for all its similarity to an English town, New York was probably more like Athens than London. In England a man's home was his castle, a place where none but family and a very few intimate friends might gain entrance, while here in New York these Americans thought nothing of stopping by a friend's house at any hour of the day or night, and might even do so even after an already long evening at the tavern. Yet, unlike pirates whose bacchanals rendered them unfit for duty for days after, these New Yorkers appeared promptly at their desk each morning and labored hard till well into the evening, only to retreat to a public house and begin another round of pleasure all over again. It was a life that might have appealed to me once, I thought, as I pushed through the crowd, but not since meeting Sarah.

I caught a serving wench by the wrist as she made for the bar with a tray of empty tankards, and asked where I might find Governor Sloughter.

"At 'is usual table by the fire," she said, jerking free and plunging into the crowd.

I looked across the room, saw his florid face glowing bright as the hearth, and started over. There were a great many gentlemen crowded round the Governor's table, all of them urging Leisler's execution no doubt, so it took a fateful moment before I noticed the gentleman seated beside him, dressed as he was in a dark frock coat and plain white scarf.

"So 'ere ye be!" Captain Kidd shouted, jumping from his chair.

"C—Captain…" I stammered, not knowing whether to run or stand.

"C'mere ye ungrateful lyin' wretch!"

"Please, sir--hear me out. I'm neither ungrateful nor a liar," I lied, as I haltingly approached the table, all eyes fixed on me. Who was this lad who could turn a peaceful man suddenly into a fire-breathing dragon?

"Don't tell me you're not a lyin' blackguard! For though ye played me once for the fool, ye'll ne'er do't again I promise ye! Get over 'ere!"

At this he reached across the table and pulled me most forcibly to him.

"'ere, what's this?" the Governor asked, as we thrashed about above him.

"This is the one!" Kidd said, twisting my ear most painfully. "Treat 'im like a son and what's 'e do… 'e runs off again, 'at's what 'e does!"

"Deserter, eh…" the Governor remarked in a slurred voice. I could see now that the Governor was quite drunk, and I feared that in this condition he might have me summarily executed.

"Pardon, sir, I'm not a deserter…"

"Don't talk to the Gov'nor till you're spoken to!" Kidd ordered, giving my ear another violent tug.

But I refused to cry out. Instead I replied, "The Governor was speaking to me! He asked if I was a deserter and I say no! And what's more I can prove it. For it was Governor Sloughter's own soldiers who arrested me and dragged me off to Mr. Oort's house."

"Oort…?" the Governor grunted.

"Yes sir. From whom I carry a message--if the Captain will but let me get to my pocket."

"Let 'im go," the Governor ordered.

Captain Kidd did as he was ordered, but not without a final hard pinch. I went into my pocket and passed Mr. Oort's letter to the Governor.

"Now what's this about your bein' arrested?" Kidd demanded, while the Governor read. "And none o' your lyin'!"

"I did not lie to you before and I'll not lie to you now," I said forcefully. "Whilst I was on the run in Carolina, I was forced to sign a contract of indenture. Being in New York I thought I was free of it. But while I was strolling innocently along the waterfront, I was suddenly apprehended by my bondholder and hauled off to Mr. Oort's house, where I have been most cruelly kept ever since. It was not until this evening, when I was entrusted with this message for the Governor, that I was allowed out of my cell."

"Ye mean you're a prisoner…?" Kidd asked.

I nodded. "Albeit a legal one."

"Legal be damned! No contract made in Carolina is enforceable in New York. Who the 'ell is this Mr Oort anyway, thinks 'e can press one o' my 'ands…! A damned Dutchman by the sound of it."

"Mr. Oort is a very powerful and influential merchant," I put in hastily, hoping to dissuade Captain Kidd from going against so formidable a man.

"I don't care a damn how powerful 'e is! This is a British colony, not a Dutch colony! Am I right, Gov'nor?"

"Right ye are…" the Governor mumbled, while staring blearily at the page in his hand. "What's 'is say?" he demanded, thrusting the letter at me.

I held it to the fire and read it quickly. "It's a request from Mr. Oort that you attend a wedding feast with him and his friends, all of them gentlemen of property and loyal subjects of their Protestant Majesties William and Mary, on Saturday evening next."

"Umm--they ain't Puritans, are they?" he asked, raising his tankard.

"No, sir," I answered. "Mr. Oort serves a fine Madeira."

"Then you can tell 'im I'll be there."

"Yes, sir," I said, then turned and hurried out, despite Captain Kidd's shouted demand that I stay.

Upon my return to Mr. Oort's house some time later, I was surprised to find the "gentlemen of property" still in attendance, waiting anxiously for word of the Governor's decision. When I informed them, after planting but one foot in the room, that the Governor was pleased to accept Mr. Oort's dinner invitation, there was a great collective expression of relief--except from Mr. Oort, who did not seem entirely pleased by the news.

"The Governor made as a condition of his acceptance, however, that there be wine at the table," I warned my employer.

"Yah, yah--dere vill be vine," he replied absently.

"And a flagon o' rum t' see it down!" Mr. Livingston exclaimed. "Which I shall gladly supply," he added, which rather took the company by surprise.

A short while later, after seeing his guest to the door, and while I was gathering up the tankards they had left, Mr. Oort came slowly into the library and sank heavily on the chair before the dying embers on the hearth.

"Are you all right, sir?" I inquired, for his complexion was ashen and his features contorted as if he were in some considerable pain. Mr. Oort did not reply immediately but instead sighed heavily and raised his pale watery eyes to mine.

"Perhaps no vorse dan any udder New Yorker, yourself included," he answered after a moment. "For you are a New Yorker now too, Christopher. But I fear you might soon vish you vas anyplace else but here."

"I do not know what event could make me wish to be anywhere else but here, sir," I answered, thinking of the lovely woman who lay upstairs in her bed at that moment. "For your own kindness and generosity is the only I have known since arriving in this mean country."

"Yah, yah, de poor can be most cruelly treated, dat is de same everywhere," he said, with the moral certainty of a man who has never been poor. "But in New York de rich are few und de poor are many, und if de Govenor executes Leisler I am much afraid dat de many vill rise up against de few.

"Then you must warn Governor Sloughter!" I spoke hastily. I began to apologize, but Mr. Oort interrupted.

"No, no--you are quite right, Christopher. But I haf given my vord to de udders, I must obey de majority."

"Even if it means an uprising?"

Mr. Oort stared at the faintly glowing coals for some time before replying, "Let us pray to God dat I am wrong."

With Mr. Oort's ominous prayer still echoing through my mind like Psalms bouncing off chapel rafters, I joined with Mrs. Oort and the household staff in preparing for the Governor's dinner on Saturday evening. It being early spring following the fierce winter of '91, it was of necessity to be a sparse feast of just root vegetables and dry peas, fish soup, venison, bacon, lamb and chicken, followed by spring berry tarts with cream; but as the wine and rum would be plentiful it was hoped the guests would overlook the paucity of garden things. Although I was new to the scullery and not much use in the preparation of victuals, the task proved to be, due to my enforced proximity to Mrs. Oort in the small steamy room, redolent with the smell of simmering pots, a most sensually pleasurable experience that rendered me somewhat light-headed and besotted.

At first, Mrs. Oort merely peeked in from time to time to offer instruction, or note my progress before rushing off to the dining room to see to some table matter or other. However, when she did finally come and stand beside me in that warm moist galley, I sensed that she too was soon overcome by the intoxicating spell of that enchanting place. While before she had called out instructions freely, now she was strangely quiet, content to teach me by her actions rather than her sweet voice, even going so far as to lay her hand on mine to guide my knife. Although this was the one scullery skill at which I was most proficient, having gutted many a fish in my youth, I was more than happy to allow her hand to rest atop mine for so long as she chose. Which was quite some time. When we'd stopped slicing the meat entirely, she looked up at me with a breathless fix to her parted lips and we stood still as statues, unable or unwilling to move and break the spell that engulfed us both. Until she abruptly pulled away, her face red as the leg of lamb that lay on the sideboard and, murmuring something I could not make out, fled for some safer precinct within the house.

My hand, still holding the knife, was trembling lightly but uncontrollably, while my staff had risen hard and stiff as the knife, and my face too was red and hot as Mrs. Oort's. That I, a rover of the world, however young, who had lain with women on two continents (including two Indian maidens together), could still be thrown into such flux at the mere touch of Sarah Oort's soft, warm hand, both mystified and pleased me at the same time. Mystified me as I was once more made aware that love, just when I thought I'd exhausted its possibilities, is in fact a condition capable of infinite renewal; while it pleased me to know that even after all my rogering--with a manipulating nymphomaniac in Lyme Bay, an opium addict in the wilds of Carolina, and a pair of heathen salvages in a murderous swamp--I had still somehow managed to hang on to a considerable scrap of my former innocence. Praised be the Lord!

I was not entirely recovered from this considerable excitement when Sarah came shyly into the scullery again, edging quietly up next to me as I stood at the table in front of the window, chopping onions.

"It occurs to me that I demand too much of you, Christopher," she said in a soft voice.

"I doubt that is possible," I replied, courteous but uncertain, for I was not yet sure of her meaning.

"Mr. Oort says you are a quick-witted lad, an opinion with which I am completely in accord and, I might add, a judgment which I am better qualified to make than my husband. For even though he is older and wiser than I, I am sure he cannot know you as well as I. When you are with him, you only *keep* books; but when you are with me, you *read* books. The one requires a cold, closed heart, the other a warm and open one. And that is the heart that is revealed to me. Is this not so, Christopher?"

"You know it is," I replied in a breathless rush. "And you say it better than ever I could, for all my books."

"But I must sometimes remind myself that Mr. Oort is wrong in one way. Thou art quick-witted, yes, but no more a lad. Not yet fully a man perhaps, but certainly not a lad," she added quickly, as she reached round and took the knife from my hand. "And though wit will serve a young man well in most affairs, there are some things that can only be learned with experience. What I mean to say, Christopher, is that no matter the wit, a young man might yet stir up the fire and burn the pot. Dost thou get my meaning?" she asked, sliding between me and the table.

"If you mean that a young man's heart betimes urges him to behave in a way he knows the wit forbids, then yes, I understand thy meaning. But if the heart should overwhelm the wit, cans't thou understand that, Mistress?"

"You forget, Christopher, I too was once young," she said, tilting her head back and round to me, displaying a neck long and graceful as a swan's.

"To me you are still young and will always be," I answered.

When she laughed, her soft, twin mounds of posterior flesh pressed mirthfully against me, causing my sheathed blade to rise with glee. "Consider the onion," she said, holding it over her shoulder for my inspection. When I pressed closer, to see it better, resting my sheathed sword between those mounds of flesh, she did not pull away, but rather anchored her thighs firmly against the table edge and spread her feet for firm support. "One might chop it too coarsely, or too finely. As a rule, men prefer it coarse, women fine. But men and women of experience prefer it sometimes one way, sometimes another. It depends upon the dish."

"And for this dish?" I asked, reaching round her and laying my hand atop hers on the knife handle.

"Not too coarse," she said, slicing the onion in two. "Nor too fine," she added, slicing it again crosswise.

Then she leaned over the table and, with my feeble assistance, chopped the onion in pieces neither too coarse nor too fine, while at the same time her rounded haunches moved against my own stiffened blade with the same urgent motion of her chopping knife, causing me to rest one hand against her hip to steady myself. Seemingly unmindful of me, Sarah reached for another onion and chopped furiously, then another and another, while all the time her bottom rose and fell to the rhythm of the chopping block, while I tried to control her wild plunging with a steadying rod placed securely abaft and between her pitching stern.

"My eyes!" she cried, causing me to stop suddenly and peer round at her. Tears were running down her cheeks. "No, tis only the onions!" she said, flicking me on the hip with the knife, and we resumed once again our chopping and grinding.

On we plunged, like horse and rider, coursing over fence and hedge to the equestrian rhythm of chopped onions. My eyes, too, now streamed tears down upon Sarah's bared shoulder (all that chopping had caused her dress to slip) and we were both bathed in sweat from the steaming kettle on the hot fire, aggravated further by our culinary exertions. Then, when Sarah had reached her last onion, I, despite the many layers of muslin, wool and linen that lay between us like a stockade fence, suddenly exploded with my own string of tiny pearl onions and a shuddering gasp, causing Sarah to collapse over the tabletop. When I looked up a moment later, I saw Mr. Oort, frozen in the doorway with a most horrified expression on his usually placid face.

"Vaht--vaht iss you doing?" he gasped.

Mrs. Oort rose serenely from the table, brushed the onions from her dress and replied, "Chopping onions." Then, holding her chin high, she strode imperiously past her husband, while he stared incredulously after her. When he looked back at me, he was glaring balefully.

"Mrs. Oort was teaching me how to cook," I explained.

"Come vit me!" he ordered.

"Yes, sir," I replied, hurrying after him.

Through the dining room, down the corridor and into the parlor. Where who should be waiting there but Captain Kidd!

"'at's 'im, 'at's my cabin boy!" the Captain cried, leaping up from his chair. "And bond or no bond, 'e belongs t' me!"

"Captain…" I began, as Mr. Oort stepped in front of me.

"Don't vorry, Captain, I haf no more vish to contest your claim," he said.

"Ye don't--?" Captain Kidd said, anger giving way to confusion.

"None at all."

"But ye just said--ye told me ye'd rather part with your right arm…"

"Dat vas den. Now I vant you to take him."

"'ere now, what's goin' on?" Kidd asked, glancing from my master to me, as if suspecting some conspiracy. "A minute ago I couldn't've 'ad 'im for all the gold in Peru, and now ye tell me t' take 'im. Who do ye think you're dealin' with 'ere, ye Dutch sharper, a Manhattan Indian?"

"Vill you take him or von't you?" Mr. Oort demanded.

"'Ow much?" Kidd asked suspiciously.

"Notting."

"Nothin'!" It was apparent to the pirate that this Dutchman intended to somehow sharp him, but he could see nothing amiss in a free offer. Yet he knew from harsh experience that no damned Dutchman ever entered a bargain from which he came away the poorer. "'e's not sick is 'e?"

"He iss strong und healthy," Mr. Oort replied unhappily.

"Then where's the rub?" Kidd demanded.

"I tell you, dere iss no rub!" Mr. Oort replied irritably. "Take him, no charge."

But the Captain didn't move. To cure the impasse, I asked to speak. "...seeing as how this concerns me..."

"You don't say notting!" Mr. Oort ordered.

"I'd like t' 'ear what 'e 'as t' say," Captain Kidd replied firmly.

"But I vouldn't! And as my servant he iss not free to speak vidout my consent. Now vill you take him or vill I gif him to the slave trader?"

"No!" Sarah cried from the corridor a moment before rushing into the parlor. "Please, you mustn't give him to the slave trader!"

"You haf no business in dis!" Mr. Oort replied.

"I know Christopher is your servant, but think of your daughters, sir!" she pleaded. "They have come to love the lad and rely upon him for their schooling, and they should be greatly distressed if he should be taken from them."

"Und I should be distressed if he remains. I pray you, sir, take him from dis house," Mr. Oort pleaded.

But Captain Kidd was no longer interested in me or Mr. Oort. He stared at Mrs. Oort as if she were a Spanish treasure ship, then rose to his fullest height and bowed deeply. "You may rest assured, madame, that the lad'll be given o'er to no slaver so long as Cap'n Kidd lives. And you 'ave my word on that, madame, as well as the word of my friend the Gov'nor, who I already spoke to about this matter."

"I am deeply grateful," she said, with a quick bow to the Captain, followed by a faint but unmistakably defiant glance at her husband.

"You iss friend mit Gov'nor Sloughter?" Mr. Oort asked, his interest piqued.

The Captain struck a pose before Mrs. Oort and replied, "Had ye been standin' on the Bat'ry when the Archangel sailed into New York Harbor last month, ye would've seen me standin' at Gov'nor Sloughter's side. Or was ye t' take yerself t' the Kings Armes Tavern of an evenin', ye'd find me sittin' at 'enry's right 'and, with Colonel Ingoldsby on me left. In fact there are a good many as would say Cap'n William Kidd is 'enry Sloughter's dearest friend in the New World. I'd not presume t' say it myself, mind ye, but there's them 'at would just the same," he concluded with a bow for Mrs. Oort to which, I was unhappy to notice, she blushed and smiled most invitingly.

"Den I am most honored to know you, Sir," Mr. Oort said, scarcely aware of his wife's fascination with the man. Nor did I understand why the wealthy merchant should wish to toady up to Captain Kidd when he already had more than enough aristocratic friends with ties to Governor Sloughter. "Und because you know him so goot, you iss the man who can tell me--you think the Gov'nor vill sign Jacob Leisler's execution order?"

"Havin' assisted the Gov'nor in the apprehension of that scalawag, 'enry and I are in close counsel regardin' the fate o' the man," he assured the beaming Mrs. Oort. "But as I'm sure ye'll understand, these deliberations are of a highly sensitive nature."

"I don't vish to pry into the secrets of government, I vas only vondering vat the Gov'nor's t'inkin' might be," the Dutchman wheedled.

"While I was wonderin' what Mrs. Oort's thinkin' might be," the Captain said with a bow to that lady.

Flustered but pleased by so unusual a question from a man, Mrs. Oort replied, "I know very little of politics, Captain."

"Then ye know more than most," Captain Kidd said, "Prithee, Madame, let us hear it."

"Well," she said, smoothing her skirts as she came a step closer to the Captain, "if I were to venture a guess I should say that the Governor will not execute Mr. Leisler."

"Indeed," Captain Kidd said, stroking his chin. "And why would that be?"

"Because it's cruel," she answered.

"Cruel…!" Kidd gasped, followed by an explosion of laughter with which even Mr. Oort joined. "Tis worthy of Coke!"

Mrs. Oort's face reddened with humiliation and anger. "And cause a great deal of harm," she added firmly.

Too amused to note her anger, Kidd asked, "Prithee, Madame, 'arm to who?"

"To you, sir, for one."

"To me…!"

"And to all men of New York who hold property or position only because they hold favor with the king. But men like Leisler, tradesmen and artisans who pay rents and taxes to these aristocrats and yet have no say in their governing--they are like dry sticks waiting to be struck."

"Enough!" Mr. Oort commanded. "I don't know vere my vife gets such ideas," he apologized nervously.

"Why, from you, sir, who else?" she replied.

"You iss mistaken, my dear. Please, say no more."

"No, I should like to hear more!" Captain Kidd exclaimed, obviously more amused than alarmed by her seditious opinions. "Do ye seriously think the execution of one man could cause a revolution?"

"I should think Pontius Pilate heard just such counsel before executing Christ," she answered.

"That sparked a religion, not a revolution," Kidd pointed out.

"Do you seriously believe, sir," she began with a mischievous glint in her eyes, "that if Christ had not been executed, we should have ever heard of Christianity?"

"Sarah...!" Mr. Oort gasped.

Even Captain Kidd, old salt that he was, came up briefly speechless at this blasphemy. If Jesus had lived, there'd be no Church of England...? The idea was unthinkable! "You would compare Jacob Leisler to Jesus Christ?" he asked, incredulous.

"I say there are certain similarities, sir, that we ignore at our peril. Just as Christ was the spirit of Christianity in His time, Leisler is the spirit of democracy in ours. Like it or not, the peoples' heads are filled with dreams of self-government. Kill Leisler and their dreams will become our nightmare. But allow him to live and the people will have no need of revolt. For in truth, sir, while Jacob Leisler might embody the spirit of democracy, he most surely has not the presence of a Cromwell. Ignore him and these New Yorkers will soon tire of this cantankerous old German and his lofty ideals, and go back to their one and only ideal--which is making money by hook or by crook!"

This was the only time in my life, up to then or since, that I have seen Captain Kidd made speechless by anyone, least of all a woman. He stood anchored to the floor, his mouth working like a fish's, apparently trying to find some place for Sarah Oort in his rigid and limited category of women, consisting only of loving mothers, dutiful wives or wanton women. Until now he'd never dreamed any woman, not even the Queen of England, could discourse so capably on politics.

"I am much impressed by the sense of your argument, madame," Kidd finally managed, with either a begrudging bow or a deep nod. "However, you fail to recognize that although the people have their democratic ideals, the aristocrats have their army."

"So did King Charles, until they beheaded him," she riposted.

"But as you said, Leisler is no Cromwell," he rejoined.

At this Sarah heaved her magnificent bosom in the air, preparatory to unleashing her argument, when her husband regretfully shut her off.

"Dot's enough, Sarah," he ordered. "It iss getting late, dere iss still much to do."

The Captain watched sadly as that lovely bosom sank like the sun plunging into the sea. Although New York women could hold political opinions that in England would get them hanged, they could only be expressed with the forbearance of their husbands.

"A most unusual woman," Kidd remarked after Sarah had taken her leave.

"More dan I t'ought," Mr. Oort grumbled while glancing crossly at me. "I hope you vasn't offended."

"Not at all," Kidd assured him. "In fact she makes great sense for a woman."

"You tink so?"

"She's 'ad a great affect on my thinkin'," Kidd remarked, staring in the direction of the scullery to which the angel had been banished.

"Und do you tink she might also affect the Gov'nor's tinkin'?"

"I think she'd have a profound effect on any man," Kidd replied.

"Den in dat case, Captain, Mrs. Oort und I vould be honored if you vould join the Gov'nor and my guests here at dinner dis evening."

"The 'onor, sir, would be mine," the Captain said, with a pleased grin.

Never had I seen two men at such cross purposes arrive at so amicable an agreement without so much as the slightest understanding of the meaning of that agreement. To see the two of them walking arm in arm to the door, one would've thought them to be the oldest and dearest of friends, with nary a thought save for the wellbeing of the other. I knew very well that such false bonhomie must end badly, yet I hadn't the slightest inkling of the full catastrophe to come. Until that time, however, their present spirit of generosity did result in one most fortuitous event that day.

"About the boy, Captain Kidd--please take him, as a gift from me," Mr. Oort urged, when they reached the door.

"Wouldn't 'ear of it," Kidd replied. "Although the boy is dear t' me and I don't give 'im up lightly, it's obvious 'e enjoys more advantages 'ere with you than 'e ever could with me."

"Unfortunately…" Mr. Oort grumbled, reaching for me. "Vich iss vy I insist you take him." he said, thrusting me at the Captain.

"You keep 'im," Kidd said, pushing me back.

"I insist," Mr. Oort pushed back.

After a bit of bandying back and forth like a shuttlecock, Captain Kidd, to my great delight, suggested that I be allowed to decide my own fate--to which Mr. Oort objected strenuously. However, when I added my own voice to Captain Kidd's, my master was forced to at least listen.

"Solomon himself could not have decided more wisely," I opined. "And like the infant in question, I am very nearly split down the middle by such a cruel choice. For it was Captain Kidd who found me, like baby Moses adrift on the water, and it is he to whom I owe my life."

"Consider the debt discharged," Kidd said.

"But," I went on with a nod to my master, "it was Mr. Oort who rescued me from the cruelty of servitude, and it is he to whom I owe my liberty."

"Vich you took," the old man muttered.

"Never mind the Bible speeches, which is it t' be?" the Captain demanded.

"I'll stay here," I replied.

"Then tis decided," Kidd said, grabbing and pumping the old man's hand before he could effectively protest.

After Captain Kidd had made his departure, and while I was attempting to sneak back to the kitchen, Mr. Oort shouted my name, stopping me in my tracks. "Sir--?"

"You may stay until I can find anodder situation for you, but den you vill go. Iss dot understood?"

"I'm sorry, sir, but I don't understand at all," I brazenly replied, "Might I know what I've done to cause you such disfavor?"

"You dare ask--after vaht I see you doing in the kitchen!" he exclaimed.

I pretended a moment's confusion, then dignified outrage. "Sir, Mrs. Oort was teaching me to chop onions," I informed him. I considered it an abject though justified lie in that a lady's honor was at stake. But watching the old man puff up like a bright red frog, I saw he was convinced by neither my false statement nor its rationale.

"I may be an old man but--but I still remember how to chop onions!" he spluttered. "Und dot vahsn't onion-chopping!"

"I understand your confusion, sir," said I most reasonably. "Until Mrs. Oort tutored me, I too thought there was only one way to chop an onion. But you know there is more than…"

"Stop, stop--!" he cried, his reddened face changing now to purple. Suddenly he grasped his chest and slumped forward, gasping, "A chair…"

Snatching a small bench from nearby, I thrust it behind him and gently lowered him to a sitting position as, a moment later, Sarah rushed into the room.

"Dear, what is it?" she cried, taking his hand in hers.

"I think he's excited about tonight's dinner," I said, when Mr. Oort failed to answer.

"Is that all?" she asked. Mr. Oort nodded silently. "There, there," she cooed, patting his hand, "you mustn't worry about a thing. Christopher and I will see to everything. Won't we, Christopher."

I assured him we would. Then with Sarah on one arm and me on the other, we helped the old man up to his bed where he could rest while Sarah and I prepared the dinner.

Owing no doubt to her imagined guilt over her husband's unfortunate collapse, Sarah remained somewhat distant from me for the rest of the day while, with the help of several servants earlier hired by Mr. Oort to help with the evening's dinner, we went quietly and efficiently about our tasks. I was greatly surprised upon answering a knock at the rear door to find that an old friend (whom I was unavoidably forced to leave waiting vainly for me in a shed in the garden of Madame Smith's Lodging house, following our first and only meeting) was to be part of this temporary staff.

"Fiona!" I exclaimed, upon opening the door and seeing her there, washing the mud and pig shit from her bare feet and ankles.

She looked up, parted the black hair that covered her green eyes and exclaimed, "So, tis you! And hardly the wonder ye didn't come back, seein' as how well ye've doen for yourself," she said, peering round me and into the house.

"That had nothing to do with it," I protested. "Didn't Reverend Mather tell you what happened to me?"

"'e told me ye went off with a coopla your mates," she smirked, with an epicene wave of the hand.

"That's not at all what happened--I was kidnapped!"

"Kidnapped was it?" she grinned.

"It was," I replied indignantly. "By two of the most horrible wharf rats you can imagine."

"Sometime ye must tell me how ye managed to escape," she said as she stepped past me and into the scullery.

"You don't believe me?" I asked, pulling the door closed after her.

"Does it matter?" she replied, casting an appraising eye round the room.

"It does to me," I assured her. "If the Reverend Mather called me a Catamite, it could only have been to further his own lustful designs on you."

"Lustful designs…? Hah! The man never so much as kissed me. Though I'd as soon he had rather than keepin' me up all night as he did, listenin' t' me confession, mind ye."

"Listening to your confession…?"

"Down t' the finest detail of every carnal sin I ever committed, even the venial ones."

"But the man's a Puritan, not a papist. Puritan's don't listen to confessions."

"Don't listen!" she exclaimed. "I promise ye, Christopher, until ye've seen a Puritan with 'is ears flarin' red and his eyes agoggle and his tongue lollin', ye've no idea what listenin' is. Though I must say," she added thoughtfully, "the penance 'e give me was unlike anything Father O'Reilly ever give."

"Penance--what penance?"

"'e put me o, 'er his knee and he spanked me bum."

"No...!"

"'e did. 'n then 'e 'ad me do the same t' him--cuz 'e said 'e'd lusted in 'is 'eart. 'n that's the way it went all night long. First I'd tell 'im a sin 'n 'e'd womp me bum; then 'e'd tell me 'e' lusted in 'is 'eart 'n I'd womp his. Until by mornin' we was both black and blue 'n I could scarcely lift me arm."

"Why the old hypocrite. I'm afraid he treated us both with little Christian charity that night," I said.

"Then ye was comin' back t' see me?" she asked, lifting her eyes and fluttering her long dark lashes.

"I was--just as soon as I could make my escape."

Then she took my hands in hers and said, "I see no shackles holdin' ye now."

She was right, there were no shackles round my wrist. Yet how to explain the chain bound tightly round my heart?

I was spared the need for an explanation by the untimely entrance of the subject of my dilema herself, who, upon seeing this strange girl standing hand in hand with me, pulled up sudden as a shied horse.

"This is Fiona, she's to help with dinner," I said, lifting her hands and peering closely at them. "Better wash them again, and this time get under the nails," I rebuked.

"Yes, sir," she replied with a short curtsy, and hurried to the washtub.

"Mr. Oort is awake and would like you to help him dress," Sarah said, while watching Fiona closely.

"Then he's no longer angry...?"

"Whyever should he be angry?" she asked, haughtily innocent.

"Quite right," I said, then turned and left the kitchen.

Sarah followed as far as the stairs where she laid a hand on mine as I started up. "Christopher...?"

"Yes...?"

"Do you know that girl--Fiona?"

"Only that she was hired by Mr. Oort."

"You've not met her before?"

I shrugged ambiguously. "Would it matter that I had?"

"I suppose not," she sniffed, then turned and hurried off.

Hoorah! I cried silently, as I spurted up the stairs, borne by the wings of Sarah's jealousy. And when I glimpsed her husband's grayed visage, seated like a ghost on the edge of his bed, I sensed that my mistress would soon be mine indeed.

"Help me," he said, holding out his arms for the clean white shirt that hung loosely from the back of a chair.

I picked up the shirt and tugged it gently over first one arm and then the other. Knowing that I would soon have what I wanted most in the world, I should have been the happiest man in that world. Yet, as I silently dressed this kindly old man who had taken me into his home and treated me like a son, I was suddenly overcome by such shame and grief for my treachery, over which I was powerless, that great tears gathered in each eye--tears of joy in the left, tears of sorrow in the right--and ran down each cheek. Then I felt the old man's hand under my chin, and when I looked, it seemed he too was near tears. But he didn't cry, he just looked at me and nodded.

Except for Fiona, who served to keep the gentlemen's cups filled and their hands busy, all the women left the table at the conclusion of the meal, leaving the men to the business of the evening--the fate of Jacob Leisler and his son-in-law, Jacob Milborne. Aristocrats all--highborn Englishmen with a few Dutch and Frenchmen scattered amongst them--who privately knew themselves to be even higherborn. Here were none who bore any sympathy for Leisler. Unless he might be John Oort or Henry Sloughter, neither of whom had much to say on the matter, Oort because he was so weakened, Sloughter because he was so drunk, thanks to Mr. Livingston who had generously supplied the rum, and Colonel Bayard who never let the Governor's cup go dry. Indeed, of all the fine gentlemen present that evening, it was Nicholas Bayard (whom Leisler had confined to the stockade for the previous fourteen months for insurrection) who was most eager to see the rebel and his son-in-law executed as quickly and as horribly as possible.

"Hang 'im from a tree, but slowly, don't kill 'im right away," the Colonel urged. "Then while he's still livin', cut out his guts and burn 'em in front of his eyes, then cut him up in five pieces."

Although it sounded terribly cruel, it was no more than the legally prescribed means of execution, I had to remind myself. However, Governor Sloughter (at least while he was still sober enough to talk) showed that he--despite his redolent surname and many heroic feats on the battlefield--had little stomach for the gruesome task. At first, getting all his information from such as Phillips and van Cortlandt and Livingston, he had believed Leisler a traitor to King and country, deserving nothing less than death. However, after listening to some cooler voices, he had begun to suspect that Jacob Leisler might be no more than a traitor to the aristocracy. He had, after all, during the two years he'd governed, executed no one (a claim no previous governor could make) and he had even managed to convene the first congress of the American Colonies (likewise something no previous governor had been able to do). And although this along with other government improvements caused the aristocrats to pay more taxes than they would have liked (in truth they didn't like to pay so much as a farthing), Governor Leisler had gone so far as to spend much of his own money to bring about the congress.

But the gentlemen assembled round Mr. Oort's table that evening were in no mood to hear anything on Leisler's behalf, not even from the Governor himself. And as to the Governor's boon companion, the stalwart Captain Kidd, whom Mr. Oort had been counting on to the tip the scales of justice in Jacob Leisler's direction--it saddens me to report that he'd been struck so balmy by Mrs. Oort that he was good for nothing save mooning about like a lovesick youth--which was the role I had already carved out for myself. And coming at a time when

Sarah and I were close to announcing our engagement, his attention served only as an unwelcome distraction. It started early in the evening when the Captain took it upon himself to change the seating chart--which Sarah had carefully drawn up with a view to mixing gentlemen and ladies, except for the Captain and Mr. Oort who should be seated beside the Governor at the head of the table.

"Where is Mrs. Oort t' sit?" Captain Kidd had whispered, catching and pulling me into the dining room while the others were yet in the parlor.

"At the end of the table opposite the Governor," I pointed.

"Then I shall sit here," he said, and boldly switched nameplates with Mr. Livingston, whom Mr. Oort had particularly wanted as far from the Governor as possible, being one of the most bloodthirsty of the lot.

When I informed Sarah of the change, expecting her to put the Captain back in his proper place, she did not react at all with the indignation I expected, but if anything, behaved almost as if pleased by such effrontery.

"If it means so much to him, then he shall stay," she said, turning in a swirl of skirts and returning to her guests in the parlor.

It took a moment, but I was quickly on to the game. Her jealousy having been aroused by the attention I had paid Fiona, she now meant to pay me back in kind--with a hoary old sea dog like Captain Kidd no less! My amusement, however, was tempered by pity for poor Captain Kidd, being so cruelly used as he was by my jealous mistress. Unfortunately, there was nothing I could do about it.

"Fiona, see to the guests!" I ordered, catching her staring at me from the doorway.

"Yes, sir," she said, and skipped to.

Twas somewhat disconcerting to be admired by two women, I was finding, although not an entirely unpleasant experience.

Even before the guests had moved from the parlor to the dinner table, it was apparent that the party had separated into factions, the romantic and the political. The former consisted of the ladies, who thought they were here to celebrate a betrothal; while the latter consisted of the men, who knew full well they were here for only one purpose--to persuade Governor Sloughter to sign Leisler's death warrant. And how they did hammer home the point.

"'ere, 'ave another drink, Gov'ner, 'n let me tell ye why the rebel's got t' be hung," came the steady refrain from the parlor.

And when Mr. Oort looked to Captain Kidd for some support for his side, he found the Captain had deserted the political faction entirely, and was tagging along beside Mrs. Oort and the ladies, listening to talk of babies and cooking and such.

Later at table, Mr. Oort tinkled his wine glass for attention and announced, "I believe hiss Excellency hass heard the opinion of everyone concerning Leisler's fate--save Captain Kidd."

"Eh—what…?" Kidd asked, tearing himself away from Mrs. Oort.

"Vaht do you tink should be done vit Leisler?" Mr. Oort asked.

"Well--as ye know, sir, my opinion's the same as yer wife's," he answered with a courtly nod to the lady.

"Vhich iss?"

"That execution is cruel."

This opinion from the bloody buccaneer was greeted by a moment's silence, followed by an outburst of rollicking laughter from everyone at table, even Mrs. Oort, who this time seemed not at all offended by the Captain's condescension. It was only when she caught my astonished eyes and looked quickly away, that I realized she was hiding her true feelings, if only in deference to her boorish guest. How my heart went out to that poor woman.

I had always thought it terribly unjust and even wasteful that perfectly intelligent women were expected to have opinions of nothing save matters domestic; yet to watch them play the fool for men, as they are often wont to do, it seems to me that far too many of that sex are most willing victims. Or at least that was the way I felt about Sarah Oort at that moment, watching her play the silly goose for Captain Kidd and his oafish cohorts, while they belauded his wit and put an end to whatever chance Jacob Leisler might have had that evening.

A short while later, when the dinner was finished and the women retired from the dining room (and Captain Kidd with them), Mr. Oort excused himself from the company of gentlemen, pleading fatigue.

My offer to see him to his bed was coolly refused, and so I was left to keep the pitchers filled with rum, no small task what with the way they poured every loose ounce down the Governor's gullet. Their intention--to get the Governor drunk and then persuade him to agree to Leisler's execution--was obvious to that wily Irishman who, even when he could scarcely keep his chins off his chest was somehow able to muster the sense to mutter "Nay" to their bloody entreaties. And when the Governor finally passed out for once and for all, after swallowing enough rum for a regiment, I heaved a great sigh of relief, for now surely Jacob Leisler was safe, at least for a time.

However, I greatly underestimated the treachery of these villainous aristocrats, I soon saw, when from somewhere there mysteriously appeared a Writ for the Execution of Jacob Leisler and Jacob Milborne and six others, ordering that they be "Hanged by the Neck and being alive their bodies he Cutt downe to the Earth that their Bowells be taken out and they being alive burnt before their faces that their heads shall be struck off and their bodies Cutt in 4 parts." I watched, horrified but shamefully silent, as these evil men gathered round that good man, did dip the quill in ink and place it in the Governor's hand--and then did guide his hand to that abominable document and affix his official seal thereto with their own hand! And then, their treachery accomplished, the cowardly assassins did slink shamefully away, leaving the disabled Governor to the care of his faithful though unsuspecting friend, Captain Kidd.

When I informed the Captain of their crime, while together we tried to bring the Governor round, he seemed surprisingly untroubled by their treachery--even when I suggested that their forgery might warrant the same fate they had spuriously designed for Jacob Leisler.

"I'd 'old on t' charges like them, lad," he warned. "For even though our friend 'ere might be the Gov'ner, them as ye would charge ain't without some power o' their own. 'n if ye was t' charge the aristocrats with forgin' a gov'ment document, who do ye think would be sittin' on yer jury? Not many Leislerians, I'd wager."

The injustice rankled but the political wisdom was unassailable. My only consolation lay in the knowledge that this was a cruel aberration in the history of New York, and never again would a few such villainous gentlemen of wealth and influence come together to so heinously abuse their power.

The next morning the sun came up over Bruklyn like a bloody wound oozing through gray clouds of bandage. The rain had fallen lightly and intermittently through the night, tamping down the mephitic stench of the Broad Street tanneries, until the fumes clung about the shoulders like a scarf of suppurating flesh. Beside it, the acrid smoke that slithered down the chimney pots and wormed its way through the nose and mouth and into the lungs, was blessed relief. Nevertheless, Governor Sloughter--who perhaps dimly realized he had been duped by his dinner companions the night before but was too embarrassed to do much about it--was one of the few New Yorkers not assembled on the parade ground at Fort William Henry on that damp and cold May morning, when they came for Jacob Leisler. (The Governor did at the last show some mercy, however, sparing the condemned the ordeal of having their "Bowells be taken out and they being alive burnt before their faces and their bodies cutt in 4 parts." Unfortunately, he could not find the courage to spare them the hanging and decapitation portion of the writ.) There was no official announcement of the execution--those who'd arranged it were careful to keep it a secret--yet everyone in the Colony, even Indians and African slaves, had somehow learned of it, and were there on that day to see the first flickering light of liberty go out. I felt myself drawn to the event despite my abhorrence, as seemed the case with almost all the others who stood about in the mud that day.

There were a few isolated calls to bring the traitors out and hang them from the gallows, but these were quickly silenced by the troublous Leislerians who made up the great majority of the crowd. Indeed, were it not for the presence of the armed soldiers, I am sure the crowd would have risen up and taken the prisoners away. It was something I dearly hoped for, the thing that drove me to this horrible spectacle in spite of myself. However, when the two men were led out of the fort, hands tied in back, barefoot, dressed in filthy rags already wet through, it was plain there would be no miracles in this debased atmosphere.

From the fort to the hanging ground at Beekman Swamp was approximately a half mile, up Broad Way and across Wall Street to William, then up to Beekman and across a muddy field to the gallows at the edge of a fetid swamp, where denuded trees floated spectrally in the morning mist. Only a short distance behind us, buildings were going up on new streets as quickly as they were laid out, yet here at the edge of the dangerous marsh where a man could be swallowed up, even the inexorable forces of civilization stayed fearfully back. Beekman Swamp was truly a place fit just for dying.

Although each of the condemned men had several times slipped and fallen in the mud on their journey here, walking with arms pinioned behind, they somehow managed to cross the last track with ethereal grace and climb the gallows stairs unaided. As they stood calmly staring out at the great crowd that had come to see them die, I edged my way through the crowd, closer and closer, as if being drawn like a compass needle, until I was close enough to look up into Jacob Leisler's face and hear his final prayer.

His voice was steady and without any rancor and, though heavily accented, the words most graceful. He generously forgave those who had brought him to this sorry end, asked God's blessing on the King and Queen, this province and its government, and urged his friends to be forgetful of any injury done him, but take care of his distressed family. Jacob Milborne said some little, but it was plain his father-in-law's words were meant for both, even though I did not see so much forgiveness in Milborne's dark stare. And when my eyes followed his, I saw they were fixed on Robert Livingston and his friends, who stood beneath a bare, tentacled tree nearby, surrounded by soldiers with muskets and fixed bayonets.

When Leisler had finished his praying, the Sheriff stepped forward and asked if he was ready to die.

"I have made my peace with God and death does not scare me," Leisler replied in a strong voice. He asked that his corpse be delivered to his wife, to which the Sheriff assented, then he turned to his brave son-in-law.

"I must now die, why must you die?" the older man asked. "You have been but a servant. And as I am a dying man, I do declare before God and the world that what I have done was for King William and Queen Mary, for the defense of the Protestant religion and the good of the country!"

But this gallows and this fetid swamp was a place for execution, not reprieve. As the Sheriff raised a black shroud to Jacob Leisler's head, the condemned man said, "When this my skin shall be eaten through, with this my flesh shall I see God. My eyes shall see him!" Then as the scarf was put about his head, he added, "I hope these my eyes shall see our Lord Jesus Christ in heaven. I am ready. I am ready."

While Jacob Leisler stood blindly by, the Sheriff turned his attention to his son-in-law, standing stiffly in the now heavy rain, and asked, "Are you now ready to die?"

At this, Jacob Milborne turned his eyes to Robert Livingston and the aristocrats, and for a time all was silent, save for a grumble of thunder rolling across the swamp. The condemned man held his accusing stare for some moments, while Livingston stirred uneasily and edged closer to the soldier at his side. Then when he lifted his chin, his voice pierced the sodden boggy air like a spear. "You have caused the King that I must now die! But before God's tribunal, I will implead you for the same!" he swore. At this, Livingston drew up his collar to cover all but his eyes.

Then Milborne turned to his father-in-law and, in quite another, softer voice said, "We're throughly wet with rain, but in a little while we shall be rained through with the Holy Spirit."

To which Jabob Leisler nodded.

"Will you not bless the King and Queen?" the Sheriff asked as he prepared to place the black shroud over Milborne's eyes.

"It is for the king and Queen I die," he answered. "I am ready. I am ready," he said as the Sheriff tied the scarf round his eyes.

He then placed the noose over each stiff neck and stepped back from the centre of the platform. A moment later the trap swung open and both men fell heavily through, danced and swung for a while, then were still and quiet as the swamp.

The crowd, too, was still and quiet, until stirred by a bolt of lightning directly overhead, flushing a great, *una voce* groan from them, pierced by some few cries of exultation. Then there was much shrieking and lamenting, and women fainting into the arms of men, or falling into the mud as the sky turned black and the rain fell on them like locusts. The soldiers grew nervous, and those anti-Leislerians who had cried out in exultation a minute before, now wormed their way tightly in behind them. Another flash of lightning illuminated the hanging bodies in an unearthly, violet glow, and suddenly the crowd surged forward, pushing back the soldiers and those they guarded, until it appeared from my vantage point that they would be overwhelmed, and the aristocrats torn limb from limb.

However, it was not blood they were after, but relics--*memento mori*. They tore at the bodies like chicken pluckers, keening and wailing most frighteningly, coming away with locks of hair and bits of clothing, reminding me of Sarah's fateful prediction: "Kill Leisler and their dreams will become our nightmare."

I watched until I could take no more of it, then turned and staggered back through the sucking muck to the high ground, and thence back from where I came.

If tis true, as is said, that death comes in threes, then surely the spirit of John Oort was also upon the scaffold that day. For by the time I returned home he was dead. I learned this from his distraught widow only a moment after closing the door, when she ran into my arms with this sad but not altogether surprising news. While thus holding her in my arms, I recited the usual litany of sympathies and reassurances, perhaps at greater length than was called for, so as to keep her in my arms the longer. Although she seemed disposed to remain in my embrace for so long as I desired, I felt it my duty to go upstairs and pay my last respects to the gentleman who had treated me with such kindness--and for whose death I was perhaps partly to blame.

"I must go to him, but I'll return," I said, prying myself loose. After all, what were a few more rapturous moments in her lovely arms compared to the lifetime of wedded bliss that now awaited me.

"I'll wait in the parlor," she called, as I started up the stairs.

The servants and his two lovely stepdaughters were kneeling silently at one side of the bed when I entered the room, a young clergyman on the other. Except for his already waxen pallor, the old man looked as if he might be asleep, having an unpleasant dream perhaps, judging by his somewhat pained expression. Was it Leisler's execution caused it, or my betrayal? Becoming aware of the clergyman's reproving stare, I realized I too was expected to kneel, and fell promptly to my knees at the foot of the bed. When the clergyman cleared his throat I thought he was about to lead us in prayer, but after several minutes of silence I realized the man must be one of those Quakers who don't hold with prayer, but would rather wait until someone is moved to speak. So I waited for someone to speak. And waited.

While I was waiting, I heard the door downstairs slam shut, followed by Sarah's cry of grief. I should have bolted to my feet at that moment and rushed downstairs to comfort her, but her muffled sobs told me that someone was attending to that duty, so I remained on my sore knees at her husband's bedside. For the better part of an hour. And still no one spoke. Finally, with little idea what I should say, I heard my voice issue forth as if divinely inspired.

"I am sure that Mr. Oort is today in heaven with Jacob Leisler," it said. "And like Jacob Leisler, who in his last moments asked only that care be taken of his distressed family, Mr. Oort cries out from heaven that someone should care for his wife and these two lovely children. And I swear by God almighty," I said, climbing up off my aching knees, "that I shall faithfully execute that duty from this day forward, until death us do part!"

It was obvious that the mention of Jacob Leisler had caused the clergyman, who stared wide-eyed at me as I made my exit, some little consternation. But 'twas no matter to me, whose place was at my beloved's side.

However, she was not be found in the parlor, I saw when I got downstairs. Nor in the dining room. I found her finally behind the closed library door, seated on the couch with Captain Kidd, her tiny hands enveloped in his great, hairy paws.

"Christopher, how fitting it should be you!" she exclaimed happily, upon seeing me. "For it was you who brought us together only a short while ago, and you who should be the first to know. Captain Kidd and I are to be married!"

Married! Her husband not yet cold in their upstairs marital bed and already she was engaged! The trollop! The money-grubbing trollop, who would jump from the bedside of her dying husband into the arms of an aged pirate, rather than into those of the young man to whom she had as much as promised herself! The fickle whore!

"Congratulations, madam," I replied dully, as Captain Kidd crossed the room and shook my hand.

"Madam…?" she said, and laughed. "If you are to stay with us, Christopher—and I pray you will—you must continue to call me Mrs. Oort. Or at least until I become Mrs. Kidd," she added, with a smile for her intended.

Jezebel would be more like it I thought, but held my tongue. And as for my staying with them, I would rather serve as a white slave on a tropical sugar plantation than be ever again anywhere near her. Oh, the lying, deceitful slut! Much as I wanted to stay and tell her how much I loathed her, I felt a stronger desire to go off and kill myself. So as soon as I could, I turned my back on them both and hurried from the house, while the grieving widow called after me to come back.

Or at least I'd like to think she did.

I slogged down to the waterfront, my tears mingling with the afternoon rain, fully intent on drowning myself in New York Harbor. But first a final draught of rum, I decided, spying a seedy tavern at the edge of the wharf from which I would make my jump. The place was dark and smelled of piss, and there were but a handful of drunken seamen strewn about the place like rotting corpses. It seemed an altogether fitting place from which to depart this world that had treated me so cruelly, I thought, as I ordered a large glass of rum from the slit-eyed barman.

"Ye got money?" he asked.

"Plenty," I replied, tapping the heavy bag of coins tied round my neck, setting off a tinkle that caused the corpses to stir. I pushed several coppers across the bar, lifted my glass and dashed it off at once. Then I ordered a second and drank it a bit more slowly, while the barman waited and watched like a hungry wolf. And that was the last thing I remembered before coming to in a muddy alley with no purse round my neck nor shoes upon my feet. Being in no shape for suicide, I staggered back home in the dark where, despite my foul state, I received a joyous welcome home from the faithless woman who had very nearly caused my death.

After washing myself from head to foot, I stumbled naked into my warm clean bed. I had scarcely fallen asleep when I was awakened by a light knock upon my door.

"Christopher, may I come in?" Sarah called softly.

"It's your house," I answered.

The door opened, revealing Sarah in golden candlelight, dressed in a white nightgown, her loosened hair trailing behind as she floated softly to my bedside on bare feet.

"The girls are finally asleep," she said. "They're terribly upset--their father lying dead downstairs…"

"Someone should be," I said.

"Why do you punish me, Christopher? Is it because I choose to marry too soon; or do you think I marry the wrong man?"

"Whom you marry has nothing to do with it," was all I would say.

"I see," she said. When she placed the candle beside the bed, I could see her body behind the thin gown. "So if now I were to choose to marry you instead of William--would you stll say it was too soon?"

"You know my answer to that."

"So now we understand that you are not motivated solely by your feelings for Mr. Oort," she observed.

"I admit that my feeling for you is greater than for any other, and I know you feel the same for me."

"I know that you are my dearest friend, and I hope that you will continue to be. And if you are a true friend, you will understand that I have children, property, debts, business affairs… In short, Christopher, your dear friend cannot afford to marry for love."

"No, Sarah," I said, catching her hand in mine. "You cannot afford to marry for anything but love. If the poets know nothing else, they know this. You've endured a cold marriage, now is the time to 'stir up the fire and burn the pot'."

She snatched her hand from mine and replied, "I have no idea what you're talking about."

"I'm talking about onions—neither too coarse nor too fine."

"You are coarse to remind me, sir," she said, crossing her arms and pulling her thin gown taut over her breasts, which hung above me like fruit on a limb.

"I'm sure it's been as much on your mind as it has on mine."

"It was a moment of weakness, nothing more. Until now I had totally forgotten about it."

"But now you are remembering---"

"I'm thinking of something else entirely."

"Then why are your cheeks reddening, just as they did in the scullery?"

"It is warm in here."

"And why are your nipples hardening?"

"Christopher…!" she gasped, bringing her hands to her breasts.

"And why are you growing moist?"

She looked down at her gown, saw that I was only guessing, and asked, "And why is your tent pole standing up?"

I looked at my blanket, standing like a lone Bedouin tent on the flat desert, and replied, "I wouldn't even attempt to deny my feeling for you, Mrs. Oort."

"Nor could you, in the face of such evidence," she said, still staring, admiringly it seemed, at my erect pole.

"And what of the evidence against you?"

"I can't deny what is plain," she answered, dropping her hands from her pointy breasts. "But I, unlike you, am not free to act upon my feeling."

"You're not yet a married woman," I reminded her. If I could not have the loaf, perhaps a slice might sate me. "And until then you are a merry widow."

At this she laughed and said, "'tis convincing logic, but still fornication."

It occurred to me then that if it were only the final act of fornication which she felt her vow denied her, there were perhaps a few other steps along the way to which she might not be disinclined.

"If you were to see me naked, would that be fornication?" I asked.

"'twould surely be temptation," she answered charily.

"So I lifted the edge of the tent that covered my stiffened pole and placed it in her hand. She held the blanket between her fingers for a moment before slowly turning it back. A pleased smile crossed her lips as her large eyes roved over my body.

"And if I were to see you naked, that would not be fornication either," I said.

She opened her mouth to speak, then realized she was a snared rabbit. "Tit for tat," she said.

She pulled the gown slowly upward, revealing her smooth white body one part at a time, her firm legs flecked with silvery down, leading to a transparent ginger veil, flared hips and pinched waist, and full, crimson-tipped breasts. When I asked her to turn slowly around, she did, showing me those rounded haunches that had such a short time before pitched and bucked against this stiffened pole that now remembered and strained upwards for another go. But not too fast, I cautioned myself.

"You're more beautiful than any Greek statue," I said. It was lame, but the best my feverish brain could conjure.

She smiled down at me and said, "As are you. Although I've never seen anything like that on a Greek statue."

"If you were to lie here beside me, like two Greek statues, that would surely not be fornication," I suggested.

"'twould be no different than standing," she said, and slid into bed beside me.

We lay hip to hip, staring up at the ceiling. I was considering my next step when, after some time had passed, it was Sarah who surprisingly broke the breathless silence. "If I were to touch your tent pole, would that be fornication?" she asked.

"Not by any definition," I assured her, as her soft warm hand found my pole.

"Nor if I were to touch you there," I said, gliding my hand over her moist nether lips, "neither could that be called fornication."

After some time, she sighed and said, "I'm glad for that."

As her pleasure increased, she began bucking and moaning as she had in the scullery, until I feared Captain Kidd might hear her even from his ship. But then she suddenly stiffened and went silent, except for the sibilant sound of air leaving her lungs. After a moment she lifted her head and regarded my still erect tent pole, then dived down upon it.

"Id dis for'cashun?" she asked.

"Not at all," I assured her.

> And thus we passed the night
> In contrived erotic delight
> Limited only by our imagination
> And our definition of fornication.

Chapter 7

The Politics of New York

If, after the last, the reader should think me a lucky man, just think of Captain Kidd. Fortune did not smile on him in the New World, so much as shake and roar with laughter. After arriving in New York with nothing more than a leaking ship, manned by a mangy crew of old seadogs scarcely fit for galley slaves, he now found himself married to one of the fairest women in the colonies, a favorite of the Governor and the aristocrats, and as much a gentleman as any Yankee might claim to be. Gone were the rainbow-hued pirate costumes of the past, replaced now by the good cloth coat of the burghers, who gathered each morning in the uptown coffee houses to discuss commerce. On Sunday mornings, however, the Captain changed to his gentleman's dress--green silk breeches trimmed with gold and silver thread, a gold embroidered blue coat, a lace shirt, scarlet and blue hose, a powdered and pompadoured wig, and a silver-hilted sword-- and, accompanied by his wife and daughters, went off to Trinity Church, where he would sit proudly in his own front pew, owing to the most generous donation the Rector had ever seen. Although the Captain had been a Presbyterian all his life, his switch to the Episcopalians--upon learning that it was the favored church of the aristocrats--was quicker than the conversion of St. Paul.

Soon after they were married, Captain Kidd moved his wife and daughters (and me) into a great house on Hanover Square, quite the most fashionable address in Manhattan. He had insisted on leaving all the old furnishings behind and buying all new things for Sarah when they moved. However, due to the war with France, few English ships managed to make it past the French blockade to New York at the time, resulting in a great scarcity of English goods throughout the colonies. Fortunately or unfortunately, Captain Kidd had other sources of supply. Needless to say, every merchant in New York traded illegally with pirates during the war, as there was scarcely any other trade to be had. Kidd, however, knowing most of those villains who frequented the waterfront dives of lower Manhattan, enjoyed a considerable advantage over other merchants when it came to dealing with them. Most merchants chose to wait uptown for the pirates to come to them with their ill-gotten goods, but Captain Kidd dared go down amongst them, trading arms and ammunition and ship's supplies for gold and silver and all manner of loot from every corner of the world. It was in this way that the house on Hanover Square soon came to be the most exotically furnished residence in Manhattan, if not all the Americas.

The parlor floor was covered by the first Turkish rug ever seen in Manhattan, a rug so large it had to be folded under at the sides to fit the room. The dining room was dominated by an oval table large enough for forty dinner guests, flanked by four enormous candlesticks fit for a Spanish cathedral (for which they were probably intended). To complement the table, the Captain added two dozen single-nailed leather chairs, a dozen double-nailed leather chairs, a dozen Turkey-work chairs, one hundred four ounces of silverware and three chafing dishes, which no one in the Colony had ever seen before. He also brought home several Oriental chests of drawers, four feather beds resembling Cleopatra's barge, rolls of silks and satins, and any number of other things whose purpose one could only guess.

Once the house was finally outfitted to Captain Kidd's satisfaction (though Sarah was dubious) the newlyweds hosted a party such as New York had never seen. All the most important people in the Colony were there--the Governor and his Council, the Philipses, the van Cortlandts, the Bayards, the Brooks, the Schuylers and the Livingstons--and dozens less august. Before sitting down to dinner, Mrs. Kidd conducted their guests from room to room, where they stared--whether admiring, mystified or horrified--while she recited the genealogy of each piece from a script prepared by her husband. Lest anyone think such exotica had come to them by other than lawful means, she hastened to explain that the Turkish rug and chairs had come from her husband's castle in Scotland, while the chests of drawers were Oriental copies manufactured by English craftsmen in England. As for the sacred candlesticks: her husband had kindly purchased them from a Baltimore priest so that he might rebuild his church that had burned to the ground; while the Madeira they were drinking had been purchased in Boston, where it had been duly taxed. The women had no difficulty with Mrs. Kidd's explanation (although perhaps with her taste), while the men grinned round their cigars at both. Nonetheless, by the end of the evening the Kidds had established themselves among the smartest hosts in New York, a place where such things were lately of some importance, owing perhaps to the social unrest that was then abroad.

In that regard, it is to be remarked that while the aristocrats rejoiced at having their town back, the Leislerians, much as Sarah had predicted, were coming together in a most ominous way. Livingston and Bayard, and the rest of that bloodthirsty pack, had assured the new Governor that Leisler's execution would put an end to the democratic movement, when instead, the Leislerians had become more fearless and vocal than ever, speaking to crowds on street corners, telling them they were the equal of any man...! They had even managed to somehow get hold of a printing press, and were circulating their own charter of Liberties, espousing the mutinous notion that neither the King nor his minions may govern without the consent of the governed! The aristocrats, however, busily dividing the spoils of victory, trading with pirates and cheating Indians out of their land, had little time to worry about the Leislerians. If they should be mad enough to rise up against the government (i.e. the aristocrats), then the Governor should loose the militia on them, and that would be the end of revolutionaries for once and for all. I knew the aristocrats were correct in this--for even though The Glorious Revolution had succeeded in England, it could never work in America--yet I was keeping my indenture papers close by, just in case the Leislerians should surprise us all. It was said that there were some Whigs in England who openly supported the democratic movement, and a few had even stood up in Parliament to denounce the execution of Leisler. So who could say how far this rebelliousness might go?

Captain Kidd, who worried little about Leislerians, profited handsomely for his part in helping capture their leader, receiving an award of 150 pounds from the Governor's Council. However, his greatest satisfaction would come before the Admiralty Court, where he would exact some remote revenge on Mason and Burgess and the others who had stolen his ship from him. While in New York the pirates had captured a French ship, the Pierre, which Governor Leisler's Admiralty Court had duly condemned, allowing Mason and Burgess to sell it to a Leisler supporter. Captain Kidd, whom I'd come to believe was really a lawyer at heart, petitioned the new Admiralty Court (staffed now by loyal aristocrats all), arguing that because Leisler was never a lawful governor, his Admiralty Court was without authority to condemn the Pierre. The new court readily agreed with Kidd's legal reasoning, the Pierre was reclaimed from its hapless owner and sold to Frederick Philipse for a pittance, who in turn rewarded Kidd quite handsomely for his legal services. The irony of a pirate claiming a ship before a court of law was not lost on the spectators.

One way or another, virtually all the wealthy Leislerians in the colony were plucked like chickens following Leisler's execution. Leisler and his Council forfeited their estates, while most of his wealthy friends were stripped naked by claims lodged against them by those aristocrats who imagined themselves damaged by the Governor. Nicholas Bayard, furious over his gaoling, filed the largest claim, for 5,551 pounds; while Bartholemeu LeRoux filed the smallest, 12 pounds for five Barrels of Porke taken from him by the 'Undermentioned Partyes'. I was not able to determine the amount of Robert Livingston's claim, but I did hear Governor Sloughter complain that, "It was too much by far, even for such a rogue as Livingston!"

Although Governor Sloughter had no great liking for Mr. Livingston, he was not averse to doing business with him, I discovered on the night of the Kidd dinner party, so long as there be sufficient profit in it for himself. As usual, the Governor became quite drunk at dinner and was the last to leave the table. Except for Mr. Livingston, who had earlier sent his wife home alone, then remained behind to wait like a cat for the time to pounce. I was quietly clearing away the china, while Mr. Livingston was pouring another brandy for the Governor, when I heard Livingston propose himself for the position of military Commissary.

"'at's an officer's role, not a merchant's," Sloughter dismissed.

"But supposin' the merchant could do it more efficiently...?" Livingston continued.

The Governor was amused by this novel suggestion. "If I was t' put you in charge of victuallin' the troops, methinks the poor soldiers' stomachs would soon be empty, and yer own pockets full o' gold."

"Aye, 'n yer's as well," Livingston replied, topping off the glass.

"Eh--how's 'at?" Sloughter asked.

It was then, as I passed in and out of the room, that the plan was hatched. Mr. Livingston would feed and supply the troops, then present a somewhat inflated bill to Sloughter, which he should then pass on to the King with his recommendation for payment. As there were already thousands of men under arms and more coming each day--what with the dangers posed by the French and the Indians and now the Leislerians--the profits from such a scheme would be enormous.

"'n what's my cut t' be?" the Governor asked.

"Ten per cent."

"Ten--! Fer the risk I'd be takin' I'd not settle for less'n half."

Mr. Livingston joined his hands as if in prayer and replied, "Jesus Christ might feed the multitude with but a few loaves 'n fishes, but I, sir, am just a mortal merchant. I cannot go higher'n fifteen percent without arousin' the suspicion o' the King or the mutiny o' the troops, either o' them bein' fatal to our enterprise."

So in the end they settled for twenty per cent.

After having been denied a garment to cover my nakedness, and then sold into slavery by Mr. Livingston—and now witnessing this devil's agreement to starve those brave soldiers who kept him and his vast estates and his fur trade safe from Indians and Frenchmen--I was sure that I had at last witnessed the fullest and most villainous avariciousness of the man. But as I was yet to learn, the well of corruption had scarcely been tapped.

While the war with France was something of an inconvenience to the merchants of New York, there was not an Englishman among them who didn't support the British cause, so long as it didn't interrupt the thriving pirate trade. And with the Navy busy as it was with the French, there was little chance of that. In fact, it lately seemed there were more black flags flying in New York Harbor than Union Jacks, and more murder and mayhem each night on the docks than off Beachy Head. There were those who complained that New York had grown more hospitable to buccaneers than Port Royale, but they were mostly Leislerians, and hence paid little heed by the Governor and his Council. So when the Governor's Customs Collector, a patriotic Englishman named Chidley Brooke, insisted that duty be paid even on illegal pirate's booty, most merchants grumblingly complied when caught (not very often), writing if off as their patriotic contribution to the war effort. Robert Livingston, however, who felt that war--as well as any other government activity--should either be prosecuted on a profitable basis or else abandoned, stubbornly maintained that a tax on stolen goods was *prima facie* illegal. Captain Kidd, who was very admiring of the legal reasoning, had to admit there was some justification for Livingston's opinion, while Governor Sloughter, practical to the bone, summarily dismissed it.

"Whether the source o' the wealth be legal or illegal don't mean a fookin' thing, the King's still entitled t' 'is pound o' flesh," he proclaimed while seated in Captain Kidd's favorite chair, cup of rum in hand.

"'n is 'e entitled to a pound o' the victuallin' fee ye gets from me?" Livingston argued.

"What fee? I've yet t' see a farthin' from that fookin' scheme," the Governor complained.

"Ye would if ye'd get the King t' pay my bill," Livingston grumbled.

The agreement they had struck, with the greatest of expectations just a short while before, had lately become a sore point between the two men--with Sloughter because he'd been paid nothing after approving the greatly inflated bill, and with Livingston because he hadn't been promptly reimbursed the great amount he'd expended. With each ship that arrived from London--and they were few and far between owing to the French blockade--Mr. Livingston could be found waiting on the dock, hoping desperately that the King had at last sent his money. Instead of money, however, the ships lately carried inquiries from the Whig government regarding the execution of Jacob Leisler, which only caused the Governor to drink even more than usual.

"The Gov'ner don't tell the King," Slaughter replied sullenly.

"This is costin' me all I got--if I don't have my money soon I'm facin' ruin!" Livingston cried out suddenly.

"I warned ye yer bill was too high t' pass muster," the old soldier, who would not tolerate panic in the ranks, growled angrily. "By now the Auditor-General's prob'l urgin' the King t' hang ye' fer the pilferin' poltroon y'are."

"Ye'd best pray he i'nt," Livingston muttered.

Seeing the suddenly fierce visage this comment caused the Governor, I now understood why Leisler had so quickly surrendered the fort to him. In a soft voice that pierced the air like a bayonet, Slaughter replied, "Ye wouldn't be threat'nin' me now, would ye, Robert?"

Mr. Livingston went white with fear, and was barely able to stammer assurances that he had meant no such thing, and if he had to dance at the end of the rope for his fraud, he would do so without a partner.

Mr. Livingston's fear did not last long, however, as Governor Slaughter died unexpectedly and mysteriously just a few weeks later, after locking himself in the fort with a barrel of rum. It was said that the Governor deliberately drank himself to death after learning that he was to return to England to answer questions concerning Leisler's execution. However, I believed this to be just wishful thinking by those Leislerians who'd been importuning the whigs to open an inquiry. If Slaughter were being summoned home, it was, from my singularly privileged point of view, more likely to answer questions regarding Livingston's Commisary bill.

There were also those who claimed Slaughter had been poisoned, and even though suspicion centered on no one and everyone, no less than six physicians were called to examine the body. No evidence of poison was found, but enough alcohol was found in the corpse to conclude that death was caused by delirium tremens. Whether 'twas accidental or intended, only God can know, but I for one would like to believe that Henry Sloughter, a brave and honorable man in most other respects, died of grief over his part in the execution of Jacob Leisler.

Captain Kidd was greatly saddened by the unexpected death of the man who, more than any other, was responsible for his enormous success in the New World. However, no one was sadder than Robert Livingston, who stood to lose a fortune without Governor Sloughter there to press his bloated victualling claims with the King. When Livingston made the mistake of going to Major Ingoldsby, who was Governor pro tempore until the new governor should arrive from London, Ingoldsby took one look at the bills and knew them to be grosssly inflated.

"'e not only refused t' intercede for me, 'e called me a reprehensible thief!" I overheard Livingston complain to kidd. "'n now I've gone and stuck me foot in it, I'm much afraid 'e'll go and blacken me name wi' the new gov'nor!"

Mr. Livingston was surely right about that. When the new Governor, Benjamin Fletcher, finally arrived the following summer, welcomed by the aristocrats with a grand parade up Broad Way, he took a quick dislike to his Victualler and his 'snivellin' pleas t' be paid *yer outrageous accounts!* And when Captain Kidd unwisely agreed to go to the Governor on Livingston's behalf, Fletcher assumed that Kidd must be a blackguard, too, and treated him coolly from that time forward.

At first the aristocrats feared London had sent them an honest man, but they needn't have worried. For Ben Fletcher, a fat florid man who delighted in jaunting about town with his wife and daughters, gowned in the latest European finery, in a handsome six-horse carriage he had brought with him from England, proved to be as rapacious and worthless a governor as ever New York should suffer. Taking a leaf from men like Livingston, who had stolen thousands of acres from the Indians, Fletcher went them one better, taking the land of American settlers in lawful possession of their homes and farms, by the fraudulent use of his office, then awarding the properties to his friends in exchange for bribes. In a very short while, Governor Fletcher and his aristocratic friends grew enormously wealthy, while hundreds of less fortunate men and women became tenant farmers on their own land. Robert Livingston, his victualling bills still unpaid, watching from the wings while Fletcher and his old friends divided up the Colony without him, was a depressed man. And desperate.

When Mr. Livingston purchased Captain Kidd's waterfront lot on Dock Street, I assumed he'd decided to get in on the feverish land speculation then going on in Manhattan, owing largely to the Governor's confiscatory schemes. But Livingston, never a man to settle for a fair profit when an unconscionable one was to be had, had far more ambitious and dangerous plans than that. Instead of building a warehouse or other commercial building on the property, and then selling it, as others were doing to great advantage, he built a dock. He was, he grandly claimed, going to send out a ship to trade with England, and damn the French blockade! It was an insane idea, everyone agreed, when he could trade most profitably with pirates and risk neither his ship nor its cargo. But Mr. Livingston would not be dissuaded and so, on a fine fall day with a stiff breeze blowing out of the southwest, his ship, the Orange, under Captain Cornelius Jacobs, set out across the Atlantic, her hold stuffed with American goods. And it was the last anyone would see of either of them, the merchants at the coffee houses predicted.

However, late one night, scarcely a month later, customs inspector Chidley Brooke was greatly surprised to find the Orange back at her dock. Going aboard despite Mr. Livingston's objections, the inspector was even more surprised to find the Orange loaded not with English goods--but French goods! He then arrested Mr. Livingston for trading with the enemy in a time of war, an act of treason punishable by death!

When word of Livingston's arrest got round, everyone agreed that this time his greed had carried him too far. Trading with pirates and dodging the customs collector did no great harm, but trading with Frenchmen who would put the pope on the throne of England, was a crime against God and country for which no penalty was too severe. About the only English patriot who remained stubbornly silent on the matter was Captain Kidd, owing to his official responsibility and lofty title--Foreman of the Grand Jury. When at last he could speak--following the discharge of his duty--Sarah and I waited anxiously to hear if Robert Livingston was to be executed.

"I'm much afraid the customs inspector's presentation t' the grand jury was rather lackin' in the finer points o' law," he began. "But fortunately my own legal reasonin' was clear as Coke hisself, with all the Latin words tumblin' out o' me mouth like the mother tongue itself, and in the end I'm satisfied that justice carried the day," he declared, while prowling about the parlor, celebratory cup in hand.

"Then is he to hang?" Sarah asked anxiously.

"That's not for the grand jury to decide. My duty's t' decide if the man should be tried for treason," Kidd explained.

"And what did you decide, dear?"

"First we had t' 'ear all the evidence," the Foreman responded.

And so did we. The captain wouldn't reveal his decision until all the factors had been laid before us so that we might better savor the drama and suspense of the proceedings, even going so far as to recite every last piece of cargo carried by the Orange when she set out, as well as each bit of French goods found on her when she returned.

"William, please, would you come to the point?" Sarah pleaded.

"My dear, these are the very points upon which the decision rests," Kidd informed her. "Cap'n Jacobs says he was bound fer England, till he sailed into a storm and was driven south to Hispaniola."

"Hispaniola!" I cried. "That's in the West Indies."

"It was a severe storm," Kidd pointed out.

"Then why was his ship not damaged?" I asked.

"The question's moot. Cap'n Jacobs then went on t' claim that while waitin' out the storm in Hispaniola, a group of heavily armed Frenchmen boarded his ship and forced 'im t' trade with 'em, against 'is will. They took all his goods 'n give 'im some goods in exchange that he claimed was worth hardly a fourth o' what they took."

"I don't understand why they'd give him anything," I put in. "Why didn't they just take his goods?"

"They was businessmen, not pirates," Kidd answered. "But not very good ones, it turned out. 'cuz when the customs inspector tallied up the value 'o' the French goods what Cap'n Jacobs brought back, they turned out t' be worth a thousand pounds more'n what 'e started out with!" the Captain roared.

"So," I said, when the laughter all round had died down, "Mr. Livingston is to be tried for treason."

"No, I set 'im free," Kidd replied.

"Set him free--!"

"Why?" Sarah exclaimed.

"Insufficient evidence," the judge replied.

Chapter 8

Boys Night Out

January 12, 1694

My Dear Father,

I'm happy to say that your letter of November made it through the french blockade and I hope this one too is so fated. I do hope you are not too inconvenienced by this seemingly interminable war.

I was sorry to hear that you were ailing and I hope that you are by now improved. It pains me that I cannot be there to help you when I am needed, but owing to my indenture and the war, it is still not possible to return home. Be assured that I shall, just as soon as it is possible.

I am well. I continue in the home of Captain Kidd, tutoring his daughters and helping as well in other ways, much to the satisfaction of everyone, I hope. However, affairs in the Colony are getting no better, I'm afraid. The new Governor has given the place over to pirates, there is no law, it is unsafe to walk the streets, and yet the rich grow richer and the poor are without hope.

Please do not be offended when I say, Father, this place
is little like your books.

I hope to be home soon, and I am, sir,

Your Respectful and Loving Son,
Christopher Rousby

How it pained me to write still another dishonest letter to my poor
father who, knowing nothing of Sarah's powerful hold on me, believed I
would return to him if I but could. I knew I should go, that there could
be no future for me with Sarah while her husband lived, but I was more
than content to live only in the present. How we awaited those times
when Captain Kidd was absent from the house, when Sarah would
rush to me, pink-faced and breathless with a new game. Although
we still managed to stop short of fornication, our games had become
so diabolical I was beginning to worry that true fornication, when it
happened, would prove disappointing.

The Captain's absences grew longer and more frequent after the
first couple of years of marriage, which was said to be usual, but I
couldn't understand it. Three or four nights a week he would dress
in his old privateer's garb and slip out of the house, supposedly to do
business, only to return home much later, sometimes quite drunk. I
was entirely pleased by the arrangement, but Sarah, who required the
devotion of both of us, was deeply hurt by her husband's mysterious,
nocturnal forays. So much so that I reluctantly agreed to speak to
the Captain on her behalf. At sea I might've been flogged mercilessly
for such impertinence, while even ashore it was sufficiently risky that
only a lovesick fool would take it on. I was pleasantly surprised and
greatly relieved, however, by the Captain's calm reaction to my awkward
concern for his wife.

"So ye want t' know what I'm about, do ye?" he asked, looking up
at me from his place behind the desk.

"It's not for me, sir--it's only that Mrs. Kidd..." I started to explain
when he cut me off.

"Very well, ye'll come wi' me tonight 'n see fer yerself," he said.

"Aye, sir."

And that's how I happened to find myself on the docks that night with a broadsword, which Captain Kidd had required I wear, hanging uncomfortably at my side. The Captain carried his old cutlass and, with his white knee breeches and blue coat trimmed with pearl buttons and gold lace, looked as much the swashbuckler as any pirate we passed on our descent to the hellish depths of the New York waterfront. We passed the stocks and the bloody whipping posts and the slave pens packed with naked souls; we passed women with infants and children begging for coins or selling themselves to poxed pirates for little more, and drugged madmen who'd slit your throat for no profit at all; we passed roving press gangs, pimps, bullyboys, cudgellers, cutpurses, cannibals and every manner of rascally yeaforsooth knave known to the devil. I'd been told Madagascar was the vilest pirate haven in the world, but I couldn't imagine anything worse than this New York. There was no cutthroat alive unwelcome in this port, providing he could pay Governor Fletcher something more than the bounty on his head. And once here there was no need to fear the sheriff, who'd long before locked himself in the fort after being publicly humiliated by Captain Tew, a notorious brigand who'd nearly brought the East India Company to bankruptcy before being chased to America by the British Navy. Tew was so bloodthirsty that not even New Hampshire would have him. Yet Fletcher, royally rewarded with East India Booty, entertained him regularly in his home!

When the Captain announced that we'd arrived finally at our destination, I was relieved. Until I saw it was the Buckmaster Tavern, the most notorious bucket of blood on the waterfront.

"This is where you pass your evenings?" I asked, halting at the door like a mule.

"Tis a place that favors masters," he said, pulling me by the arm.

If Kidd thought I'd be put at ease by the quality of the company, he was mistaken, as the only captain I could think of as I stepped inside was Thomas Tew, whom I hoped was at home with the Governor this evening. But if he was, there were still more than enough unsavory villains to take his place, drinking, wenching, shouting, laughing and singing, but ready to turn ugly in just the flick of a knife. The place was so filled with smoke and stuffed with sweating sailors and their half-naked whores painted up like figureheads, that we could scarcely find a place to stand. Seeing us, the barman hailed Captain Kidd familiarly and made room for us at a place half way down the bar, where we were engulfed by privateers (I would never call them pirate) just off their ship, judging by the mood and the look of them. The Captain ordered rum for both of us, but the privateers wouldn't let him pay. They pushed all manner of specie at the barman, a profession that more valued money-changing skills than those of publican. Indeed, it was not unusual in such places for a drunken sailor to pay for an ale with a piece of Araby gold worth a whole brewery, or a night of debauchery with a precious stone sufficient to hire a harem--or else it might just fall into the sawdust and be lost forever. This was New York in 1694.

"D' ye miss it?" Captain Kidd asked me, as he surveyed the celebrants from our place at the bar.

I was amazed at such a question. That a man like the Captain, who lived in a castle with a beautiful queen and two lovely princesses, could still be attracted by such as this, made me suddenly aware of the terrible hold buccaneering takes on some men. But certainly not me.

"I should sooner go to gaol," I replied, little knowing I would live to do both.

"Yar, the likes o' these gives privateerin' a bad name," he said, turning back to the bar.

Then, as if the point hadn't been already made, a fight broke out in the middle of the room, not between pirates but between two whores vying for the same customer. The larger woman, who from the look of her was no stranger to this method of settling business disputes, quickly bloodied the nose of the smaller woman and pummeled her to the floor--which should have been the end of it. However, the mob hadn't yet seen enough, so they threw water on the dazed woman and pulled her to her feet, so that her opponent might have at her some more.

Which was when I leaped thoughtlessly from the bar and plunged through the bloodthirsty rabble to put an end to these ugly proceedings. The smaller woman, her blouse torn away, stood dead on her feet, fists pawing feebly, while the blood coursed down between her breasts like a mountain stream between a high gorge. I stepped between the two women and pushed the larger one away--when her place was immediately taken by a group of angry cutthroats who promised to have my blood in lieu of the entertainment I'd deprived them. Cutlasses flashed in the lamplight, while tables and benches were knocked to the floor in the rush to get out of sword's length, as I pulled my broadsword from its sheath and prepared to die. My attacker's first sword-swipe struck a rafter and I lunged low, striking flesh and bone and setting off a startled cry. I was winning! But the remaining two were not given pause by my skill. They flanked out left and right and stalked me hungrily, while I feinted, first one way then the other, never disturbing their salacious smiles.

Until quite suddenly those smiles disappeared and I saw Captain Kidd standing beside me, his heavy cutlass whistling through the air like a snapped halliard. Pleased with the result, I made my own broadsword whistle an accompanying tune, which sent my would-be assassins stumbling and scrambling away while their fallen comrade crawled bleatingly after them. Although terrified but a moment before, I was suddenly exalted as I turned to my comrade in arms with a triumphant smile--and was dealt a stunning blow to the side of the head.

"After all I've taught ye, 'ave ye no more sense than t' risk yer life for a thruppence chippie?" he shouted at me where I lay in the sawdust.

"Sorry, sir..." I stammered, climbing woozily to my feet as, a moment later, I heard my name spoken nasally.

"Chridopher--id id you?"

I blinked and stared hard through the smoky haze at the half-naked, thruppence whore I'd just saved, and though her image quivered like rings on a pond from a thrown pebble, and though the face was worn by hard use (especially the nose), it was unmistakably that same young woman who had first introduced me to the considerable pleasures of love.

"Rebecca!" I cried. "What are you doing here?"

"Idn't id obvious? I'm a thruppence chippie," she replied, spewing blood in Captain Kidd's direction.

"Somebody get 'er a towel," the captain ordered, standing back to inspect his white breeches. "'ow d' ye come t' know a slut like 'er?" he demanded.

Although until a few years ago the Captain knew only sluts 'like 'er', it seemed he'd learned the prudery of the burgher soon enough. "It is owing to Rebecca Hay that you found me adrift in the Atlantic," I informed him.

"'ow's 'at?" he asked, looking appraisingly at Rebecca.

"Shall I tell him?" I asked her.

"You mide as well," she said, head back, finger under her nose.

So I retrieved Rebecca's torn blouse and the three of us sat at a nearby table (vacancies were suddenly easy to come by for the Captain and me) while I related the tale of my flight from a false paternity charge.

"'Tis true, the baby warn't 'is?" Kidd asked Rebecca, passing her the wet towel the barman had brought to our table.

"Possibly not," she admitted, wiping the blood from her face and chest while still holding her head back to slow the bleeding. "Bud you were wrong aboud d law, Christopher. After I god your ledder I wen do d magistrate and swore out an affidavit naming Percy Duns'on de fadder of my child, bud he pud me in jail."

"For what--how could he do such thing?" I exclaimed.

"Id wad easy enough, after de lies Percy's fadder told. He told de magistrate I came round and told him I wouldn' be cleaning hid house anymore cuz I wad geddin' married and going do America. Den he claimed he gave me two gold pieces for a wedding gift and wished me well."

"The varlet...!"

"Yer sayin' the man perjured hisself?" Kidd asked.

"I'm sayin' he fookin' lied!" she exclaimed, spraying blood in the air. "I told the magistrate he wad lying, but Percy claimed he wad in de house at de time and witnessed de whole thing."

"'e accepted the testimony o' the accused...?" Kidd interrupted.

"Not only that, Percy claimed he saw me give de money to Christopher, which proved you were de fadder and nod him."

"Percy was nowhere near the square!" I protested.

"Wait a minute!" Kidd interrupted. "Did she give ye two pieces o' gold?"

"Just one," I corrected. "Which I used to pay my passage to America."

"And your runnin' off like dat didn' help my case any, I can tell you!"

"Should I have stayed and fathered another man's child!"

"Hold up, both o' ye!" Kidd ordered. "A minute ago ye said Mr. Dunston give ye no gold, now yer admittin' 'e did."

"No--I said he gave me no wedding gift," she corrected. "The gold pieces were a bribe to get me to drop my claim against Percy."

"And name me in his place," I grumbled.

"Whad's a poor girl to do?" she shrugged. "I knew id had to be one or the other of you, so I chose the rich one first."

"And failing that, you settled for me."

"Aye, and when you fled, taking my gold piece and leaving me with nothing but bad legal advice, I went back to Percy. Resulting in my getting three years in the workhouse for trying to extort money from a gentleman. So you're not entirely without blame in this affair yourself, Christopher Rousby!"

"Let that be a lesson, free legal advice is worth what ye pay fer it," Captain Kidd said.

"Is there really a chance the baby might be mine?" I asked.

"Id's possible--"

"What happened to it?"

"They took him from me and pud him in the charity house."

"Your father wouldn't take him--?"

"My father died from the shame of it."

"I'm sorry," I said.

"Ye should be."

"A boy you say…"

"Was…"

"Was…?"

"He died in the fire at the charity house."

"My God…."

"They never told me. On the day I got out of the workhouse I went to get him, but there was nothing left but charred wood and ashes. I just sat there for a couple of days--until it sank in--then I went home. Only it was no home for me anymore, with Father dead and the house gone, and the women spitting on me and calling me whore. So I drifted up to Bristol where I signed on to a ship sailing for America."

"How the hell'd ye manage that?" Kidd asked.

"I cut my hair and dressed like a boy. It was a slave ship, they weren't too particular."

"I reckon you warn't neither," Kidd grunted.

She shrugged. "I thought no worse could come to me than already had. But just when things are blackest, they can get blacker still."

"What happened?" I asked.

She removed the towel from her face and poked testingly at her nose. Getting only a trickle, she tossed the towel aside and pulled her blouse closed. "I managed to keep up the deception for most of the voyage. Until some old pederast got a hand in my breeches while I was sleeping, and finding naught where something ought, he let out a cry and all hands came running. First they stripped me naked and tied me to a spar and dunked me til I thought I'd died and gone to heaven, when in truth I was still in hell--where the captain of the ship ordered the slaves to tar me from head to foot."

"No--!" I gasped.

"And that's the way I landed in New York, blacker and nakeder than any slave aboard the Pierre."

"The Pierre!" Captain Kidd exclaimed, for she was the very ship he'd claimed from the Admiralty Court for Frederick Philipse a few years ago. "Who's 'er master?"

"Captain Burgess."

We were both stunned at hearing this familiar name. "Not Samuel Burgess--?" Kidd asked carefully, hopefully.

"That would be his Christian name, though he has no right to one," she replied. "Do you know him?"

"Aye, I know 'im," Kidd nodded. "'e's the man who's responsible fer all o' us bein' 'ere. 'e stole my ship."

"Then you have as good a reason as mine to prosecute the man," Rebecca said, clutching my hand.

"Once, but no more," Kidd said, shaking his head, "T' be sure, there was the time I would've flayed 'im alive n' fed 'im 'is own flesh, but no more. Cuz by bringin' me t' New York that thievin' devil did more fer me than ever God did." Suddenly he lifted a glass in the air and shouted, "To Sam Burgess!"

"'o's lookin' fer 'im?" came a shout from the bar.

I twisted round to see a salt in a gold-trimmed coat, hung from the shoulder by a scarlet sash, standing next to the bar. It was apparent from his outlandish dress that he fancied himself a swashbuckler, but it was only when he lifted his broad, three-cornered hat that I realized he was the same swashbuckler who had chased me o'er the walls of Charleston and into the canoe of Chindomacuba.

"Burgess--!" I gasped, but Captain Kidd had already seen him.

I watched as he pushed across the room with a pleased grin on his weathered face, expecting to find an old friend toasting his health, then saw that grin change to a ghastly grimace of unholy terror when he recognized his well-wisher. Kidd's chair crashed to the floor as he leaped to his feet, cutlass once again in hand as, an instant later Burgess's cutlass, too, flashed in the yellow glow of the oil lamps hanging from the rafters, and once more the crowd scrambled out of the center of the room. When I unsheathed my sword and tried to take up a position beside my comrade in arms, Kidd pushed me aside like a clumsy puppy as he moved in a wary circle, probing the space between himself and Burgess, as if seeking an opening in an invisible wall.

"Tis a mystery t' me how ye come t' be 'ere at the very moment I was drinkin' t' yer 'ealth, Sam. But twould be a tragedy if I was t' hafta follow so soon with yer eulogy," Kidd said, making circles with his sword.

"Or me yers," Burgess replied.

"So what d'ye say we put up our swords?"

"So's ye c'n run me through the moment I do?"

"What's past is past, Sam. Ye know I'm not one t' keep a grudge."

"Hah! Ye chased me from Nevis t' New York without ever gettin' over yer grudge, so why should ye now?"

"Cuz as I was just tellin' the lass, it's t' Sam Burgess I owe me fortune."

"Took a prize, did ye?"

"I took New York," Kidd answered.

"How's 'at...?"

"I'm a propertied gentleman now, Sam, with friends in high places."

"Then why're ye tricked up like a flamin' freebooter?"

"I'm here t' see old friends and trade with 'em. I got a warehouse uptown stocked with more goods 'n you n' me ever saw in all our days in the Indies, Sam. That ship yer sailin', the Pierre--I claimed 'er fer yer employer, Fred Philipse."

"How the hell'd ye...! Ye know Mr. Philipse...?"

"Very well, 'e's one o' me closest friends. Now will ye put up yer sword and 'ave a drink with me, Sam?"

Burgess considered for a moment and replied, "You first."

"Both together."

Precise as a military guard, they sheathed their swords, then shook hands warily as the twice deprived customers grumbled disgustedly. I righted a table and four chairs while Burgess called for a bottle of rum and we all sat, Rebecca close by my side. I could feel her body trembling against mine as she stared across the table at the man who had tormented her so cruelly and now failed to recognize her. He did recognize me, however.

"The boy's growed," he remarked.

"It's been more'n five years," Kidd informed him.

"'as it now...? And the years 've been good t' ye, ye say...?"

"Very good," Kidd said, knocking on the table.

"Ye must tell me all about it."

"And you me," Kidd said.

So Rebecca and I listened as the two men drank and heaped lies on the table higher than a skysail. I was equipped to tell when Captain Kidd veered from a true course--he listed heavily on the side of respectability--but I had no way of knowing what of Burgess's tale was fact and what was fancy. Rebecca and I both noted, however, that he left the tarring and slaving chapter out of his story. Nonetheless, he certainly looked the prosperous privateer, with rings on every finger and both ears, and a gold necklace and silver bracelets, all of them taken from one or another ship of the English East India Company.

"I tell ye, Bill, with the Royal Naivy off fightin' the Frenchies, the Indian Ocean's the sweetest plunderin' ye ever did see, like shootin' ducks in a tub. We'd be waitin' at the strait o' Babs-al Mandab when they come down out o' the Red Sea--"

"Aye, a good place t' surprise 'em," Kidd commented knowingly.

"Hell, we had no need t' surprise 'em!" Burgess scoffed. "Or even fight! All we 'ad t' do was raise the black flag n' they gladly give it up. Then it was back t' Madygascar fer a bit 'o pleasurin'."

"Madygascar, there's a place," Kidd reminisced.

"Privateer's paradise," Burgess confirmed.

"What sort o' booty?"

"Whatever kind ye want! They print it on the mainsail: gold, silk, jewels--! Take yer pick!"

"So if it's all that easy, why ain't ye there now?" Kidd questioned.

"Cuz I choose t' be here. Any reason I shouldn't?" he asked, ready again to fight.

"None atall," Kidd smiled.

"Jus' so..." he nodded, satisfied for the moment. "I heerd Gov'ner Fletcher was friendly t' the Brethren if ye 'ad the price, so I decided t' make a 'onest man o' meself while I 'ad the chance. It cost me my ship n' eighteen hundred pounds, but I got me pardon papers right 'ere," he said, patting his breast pocket, "n' I c'n go anywheres in the world without no fear o' the British Naivy."

"Workin' for Fred Philipse..." Kidd added, his disapproval unhidden.

"Aye, workin' fer Mr. Philipse, the shrewdest trader in New York."

"Yer lookin' at the shrewdest trader in New York right 'ere," Kidd said.

"Is 'at so?" Burgess asked, an amused grin spreading over his weather-beaten face.

"'at's so."

"Ye says ye come down here to trade direct wi' the Brethren 'n cut off the uptown merchants...?"

"'at's right."

"Well Mr. Philipse goes ye one better. 'e sends me out t' trade direct wi' pirates in Madygascar."

"Madygascar...!" Kidd laughed. "What kind o' fool'd go all that way when 'e's free t' trade with pirates right here in New York?"

"A monoply fool, 'at's who. In New York Mr. Philipse's got t' compete wi' every merchant in town; but in Madygascar, don't ye know, I'm the only ship in port. Ye get me point, Cap'n?" he asked.

Captain Kidd got the point all right, as shown by his flushed face. It was a plan so obvious any fool could have thought of it, but so far only Mr. Philipse had, which clearly made him the shrewdest trader in New York. At least for a while. For owing to his Captain's loose tongue, word of the Red Sea Trade would quickly spread, and soon nearly all the merchants of New York would be sending ships to Madagascar to trade guns, powder, naval stores and rum, for gold, silks and jewels. But this future development could afford Kidd no satisfaction that night. He was furious.

"And do ye also do a bit o' slavin' on the return voyage?" he asked.

"Sam Burgess ain't no slaver, n' jus' show me the man who says I am!" he demanded, striking the table with a clenched fist.

"'ow's about a woman?" Kidd responded.

"A woman...?"

"Remember me...?" Rebecca said, pulling her hair back to refresh his memory.

"You!" he exclaimed, remembering perfectly. "All right, so I conveyed a ship o' slaves on one occasion--it's completely legal."

"But half drownin' and tarrin' a woman ain't."

"It was the men, it warn't me! She was passin' herself fer a boy!" Burgess exclaimed, hand inching for his sword.

"Hands on the table!" Captain Kidd ordered, halting Burgess's hand.

It was only then that I saw the bare point of Captain Kidd's cutlass--which he'd somehow managed to remove from its sheath without anyone seeing--peeking out from under the table, pressing up against Burgess's ballocks.

"One move n' it's ye'll be changin' yer sex--which fer you ain't that big a leap anyway. I always knew ye t' be a lyin' thievin' pederast, but I never thought ye'd sink t' slavin' n' tarrin' a woman fer sport, ye putrid vermin."

"Twasn't me, twas the men! A woman's bad luck on a ship, you know that! I couldn't control 'em, Will'am, I swear!"

"Liar!" Rebecca cried. "He was the one who ordered it!"

"I 'ad no choice! Oww!"

"Don't move!"

"I ain't!"

"What would ye 'ave me do with 'im?" the Captain asked Rebecca.

"Cut his cullions off," she replied.

"No!"

"Shut yer gob! Christopher, take 'is cutlass."

"Yes, sir." I jumped up and snatched the sword from its sheath while the crowd stirred at the renewed prospect of blood.

"'is 'e goin' t' cut 'is cullions off?" one of the whores asked me.

"I'm afraid so," I answered.

"My God…!" her client gasped, clutching his own cullions.

"Will'am, please--I'll make it up t' the girl!"

"'at ye will, Sam, 'at ye will. Stand up and drop yer britches."

"What…!"

"Ye heerd me, get 'em off!" Kidd ordered, jabbing hard.

"Oww!" Burgess cried, scrambling to his feet.

"'e's goin' t' do it,' the whore said, as Captain Kidd stood.

"Oh my God…" her client groaned.

"Will'am, I beg ye, don't do this!" Burgess pleaded.

"Would ye rather I cut yer 'eart out?"

"I'm sorry we took yer ship, I'll give ye me own!"

"Ye got no ship, ye're Fredrick Philipse's hired slaver. Now drop 'em, Goddamnit!" he shouted, slapping the flat of his blade across the table with a frightening noise that caused Sam to flinch and begin to tremble.

"No, no--please, please..." he begged, as tears began to roll down his cheeks.

"Rebecca, would ye do the honors?" Kidd motioned impatiently.

"Gladly," said Rebecca, leaping to the task. She quickly undid Sam's belt and pulled his breeches down to his ankles while the whores hooted and whistled. "Would you look at that little bird hidin' in the bush! He looks scared half to death, he does!" she exclaimed, setting off a chorus of raucous laughter from the whores who were pressing about to see their first castration.

"'Tis no wonder 'e prefers little boys," Kidd remarked as he motioned the crowd back with his cutlass. "Now 'old that needle aside and put yer ballocks up on the table."

"Please, Will'am, don't do it..." Burgess sobbed.

"Now!" he ordered, smacking the table again. "Unless ye'd 'ave me do away with the whole kit--which I might just as well do, as one ain't much good without the other."

"No!" Sam cried, grabbing the wee thing.

"Christopher, 'elp 'im," Kidd ordered. Seeing my reluctance, he added, "Lest ye ain't got the stomach fer it, I'd advise ye t' think o' the mess I'd surely make o' the surgery without yer assistance."

So I pulled Sam's arms behind his back and pushed him up to the table while Rebecca placed his ballocks on the corner of the table.

"Release one hand," Kidd ordered me.

"In God's name..." Burgess wept.

"Grab it er lose it," Kidd said, raising the sword over his head.

"Wait!" Sam said, grabbing the poor wee thing and pulling it up out of harm's way.

"Ye ready now?" Kidd asked.

"Ready," Rebecca answered.

"Ye'd best hold it in tight, Sam, as me sword arm's a bit rusty," Kidd advised, as he practiced his stroke. "n' you, Christopher, ye'd best get yer feet back a ways as 'e's bound t' shit hisself when I chop 'im. On the count o' three then. Rebecca, ye c'n do the 'onor."

Sam was now weeping and praying at the same time, which came out in the strangest sounding liturgy ever heard, while all around me the whores stared glittery-eyed, while the men stared open-mouthed and clutched their own ballocks most tightly.

"One!" Rebecca called, and Captain Kidd placed the cutting edge of his cutlass on the table beside Sam's shriveled sack.

"Could've used with a bit o' sharpenin' " he observed.

"Two!" she called, and the Captain raised the blade as high as the rafter.

"Three!"

At this Sam collapsed in my grip and fell across the table under the falling blade, as at the same time I heard a wet squish followed by a most putrescent odor, then a resounding whap of steel on wood, followed by a collective cry from the bloodthirsty rabble, as the victim slid unconscious from the table into his own feculent pool. But there was no blood, as the cutlass had landed broadside on the table some distance from Sam's ballocks. As was obviously the Captain's intention from the beginning, as his sword arm wasn't that rusty. When he replaced his dry cutlass in its sheath, there arose an almost palpable sense of relief from every man in the place, while the women began to grumble, and Rebecca was loudly dissatisfied.

"Give it to me, I'll do it!" she cried, going for the Captain's sword.

"Let 'im be," Kidd ordered, catching her wrist. "When Sam comes to, 'e'll find 'e's lost more'n 'is ballocks." Then he dug into his pocket and came out with a pair of gold coins which he placed in her captive hand. "These'll pay Christopher's debt. 'n ye'll find they're worth a lot more'n Sam Burgess's balls," he added.

"Thank you--thank you, sir," she stammered, staring at the two shiny gold pieces.

Then Captain Kidd threw an arm over my shoulder and led me out of the notorious Buckmaster's Tavern and home. I'd not seen him enjoy himself so much in a very long time.

Chapter 9

London

I stood on the dock in the rain like the family dog while Captain Kidd bade farewell to his wife and daughters. Then, as he bent over to wrap an arm around each little girl, Sarah walked across the dock to me. When she looked up at me and I saw the tears mixed with rain running down her cheeks, my own eyes immediately welled up and we stood very still in the rain for some time, neither of us able to speak. When Captain Kidd called to me to board the ship, she kissed me quickly on the cheek and whispered, "Thank you." Then she turned and hurried back to the children, as I followed her husband up the gangplank and onto the Antigua.

"Prepare t' cast off!" Captain Kidd called, as I went aft to my place in the stern.

Then the lines were cast off and the sails unfurled and sheeted home, and we were running with the tide to the sea that would carry us back to England. The last I saw of Sarah, she was standing on the end of the dock in the rain like a beacon, whether for her husband or me or both of us, I didn't know. I could only remember her words: "Hard as it is to ask you to go, twould be harder still for me if you were to stay."

Why, I asked myself as I stood on the deck in the pelting rain, had I been so eager to do the honorable thing? The thought that I could now be at home with Sarah, sitting before a warm fire while Captain

Kidd ran this damned fool's mission by himself, filled me with such despairing regret that I wanted to leap over the rail and into the sea. For I might just as well die in American waters as French, as our chances of slipping through the French blockade on a merchant ship loaded with rum and sugar weren't much better than swimming from New York to London. Nor was there any overriding commercial reason for this voyage that I could see, as the entire cargo wouldn't bring more than a thousand pounds, even if we did make it to London. As best I could see, the only reason the Captain would undertake such a useless and dangerous voyage as this one, was either because he had become intolerably bored with the life of the wealthy burgher, or had taken complete leave of his senses--which to me amounted to the same thing.

That there was a bit of madness in Captain Kidd I had no doubt, (how else to explain his two year pursuit of Burgess and Mason?), but I'd lately come to believe that all ambitious men were a little mad. Surely Robert Livingston couldn't have grown as rich as he had without a cord of madness to fuel that ambition. But although madness might drive ambition most ruthlessly, it was certainly no guarantor of success, as demonstrated by Livingston's collapse owing to Governor Fletcher's refusal to approve his victualling bills. Much as I despised the man who'd made a slave of me, I didn't take nearly so much satisfaction in his sad end as I'd always thought I would. So when the Governor, annoyed by Livingston's constant pleading, challenged him to a duel, which Livingston declined, I was almost sad to see him lose his self-respect as well as his money. Almost. Livingston was so distressed by it all that he had recently left New York and sailed for England, a desperate and unlikely voyage for a coward, to appeal directly to the King for his money. So, I asked myself, if it were only the mad and the desperate who would attempt such a passage as this, what was I doing aboard this ship? Or was love the maddest obsession of all?

When we were three weeks out, Captain Kidd was to shed some light on his own obsession, when he called me into his cabin and showed me a sealed letter.

"Ye've doubtless thought me daft goin' on a voyage such as this," he observed correctly. I did not deny it. "But ye came without question n'

I decided ye deserve an explanation. It's becuz o' this 'ere letter, not the goods in the hold 'at we're sailin' fer England," he announced, holding it for over the chart table like a guiding star. "Ye know what this is, Christopher?"

"It appears to be a letter."

"Aye, a letter," he said, regarding it as if it were the Holy Grail. "A letter from me good friend Jim Graham to 'is good friend, Sir Will'am Blathwayt. Ye've no doubt heerd o' 'im, 'aven't ye?"

"I don't think so."

"What…! Ye've not heard o' the Secretary o' war? What's the sense o' readin' all them books if it don't tell ye who's the Secretary o' war? Never mind. The point is, when Sir Will'am reads this letter tellin' 'im o' my service t' the King in the Caribee, he's bound t' go t' the King n' get me a letter o' marque! What do ye think o' that?"

I was aghast. "You're going pirating?"

"Privateerin' damn it! With a letter of marque we c'n take any French or Spanish ship what crosses our bow, n' there ain't a ship o' the Royal Naivy c'n stop us! Ye're with me on this ain't ye?"

"If you mean, do I understand? the answer is no," I replied, feeling the anger rising heedlessly. "If you brought me along on what I was led to believe was a trade mission, intending all the time to go pirating, then I don't understand you at all."

"Wait a minute, wait a minute!" he called. "If ye'll remember, it warn't me asked you t' sign on, it was you asked me."

"But couldn't you have told me what I was signing on for?"

"So's ye could tell Sarah?"

"What…! You intend to pillage and plunder the French and the Spanish but you're afraid to tell your wife?"

"I ain't afraid! I just didn't want t' cause 'er no grief, 'at's all. Anyway ye've made yer point, ye c'n get off in London."

"And how will I get back to New York?"

Kidd cocked his head to the side and peered at me with one raised eyebrow. "And why should ye want t' go back t' New York?"

With all the dignity I could muster, I replied, "I should not want to go anywhere I'm not wanted."

"Nor apparently where ye are," he grumbled, replacing his precious letter in the chart drawer. Our meeting was at an end.

Except when we were forced to communicate in the line of duty, we kept largely to ourselves after that. And because life on a merchantman is boringly routine, barring bad weather, those occasions were thankfully few. The only excitement was dry gun practice, when I found myself on the gun deck relaying Kidd's instructions to a bunch of lubbers who knew as well as I that we'd never be called upon to fire at a French warship, as it would be tantamount to suicide. After that we went back to our sullen silence. Until, when we reckoned we were but a few days off the British coast, our foretopman spied a sail on the eastern horizon, sending all hands, including the Captain, to the port rail.

"She could be English," Kidd said, if only to calm the lubbers. But the few seasoned hands among us knew how unlikely it was that a British ship might be skylarking alone amidst the French blockade.

True to form, the foretopman called down a few minutes later that she was French, and the Captain ordered all hands to their stations. My station was with the Captain, who looked to the north from where a light wind was blowing, then to the west where the sun lay on the sea like an egg yolk, and came quickly to some private decision. I fell in behind as he rushed to the helm, calling out instructions to me: "Furl the staysails! Blanket the headsails!" which I blindly relayed to the crew while he brought the ship round to starboard and pointed her south til she was running dead before the wind. If he was planning to outrun the Frenchman it was soon apparent that he'd underestimated her speed, as she was gaining steadily even while angling towards us from the port side. She was a corsair, a pirate ship not a man o' war, but a deadly threat just the same to our small crew of tradesmen and ploughmen. And she was much faster than our rum barge.

However, it was not the Corsair Captain Kidd was racing, but the sun. Although it had already dropped quickly behind the sea, the reflected light remained much longer than it would over land, so that when I last saw the French ship being swallowed up by the darkness, she was scarcely a mile off. It was then that the Captain brought the Antigua hard to port--and aimed her directly for the coast of France! It was a frightening but shrewd move, I quickly realized. The Frenchman would know from the clatter of spars and rigging that we had changed course, but they would expect us to turn out to sea and then towards England, not into the arms of the French navy. However, it was also possible that we might lose one pursuer, only to acquire a host of others.

At the Captain's instructions, I moved quietly among the men, telling them to neither speak nor show a light while we crawled slowly in the direction of France. If we did not reach far enough by the time the Frenchman passed our turning point, our white sails would stand out in the night like a beacon. After what seemed hours but was only minutes, we heard French voices on the water and glimpsed a yellow lantern gliding eerily by in the dark. We stood statue still and silent as death until the light was swallowed in blackness and the only sound in the night was the rippling of the water under our stem. After another hour of this silent eastward running, Captain Kidd brought the ship round to the north and we made for England.

The new day dawned with great promise, the bracing air smelling sweetly of Mother England, the sky cloudless and the sea as soft and green as the rolling meadows of my youth. Although I'd not been aloft since serving naked on Robert Livingston's shallop several years ago (nor was it something I missed), today I wanted very much to be the first man to see England. With the sun hardly up and there no watch yet in the top, I jumped up onto the bulwark and began climbing the ratlines, being careful not to look down until I'd reached all the way to the top. There I sat, arms laced through the topmast rigging, legs dangling in space, looking down at the spear-shaped deck slicing through the dark sea, edged by a collar of dawn-white lace. And standing on the quarterdeck now with the helmsman was Captain Kidd, no bigger than a chameleon, and all around me, water--water, water, water--but no England.

So I climbed higher, all the way up to the topgallant crosstrees where I wrapped one hand around the spreader lift and leaned out against the sky until it seemed I should tip the ship. And yet I saw no England.

But I did see a ship in the distance and cried out as loudly as I could, "Ship ahead!"

"What flag?" Kidd called back.

Having no glass I couldn't make out her flag, but there was no doubt--she was the same corsair that had come after us the day before. "French!" I shouted. "The corsair!"

Even from so high up I heard Kidd's curse, followed by a barked, "All 'ands! All 'ands!"

A moment later, dozens of crewmen were darting across the deck like chameleons while Captain Kidd shouted orders, and I stood watching the progress of that dogged Frenchman. He'd obviously caught on to our game after failing to overtake us, but rather than double back he'd simply gone to the mouth of the Channel to wait for us. And here we were, sailing straight for him. Why the hell didn't our Captain turn off?

I waited until the look-out started aloft, then slid quickly down the shrouds, passing him on the way, and ran to the quarterdeck where the Captain stood shouting orders to our flummoxed crew. "The guns, damn ye! Man the guns!"

He meant to engage them...?

"Captain, there's time to turn off!" I shouted

"And go where?" he shouted back. "Get these men on the guns!"

"Captain, there's hardly a gunner in the bunch," I explained.

"Then teach 'em!"

"Teach them...!"

"That's right! Cuz behind us lies the whole fookin' French naivy, while ahead lies one fookin' French ship and England. Now would ye rather engage the whole fookin' French naivy, or blast that little fooker out o' the water and go on t' England?"

"I'd rather surrender and save our fookin' skins!" I replied firmly.

"That's enough," Kidd warned.

"I agree wi' the boy," the helmsman spoke tersely from behind us.

Captain Kidd turned to the old man and opened his coat to reveal a pistol. "It's true, Mr. Brand, if ye choose t' fight, them French rapparees might kill ye. But if ye don't, I *surely* will," he said in a calm voice that belied his purple complexion.

"Yes, sir..."

"Now get down t' the gun deck!" Kidd ordered, turning back to me. "I'll pass t' their port side!"

Pass...? More likely they'd board from that side, I said to myself as I rushed to the gun deck. Before dropping through the hatchway I glimpsed the corsair's topsails in the distance and reckoned that even in this light breeze she would be upon us in less than half an hour. When I got below I found half the men in position on one side of the deck, half on the other, as if we were going to split the corsair down the middle and each take a side.

"Get to the port guns!" I shouted, driving them across the deck like crabs, hauling their deadly equipment after: cartridges, shot, funnel, reamer, powder horn, vent bit and auger, rammer and sponge, and still more odd little tools that appeared more suitable to carpentry than death.

The slow-matches were beginning to smolder in the fire tubs (the pirates probably had flintlocks) and the powder kegs were filled and ready. We had six men who claimed some experience with the twelve-pounder, whom the Captain had named gun captains while we were yet tied to the dock in New York. But except for the single dry run at sea, they had no real experience with these guns. And as any experienced gunner knew, no two guns behaved alike. If we were to prevent the pirates from grappling and boarding us, we would have to inflict some serious damage to the corsair while she was still far off, yet I worried that these men couldn't hit a barn from ten yards. And if they missed with the first volley it was unlikely they could reload the fire in under four minutes, while any pirate team might do so in little more than a minute. We were fookin' doomed.

By the time the guns were loaded, the corsair was no more than a quarter of a mile off our port quarter, going large, meaning to come straight at us so as to avoid our guns: while Captain Kidd was reaching to starboard, intent on passing her with port guns blazing. It was a fanciful notion, because even if the Captain should manage to get abeam of the corsair, she could simply steer out of range of our guns and come back at us from abaft. But if those French rapparees could see these farmers and clerks trembling beside their guns, they would simply sail up beside us and step aboard. The Captain was going to kill us all for a cargo of rum and sugar. The corsair was now close enough for us to see the screaming rapparees hanging in the rigging, cutlasses glinting in the sun.

"Cast loose your guns!" I ordered. The tackles were cast loose and the trucks squeaked, as a man on each side of the gun carriage gripped the side-tackle to hold the gun firmly on the deck. "Level your guns!" Each sponger edged a handspike under the back of his gun and lifted, as the captain slid a quoin in under the breech, wedging the barrel up to what each judged a satisfactory pitch. I saw that no two were alike, but having no opinion myself, I left it to them, hoping that at least one of them had the correct angle. "Out tompion!" I called and the plugs were pulled from the muzzles. "Run out the guns!" They pushed the gun carriages forward until they rested against the wall and the barrels poked out through the ports. At this show of belligerence we heard a faint but ferocious cry from the French that struck terror in every American, save perhaps our mad Captain. Only with the gravest misgivings did I give the order, "Prime!"

The captains pushed their reamer through the touch-hole, piercing the flannel cartridge in the gun, then poured powder from the horn into the vent. The guns were ready for firing. All that remained was for the spongers to jam the slow-match down onto the priming and six twelve-pounders should go hurtling at the French, crashing through a foot of hard oak and sending them to the bottom of the sea. Or more likely the iron balls would fall harmlessly into the sea and sink unaccompanied to the bottom. They were closing fast but they would, thanks to our Captain's undeniable skill, come up on our port side. We would get our chance!

"Hold your fire, hold your fire," I cautioned the nervous gunners as I moved back and forth behind them. "And you'd best not be standing there when that gun goes off," I warned a frightened powder-boy.

Finally, when the French were scarcely a hundred yards away and the first musket shots began pinging against the hull, I gave the order, "Fire!"

The spongers brought the slow-matches down onto the priming, followed by a quick hiss and a flash, then a series of deafening explosions as the guns bucked and recoiled across the deck, until they were snapped up sharply by their breeching. I saw two brief plumes, short and long of the corsair, but no sign of the other four. Two of these were accounted for when I saw that the two forward guns had failed to fire, but one or two of the others must have struck the corsair a good blow, as she was suddenly veering away from us, as at the same time I heard a great cheer from the decks above.

"Reload your guns!" I shouted. "And worm and draw those other two!"

No sooner had we set to the task when a man above stuck his head in the hatchway and shouted, "They're runnin' off! The Brits're 'ere!"

When I joined our jubilant crew on the main deck, I did indeed see a squadron of British warships in hot pursuit of the French. I was standing at the rail, cheering loudly as any man, when I chanced to glance up at the quarter deck to see Captain Kidd staring smugly down at me, as if he'd know all the time that the British were waiting just over the horizon. Damn the madman! But he'd been right, and I'd been wrong. I went to my cabin and remained there until we fetched up the Scilly Isles the next day.

We passed Lyme Bay sometime during the night and, much as I wished to disembark there and not go on to London, I was no more inclined to ask a favor of Captain Kidd than was he to grant one. I would fulfill my contract, go on to London and see to the offloading of the ship and then return home. I would be done with Captain Kidd and America forever. And sadly, Sarah, too. But there was nothing else for it, I'd finally decided. I had no future with Sarah and I desired no future in America. It was a place, as best I could see, bent upon its own destruction. The countryside was overrun with antediluvians intent upon killing Indians and each other over land (although there was more than enough for everybody), while the towns were run by corrupt politicians and venal merchants intent only upon lining their own pockets with money. And more's the pity, for until the death of

Leisler and the democratic movement, it seemed to me that this New York might be the second flowering of Athens.

However, I'd not yet seen London.

Upon rounding the point at Greenwich we were greeted by a forest of masts belonging to fully a thousand ships, so thick upon the Thames that it seemed a man might cross the river by jumping from deck to deck, yet each master threaded his way up or down that great estuary with an arrogance that somehow precluded any serious collision. There were East India merchantmen from Africa and the Orient running safely beside men-of-war, luxurious private boats, many-oared guild and government barges, eight-oared wherries with upholstered benches and bright awnings, thousands of lighters for loading and unloading the many ships that could find no dock, and two-oared ferry boats thicker than water bugs to be hailed like cabriolets in the street for a short ride. Indeed, the Thames was not so much a river as a grand highway paved with water.

The buildings, too, that stretched down from the hills and pushed up to the waterfront on stone steps, were crowded together tight as a bag of musket balls, separated by cobbled lanes barely wide enough that two carts might pass. Yet it seemed there were more than a hundred carts in each street, being loaded and offloaded from ships of every flag, tied two deep at the wharves, while hordes of humankind thronged over the waterfront like frenzied rats. That there were still hundreds of thousands of souls in this swarming metropolis, despite the plague of '65 and the Great Fire of '66, was more than proved by the putrescent stench of waste that reached even out onto the river, tamped down by gray skies heavy with coal smoke spewing from manufactories. Because the fire had scoured four-fifths of the city just twenty-nine years before, I expected to see some blackened spots and charred remains where great buildings had stood, but from my place on the deck of the Antigua that day, it looked as if London had been there from the first day of creation, spreading out like poisonous mushrooms in a bog.

Yet for all the crowding, we still passed a great many palatial houses surrounded by pleasant green gardens as we made our way slowly up the river, and, by the time we docked at Wapping on a Sunday evening, I was most eager to go ashore and see this place. When the dockmaster warned Kidd of the Mudlarks and Scuffle Hunters who could strip a ship to its keel in the blink of an eye, we were forced to remain aboard the ship that night to guard the cargo. By the time our goods had found a buyer and were finally offloaded, I was ready to jump ship. However, Captain Kidd had further plans for me.

"I might've spoke too hasty," he said, after calling me into his cabin.

"Sir…?" I had no idea what he could be talking about, as he'd scarcely spoken to me at all since the episode with pirates.

"Back there," he said, thrusting a thumb over his shoulder. "Ye can come back t' New York if ye like."

It took me a moment to understand--for I'd never seen it before--the man was apologizing! "Thank you, sir, but I've decided to return home," I replied as firmly as I could, for I was in truth somewhat touched.

"O' course--a lad should spend some time with 'is father," he allowed "But that ain't a career. What I got 'ere," he said, laying a hand on the chart drawer where his precious letter to Sir Blathwayt lay, "'at's a career. Go 'ome, see your father, then come back and serve with me and I'll make ye a rich man. And ye'll be servin' yer King besides."

"I believe I can best serve my King by becoming a schoolmaster," I replied.

"A lad 'at can command guns is no schoolmaster," he said, shaking his large head. "At least not yet. Serve with me, make yer fortune, then become a schoolmaster."

"I've made up my mind," I said.

"And 'ave ye thought o' the children? They'll be grievin' terrible fer ye, ye know."

"And I for them."

"And Mrs. Kidd…"

"For her too."

"…will be angry with me fer losin' ye."

"Of course--but--she'll find another tutor," I assured him.

"Aye, a tutor. But ye're more'n that t' me, Christopher. Even though ye warn't born to it, y'ave the manner of a gentleman--much like myself. And damn it, I come t' rely on ye."

"As a gentleman's servant…?"

"'ave I ever treated ye as a servant?" he demanded.

"I have served in that capacity," I reminded him.

"From time t' time, at Mrs. Kidd's request, and I don't remember ye complainin' at the time. The point is, I find myself in need of an aid-d'-camp."

"An aid-d'-camp?" I asked, for I'd never heard the word.

"It's fer me meetin' with Sir Will'am Blathwayt. An officer n' a gentleman is expected t' 'ave an aid-d'camp."

"I see," I said, thinking of my pay for the voyage over, which unfortunately had never been discussed. "And if I serve as your aid-d'-camp, I'll then be free to leave?"

"Ye're free t' leave whenever ye like."

"I'm not able to go anywhere until I've been paid something," I prodded.

"We can discuss that after you've served as my aid-d'-camp," he smiled.

So I signed on as aid-d'-camp.

Early the next day, dressed as an aid-d'-camp in a kind of naval officer's uniform Kidd had scraped together and forced me into, the Captain and I proceeded through the clogged streets of London in a hired coach, until we arrived finally at Whitehall, verily a city of grand buildings all by itself. We entered a vast, arched corridor where men in ornate military raiment skittered about in all directions, like rare birds in an aviary. The Captain and I looked absurdly drab amongst these elegant cocks, some of whom ill-concealed their amusement. When Captain Kidd stopped one of these foppish gentlemen, I thought it was to teach him some American manners, but instead he merely inquired politely as to where he might find the office of the War Secretary. The officer directed us through a maze of corridors which soon had us entirely lost, but after asking directions twice more we finally found Sir William Blathwayt's headquarters.

"The Secretary is unavailable," we were told by a young officer who limped about the large office on a walking stick.

"Could ye tell me when 'e'll be back?" Kidd asked.

"That's hard to say. What did you wish to see him about?"

"Well--I got a letter fer 'im from 'is friend in New York, Mr. James Graham…?"

"Let me see it," he said, opening his hand. "Or keep it and go," he added, when Kidd hesitated.

Captain Kidd looked uncertainly at me, then handed him the letter. A faint smile gathered in the officer's face as he read.

"You wish the King to send you pirating--?"

"Privateerin', sir."

"Has word of the war not reached the colonies then?"

"It was thought by Mr. Graham that I might be of considerable service to the war, sir."

"If you wish to serve the King--*Mister* Kidd," he said, pointedly ignoring the title plainly inscribed on the document at hand. "the Royal Navy desperately needs men."

"I wish t' serve where I c'n be of most use, sir. So if you'll just give me my letter, we'll come back at a more convenient time."

"Sadly for you, sir, I can see no convenient time in the future. Being ignorant of the war, I expect you know nothing of politics. Or if you did you'd know that in last month's elections, the Whigs, much to the King's pleasure, swept those peace-loving Tories out of Parliament and back to their estates. And your intended sponsor, unfortunately for you but not for England, is a Tory. Need I say more--*Mister* Kidd?"

"Ye've said enough," Kidd replied, taking back his useless letter.

"Well, does it give ye pleasure t' know I come all this way on a fools's errand?" Kidd asked as he hauled me down the corridor.

"I had only hoped that we might both have what we wished," I replied.

"Ye'll be schoolmaster soon enough, but I'll be no pirate hunter," he growled, tugging me from my intended course.

"I believe the door is that way," I pointed.

"It's this way," he said, pulling me into a long, dark labyrinth which I was sure I'd not seen before. I continued to make my opinion known, though not forcefully as I was sure all tunnels must lead eventually back out onto the Street, while the Captain continued to pull me through the twisting ways of Whitehall. After a few turns into ever narrower and darker corridors, however, I became less confident of the light at the end of the tunnel. And when I saw a somehow familiar man, wearing a dark greatcoat despite the summer's heat, coming at us with a satchel, I worried that the gatekeeper of Hades had come for us. But it was not the devil.

"Mr Livingston!" I exclaimed.

"What--by God it is!" Captain Kidd affirmed. "What the 'ell are you doin' 'ere, Robert?"

"Will'am--? My God man--what're you doin' 'ere?"

"Wastin' a great deal o' time it seems," Captain Kidd said, then began to tell Mr. Livingston of his dangerous voyage to England, but was quickly and rudely interrupted.

"Dangerous…? Hah! Did ye lose yer rudder in a storm n' drift fer weeks, till ye was near t'thirstin' n' starvin' t' death?" Mr. Livingston asked.

"Our death would've been quicker if it hadn't been…" Kidd began.

"Fortunately we was fetched up on the coast o' Portugal by the hand o' God at the last minute, only t' be set upon by Catholic brigands n' stripped o' all we 'ad!"

"Stripped naked?" I asked wishfully.

"All but! When I got t' London I 'ad nothin' save my victuallin' receipts n' a letter t' Sir Will'am Blathwayt, which ain't worth nothin' now the damn Whigs are in power."

"You too?" Kidd exclaimed.

Then the men fell to comparing their worthless letters and roundly cursing Mr. Graham for sending them on a fool's errand.

"But I've made a new friend who might yet get me my money," Livingston said, returning his worthless letter to the satchel. "Come with me t' my coffee house and I'll tell ye all about 'it."

Being the aid-d'-camp, I fell in behind my commander as Mr. Livingston guided him out of the building. At one point, as we walked along Whitehall Street searching for our coach, Mr. Livingston looked back at me and inquired of the Captain, "Who dressed the boy?" to which my tailor muttered evasively.

We found our coach, and plunged into the tide of cabs and cursing drivers and whinnying horses, as Mr. Livingston shouted directions to our hired man. Along the way Mr. Livingston pointed out the splendid edifices of trade and commerce (a bit wistfully it seemed), including the very bank where their Majesties William and Mary kept their considerable fortune. Captain Kidd seemed little interested in the Royal Exchange or Lloyd's of London, but when we passed the opulent Greek temple that was the home of the East India Company, he smiled approvingly. Mr. Livingston's coffee house lay close by.

The large room was scarcely less crowded than the streets, hot as Hades and thick with blue pipe smoke, yet the customers seated at the long tables, whether locked in animated discussion or quietly reading, seemed most comfortable. Young boys in white aprons rushed about with clay pipes for any who wished them, while a chubby, red-faced woman brewed coffee from behind a tall counter, and across the room a sweat-bathed baker made cakes at the oven. We found a place at a table near the oven that was not so crowded, owing to the great heat, and ordered coffee and cake.

"Tis a fair place," Kidd said, gazing this way and that.

"Tis a Whig place," Livingston said.

"What…!" Kidd exclaimed.

"Hear me out," Livingston cautioned, laying a hand on the Captain's arm. "In New York we must be Tories because everyone knows we are Tories, but 'ere in England we c'n be what we like. And seein' it's the Whigs 'at 'as the power, I think ye'd very well better become a Whig like me."

"Never! I'm a King's man now and always will be!" Kidd swore.

"Especially," the new Whig went on as he leaned across the table, "in view o' yer considerable part in the apprehension o' Gov'ner Leisler."

"*Gov'nor* is it!" Kidd exclaimed.

"Not so loud…!" the Whig cautioned, glancing left and right. "*We* may know what a dangerous rabble-rouser 'e was, but these Whigs think 'e's Jesus Christ hisself. And what's more, the King ain't all that unhappy wi' the Whigs no more neither, not since they're supportin' 'is war and the Tories ain't. "So ye see, Will'am, ye c'n be a Tory in America, but 'ere in England it's yer patriotic duty t' be a Whig."

Kidd just sat there shaking his head at the idea, and I understood why. He had finally become a gentleman, a Church of England Protestant with a pew of his own in Trinity Church, a wealthy man of property, if not estates, a man with every right to call himself Tory, and now he must call himself Whig...? Even if only a temporary title of convenience, it was an appalling demotion. When he tried to explain his resistance to conversion, Livingston--who was willing to become anything for profit, even a treasonist who would trade with the enemy--stared uncomprehendingly.

"I c'n see I'm makin' no sense t' ye," Kidd concluded correctly. "I'm no a man fer politics."

"Yer as shrewd a man fer politics as any I know," Livingston said. "And that's why ye'll understand when I tell ye--my new sponsor's a Whig."

"Why didn't ye say so? What's 'is name?"

"Richard Coote, the Earl of Bellomont," Mr. Livingston announced proudly.

"An Earl is 'e ..." Kidd remarked approvingly.

"But alas, not a rich one. 'e was just named the new gov'ner o' the Massachusetts Bay Colony, but the salary's not enough t' pay off 'is debts."

"Up to 'is ballocks in markers, eh...?"

"More like 'is eyeballs. So 'e's petitioned the Lords o, Trade n' Plantations t' be named t' the post o' Gov'ner o' New York as well--so's 'e c'n 'ave *two* salaries."

"The greedy bugger. But what's t' become of Gov'nor Fletcher?"

"That's the best part--we're goin' t' get rid of 'im," Mr. Livingston said. "And when 'e's gone, Gov'ner Bellomont'll approve my victuallin' bills. I tell ye, Will'am, ye couldn't've come at a better time!"

"Why's 'at, Robert?"

"Cuz I'm lookin' fer some prominent New Yorkers like yerself t' go before the Board o' Trade n' Plantations n' testify as t' Fletcher's corruption. I already 'ave a coopla 'onorable New York gentlemen like yourself willin' t' bear personal witness as to 'is 'igh crimes and misdemeanors while in office, n' wi' you we'll 'ave more'n enough to send 'at scalawag packin'. If ye'll do that fer us, Will'am, I'm sure Lord Bellomont'll go t' the King fer ye n' get ye yer letter o' marque."

"But I know nothin' personally--the Gov'nor's always kept me at sword's distance," Kidd reminded him.

"No mind, I'll supply the information," Livingston promised, although he'd never been allowed closer than lance's distance himself.

"But if I was t' testify against Fletcher and ye was t' fail t' unseat 'im, I'd not 'ave much t' go 'ome to," Kidd pointed out.

"Ye're on'y riskin' a few properties, I'm riskin' Livingston Manor. Do ye think I'd throw in wi' Lord Bellomont if I warn't sure o' the man?" Livingston asked.

"I don't doubt 'e's a powerful man, bein' an Earl, but I know nothin' of him."

"Then ye shall! Ye'll meet 'im this very day," Livingston said, rising from his chair.

Lest my judges think I seek to avoid giving evidence as to that meeting, be assured that I was not in attendance. Captain Kidd at first insisted that his aid-d'-camp should attend him, but Mr. Livingston managed to convince him that my attendance might inhibit Lord Bellomont's expression, and I was therefore ordered back to my ship.

When Captain Kidd returned to the Antigua after his meeting with Lord Bellomont, he pulled me out of my snug bunk in the Officers' Room and insisted I join him in his cabin for a glass of rum. Reluctantly, I joined him, where he proceeded to tell me what a grand fellow Lord Bellomont was, and that he would most certainly soon have his letter of marque. I of course had no intention to go pirating, but because Captain Kidd still owed me an uncertain sum of money, I kept quiet that night, and for a great many nights thereafter. Whenever I brought up the money, Kidd rewarded me with a small advance, sufficient for a few nights ashore, but not enough to get me to Lyme Bay and back. Or so I told myself.

For in truth, London held many attractions for a young man. There was St. Paul's cathedral which was then nearing completion; there were halls and gardens where one could drink tea and eat cakes and hear wonderful music played; and there were the booksellers' stalls where once could browse through all the latest publications; and the literary coffee houses where poets read their work aloud, and the discourse was loftier than that of the ancient Greeks; and there were public galleries where great paintings of Kings and saints could be seen. But alas, I did not see as much of these places as I would have wished, owing to the many base attractions that competed for a young man's attention at the time. I would not attempt to excuse my attendance upon some of these sordid attractions, except to note that had it not been for my chance meeting with Chester Tweakham, I should not have plumbed the depths of depravity so deeply as I did.

I met Chester on one of my several mornings ashore when, with no purpose in mind, I was drawn by the din of hawkers and the smell of food to the Piazza at Covent Garden. The customers in this vast market were mostly maids and their ladies buying fruit and flowers, many of them young and beautiful, and more than a few with an eye for something other than tulips and melons. And when I saw the many young gallants, who'd obviously been roistering all night, swaggering through the crowds with no more interest in tulips and melons than the ladies, I realized that this was a marketplace of another order.

Before I'd perambulated very far beneath the arched walkway flanking the Piazza, I was appraised so brazenly by an attractive older woman, that I fairly stumbled as I passed her by. Which Chester Tweakham observed.

"Not to your taste, eh sailor?" he remarked.

I turned to see a most outlandish fop leaning against a downed sedan-chair, regarding me insolently from beneath a ridiculously wide beaver hat with a tall white feather poking up. He had a long gaunt face and soft blue lips that looked to have been stung by hornets. I'd seen the type on my perambulations about town, rich young men with a look of boredom bordering on pain, but never such a costume. His wrinkled cloak was of crimson velvet, from beneath which peaked a black silk coat embroidered with gold lace, held together by enormous gold buttons. He wore a silver chain about his neck and silver spurs on his heels, a thin sword with a jeweled hilt good for a straight thrust but no parry, and boots to his knees to guard, I supposed, against London rattlesnakes.

"A woman of quality but too many years," I replied, laying a hand lightly on my cutlass, for she was more than thirty and he a mannerless pup.

He tilted his head back, as if laughing silently. "By your costume I thought you'd dressed early for Guy Fawkes, but you are truly a Bedlam fool, are you not," he said. When I clenched my cutlass, he waved a finger yea and nay and said, "Careful lest you bring the Mohocks down on you." He threatened.

He was referring, of course, to that infamous band of young gentlemen who robbed and killed for sport, but being gentlemen, they were seemingly immune from prosecution. I didn't know if he was one of them, or just a braggart; but seeing as he fought with words not weapons, I relaxed my grip.

"Where are you in from?" he asked.

"New York."

"An American…" he mused. Have you ever swived an Indian maiden?"

I was appalled by such coarseness, yet I replied, "Two."

"Two…?" he asked, plainly dubious.

"At the same time."

"Mama mia," he said. "Tell me more."

So I reluctantly told him of my romp with Orsa and Unca, including their horrible torture and death, all of which endured me immediately to Chester Tweakham.

"We have nothing so sweet as that in London, I'm afraid. But if you'll come along with me, I'll show you things that might tide you over till you get home." He promised.

And that was how Chester Tweakham became my guide through the London underworld.

As it was Hanging Day, he took me first to Newgate Prison, where we stood in a great throng until a batch of poor wretches were brought out in a horse cart. With the executions of Leisler and Milbourne still vivid in my mind, I had no desire for more, but Chester, convinced that I was merely jaded after so many scalpings and roastings, promised that if I would but indulge him in this, he would later show me something more exalted. So I fell with him into the merry procession, following the horse cart up Holborn Hill and along the Oxford Road.

One of the condemned, a handsome highwayman, was a favorite of the crowd who showered him with flowers and gave him spirits to drink. Women threw kisses to him and some showed him their breasts, which might've been cruel however well-intentioned, yet the condemned man became increasingly cheerful as the parade rolled on. Some of the others who'd been convicted of meaner crimes did not fare so well at the hands of the crowd, and by the time they reached a tavern near St. Giles, where all the condemned were given a free bowl of ale, one man was nearly dead from the clubs and stones he'd taken along the way.

There were already thousands of howling celebrants in our raucous cortège, yet when we reached the hanging tree it looked as if all the rest of London had gathered on the killing ground. There were wooden stands that provided the gentry with an unobstructed view of the hangings, while small children hung from the topmost branches of the surrounding trees, and hawkers moved through the crowd selling meat pies and cakes and ale.

"On a good day the hangings will last for several hours," Chester apologized, as today there were no more than a couple of dozen.

I was surprised that children were allowed to witness such a bloody spectacle but my companion was convinced that it taught a cautionary lesson, and the fact that the hangings had been doubling and tripling for each of the past ten years, did nothing to disabuse him of his certainty. By standing behind a very tall man I was able to avoid seeing the first few hangings, and my companion, intent on the proceedings, was none the wiser. After nearly an hour of this, Chester removed a beautiful gold watch from his vest, looked at it and announced, "Time for the next event."

We pushed our way through the crowd to a place in the road where the hackney coaches waited, and, by generously bribing a hackman, Chester was able to obtain a cab meant for a gentleman and lady still sitting obliviously in the stands.

"What is the next event?" I asked, during the ride in.

"The law in all its majesty," he replied.

"You're interested in the law?" It seemed unlikely.

"I am a student of it," he replied. "Though not a keen one."

After some stubborn questioning (Chester was more interested in Indian maidens than anything else) I learned that he resided at the Inns of Court, a walled Temple where lawyers and their students resided together in several inns to *read the law*. Although it seemed to me a wonderfully privileged existence--Shakespearean plays were performed and all the great wits of the day were invited to speak--Chester found it terribly boring. He supposed he would become a barrister in six or seven years, although his more eager classmates required only five.

"Anything worth doing is worth doing slowly," he opined.

And it was more than just talk, I learned. After graduating from Oxford he had taken several years to do The Grand Tour of Europe--until his father called him back and enrolled him at Gray's Inn. He had spent nearly all those years in Italy, which explained his foppish clothes, and wanted only to get this barrister thing behind him so that he might get back to those fleshy brown women. This put him again in mind of Indian maidens, and I therefore heard nothing more of Chester Tweakham's languorous life for the rest of the trip to Bridewell.

"It is the place where justice is administered to the female criminal," he said, as we passed into a long corridor where women were furiously beating hemp, while they in turn were being beaten by a male overseer with a switch. "Come along," he said, pulling me into a stairwell.

We started up the stairs and, while I was yet pondering that cruel scene below, stepped into a grand law chamber stuffed with spectators, where court was already in session. A beautiful young woman, in the blue apron of a lady's maid, was standing in the dock while being questioned by a grave Judge in a curled white wig that hung down to his black robe. It was not so much a face poking out as a scowl, soured no doubt by the endless parade of thieving whores and husband-poisoners that came before him each day--although this fresh flower in the dock should have relieved that dour countenance at least for the moment, as she could certainly be guilty of no crime worse than arousing the jealousy of her ugly mistress, who now stood giving evidence against her.

"...and solid silver it was, Your Grace, a gift from my husband," she said, with a nod at the poor man huddled on the bench behind her.

"Please, ma'am, as God is my witness, I did not steal it!" the girl cried piteously.

"Silence!" the Judge cried, bringing down a hammer-blow that resounded off the rafters like a bolt from heaven. "You were charged with keeping the silver, were you not?" he asked the cowed girl, who said nothing in reply. "Answer me!"

"Yes…! Your Grace."

"And now a valuable cup is gone, is it not?"

"Yes, Your Grace."

"Hence you either stole it or allowed it to be stolen. *Res ipsa loquitor.*"

When Chester looked questioningly at me I explained, "The thing speaks for itself."

"Aha."

"You say you are innocent, but you offer no character witness other than a neighbor's servant, a girl like yourself," the Judge went on.

"I know no one else, I only just arrived from the country," she said.

"It is not the court's fault if you did not prepare an adequate defense," he said, hammering again. "Your mistress and master, a most honorable lady and gentleman, say you are a thief and that is…"

"My master does not say it!" she cried.

"He does so!" the mistress shouted.

The husband burrowed deeper into his coat but said nothing.

"Enough," the Judge said, bringing down his gavel. Next he spoke in a loud voice to the assembly, "All you who are willing Abigail Burke should have present punishment, pray hold up your hands!"

I believe every hand in the court save my own and that of Abigail's master went up. When the judge ordered that the defendant should be given one hundred lashes with a stout whip, as the cup she stole was worth near a pound, a bailiff come forward and quickly stripped the poor girl to the waist. Then a pair of doors to the side of the courtroom were opened, revealing a large room, empty but for a clawed and bloodied whipping post, to which the trembling, half-naked girl was dragged. Her hands were tied around the post and hung from a hook so that she should not slip down after passing out, which, judging from the buggy whip now whistling experimentally in the air, could not come too soon. The first lash gave rise to a great scream and a fine red stripe across her bare back. I did not see how there could be room on that small back for ninety-nine more, nor did I think she would live to see them.

When she finally passed out from the excruciating pain, I assumed the bailiff would proceed to kill her mercifully in her sleep. But I was ignorant in the ways of English justice, as she was revived by a bucket of water and the flogging resumed. The ordeal was interrupted several more times by this baptism, yet none in the audience, least of all the poor wretch's glittery-eyed mistress, would have voted to stop it.

When the count reached sixty and the woman's back was pulpy and blood-soaked from shoulders to waist, the court physician was called to examine her. When the physician informed the judge that she could take no more blows to the back, I thought at last the ordeal was over. But again I was wrong.

"Then strip her down and have at the rest," the Judge ordered.

When the bailiff removed the rest of her clothes, revealing a firm, white, unmarked bottom, the crowd stirred with renewed enthusiasm. By the time he'd finished administering the forty blows remaining, there was no difference between her back and buttocks, it was all just chopped meat.

"I daresay, she'll never steal again," Chester said, as the half-dead woman was carried off on a litter.

"If she ever did," I answered.

"There can be no doubt about that, the court has spoken," the law student informed me.

"Pity the husband did not."

"If he had, she'd've been tried for a whore and bound over to America," he replied. "So whichever way you look at it, justice has been done."

I didn't understand the English judicial system.

Chapter 10

Hockley-in-the-Hole

When Captain Kidd told me I might be called upon by the Lords Commissioners of Trade and Plantations to testify against Governor Fletcher, I became quite upset and told him so. If he wished to commit perjury before a Parliamentary Committee in the hope of obtaining a letter of marque, he was free to do so, but I was not willing to risk my skin for nothing.

"If won't be for nothin', lad. If Bellomont gets New York, we get our letter of marque," he urged.

"Captain, with all due respect, I do not wish to be a privateer," I began patiently, before he leaped in again.

"But if Lord Bellomont…"

"Bellomont has nothing to do with my decision," I said abruptly. "I hope for your sake he's able to help you. But I must tell you, Captain, I cannot believe the King would allow you to take a hundred Englishmen privateering when his press-gangs are reduced to taking old men and boys to fight the French."

"'e will if 'e comes in for ten per cent of the booty," Kidd replied surely.

I stared incredulously at him for a moment. "You think the King of England will sponsor a pirate?"

"The King's a man, not a saint."

At this, I regret to say, I laughed in his face.

"Get out!" he shouted, pointing to the hatch.

"Captain, I'm sorry--it's just that…"

"Out!"

"So I left his cabin, vowing not to try to speak to him again while he remained under this insane delusion. That the king would join with pirates…? Might as well tell me he'd trade with the enemy!

My disagreement with the Captain resulted in some good, I'm happy to say, when he stubbornly refused to call me to testify against Fletcher, in spite of Mr. Livingston's plangent entreaties. Nor was it necessary, as it turned out, as the several New Yorkers Livingston brought before the Lords proved sufficient by themselves to satisfy them that Fletcher was corrupt and should be called to London to answer charges. I was of course pleased by this decision, and hopeful that New Yorkers might again have a fair governor who would make the streets of their town safe once more.

However, when I learned that Lord Bellomont had succeeded in getting himself appointed governor of New York as well as Massachusetts, I knew that New York would suffer, as no one man could possibly do both jobs. Although New York was the richest of the colonies, these Englishmen plainly did not favor her so much as the others (probably because so many foreigners resided there), or else I'm sure New York would have had a governor of her own. Kidd, however, was little concerned with the fate of the colony, as he once again enjoyed the patronage of her number one citizen. I was beginning to think that he could do no wrong and I could do no right.

I didn't see much of Captain Kidd for some time after that, which I attributed to his impatience with my gloomy aspect. However, that was only part of the reason, I learned, when Kidd returned unexpectedly one day and proudly announced, "We're gettin' a new ship!"

Ever the pessimist, I asked, "What's wrong with this one?"

"Too small for huntin' pirates," he replied, pouring two glasses of wine, a sign of my absolution. "The new one's t' be three hundred tons and more'n thirty guns."

"To be…? You're building this ship?"

"Aye, at Castle Yard in Deptford. She's the only civilian ship under construction," he boastfully informed me. "How's the Adventure Galley sound t' ye as a name?"

"Appropriate," I said, as it was adventure, not profit Kidd was in search of.

"Then here's to the Adventure Galley!" he toasted, handing me a glass.

I repeated the toast and sipped my wine. "It's not very sweet," I said.

"It's not s'posed t' be," Kidd replied. "It's Sicilian, Lord Bellomont's favorite."

It certainly wasn't mine. But perhaps any wine would have tasted sour just then, as the Captain was talking of building a new ship when he still hadn't paid me the little I had coming.

"Pardon my curiosity, sir, but isn't it quite expensive to build a ship?

"I have investors," he replied.

"Investors…?"

"Aye, me n' Robert's formed a comp'ny with Lord Bellomont n' some o' his friends." Then, like a proud collector describing each of his treasures, he named the half dozen lords, earls and dukes he now counted his friends and business associates. "And we got another partner--a big partner," he said, grinning smugly.

"Another partner…?"

"A secret partner."

"Aha…"

I didn't probe further. Instead, after congratulating him on his success, I took advantage of his sanguine mood to ask about my pay.

"I'm afraid that'll hafta wait, lad," he said, returning to the sour wine. "This new venture o' mine's takin' every pound I c'n get me hands on."

"But, sir, surely you're friends aren't requiring you to put up your money as well as your services, are they?"

"Only a wee amount, just t' evidence our good faith."

"Our…?" I asked, fearing he had pledged both me and my money to the venture.

"Me n' Livingston n' Bellomont's promised t' come up with two thousand pounds."

"Two thousand!" I exclaimed. I could live like a king for the rest of my life on but a tenth of that.

"But I'm only responsible for a third," he added.

"Then there might still be a little for me..." I pleaded.

"There will, o' course, but not just yet," he replied. "'cuz unfortunately Robert and Lord 'Bellomont's both a bit pinched at the moment, so I had t' stand em their share. It's just until Robert's vicutallin' bill is paid and Lord Bellomont gets 'is Gov'nor's pay, ye understand."

"But that could be months!" I wailed.

"No, not months. 'Ere, 'ave a little more wine. What's the sense o' worryin' about a few pounds when we're soon gonna be richer'n all the pirates in Madygascar?"

I tried again to explain that I did not wish to be richer than any pirate, nor did I intend to be one, but I fear I made no more impression this time than before. In the end he gave me five pounds to tide me over for a few weeks, just until Livingston or Bellomont should repay their loans.

So with a few pounds in my pocket, I made my way to Gray's Inn to call upon Chester Tweakham. Although he had a great many cases piled upon his desk that had to be read by the next day, he nevertheless proposed a visit to Hockley-in-the- Hole.

"What's Hockley-in-the-Hole?" I asked as I hurried after him.

"You'll see," he promised as he stepped into the street. "Driver!"

When we were settled in the cab, Chester returned to his favorite subject. "I've heard that Indian maidens go about naked all the time."

"True," I agreed.

"Without even body hair."

"True."

"The men too?"

"True."

I continued to confirm everything Tweakham said as we jounced along the rutted road in a hired cab, as the poor man was in need of cheering up after badly failing a Torts examination. It was nearly a two hour ride to Hockley-in-the-Hole, owing largely to the clogged traffic on London Bridge, the only way across the Thames. It was not so much a bridge as a town, with buildings as high as seven stories housing thousands of people who worked in the shops and manufactories below--and even a church of its own named after St. Thomas Beckett. Indeed, a man could spend his whole life on London Bridge and want for very little other than fresh air, as the fetid stench when the tide was out could be overpowering.

Hockley-in-the-Hole proved to be nothing more than a dip in the field north of Clerkenwell Road, made up to resemble a traveling fair of a sort, announced by flying pennants and streams of riff-raff bound for a day at sport. I was relieved to see, when we stepped down from our cab in the staging area, that there were also a goodly number of gentlemen in attendance, as well, and more than a few ladies. After the last event Chester had taken me to, where a bull, a bear and a dog were dressed with fireworks and turned loose--within steps of the site of Shakespeare's theater no less--I was a bit wary of his judgment. There were more than enough footpads and ruffians about such places, that anyone who looked as if he might have a few bob in his purse was in danger of having his head caved in or his throat cut. By dressing plainly we hoped to divert attention from ourselves on our nether world forays, but there was still no way we would ever pass for one of these sooty, scarred, toothless, mud-caked unfortunates now jostling along beside us.

There were several raised and roped stages for wrestling and boxing in the center of the grounds, mixed with hay-strewn animal pens for fighting cocks and dogs, and flanking all this were a great many beer gardens with musicians and dancers and food stalls providing everything from soup to nuts. Hawkers and punters streamed through the crowd, proffering broadsides announcing the attractions and offering odds on the contestants. I ignored the latter, preferring to bet at ringside with a gentleman who knew no more of the professional combatants than I did, rather than a sharper who'd watched them fight for naught oe'r the favors of an alehouse doxy the night before.

"To which of the boxing matches shall we attend?" I asked, as we surged along on the human tide, past a stage where a pair of stripped-down boxers exhorted the crowd with pledges of mayhem.

"Boxing! Did you think we'd come all this way for pugilists?" he exclaimed, thrusting a broadside in my hand.

I, John Scully, being born on Highgat Road ad being a most Loyal Subject of King William and Queen Mary, who didst most recently serve Them and England most valiantly against the French at Beachy Head, notwithstanding that result, and having been lately discharged from the ship o' the line for injuries suffered thereon, but have heretofore ne'er truckled to any man's sword, do invite George Hill, who would call himself Champion of Hockley-in-the-Hole, to meet and exercise at these following weapons, viz., backsword, sword and dagger, sword and buckler, single falchion and case of falchions.

And in reply the Hockley-in-the-Hole Champion had written:

I, George Hill, master in the noble art of self-defense, who did take the stage against all comers and left it to none of them, will not fail, God willing, to meet this courageous challenger at the time and place appointed, desiring sharp swords and from him no favour.

"Swords!" I exclaimed. "Someone could be killed."

"Such is the intent, if not always the result," Chester replied.

I couldn't believe that such a thing could be allowed. This was the Seventeenth Century after all, not ancient Rome. Yet when we arrived at the main stage, I realized that we were indeed in the Coliseum, surrounded by bloodthirsty Englishmen who had profited not a whit in almost two thousand years of civilizing. I could believe it of some of them, the drooling lunatics who looked to have escaped from Bedlam, but what of Chester and the snuff-sniffing gentlemen and their ladies who crowded round as eagerly as anyone.

"Barbaric..." I muttered, as I watched the first contestant, attended by his wife it seemed, climb up onto the stage.

"Do you not fight duels in America?" Chester asked.

"For honor, not amusement," I replied.

"Do you think the Challenger fights for amusement? Look, he has a wife and no doubt children. And look how he limps. The result of a wound suffered at Beachy Head, I should think, but not one to merit a pension. He can't work with his bad leg, but his sword arm is still good. One lucky thrust and he'll be a rich man. Is he the barbarian, or is it the gentleman who fights for honor?"

"The king should put a stop to both," I said, smarting at the position I'd somehow been put in, for I was no defender of the duel either.

"I thought you Americans prized your freedom," he said with an amused smile.

"I'm as English as you are," I answered, hoping to abandon the argument.

"I don't think so," Chester said.

I was spared a rejoinder to this insult by the arrival of the champion. He stepped into the roped square wearing a red velvet cape, then sauntered about the stage for the delectation of the crowd, while the hapless challenger and his wife stood awkwardly by. When he'd finally swaggered more than enough, he came and stood with his back to the challenger, then lifted the cape from his shoulders. Without thinking, poor scully took the cape from him, setting off a gleeful roar from the crowd as, a moment later, his wife snatched it away from him and thrust it back at Hill. Then she stepped down from the stage and took up a place at the corner as the combatants prepared to kill each other.

Nearby, an older gentleman with a young strumpet on his arm raised a note in the air and called, "Hear, hear, I'll lay five on the Champion! Any bets?"

"What are your odds?" Chester asked.

"Three to one!" he said, to a chorus of derisive laughter.

"The punters are offering that," Chester replied.

This was true, but they dealt in shillings, not pounds. They settled on five to one and the money was handed over to the strumpet, who tucked the notes between her large breasts. It was a poor bet even at ten to one, I quickly decided as I watched the swordsmen circling and parrying. Poor Scully, the shorter of the two, lurched badly when going to his right, and had difficulty backing up. Whether owing to his injury or his nature, Scully favored a slashing charge, while Hill, who moved like a dancer and worked his sword like a conductor his baton, easily parried his violent slashing and let him rush by like a mad bull. It would have been easy for the Champion to follow and finish scully off as he turned back, but he preferred to stroll about the ring after each charge and enjoy the cheers of the crowd.

"I'm afraid your fiver has been consigned forever to the depths of that bosom," I informed my companion.

"Every dog has his day," Chester replied, as steel clanged and Scully stumbled forward, falling on his face.

I expected Hill to finish him off now, but there was apparently a rule against this, doubtless owing more to the expectations of the crowd than chivalry. With his wife urging him on from stage side, the challenger climbed gamely to his feet. His next charge, however, was not so strong as the last, and the Champion slipped by it with remarkable ease.

"If your dog is to have his day, I fear it must be within a very few minutes," I said to Chester.

"Have faith," he said, watching closely. "There, you see!"

I hadn't, but scully had somehow landed a blow to the Champion's head that left him dazed, while the blood gushed from his forehead, filling his eyes and pouring down his face. He stood in the center of the stage, thrashing blindly and uselessly, while Scully stood off to the side and his wife screamed at him to finish the man off. But before he could, the judge and two more men jumped up onto the stage and came to the aid of the Champion, while the crowd shouted excitedly, whether for scully or Hill or just the blood. They laid a flap of skin back against Hill's skull and wrapped it several times around with a white bandage, then wiped the blood from his eyes. When the judge was satisfied that the champion was fit to resume (it would have been worth his life to decide otherwise) he jumped down from the stage and the battle was once again taken up.

It was plainly not the same Champion, who this time but barely managed to evade Scully's hacking charge. He seemed still stunned by the blow, and the blood continued to flow into one eye despite the bandage. The roar of the crowd was deafening, as they sensed they were about to witness the demise of the old Champion and the crowning of the new, and Mrs. Scully's cheers were the loudest of all. The challenger turned and came back at the Champion in a slowly assured manner this time, feinting one way then another, measuring Hill's bloody vision and dulled response. When scully pricked a shoulder, Hill responded like a blind bear to the whip, lashing out too late in that direction, as Scully stung him again with a slash along the ribs. Now the Champion stood flat-footed in the center of the square, his arm tucked against his bleeding side, his hand clamped over his bleeding shoulder and his sword dangling loosely in front of him. Still, scully stayed off, wisely choosing to prick him a few more times and let him bleed to death, rather than risk a last, gasping death lunge from the disabled though skilled swordsman. Now it was Scully's turn to cavort for the crowd, whistling his blade in the air with the panache of a fencing master, preparing to assume the role of Champion.

While he stood like King Arthur with his sword raised above his head, Hill sprang suddenly out of a low crouch, swinging his sword in an ungainly but strong swath, catching scully high on his good leg with the razor-sharp edge of his steel blade, severing and snapping muscles and bone like shrouds in a gale. Scully went down like a tree, sword clattering across the stage, while Hill stood over him, his sword pointed at his heart, still Hockley-in-the-Hole champion.

A moment later, the judge and his two physicians climbed up onto the stage, followed by Scully's wife. When Hill was declared the winner once again, he somehow managed to lift his bloody sword into the air and was rewarded with a resounding cheer from the frenzied crowd. They had seen a good fight, lots of blood, and their Champion would live to fight another day.

About Scully, one could not be sure. While a few strong men held him down and the crowd pressed up close to see the wound, the physicians stitched his horribly gashed leg. Through it all, Scully screamed with pain--which was a good sign--although it seemed to offer little hope to his wife, who sat beside him with a look of utter defeat bordering upon hatred, whether for their future or just her failed husband, left now with not one but two crippled legs.

Chester was unaffected by either the blood or the loss of five pounds. "Let's go watch the women," he said, pulling me after him.

"What do the women do?" I asked, thinking perhaps they ran a footrace for the men's' amusement.

"They box, the same as men," he answered.

"What! With bare fists?"

"More than that."

And indeed, I did that day witness two half-naked women boxing upon a stage with all the ferocity of any two men I'd ever seen. Before the third round was over, both young women were gasping through broken, bloody noses and split lips, and one had lost an ear to the sharp teeth of the other. Each round lasted until a knockdown, when the women were allowed to rest for a few minutes while they were attended to by their husbands. Then the battering resumed, lasting for the better part of an hour, by which time each woman was red as an Indian with blood, sweat and tears. It amazed me that the two would stand and pound each other with clenched fists and never go to wrestling or hair-pulling, until I learned they were each holding a crown in one fist, and the first to drop her coin was the loser. The winner that day, a pretty milkmaid who'd been accused of adultery with her opponent's husband and had accepted her challenge, was awarded two crowns and the loser got none.

Chester lost a pound each on this and the next bout, then wandered over to the dog fight to wager on a scarred bulldog who looked a sure thing. But alas, the favored beast grew careless as scully, and the terrier locked onto his throat and would not let go till he was dead. Chester looked into his purse and decided it was time to go.

It had been a costly day for Tweakham, but it did nothing to harm his appetite. We supped that evening at an inn near the waterfront, where fish and oysters and fowl and roasted meats were heaped prodigiously upon our communal table. Most of the men at our table were sailors or dockworkers from nearby, attracted no doubt as much by the steady parade of pretty maids who served us, as by the food and drink. When I remarked that the girls were unusually bonny, Chester said, "They do double duty."

"Double duty?"

"They're fluters."

"After today I should welcome some flute playing," I said.

"They don't play, they perform," he said, struggling to open an oyster.

"At what?"

"Tumbling and frisking."

"They're acrobats?"

"Back benders, surely."

"You mean they're...?"

"Sausage-grinder, nutcrackers..."

"Why couldn't you have just said so?"

"I did. Are you game?"

"I wouldn't want to arrive home with the pox," I said, although one fulsome beauty was most attractive to me.

"You'll not get poxed by a fluter," he assured me.

I was thinking about it when someone in the front room shouted, "Press gang!" and by the time we were up and out of our chairs, the place was aswarm with men pointing pistols at us. We were all talking at once, explaining why we should not be pressed, when a naval officer stepped in and ordered us to be silent. Confident that the order did not apply to him, Chester informed the officer in a withering voice that he was, "... Sir Archibald Tweakham's son and a student at Gray's Inn."

The officer crossed to him, looked him up and down, took the lapel of his homespun coat in his fingers and said, "Your judicial robe?"

"Merely a gentleman's disguise," Chester replied impatiently.

"More a liar's coat I should say," the officer said, to a laugh from the pressmen.

"You insolent Tar!" Chester exclaimed, and was immediately cudgeled to the floor by a pressman, where he lay quite still in the sawdust, groaning softly.

"Any more law students here?" the officer asked. No one said anything. "All man o' war's men are we then...? You?"

"I'm no law student," I said.

"Good. Pick him up and let's go."

With Chester hanging half conscious over my shoulder, we were led out into the dark courtyard and down to the embankment, where we turned away from London Bridge and marched east towards the sea. I looked for a chance to break and run but the armed guard was pressed tightly together on our right, and to the left lay the tidal mud flats that would swallow me to my hips if I jumped. Too, I could not abandon Chester, who plainly lacked the sense to survive in this unfamiliar world. And there was nothing to worry about, Chester's father would get us out of this.

After stumbling along in the dark for a mile or so, we were marched up onto a dock where a group of naval officers sat at a lantern-lit table, recording the names of the other unfortunates who'd been captured that night. Although every man in the line knew he'd be viciously cuffed for it, nearly every one of them pleaded to be released. Most claimed wives and children, some had already served, and the rest were too sick to serve. I would have entered a desperate plea myself, but our officer effectively robbed me of the little chance I had.

"This one with the knob on his head is a nobleman, see he gets a good cabin," he said.

I tried to confirm this, but we were thrust roughly into the barge before I could get the words out. When the last man was shoved in, the hatch was closed and we were left in the dark. All around me, men were groaning and sobbing at their cruel fate. The residual stench of our prison--there were only a few barred windows at the top of the sloping walls--was already nauseating, but when the drunken men began vomiting and relieving themselves, it became overpowering. Chester was perhaps a bit more fortunate than I, as he remained partly senseless through most of the night.

When the first of the dawn light began poking through the bars above, I shook Chester awake and forced him to pay heed.

"We must get word to Sir Archibald," I said. "Where is he?"

"Dead," he mumbled.

"No…! Someone else then, an uncle or a brother--"

"Uncle Jacob--never come--hates me…"

"Why?"

"I inherited everything. I get killed--it all goes to him."

"Shit. Shit shit shit! Do you have any money?"

He went through his pockets, muttering that he'd lost a bit at Hockley, and came up with but a pound. It was no more than I had. I took Chester's pound, left him there and worked my way over and through the grumbling crowd to the hatch. I rolled one of the pound notes like a cigar and stuck it through the small peephole near the top. It took only a moment before the note was pulled from between my fingers.

"Thanks, mate," the grateful sentry said.

"Would you like ten more?" I asked through the hole.

"Let's see it," he answered.

I inched the second note partly through the hole, then snatched it back when he tried to pull it the rest of the way through.

"Take a message to my Captain," I said.

"First the money."

"Bring him here and you'll be paid," I promised.

He wanted half now and half when he delivered, but I held firm and he soon agreed to my terms. One pound was a lot of money for a Royal Naval Seaman, but nine more was a fortune. I gave him Kidd's name and told him where to find the ship, and he promised to go there as soon as he was relieved.

We spent the rest of the day in our fetid prison without food or water, and no matter how much we howled and pounded, the hatch would not be opened. I was beginning to think our guards had deserted us and my Hermes had fled with my pound, when suddenly the hatch was thrown open and my name shouted out.

"Come, Chester," I said, pulling him to his feet, "We're getting out of here."

Although his senses had returned, his head pained him so sorely that he had done little else all day but lie on the deck and groan. It was difficult getting to the hatch, as the prisoners had lunged for the light the moment they saw it, begging for food and water, but a couple of tars with cudgels managed to clear the way for us.

"Which one's Rousby?" the officer at the hatch demanded.

When I said I was he, I was pulled out onto the dock alone and the hatch slammed behind. I tried to explain that Chester should be allowed to come along, but the officer had been ordered to bring out me and none other. Captain Kidd, accompanied by the young tar who had carried my message, was waiting beside a cab on the embankment.

"Thank God, sir, you found me!" I gratefully exclaimed.

"It was no small matter gettin' ye out" he said churlishly. "Did ye promise this man ten pounds?" I said I did and Kidd gave him the money. "Get in the cab."

"But I've left my friend in there," I said, pointing back at that hellish barge.

"Then 'e's a naivy man now," Kidd said, pushing me into the cab. I tried to explain that Chester was a law student and the son of a nobleman and unfit for a man o'war, but Kidd was unmoved. "I'll 'ave ye know, Lord Bellomont 'ad t' go t' the Treasurer o' the Naivy hisself t' get ye out o' this. And it's only cuz 'e's a member o' the syndicate n' Bellomont told 'im ye was indispensable t'our venture that I was able t' get even you out. So ye c'n forget about Chester. Take us t' Deptford!" he shouted, and the cab moved off, leaving Chester to his new career.

I spent much of the little time remaining to me in London looking for someone who might be able rescue Chester, but alas, I had no luck. His mentor at Gray's Inn, the same barrister who had found him wanting in Torts, listened patiently to my account of his student's plight, then coldly informed me that Chester's misfortune might be for the best.

"The young man does not think like a lawyer," he said.

If lawyers don't think like the rest of us, I pondered as I left Gray's Inn, why do we trust them to make our laws?

I next found my way to a kind of eating house in Lombard street, where Chester's Uncle Jacob worked at insuring ships' cargoes. He was at first too busy to speak to me--running between tables as he was with slips of paper, jotting down names and sums--until I blurted out the reason for my coming. Then he stopped, calculating his nephew's chances of survival aboard a man o' war no doubt, and smilingly informed me there was nothing he could do.

A short while later I found myself again pressed, this time aboard the Adventure Galley with Captain Kidd and seventy privateers, bound for New York.

Chapter 11

Homecoming

Lest my Judges leap to the conclusion that my presence aboard the Adventure Galley meant that I intended to go privateering, let me assure you that I was only there because I, like a transported convict, had no choice in the matter. Kidd claimed he had only been able to obtain my release from the Royal Navy after convincing Lord Russell (his partner and Treasurer of the Navy no less) that I was a keen gunnery officer (they were in short supply owing to the French war) and therefore vital to the success of their mission. This was of course balderdash but, indebted to Kidd as I was for my freedom, I felt I could not then forsake him. But I swear, Your Honors, I had every intention of abandoning Kidd and his enterprise just as soon as we arrived back in New York, where we were headed to enlist more volunteers. And that, my respected Judges, was the only reason I happened to be aboard the Adventure Galley when she sailed from London that late winter's day in 1696, so help me God.

The sun was barely risen when we slipped quietly from Deptford, where Mr. Livingston, Lord Bellomont, the Earl of Romney and several lesser well-wishers had gathered to bid us bon voyage. The five other Whigs who made up the syndicate, including the King, had chosen to send their representatives to the launching, which caused me to wonder if this was really the patriotic enterprise Lord Russell claimed it to be.

Although I had decided while in England to end my friendship with Sarah, I must admit that I was pleased at the prospect of seeing her again, if only to say good-bye forever. For I was firmly decided that after arriving in New York and collecting my pay from Captain Kidd (which he was still dangling before me like a carrot on a stick), I was going to take the next ship home. Perhaps not the very next ship, as I might stay in New York for a fortnight or so, just to spend a little time with Sarah's two lovely daughters, whom I'd missed very much. It gave me a good feeling to be sailing to New York with, for the first time in my life, a firm life's plan in mind.

However, owing to Captain Kidd's bloated arrogance, I very nearly found myself back on a British man o' war along with our entire crew, before we'd even sailed as far as Greenwich. Kidd was loathed by the officers of the Royal Navy, who'd been able to do nothing but watch helplessly as he strutted along the waterfront in one or another of his flamboyant new uniforms, bragging about his Royal Commission to hunt pirates, while freely recruiting seamen desperately needed for the war. Once on the water, however, the privateer was required to pay proper military homage to any Royal Navy vessel he encountered, or else suffer serious consequences. I was therefore incredulous when, as we were approaching a menacing man o'war, Kidd stood silently on the quarter deck, arms crossed, chin jutting out like a bowsprit, while the crew waited tensely for his order to dip the colors and fire a salute. But no order came. Not even after the man o'war fired a warning shot across our bow! Emboldened by their foolish Captain, the men climbed up into the rigging, turned their backsides to the Royal yacht, dropped their breeches and clapped their butts. I was sick with fear.

Naturally, this was too much for the Royal Navy and so, before we'd proceeded much farther down the Thames, our way was blocked by another Royal yacht, and we were boarded by armed marines. Kidd was arrested and confined to his cabin, while the rest of us were herded together and taken aboard the Duchess, where we were locked below decks. Suddenly Kidd's crew of arrogant civilians was a sorely humbled and woeful group of man o' war's men, along with one innocent boy. We remained in this sorry prison for nearly a fortnight, when, to my great surprise, we were ordered released by Lord Russell himself. It was the second time I'd been saved by the Treasurer of the Navy, and I was once again a most grateful privateer. But as I looked up at the Captain of the Duchess, glowering at us from his quarterdeck as we returned to the Adventure Galley and her gloating Master, I had the uncomfortable feeling that his long face was matched by a long memory. Captain Kidd, however, with a grand ship and the patronage of the King (so it was said) and Junto, was little concerned about the hurt feelings of the Royal Navy. He broke out a ration of rum to celebrate his crews' homecoming, and by the time we reached Greenwich we were a ship of drunken sailors.

Our voyage, by way of the shorter northern route rather than south to the West Indies and then north along the American coast, took just over six weeks, which Captain Kidd felt was fine time for the Adventure Galley's maiden voyage, fetching us up to Robert Livingston's dock on a beautiful spring day in 1696. Sarah and the girls, hats and ribbons billowing in the wind, were there to greet us, which, owing to my vow, thrilled me even more than I wished. And when Sarah chastely kissed my cheek, under her husband's watchful eye, I sensed that she was equally thrilled to see me. And when Captain Kidd enlisted me to see Sarah and the children home, as he had to stay and secure the ship, I worried that my vow might be sorely tested.

I tried to explain to Sarah, as we rode to the house in her carriage, that I should not be staying long in New York, and she should therefore drop me at an inn. But neither she nor the children would hear of it. Owing to my weary state after the long voyage, I consented to remain in my old room that first night, but insisted that I would be moving the next day. And after that first night back, listening to the grunting and squealing and bed-banging that came from Sarah and the Captain's room, I was more convinced than ever that I must get out of that house as quickly as possible.

However, when Kidd returned to see to his ship the next morning, after telling his wife he'd be quite busy for the next few days, I reluctantly agreed to stay and keep Sarah and the children company. But only until the Captain should be free to take up that pleasant duty himself. There were naturally a few minor repairs to be made to the Adventure Galley after her shakedown cruise, and almost a hundred more sailors had to be added to her crew. The King had been willing to allow Kidd seventy men--half experienced seamen, half lubbers--but any more than that when the French were threatening to invade England, would appear unpatriotic if not treasonous. So the rest of the crew had to be picked up in New York. Unfortunately, Governor Fletcher (who'd not yet returned to London, claiming hostilities with the French and the Indians kept him in New York) was no more willing to part with men needed for the war than was the Royal Navy. Fletcher showed up shortly after we'd arrived, hoping to find Robert Livingston aboard the Adventure Galley, so that he might kill him for his role in his recall.

"Livingston's not here!" Kidd called down from the deck.

"I'm comin' aboard t' see for myself!" Fletcher said, starting up the gangplank.

"Ye 'ave no rights aboard this ship," Kidd said, blocking his way.

Seeing seventy fearsome privateers ready to do Kidd's bidding, Fletcher halted near the foot of the gangplank and inquired hesitantly, "Says who?"

"The King o' England," Kidd said. Then he carefully removed his letter of marque from its envelope and slowly read it aloud to the Governor from beginning to end.

"What the hell's 'at supposed t' mean?" Fletcher called up when he'd finished.

"It means I'm authorized by the King o' England t' take a hundred New Yorkers privateerin'," Kidd replied.

"And where d' ye think you're gonna get 'em? Every able-bodied New Yorker is either up fightin' the French or hidin' out in the Jersey swamps."

"They'll come when they 'ear my offer," Kidd replied confidently.

In the end, Fletcher went away, chastened but satisfied that Kidd would never find a hundred men to crew his ship, letter of marque or no letter of marque.

Yet within a very short while, word of Kidd's Royally sanctioned privateering expedition reached far back into the deepest and darkest corners of the Jersey swamps as, one by one, the dodgers and deserters flitted into town by the dim light of the moon and made their way to the Adventure Galley. I was surprised and a bit troubled to learn that Sarah's young brother, Samuel Bradley, a somewhat fragile boy, was among those who wished to join his brother-in-law's crew. When I heard this from Captain Kidd, I went looking for Sarah and found her in the root cellar at the back of the garden, twining dried flowers and vines together into fanciful patterns. When I asked what she was doing, she jumped.

"Christopher, you startled me. I'm afraid I'm wasting my day," she said, displaying a flower-laced crown of thorns.

"Not at all, they're beautiful," I said, stepping down into the small room. I lifted one up and held it to the light from the open door. "It looks like a star encrusted with roses."

"I never know what shape they'll take. Or at least I try not to know--to do them without thinking. I suppose that sounds much like a woman."

"I suppose it's all right to do some things without thinking," I said, laying down the star. "The Captain tells me your brother is sailing with him."

"Yes."

"The voyage will be rigorous, Sarah. I believe you should urge him not to go."

She looked up from the crown she was weaving and smiled. "It's too late. William has already filled Samuel's head with visions of gold. But he's promised me that he'll keep him away from any danger," she said, with her beautiful but innocent smile.

"Sarah, there is no place on a pirate ship that's safe from danger," I explained. "Even if the Captain should somehow keep your brother out of range of swords and guns, there's still scurvy and storms and shipboard accidents and maggoty bread, and water that must be sucked through the teeth to keep the vermin out, and strange poxes that can wipe out a whole ship in a fortnight and…"

"Christopher, stop! How you do talk," she laughed. "William has been sailing all his life and nothing has yet happened to him. So why start worrying now?"

Knowing her brother would go, with or without my blessing, I said nothing more to rob her of her blissful ignorance.

"I shall pray that they make it back," I said, which wasn't strictly true, but I was leading up to something having vaguely to do with religion.

"And I shall pray that all three of you make it back," Sarah replied, which was not the response I'd hoped for.

"Sarah, I'm not going with them," I said.

"Not going...? But of course you are. William told me so."

"I haven't told him yet. You're the only one I've told. I intend to go back to England, Sarah."

"England... I see." She bit down on her lower lip as she often did when troubled. "There's a girl...?"

"No, there's no girl."

"When you spoke of prayer just now--I thought you wished to confess your lust."

"My lust is only for you, Sarah."

"And mine for you, Christopher." She pressed the flowers to her breast and looked down at her muddy feet. "I have sinned much in my mind while you were away."

"Not so much as I."

"My sins were very black."

"Mine were blacker."

"Shall I confess my sins to you?" she asked. "Or would you like to confess yours to me?"

"I should not like you to kneel in the mud," I said.

"I could raise my skirts," she said, lifting her eyes shyly to mine. "Shall I?"

I inhaled deeply and replied, "Yes."

Slowly she lifted her skirts, up past her thin ankles and swelling calves, inching the hem slowly, up to the knees themselves, pink and dimpled, then finally over the top, and I could not restrain a faint gasp before she sank to her knees in front of me.

"While you were away, I dreamed of you every night," she began. "And my dreams were so real that in the morning I felt you had been with me. I could see the place on the bed where you had been, and it was still warm and I could still see you there."

"Was I naked?"

"Yes. You were completely naked. And so was I. I shouldn't say such things, I know, but it was only a dream."

"We're not responsible for our dreams," I said.

"Thank you."

"Did you see my sex?"

"Yes, I saw your sex. It was standing up like--like a strong plant. Like a thick, stiff root. Huge. Unlike any I'd ever seen. I wanted to see it better so I got closer."

"How close?"

"This close."

"Did you touch it?"

"Yes--yes--I couldn't help myself. I wrapped both hands around it. Then I put it between my breasts…"

"Were they big and soft?"

"Huge--and soft as pillows."

"But your nipples were hard…?"

"Hard as diamonds. And they glittered like rubies. And you kissed them and licked them and bit them. And then I kissed you and licked you and bit you. And then we did things that no man and woman have ever done before."

"What things?"

"I can't tell you."

"It's a dream, you're not responsible."

"All right, I'll tell you."

Then she told me of our lovemaking in her dreams, and in truth it was even more fantastic and exciting than anything we'd ever done before. So much so that when it came my turn to confess my lust, I'm very much afraid that my imagination was no match for her dreams. But it didn't matter, as Sarah's enthusiasm was more than sufficient for the two of us, and by the end of the afternoon we were both more spent and satisfied than ever we'd been before.

And more I saieth not.

Except to acknowledge Cotton Mather's small contribution to this--
this game of priest and penitent which I had earlier introduced to Sarah,
and which we thereafter together greatly improved and enlarged upon,
until it attained for us the glory of a sacrament. The dream element,
however--which I thought nicely freed Sarah of whatever few inhibitions
remained with her until that time--was something new, something I
thought had arisen quite spontaneously and would most certainly be
kept in the act. When Sarah later confessed to me that she had only
made up her dreams, I was amazed. Could it be that women were
sexually superior to men both physically and mentally? Or was it just
that Sarah was not the same as other women, that there had been some
confusion at birth and she had somehow been endowed with the lusty
proclivities of the male of the species? It was perhaps an unfortunate
condition, but one which I could overlook.

There were many new faces in New York that summer. They came
from as far away as Philadelphia and Boston, alerted by Captain Kidd's
expansive broadsheet promising *Great Wealth and Riches under Legal
and Lawful Commission of Their Royal Majesties King William and Mary*.
They were mostly desperate men, unemployed bakers, shoemakers,
carpenters, clerks and the like, men whose services and goods were no
longer required, owing to the war with the French. And like poor Scully
of Hockley-in-the Hole, they hoped, against all odds, to land one lucky
blow and come home rich and wealthy men.

Many of these men arrived half-starved, in ragged clothes, lacking
funds to outfit themselves for a *no prey no pay* voyage. Every sailor was
required to provide his own pirate's tools--musket, pistol, cartridge
box and musket--and he'd better bring along a supply of clothes and
supplemental rations, lest he soon become a naked skeleton. A single
man might require ten or fifteen pounds to get him over a voyage of one
or two years, but a married man with children might require thirty or
forty pounds to support his family while he was gone. This presented a
problem to Kidd, whose own resources were too crimped to permit even
a small advance to these impoverished but ambitious men. However, the
bankers of New York, who seemed somehow able to make money out

of any situation with just paper and quill, quickly devised a scheme to enrich themselves handsomely, at the considerable expense of those poor sailors who could not make the voyage without some financial backing. These well-dressed businessmen could be found on the dock each day, offering loans to sailors in exchange for a percentage of their expected plunder, anywhere from a quarter to three quarters, depending upon the man's prospects and how desperate he was to make the voyage. An experienced sailor, who was entitled to a full share, could negotiate a larger advance than a lubber, who was entitled to just half. Although the profit to the bankers seemed to me unconscionable, sometimes more than half a poor sailor's take, so too did the risk. Collecting a debt from a pirate, after all, is not the same as collecting from a merchant. But these bankers were no fools. Before they would loan a sailor a shilling, they first required that Captain Kidd guarantee that his crew would not be paid until their sponsor's debts had been satisfied. And to protect themselves still further (should the ship be sunk and there be no fortune), these wily bankers then gathered their contracts in piles and sold them off to their customers. So whether the venture succeeded or failed, the bankers had already secured a handsome profit for themselves, if not for their customers.

Besides the impoverished lubbers, there were also a good number of experienced pirates in the group, men willing to abandon their usual ship so that they might sail under the protection of a letter of marque, a few of whom had sailed before with Kidd. These professional buccaneers weren't interested in coming home rich and wealthy men and resuming the duties of husband and father, but only in continuing in the life of rape and plunder, safe from the Royal Navy, if not from the guns and swords of their prey. It occurred to me as I sat at the table beside the Captain, making notes while he interviewed each applicant, that putting together a crew with such cross-purposes might present discipline problems later on. I was moved to express my concern following an interview with a mean-eyed gunner named William Moore, who was unabashedly more interested in plunder than the conditions of Kidd's commission. Captain Kidd, however, saw no danger in the mix.

"'ere's nere been no mutiny on any o' my ships," he stated, fanning at my caution..

"Was it not mutiny when your crew stole the Blessed William?" I posed.

"'at was an unusual situation--they thought I was goin' t' make Royal Naivy men outta them."

"And are you not trying to make lawful privateers out of pirates? Do you expect a man like Moore to be content preying only on other pirates, when he sees the ships of the East India Company wallowing by, stuffed with gold and jewels but hardly a gun in sight?"

"They know the rules by which we sail," he replied confidently.

"Aye, sir. And the farmers and clerks will have no trouble obeying them. But pirates don't sail the same course."

"Privateers, damn ye! They'll sail the course I set for 'em or they'll swim for shore. Now let's 'ave no more talk o' mutiny lest ye be puttin' a hex on us. Bring in the next man."

"Yes, sir," I muttered, crossing to the hatch. When I threw it open I saw a sight I'd long ago decided sadly that I should never see again.

"Chindomacuba!"

"Christopher…?" he asked, in his high-pitched voice, while staring incredulously at me.

"Yes, it's me!"

"Good gosh, I tot you be dead!"

"And I thought *you* were dead!" I exclaimed, happily embracing the healthy, black giant.

"'ere, what's all this?" Captain Kidd asked.

"It's Chindomacuba! The man who rescued me when I was being chased by Mason and Burgess and Culliford!" I reminded Captain Kidd. "I thought he'd been killed with the Stono people, but here he is, alive and well! However did you escape?"

"I doan escape, I be off huntin' when dey come. Den when I get back, eberybody dead. I find your clothes, I tink you be dead too. But here you be, alive like me! Ain't dot a joke?"

"A horrible joke. But what are you doing here?" He was a strange sight, dressed all in buckskins decorated with feathers and beads.

"I goan be a pirate like you tole me. I shouldda listen to you den, steada go out west. I tell dem Indians de white men comin' t' get 'em, but dey jus' laugh at me. So fuck 'em, I go be pirate, get rich," he said, showing me one of Kidd's broadsheets from somewhere out west.

"And you shall," I said, turning to Captain Kidd, "I urge you to sign him, sir, for you'll not find a better man than Chindomacuba."

"I don't doubt that, just from the look of 'im," Kidd said. "But I can't 'ave a black man servin' in me crew."

"Black or white, sir, Chindomacuba is one of the finest men I've ever known," I informed the Captain.

"'at may be but 'e's still a slave. And as I been charged by the King t' fit out a legal ship, I can't steal somebody else's property."

"He's not property, he's a man!"

"I can see 'e's a man, but the law can't!" Kidd fired back. "Now I can't take 'im n' 'at's final. So show 'im out n' bring in the next man."

"Bring him in yourself, I quit!" I blurted.

"What ...!"

"And don't forget you owe me for two voyages! Come," I said, pushing Chindomacuba to the hatch.

"Ye walk out n' ye'll nere see a farthin'!" Kidd called after me, as I slammed the hatch.

Pulling Chindomacuba after me, I strode past the line of prospective pirates and down the gangplank, pushing through the greedy bankers waiting there, shouting out their offers like Hockley-in-the-Hole punters.

"I tink mebbe you talk too fast, Christopher," Chindomacuba said, padding beside me in deerskin moccasins.

"I was going to quit anyway," I answered. I regretted that I would now probably never see my money, but not enough to go back and apologize.

"Where we goin'?" he asked.

"To Captain Kidd's house to collect my things," I answered.

"You libin' wid de Captain?"

"I was."

"I'm sorry you losin' your house too."

"That's the least of my loss," I said, as we turned up the street to the house.

Sarah stared in amazement as Chindomacuba stooped to enter through the front door. I introduced him briefly and, without asking her permission, told him to wait for me in the parlor while I went upstairs. While I was filling my bag with my few possessions, Sarah entered the room.

"Chindomacuba told me what happened," she said, speaking softly. "He thinks you might have acted hastily. So do I."

"You know I never intended to make the voyage, Sarah. I had to tell him some time, so it might just as well be now as later," I said, stuffing a shirt into the bag.

"I know," she said. "But I hoped you would change your mind."

"Why--so that I might look after your husband and your brother? Well no more, Sarah. I have to start looking after myself."

"Then who will look after me?" she said, laying a hand on mine as I attempted to draw the rope closed.

"Sarah, I would look after you for the rest of my life if you would but allow it."

"Allow it? Dearest, I desire it more than anything."

"Do you mean it?" I fairly gasped.

"Of course."

"Then I'll stay!" I said, knocking my bag to the floor as I reached for her.

"But you can't," she said, dancing out of my grasp.

"But you just said..."

"I said it only because I'm a weak woman. And being a weak woman I can't trust myself to be here alone with you in the house."

"Oh, Sarah..." I groaned, collapsing to my knees, elbows on the bed. "Pr'ythee, what more can happen. We've been naked together, we've done everything *but* fornicate, and I'm not sure we haven't done that."

"Christopher!" she exclaimed, clapping her hands to her cheeks.

"But it's true! And I've loved you with all my digits save one."

"No!" she shrieked.

"Yes! We've sinned so often in so many ways that there's no reason we should not commit the final sin!"

"We haven't, Christopher, we haven't! All we've done is play games together! Innocent childrens' games!"

"Innocent! Sarah, our games are more infernally diabolic and maddeningly lustful than any sweaty, rutting, sexual act I have ever known."

"You haven't! You told me you were innocent!"

"No, Sarah. I said it was only after you that I realized how innocent I had been. You've shown me things I could never have dreamed on my own, not with the help of all the whores of Babylon."

"How you talk--I won't hear it!" she cried, covering her ears.

"Listen to me!" I demanded, pulling her hands down. "You've destroyed me, Sarah--you've ruined me for any other woman."

"How can you say such horrid things! They were just games, you said so yourself!"

"No, they were lies we told each other so that we might have our pleasure without any guilt. But we can't be children forever, some time we must face the truth. Do you love me, Sarah?"

"I do, like a brother."

"No! Like a lover!"

"You mustn't say such things!"

"It's time they were said! Answer me! Do you love me like a lover?"

"Very well, yes. I love you--like a lover."

"Thank you," I sighed, releasing her hands.

"But you can't stay."

"No, Sarah, no..." I groaned.

"Forgive me, Christopher. I know my brain is addled, but it's only because I'm a poor woman. I'm married to one man, yet I love another. But I must pretend I don't, else I'm in danger of throwing everything up and running off to the wilds of Jersey with my lover."

"Do it, Sarah! Throw up everything and run off with me," I urged.

"What, give up this house...?"

"I'll build us a house."

"But what should we live on? No, Christopher, it isn't possible," she said, shaking her head.

"Houses and money aren't important, love is important! You must choose between Captain Kidd and me."

"My darling no--I could never do that! I love you both too much."

"Then spare me harm and choose me. Or spare Captain Kidd and choose him. Or spare us both and allow me to stay here with you while he goes pirating."

"The temptation would be too great," she said shaking her head.

"You haven't heard a word I've said!" I exclaimed.

"Christopher, I have! It's only because I'm a woman that I might not've understood it all."

But I was beginning to think she understood all too well. I knew that she loved me more than her husband, yet her love for her children and her house and her furnishings and her steady income was sufficient to offset whatever advantage this represented to me.

"Do you mean you would love me more if I were rich?" I asked.

"I could never love you more than I love you now," she pledged. "Therefore someday I must love you less. And on that day it would be good to be rich."

"I see. So if I sail with your husband and come home a rich man, then you would be willing to come with me to New Jersey?"

"Well, maybe not New Jersey," she answered.

"But you would come away with me..."

"I would see less objection to it," she replied.

It was as good as I would get. "Very well, I'll make the voyage."

"Dearest!" she exclaimed and kissed me on the cheek.

"Providing the Captain will take me back," I cautioned.

"Don't worry, I'll see that he does," she promised.

Suddenly I remembered the man downstairs who had saved my life. "Chindomacuba--I can't leave him!"

"Why not?" she asked innocently.

When I told her how he had saved me from pirates she agreed, much to her credit and the shame of her husband, that something had to be done.

"We must convince William to take him along," she said firmly.

"He'll never do that," I assured her. "Since becoming a favorite of the King and the Junto, he's become a great stickler for law and order. The law says Chindomacuba's not a man, but the property of a white man."

"Then he shall be your property," she replied easily.

"You mean I should become his master...?"

"Why not...?"

"Because someone else holds his ownership papers," I explained.

"Then get a lawyer to draw up new papers," she replied with an easy shrug.

"Unless you know an unprincipled lawyer who will swear to anything for the right amount of money, I'm afraid that's impossible," I said.

"I know of no other kind," she said, grabbing my hand and pulling me through the door.

And so, that afternoon I became a legal slaveholder. And when Chindomacuba and I sailed out of New York with Captain Kidd on September 6, 1696, I became the first cabin boy in history to sail with his own personal slave.

Chapter 12

Letters Home

Isle of Madagascar
April 30, 1697

My Dear Father,

I am very sorry that it has been so long since I last wrote, but when I tell you the reason I'm sure you will understand. You see, I have been on a ship for the last eight months, sailing from New York to Madeira, then to Brazil, then down around the Cape of Good Hope and up the east coast of Africa to the Isle of Madagascar. Let me quickly explain, before mention of that notorious pirates' haven give you fright, that Captain Kidd and I have been commissioned by King William to hunt and take pirates, not join them. And don't worry, Father, the mission is not so dangerous as it sounds, as the Adventure Galley is a mighty ship of 34 guns and forty oars, manned by 150 of the bravest and finest English and American seamen afloat, and my official duty is but cabin boy to the Captain. Unofficially, however, I am a skilled gunnery officer and, should the need arise, capable of filling that post as well.

I know that despite my assurances this must sound like a dangerous adventure, but believe me when I tell you it is mostly boring labor. So far we have not seen a single pirate ship, and lately all of our time has been spent *careening* the ship--running her up on the beach, propping her first on one side then the other, scraping, caulking, recoating and then refloating her. The Captain says we will be ready to sail within a few days, and with any luck we should capture our first pirate very soon.

I of course only volunteered for this voyage because it is my duty as a loyal Englishman, but if we are successful I also stand to make a fortune, and for that reason, Father, I have made out my last will and testament, leaving everything to you. I don't mean to alarm you, as I fully expect to arrive home hale and hearty within the next several months, but as you always say, better to be safe than sorry. Meantime, be assured that I'm enjoying a relaxing cruise with a wonderful bunch of fellows, and when I next write it will be to tell you of our great success.

Until then, God bless King William and Queen Mary, and you my dear Father.

Your loving son,
Christopher

Isle of Madagascar
May 1, 1697

Dear Sarah,

You can have no idea what a miserable voyage this is turning out to be. By the time we finally reached land, after the slowest and most miserable voyage I've ever endured, half the crew, including your poor brother, was sick with scurvy and had to be put ashore for several weeks to recover. Some might say they're the lucky ones though, as this ship is so hot that no sailor can survive below deck for very long, and to walk the deck is to dance on the griddle. And it's little wonder Samuel became sick after the cruel way the crew treated him when crossing the equator, hauling him up on a plank and dropping him three times into the sea from the mainsail spar. I truly thought they would drown him, but despite my entreaties you husband would do nothing to help his brother-in-law, insisting that he be treated no differently from anyone else. All I can say to that is, if relatives and friends of the Captain are to be treated no differently from anyone else, then from now on I shall give the man wide berth. However, you may rest somewhat easily, as I have since enlisted Chindomacuba to keep an eye out for Sam, and I trust this will spare him the worst.

No sooner had the men recovered from the scurvy- -including your brother I'm happy to say--than we were struck by some mysterious pox that took thirty of our men, some fine New York boys among them, all of them now buried in the sand near the place we careened the ship. Needless to say, with our crew reduced to 120 men, we were scarcely in a position to attack any fully-manned pirate, so the Captain has been forced to shore up our crew with thirty of the most black-hearted, Madagascar seamen I've ever seen, most of them Frenchmen!

The Captain has also insulted the Royal Navy once again, this time far more seriously than the last. By a strange coincidence, on the way over we happened to stumble upon a naval squadron in the South Atlantic commanded by Commodore Warren, the very officer who had ordered our arrest after the back-slapping incident on the Thames. Needless to say, the man does not hold your husband in high regard. He said he'd lost almost a hundred men to scurvy and demanded we send over thirty replacements, which the Captain promised he'd do first thing in the morning. In view of the earlier offense to his dignity, I thought the Commodore was acting with considerable fairness and restraint; an opinion not shared by your husband, however, who waited till dark, then quietly dipped his oars in the water and slipped away. I knew this treachery would come back to haunt us, but you know William, he's convinced that his friends in high places will get him off anything.

And, true to my prediction, it did come back to haunt us. After arriving in Madagascar three months ago, without yet having taken a single pirate ship, we were of course out of supplies and money. But the Captain wasn't worried, he would simply draw a bill of exchange on the King. Hah! It seems Commodore Warren has spread the rumor that we are a pirate and therefore our letter of marque is no longer legal! This is of course false, but because of the position it has put the Captain in, I fear it might yet become a self-fulfilling prophecy. Being broke, he had to either return to England (and face his unhappy investors), or borrow money where he could--from those thirty French cutthroats I now count my shipmates. I don't know what promise your husband was forced to make in exchange for this loan (he keeps close counsel lately), but I can tell it is not to his liking. However, I'm quite sure that our new crew members would much rather attack merchant ships then pirates. I must say, Sarah, I wish to heaven I had not allowed you to talk me into this desperate voyage.

Which brings me to the real purpose of this letter. I have had eight months to think about us and have finally come to the sad conclusion that we can have no future together. Not because I don't love you, but because you don't love me--at least not as much as wealth and security. I was willing to undertake this voyage so that I might have those things and you too, but I've since realized that you played me for a fool. Yes, Sarah, a fool. For my love for you is for better or for worse, while yours for me is only for better. What would happen if I should become a bankrupt? Would you leave me for the first rich man to come along? Or if I should become sick--? Would you unburden yourself by running off with my physician? And when my root ceases to be thick and stiff as a strong plant, would you then run off with the first young swain to come along?

I'm sure you think these charges unfair, Sarah, and by some measure they are. For I've decided that you are a child, and it's unfair to charge a child with the responsibilities of an adult; the responsibilities of loyalty, devotion and constancy. I know you have always considered me the child and you the adult, but in our lovemaking it's you who stubbornly insists that we are but children innocently playing childrens' games, not I. I know that when we were in the potting shed, we were not acting like children. And when we were in my bedchamber, we were most surely acting like two sexually mature adults who knew full well that what they were doing under the cover of silk and lace would have shocked and outraged New York society. And when we were in the Town Square, and in the graveyard beside St. Luke's, and again in the bell tower, we knew very well that what we were doing was beyond the pale of both Church and State.

I am sorry to shock you with these things I know you would prefer to pretend are otherwise, but I hope my doing so will cause you to realize how unfairly you have used me, and understand when I tell you that I am not coming back to you. This is the hardest thing I have ever done, for I continue to love you more than I can ever love any other woman, and knowing you has been highly educational. Yet I cannot pledge myself to you who loves me less than I love you, and so I must sadly say good-bye forever, my Dear Sarah.

With all best wishes for the future, I am

Your former playmate,
Christopher

P.S. I'm sure I need not remind you to destroy this letter.

May 25, 1697
Zanzibar, Africa

My Dearest Sarah,

Last month I mailed a letter to you which I now realize was the greatest mistake of my life, and I now beg you to forgive me what I wrote. The letter was written in a fit of anger and a mood of despondency brought on by a harsh sea voyage, which I unfairly blamed on you. Since then I've realized that I'm the one who is acting like a child, not you, and I have no one to blame for my present state but myself.

There is so much I wish to say--I could write volumes telling only of my love for you--but the pilot is returning to shore at any moment and I must rush this letter to him before he leaves. I will write more fully and explain everything when we next touch shore, which should be only a few weeks.

Meanwhile, I love you with a passion that knows no reason and I am forever,

Your undeserving slave,
Chris

P.S. Don't forget to destroy this letter.

My Dear Father,

As you have no doubt noticed, I have neither dated nor located this letter as I am presently unsure of both. I know only that we are somewhere on the Arabian Sea, where we have been for the last few months, without yet sighting a pirate ship. Despite this, the men's spirit remains reasonably good, and once we find and capture a pirate, which should be any day now, we will all give thanks to God for the success of our mission, and ask that He bless the King in whose name we sail. Meanwhile, we sail on, seeking, seeking, seeking--

I remember what you taught me, Father, that the unexamined life is not worth living, and I've been thinking much about my own life lately. What an odd shape it seems to have taken, despite my efforts to twist it into something graceful and useful. Like a sculpture woven from dried leaves and flowers, one never knows what form it will assume. And what a strong role love plays in the shaping of our lives. Had it not been for Rebecca Hay, I should have never gone to America, or met Captain Kidd and Sarah. Last year I had finally decided what to do with my life--to return to Lyme Bay and become a schoolmaster like you. It should have been a simple thing to do, yet instead I find myself on a ship bound for God-knows-where, and suddenly my future is again no more certain than before.

I'm sorry to bore you with my desultory thoughts concerning my life, but as there's nothing momentous to report, it's the best I can do. I will pass this letter on to a westbound ship or post it when we next touch land, whichever comes sooner.

I am, sir, your loving son,
Christopher Rousby

September 4, 1697
Carwar, India

My Dear Sarah,

No doubt you are confused after receiving one letter saying I should never see you again, then a second begging forgiveness for that hasty letter and the promise of an explanation to come--then nothing for four months. Unfortunately, we have scarcely seen land in all that time, and the situation aboard the Adventure Galley has deteriorated so badly since we sailed from Madagascar, that it is painful for me to write of it.

After leaving Madagascar, we sailed up the cost of Africa to the strait of Babs-al-Mandab, where the Red Sea empties into the Arabian Sea, a place where we were sure to find pirates waiting for the pilgrim fleet from the Arabian port of Mocha--or so our Captain claimed. When the Mocha fleet came through the strait, the Captain eyed a straggler and, thinking her a pirate, ordered the attack. When I saw that she was not a pirate but a merchant ship and shouted it out to the Captain, Gunner Moore and one of the new Frenchmen knocked me to the deck and kicked me.

But not before the Captain heard me, I'm sure. In the end it made no difference, as we were driven off by an escort ship, which left the Captain no more popular with his cutthroats than with me, though for a different reason. When I asked him later if he knew he'd gone after a merchantman and not a pirate, all he'd say was, "I know what I'm up against," and then he ordered me out of his cabin.

After that the crew divided into two groups, pirates on one side, honest men on the other. The honest men wanted to go home, but the pirates wanted to sail to India. So they called an election and the pirates won. I don't know what would have happened if the Captain had refused to honor the vote, but he didn't, and so we set sail for the Malabar Coast. And that's when things began to come apart.

There was a lot of fighting between the pirates and the honest men, and the Captain had to go about with a cudgel and loaded pistols to keep order, knocking more than a few of them on the head from time to time. And as if threatened mutiny weren't enough, the ship was beginning to leak badly, and some of the hard men were refusing to take their turn on the pump, which the Captain could do nothing for, save flog one of them, which would almost certainly set off a mutiny. I tell you, Sarah, this is not so much a ship as a keg of powder, and all the sailors have lighted cigars.

When we were just off the Malabar Coast, we stopped a local trader skippered by an Englishman named Thomas Parker. While the Captain was interviewing him aboard the Adventure Galley, some of our pirates went aboard his ship and tortured his Indian sailors until they gave up their money. Maybe that wasn't the Captain's fault, but nobody forced him to take poor Parker captive after that, which he did.

He claims he needs his local knowledge to hunt pirates, even though all the pirates are back in Madagascar, not India.

When we put into Carwar and the manager of the East India factory rowed out to meet us, I was struck dumb at the sight of William Mason climbing over the rail. You may remember--he was one of the pirates who stole your husband's ship and chased me out of Charleston seven years ago. He was in command of the Jacob when she sailed from New York with your husband's old crew, but by the time he and Robert culliford got to India, they decided they were tired of the pirate's life, so they took an honest job with the East India Company. How the company could have been hoodwinked by two such rapscallions as these is beyond me. In any event, your husband and his old shipmate spent much of the morning trying to convince the other that he was now an honest man, but I don't think either of them succeeded. However, I'm sure the Captain convinced Mason that he was still a harsh disciplinarian.

While they were talking, a bunch of our men deserted, but the Captain took a search party into town and managed to recapture all but ten of them. And when he got them back to the ship, he gave them the worst whipping of their lives. Which didn't sit well with the honest men, as it was their mates who had tried to escape.

I don't wish to worry you, Sarah, but if things turn out badly for us, it's important that someone know what happened aboard the Adventure Galley. William asked me to write to you as he's too busy--we both know he has trouble getting the words in order but can't admit it--and tell you he's fine. But he's not fine. He's a very desperate man. His sponsors want him to take a pirate ship and make them rich, while the pirates among us want him to take a ship of the East India Company and make *them* rich. So far he's managed to keep these rogues in their place, but I'm not sure he can do it much longer.

I'm sorry to write such a gloomy letter, and I hope the next will be filled with good news. Sam is well, except for a stomach cramp, due no doubt to the rich Indian food here in Carwar.

Until you next hear, I am,

Your devoted servant,
Christopher Rousby

P.S. Please keep this letter.

May 30, 1698
Isle Saint Marie

My Dear Father,

At last our mission is done and we will, when the winds freshen in a few months, be setting sail for America. I wish I could say it has turned out to be the great success we had all envisioned when we sailed from New York almost two years ago, but alas, it has not been so. We took no pirates--indeed, until we arrived here (Saint Marie is a small island off the east coast of Madagascar), we didn't even see any--and we failed to secure the kind of riches we had hoped to present to the King. Yet though I return with neither riches nor Royal acclaim, I have learned that virtue for its own sake is more than sufficient reward. The voyage has been long and hard, I am exhausted beyond my twenty-one years, and yet I know I am wiser and stronger for it. But if any harm should come to me because of it, or if you should hear any accusations against me, you have my word, Father, that I never once strayed from the righteous path, and did my best at all times to be a credit to you, to my King and to my country, so help me God.

I shall write again when I reach New York, hopeful that by then I'll know better what my plans are.

Until then I remain as always,

Your loving and dutiful son,
Christopher Rousby

May 30, 1698
Isle Saint Marie

My Dear Sarah,

What a disaster this has been. We were sent out to capture pirates, but instead we have captured a merchantman owned by the most powerful Mogul in India, and once word gets back to London we are surely doomed. Her name is the Quedah Merchant, and in a few months we hope to be sailing her back to New York, as the Adventure Galley now lies rotting on the beach. When I say we, I am speaking of just seventeen men, your husband and long-suffering brother among them.

I'm afraid I was wrong about the rich Indian food, Sarah, as your poor brother's been sick the whole time, but at least he's still alive. A third of our crew was wiped out by the pox, a few by Portuguese gunners, and almost a hundred chose to go pirating with Robert Culliford--who happened to be in Saint Marie when we arrived. That was a dangerous moment, as Culliford expected us to attack him, when in truth we were in no condition to attack anyone. But when he saw that our men were now more interested in *becoming* pirates than *hunting*

them, we both pulled in our guns. The fact that even
our honest men chose to throw in with a treacherous
dog like Culliford, rather than risk a trial, should give
you some idea how desperate our situation is.

I'm happy to say that Chindomacuba didn't go with
them. However, he won't be returning with us either,
as he has married a Madagascar princess and become
the king of her tribe. He has declared war on the slave
traders of Madagascar and is at last a very happy man,
even if, alas, the only one this voyage has produced.

Your husband, meanwhile, is quite convinced that he's
done nothing wrong, but even if he did, his Whig friends
will get him off. He believes his seizure of the Quedah
Merchant was legal because she was flying French colors,
while conveniently forgetting that he tricked her captain
into raising the French flag by showing a French flag of his
own. Then he went aboard with one of his French pirates
who pretended to be our captain, and when the Quedah's
master--who anybody could see was an Englishman--
produced a forged French pass, Kidd pounced on him.

He did the same thing a couple of months before,
when he took a Dutch ship exactly the same way, which
turned out to be hardly worth the trouble. In fact her
Dutch Captain was so poorly paid by his employer,
that he quit his ship and joined Kidd's crew. Even the
Quedah Merchant wasn't a very rich prize, but I'm sure
nobody will believe that when we get back. I think these
Indians can't distinguish one Englishman from another,
for every piracy in the Indian Ocean is blamed on us,
when there are dozens of real pirates, like Avery, taking
fortunes from these waters.

Your husband thinks we shall be saved by the *word*
of the law, not prosecuted by its *spirit*, but I am not so
sanguine. Even if he does prevail with his French passes,
which he carries about like the bones of the saints,

there's still the matter of William Moore, the gunner he hit on the head with a bucket. The Captain says he had to do it or there'd surely have been a mutiny. And it's true the crew came close to mutiny just a short while before, when the Captain refused to attack a ship of the East India Company. By that time they'd been out for more than a year and they hadn't yet made their voyage, and they were becoming impatient. So when Moore wanted to attack a Dutch ship, and the Captain reminded him we were only commissioned to attack pirates, the Gunner said, "That's all well and good for a rich gentleman like yourself, but what about us poor sailors who got nothing to go home to if we don't take a prize?" Then the Captain called him a lousy dog, and Moore said it was him who had made him so. And that's when your husband lost his temper, you know how he is. He just grabbed the bucket that happened to be lying there and smashed it down on Moore's head. Which wouldn't have been so bad if he hadn't died the next day. The Captain says it was a legal execution of a mutineer, but I'd be a lot more comfortable with that if he'd died at the end of a rope, rather than a bucket.

We will be sailing for New York in late summer, when the winds are favourable, but I doubt we will make it in our Indian Ship. Not that she isn't seaworthy, but her unusual design and color will surely attract the attention of the British Navy. I know there are things between us that remain unresolved, Sarah, but in view of the danger we're facing, it seems foolish to plan for the future. Let us hope that my gloomy assessment is unwarranted, and that when I see you next it will be under the best and happiest of circumstances.

I remain your faithful and loving friend,

Christopher

Chapter 13

Limping Home

We finally set sail for America on our Indian barge in November of '98 and didn't fetch up in the West Indies until April of '99. After five months of listening to the Captain's assurances that we would be got off, I was almost ready to believe that my reunion with Sarah might yet be under the best and happiest of circumstances. However, when he chose to avoid the English colonies and put into the Danish island of St. Thomas, it was clear to me that he hadn't even convinced himself that would be safe in America. And when the Danish Governor told us the worst, that the government had declared us pirates and put a price on our heads, I knew then that I should never see Sarah again under any circumstances.

When we sailed out of St. Thomas two days later, five men remained behind, including Sarah's brother whose condition had worsened terribly on the long voyage over. When the Captain urged me to stay and save my own skin, even while knowing that I was one of the few who would testify in his defense, I could do nothing else but sail on with him. I had the feeling at that moment that a kind of transaction had taken place between us, as if the Captain's loss of confidence had somehow strengthened my own. Or maybe it was simply an attempt to atone for my indiscretions with Sarah. Whatever the reason, I decided then that I would see him through this to the end, which was probably no less foolish than my decision to go with him in the first place.

Our only chance was to get to New York where we might enjoy the protection of Governor Bellomont, but dodging the English Navy and the bounty hunters who would surely be waiting for us along the coast, would be all but impossible in our flamboyant Indian ship. So we set sail for Hispaniola, the only place in the Caribbean where we might be welcome, hoping to trade some of our cargo for a new ship. And when we made the acquaintance of John Bolton there, a more loathsome and wily trader than even Robert Livingston, Kidd was sure he had met his man.

While Bolton sailed south to Curacao to bring back some Dutch traders, we concealed our ship up the River Higuey and waited. Presently they arrived and we traded most of our bulky goods, bales of silk and calico, for a couple of thousand pounds and a small ship, the San Antonio. We of course did not get a fair price for our goods, as those Dutch sharpers knew we were in no position to drive a hard bargain, and they therefore pressed us till we fairly bled.

After the first wave of Dutchmen left with their holds stuffed, Kidd commissioned Bolton to trade the goods remaining in the Quedah Merchant, and send a bill of exchange on to him in New York. I thought at the time that the chance of Bolton's bills ever arriving in New York were even less than our own. Then the next day we transferred our chests of gold, silver and jewels, and as many bales of cloth as could be stuffed into the San Antonio, and set sail for New York.

We made our way up the American coast in our small sloop as inconspicuously as possible, anchoring offshore from time to time while I rowed in to gather information, much as I had almost ten years before when chasing Mason, Burgess and Culliford. I was sure I had seen the last of those villains after losing them in the swamps of Carolina, and yet how devilish it was that our paths had continued to cross, and might yet again. At each place we stopped, I listened to ever grander stories of our exploits and the treasure we were supposedly carrying. In Georgia it was three hundred thousand pounds, in Carolina four hundred thousand, while in Maryland a publican swore to me that Robert Livingston himself had told him Kidd was carrying five hundred thousand pounds sterling. Another man, who should write romances, told me Kidd was carrying an Arabian princess, more beautiful than any other woman in the world. He had intended to hold her for ransom, but he had fallen hopelessly in love with her and had rejected the king's offer of a million pounds for her release. If any of these stories were getting back to Kidd's backers--and I didn't see how they could not, as they were on the lips of every man and woman I came across during our voyage--they were in for a bitter disappointment.

More alarming than the inflated tales of our wealth, however, was the hysteria Governor Bellomont had set off by closing New York to pirates. Unable to land safely there anymore after arriving from Madagascar, the buccaneers were abandoning their ships wherever they could, taking whatever plunder they could carry, and disappearing into the countryside. Up and down the coast, the jails were said to be filled to bursting with pirates, and the hills were filled with bounty-crazed farmers and merchants chasing them down with pitchforks and muskets. It was for this reason that Captain Kidd decided he would avoid New York, and send a messenger by land to request that his lawyer meet him on Long Island.

"I'll go," I said.

Captain Kidd shook his head. "It's dangerous, I cannot afford t' lose ye."

"There's no one else you can rely on," I said. The others were either not wily enough to get through, or, given a horse and a few pounds, it was likely they would run off. But the real reason I wanted to go was to see Sarah. I suspect the Captain realized that my devotion to Sarah might get me through, where another messenger would fail. And so, whether he liked it or not, he allowed me to go to New York.

I was put off on the Jersey side of Delaware Bay from where, after purchasing a horse from a larcenous blacksmith, I started out for New York. Two days later I arrived at Sandy Hook, traded my horse to a packet skipper for passage to Manhattan, and arrived at Sarah's house late the next evening.

When she opened the door and saw me standing there in a muddied cape, wearing a beard she'd never seen before, it took a moment before she recognized me.

"Christopher!" she exclaimed, coming into my arms. "You're home!"

"Yes, Sarah, I'm home."

There followed a most warm homecoming, and more I saieth not.

Two days later, accompanied by James Emott, Kidd's lawyer, Sarah and I and her two daughters went by coach to Oyster Bay on the north shore of Long Island to await Captain Kidd. He was of course pleased to see his wife and children for the first time in almost three years, but he was much too concerned with the fate that awaited him to give them his full attention. So while he and Emott discussed how to proceed, Sarah and I and the two girls spent a lovely summer afternoon on the beach at Oyster Bay. By the time we returned to the ship, a course of action had been decided. Emott was to return to New York the next day with Sarah and the children, then go up to Boston the next day, where Governor Bellomont was now headquartered, and present his brief on Kidd's behalf.

"James will tell 'im we took but two ships, both legal prizes, and present 'im wi' the French passes t' prove it," Kidd announced.

It was the same story I had heard countless times on the voyage back--Kidd going about with cudgel and side arms to keep his crew from turning pirate, until they finally deserted him at St. Marie to go off pirating with Culliford. The story was essentially true, but it left out a few things and added others. Such as the claim that the Quedah Merchant had been safely hidden somewhere in the West Indies with thirty thousand pounds worth of goods in her hold.

"Are ye comfortable with that?" the lawyer asked me, after Kidd had finished with his defense.

"Shall I be frank?" I asked the Captain.

"Ye c'n say what ye will t' your lawyer," Kidd allowed.

"With all due respect, sir, I don't think the goods in the Quedah Merchant are worth nearly that much," I informed the lawyer. "But even if I'm wrong, they've surely been stolen by John Bolton by now."

"It don't matter, it's just a negotiatin' point," Emott assured me.

"A legal technicality," Kidd added. "With the ten thousand pounds we got 'ere, plus the thirty what we c'n get, it'll be more'n worth it t' Bellomont t' give us a pardon."

"But if we aren't guilty of anything, why should we request a pardon?" I asked.

"It's just a legal fiction," Emott said.

I was not reassured. If the Governor granted that Kidd had obeyed the law and his investors, Bellomont stood to come in for very little, after expenses and shares to his partners, including the King. But if he arrested Kidd as a pirate, he'd be entitled to a third of everything. However, when I brought this up, Emott assured me there were legal reasons the Governor would never do such a thing.

"And besides that, 'e's a gentleman and a friend," Kidd added.

The next morning, I bade good-bye to Sarah and the children, then remained aboard the Antonio while Captain Kidd accompanied them and Mr. Emott to their coach. The Captain left the ship with a large chest which, he told me upon his return, contained *a few household goods* for Sarah. Then we weighed anchor and made for Gardiner's Island near the eastern end of Long Island, where we sailed about for the next several days, while waiting for word from Emott.

During that time we were visited by three sloops carrying friends of the Captain, each of whom left with a portion of our cargo. We also twice visited John Gardiner on his island, first to buy food and wine, then to leave off fifty-two pounds of gold, five bales of cloth, and a chest of fine silver. I didn't understand why Kidd was stowing his cache in various places if he was so sure Bellomont was going to strike a deal with him, but I said nothing, as the man was already under a great strain.

Finally a letter arrived from Governor Bellomont, filled with kindness and assurances that Kidd would surely be pardoned. He instructed that we should sail to Boston as soon as possible, where our goods would be placed in safe trust, until he should receive orders from England regarding their distribution.

"What did I tell ye?" Kidd exclaimed, waving the letter happily in the air.

I had to admit, he was right again.

We arrived in Boston Harbor on June 30, filled with hope and trepidation. I offered to accompany the Captain when he went to see the Governor, as his aid-de-camp, but Captain Kidd insisted on going alone.

"I could be gone a long time, as me n' the Gov'nor got a lot o' catchin' up t' do," Kidd said, brushing the salt from his best blue coat.

"Yes, sir," I said, and helped him on with the coat.

Young Barlycorne and I rowed him ashore in the skiff, and wished him luck as he stepped onto the beach. He thanked me, then drew himself up and gave me a sharp naval salute, which I returned a bit sloppily. Then I watched as he marched smartly up the beach to his appointment with Governor Bellomont. And that was the last I saw of him.

Early the next morning, a boatload of soldiers boarded our sloop, arrested me and Barlycorne and the rest of the crew, and marched us to the Boston jail, where we remained for the next nine months. Then, on a bitterly cold day in March, I was shipped to England along with thirty-one other prisoners, including Captain Kidd, who was locked somewhere alone in the bowels of the frigate. And to this day, even though, at this writing, we are both confined in Newgate prison, I have not yet seen Captain Kidd. Perhaps we'll meet again on the gallows.

Chapter 14

The Letter of the Law

It took some time to convince myself that I was not dreaming, that the familiar voice calling my name in the darkness was indeed that of my father, and the face I saw when I opened my eyes, though now lined and white-maned, was truly that of my dear father. I could not speak. I could only wrap my arms around him and bury my face against his chest, and cry as I had not since I was a small boy.

While my father patted and stroked me, and spoke to me in familiar, reassuring tones, I became aware that there were others in my dark cell. And when I wiped the tears from my eyes, I recognized the sharply-angled, dark-eyed countenance of the Admiralty lawyer who had commited me to this dungeon.

"Is it time then?" I asked.

"Time...?" my father asked.

"For my execution."

"No, my boy, no," my father said, clasping me again to his bosom. "Mr. Tweakham has seen to that."

"Tweakham...?"

"Aye, mate," I heard, and saw for the first time, Chester Tweakham, standing just behind the Admiralty lawyer.

"Chester!" I exclaimed, getting to my feet. "What are you doing here?"

"Your father has hired me to represent you," he said, grasping my hand.

"We've both been trying to see you for weeks, but with no results," my father explained. "Then we happened to meet at the Old Bailey, and together we've moved mountains."

"You're a lawyer...?" Surely I was doomed.

"Aye, mate. And quite a good one I should say, thanks to the Royal Navy. A few months on a man o' war will straighten anyone up, I'll testify. Certainly would've done you a bit of good to've come along with me," he said, glancing about my sordid place.

"I only wish I had."

"Aye, mate, I'm sure you do. But never mind, you're as good as free now."

"Free...?" I repeated, glancing over at the Admiralty lawyer.

"Dr. Newton has agreed to release you!" my happy father exclaimed. "Thanks to the letters you wrote."

"Letters...?" I said, taking them in my hand. I had all but forgotten, but there they were, the three miserly letters I had written to my poor father over three long years, disgusting, hypocritical documents, blaming everyone for my fate except myself.

"It's plain from those letters that you thought you were serving your King when you sailed with Kidd," Dr. Newton said. "Though I don't know how anyone could remain so naive for so long."

"The lad has always been of a most trusting nature, sir," my father offered.

"I can testify to that," Chester added.

Thank God they hadn't seen Sarah's letters, I thought.

"Still, there is the matter of your statement," Dr. Newton said, holding a page before me.

"What's this?" I asked, beginning to read.

"'Tis but an affidavit swearing you have no knowledge of the King's role in Kidd's syndicate," Chester supplied.

"As well as assurances that you will not testify at Kidd's trial," Dr. Newton added.

"But--I cannot sign such a document," I replied.

"Then you shall be tried for a pirate," Dr. Newton said.

"Christopher, you must…" my father began.

"There is no reason you can't sign," Chester said. "Kidd already has more than enough witnesses."

"Still, I cannot sign until I hear the same from Captain Kidd."

At this, Chester turned to Dr. Newton who, after a moment, shrugged and replied, "It can be arranged."

And that was how I came to see Captain Kidd for the first time in almost two years. He was thin as a skeleton and pale as a corpse, yet he recognized me, even in the dim lamplight, the moment I stepped into his cell.

"Christopher…?" he said hoarsely, struggling to rise from his palette.

"Don't get up," I said, hurrying to him.

But he did, and gripped my hand with surprising strength. His first concern was for me. Only when I assured him that I was well enough, would he answer about himself. He had been sick ever since his passage over in a cold black cell in the bottom of the frigate that brought us, but since being allowed a physician, he claimed to be feeling somewhat better. If so, he must have been near death before, as he was scarcely fit for the noose as it were. I led him back to the palette and sat him down. I began to tell him why I had come, but he wanted to talk more.

"I been before the Admiralty and Parliament, but I ain't yet changed me story. I may go down, but them as put me 'ere is goin' with. Ye know the House voted t' impeach Somers, Orford and Halifax, don't ye?" he asked, turning his feverish eyes on me. His hair was nearly gone, but for some greasy gray strands that hung down from the sides and back, like shrouds from rotting spars.

"I know," I said. "What about the King?"

"They don't care t' 'ear nothin' about the King. I give up on that a long time ago. Ye was right, Christopher, I was a fool t' think I could trust gentlemen. Where there's money at stake, they're no different from pirates--even worse. A pirate'll stab ye in the 'eart, a gentleman in the back. But ye 'aven't told me, Chris, why'd they let ye come?"

"They want me to stab you in the back," I replied.

"Eh…?"

"If I agree not to testify at your trial, they'll set me free."

"I see," he said, nodding thoughtfully. "Then ye must do what they ask."

"Never."

"Ye 'ave no choice."

"I can't."

"Course ye can. I already got more'n enough witnesses willin' t' lie for me. Surely ye don't think I want a 'onest lad like yourself fookin' up me case for me, do ye?"

"I appreciate what you're trying to do, but I'm going to testify," I said.

"No you're not, 'cuz I ain't goin' t' call ye. And if I don't call ye, n' the Crown don't call ye, there's no way ye c'n take the stand."

"So, you've been reading the law," I said, thumbing the papers that rested on the table.

"Much as I can. 'Tis a shame all this education'll be goin' t' the gibbet wi' me."

"Maybe it won't, if you'll allow me to testify."

"Don't flatter yourself, lad. They're goin' t' 'ang me all right, I got no illusions about that. So if you're serious about 'elpin' me, ye'll keep yourself alive n' see t' Sarah n' the girls after I'm gone. Will ye promise me that?" he asked, lifting his eyes to mine.

I couldn't tell if he was thinking of Sarah's welfare or my happiness when he proposed this, but I willingly accepted the charge. "You have my word on it," I said.

"Thank you," he said, squeezing my hand. "I c'n promise, ye won't be sorry."

I wasn't sure of his meaning, but neither did I want to get into it.

When he bade me good-bye some time later later he said, "Takin' care o' Sarah, 'at shouldn't be too much a burden on ye, should it?"

I could not be sure in that dim light, but it seemed, even in the hall of the condemned, that there was some mischievousness behind that deathly grin. I assured him it was no burden, but even if it were, it was one that I would gladly assume. Then I took my last leave of Captain Kidd.

When I left Newgate Prison that day, accompanied by my father and my solicitor, Chester Tweakham, I was sure that I should never again be so happy in this life. Until I arrived at my father's inn on the Chelsea riverbank. There, in a garden bursting with spring flowers, sat a boy of about ten years, more beautiful than any Greek statue, with hair like golden sunflowers and wide eyes green as jade, that were somehow familiar. He looked at my father, then at me and asked, "Papa…?"

My father nodded, then said to me, "Your son."

"My son…?"

"He is called John, after Vicar Hay."

"Rebecca--he's Rebecca's son…?" I stammered.

"And yours."

I started to explain that Rebecca's son had perished in a fire at the charity house, or even if he hadn't he was Percy Dunston's son, when the lad came across the garden, hand extended. And when I took it, felt his firm grip and stared at that radiant face, strong and honest and gentle, I knew at that moment that he could be no one's son but mine.

"My son," I said, falling to my knees and wrapping my arms around him, holding him tightly and pressing my face to his. I could not speak or move until, after some moments, I heard my son say, "Papa is crying."

"Yes, Papa is crying," my father said in a chocked voice.

"We're all crying," Chester said.

"But I'm very happy," I assured my son.

Then I rose and we went into the dining room, where we all sat down to a great feast celebrating my son, and his father's release from jail. Now I was sure that I would never again be so happy in my life.

When I finally dared ask how the boy had escaped the fire (for I dreaded and feared the possibility he wasn't Rebecca's son, and might yet be taken from me), my father, fortunately, had an easy answer.

"Those false rumors you spoke of in your farewell letter did eventually reach me," he said, as he carefully replaced his wineglass on the table. "But by that time Rebecca was in the workhouse for extorting

Mr. Dunston, her poor father was dead, and her baby was in the charity house. I did not doubt that the rumors were false, just as you said, but I nevertheless felt it my Christian duty to rescue the poor child, and so I took him from the charity house, claiming he was my own. I intended to keep him for just three years, until Rebecca returned home from the workhouse to claim him. But during those three years, as I watched the boy grow, I became aware that you were wrong, Christopher. John could only be your son.

"Then Rebecca came back to Lyme Bay, but I only learned about it after those vicious fishwives had driven her off, and I was never able to find her. I managed to trace her as far as Bristol, but there the trail ended."

"And it was there that I picked it up," I said.

"You've seen her?" my father asked.

"Yes," I answered, and proceeded to relate a considerably expurgated version of my meeting with John's mother at Buckmaster's Tavern.

"What is she like?" my son cried excitedly, at learning both his parents were now accounted for.

"Well--she's--she's quite nice."

"Is she beautiful?"

"Not so beautiful as she once was, but she's pretty," I said.

"When will I see her, papa?" the little boy asked.

"When--? Well--New York is quite a way off--"

"But you'll take me to her, won't you, Papa?"

I looked at his large green eyes, so much like Rebecca's, already beginning to well up, and suddenly I realized the fuller implications of my joy. I was not just a father, I was also a husband! Like it or not, I now had to do the honorable thing. I had to marry Rebecca Hay. But worse, I must give up any thought of ever marrying Sarah!

"Yes, son, I'll take you to her," I promised.

And that is how I found myself, one month later, standing hand in hand with my son John on the deck of the Jan Kees II as we drifted down the Thames on the outgoing tide, bound for New York. As we approached the execution dock at Wapping, where the bodies of several pirates, wrapped hideously in chains, hung from the gibbets that lined the riverbank, I tried to direct John's attention to the opposite shore. But John, like all London, was deeply interested in the pirates swaying in the breeze, a horrible reminder to all outgoing seamen of the terrible fate that awaited them should they decide to go on account.

"Which is Captain Kidd?" he asked.

"The first one," I answered.

"Was he a bad man?"

"Sometimes he was bad, sometimes he was good," I answered.

"Like me," he said.

"Like all of us," I said, resting my hands on his shoulders.

"But he repented at the end...?" he said, looking trustingly up at me.

John, like all literate London, had read Daniel Defoe's True Account of the Last Words of Captain Kidd and, unlike those of us who were there that bleak Friday, believed that at the last he had confessed his sins to God and forgiven his accusers. Hah! In truth the Captain arrived quite drunk for his execution, and roundly damned the King and the Junto for their part in his murder, which poor Mr. Defoe could scarcely publish, lest he go the same way himself for treason. Nor did he mention that the first hanging attempt failed because the rope broke. Poor Darby Mullins and a pair of Frenchmen were dispatched well enough, but the most notorious pirate in all the world couldn't even have a new rope.

When the hangman threw him off the ladder a second time, the rope held and Captain Kidd hung choking and strangling for but a few seconds, as young Barlycorne and I were waiting beneath the scaffold to pull on his legs and break his neck. It was a hard thing to take part in the Captain's execution in such a way, but it would have been much harder for him if he'd been left to strangle slowly to death. Barlycorne was there because he and two other boys, being only innocent servants, were found not guilty and released. Yet if I'd been in the dock with my fellow servants, shouting out that the king was involved! there would now surely be one servant hanging in chains beside his master.

"Yes, he repented at the end," I answered.

When we went round the bend at Limehouse, I hoped I was putting it all behind me. But of course that's not possible. I'll remember Captain Kidd and that fateful voyage till the end of my days.

What of the trial, you ask? Hah! Captain Kidd was right, they meant to hang him and they wouldn't let any trial get in the way of that. It lasted two days in the Old Bailey, and before the end of the first day he was found guilty of murdering Thomas Moore--by wooden bucket, and on the next day he was found guilty of piracy. The prosecution produced two witnesses against Kidd--both of whom had joined Culliford's pirate crew and were later captured, along with Culliford--and offered them a pardon in exchange for their testimony. Kidd insisted that his French passes would exonerate him, but the court had somehow misplaced them, and they weren't found until after he'd been hanged. It would've made no difference anyway, as Moore's death was more than enough to hang him. 'tis little wonder he finally gave up his defense, for as he said at trial, a man can be hanged but once. Little did he know—he was wrong again.

There is much irony here, but perhaps the most has to do with Culliford and his crew, who were captured and tried on the same day as Kidd, but in a separate proceeding. All Culliford's crew were found guilty of piracy, but the two who testified against Kidd were pardoned--and Culliford's conviction was set aside! And the reason...? Culliford had agreed to testify against his old shipmate and lover, Samuel Burgess! I shall do everything in my power to see that my son does not become a pirate or a lawyer.

We arrived in New York on a hot July day and proceeded directly to Sarah's house to offer our condolences. Being a well experienced widow, I found her in little need of consolation. Or perhaps it was the curious presence of the young boy waiting in the next room that served to distract and cushion her grief. After a sad moment, she smiled bravely and asked, "Whose beautiful boy is that?"

"He's mine," I replied.

"Yours...? You've adopted a son?"

I shook my head. "He's my natural son."

"Pr'ythee, sir, do not jest with me while I yet bereave," she admonished.

"I do not jest, madam. He is my flesh and blood."

"But--he looks to be ten years or more..."

"I fathered him when I was but fifteen."

"Fifteen..?"

"With the vicar's daughter, an older woman. I left England because I thought Percy Dunston was the father, but I've since learned that I was mistaken. He's truly mine, Sarah. And I intend to make him a proper father."

"Of course you shall, my dear, of course!" she exclaimed, clasping my hands in hers. "He is such a beautiful boy. He'll make a wonderful brother for the girls!"

"There is yet another matter, Sarah…"

"What is that, dear?"

"John's mother--- I've decided to marry her."

"What…!" she gasped, her hands bolting from mine.

"It is not what I wish for myself, you must know that!" I cried. "But it is my duty to her, and to our son."

"No…! No, no…!" she said, shaking her head incredulously from side to side. "Just when we're at last free---This is too cruel—too cruel…"

"I know, I know… I've been thinking about it until my head would split, but there's nothing else for it. If I don't do the honorable thing, I am but a cad and a bounder, and I could never expect you to love such a man as that."

"But if you do the honorable thing, we will not be able to love each other at all! We must think, Christopher, we must think," she said, clasping her hands together and pressing them to her lips.

"I've been thinking of nothing else the whole voyage. There's no way I can marry one woman and yet live with another, not even in New York."

"Yet you lived with me while I was married to William--albeit chastely."

"I was a servant, it was not the same."

"There must be some way," she fretted.

"There is none," I replied sadly. "Not if we wish to keep our honor and our dignity."

"And we do, of course."

"Of course."

"Then it's decided…." she said in a weak, resigned voice.

"Yes, it's decided."

"It isn't fair!" she cried suddenly. "I've been made a widow twice in one day."

"I'm so very sorry," I said, opening my arms to her.

"When will you go back?" she asked, pressing her face against my chest.

"Go back...?"

"To England--to marry."

"No, no--she's here, in New York. I don't know exactly where she lives. I only know that she works in taverns."

"She's a barmaid...?"

"More an entertainer."

"I see. And where will you stay while you look for her?"

"I haven't decided. I suppose I must find an inn suitable for a child."

"I doubt you'll find one of those in all of New York," she said. "You could leave him here with me."

"If he wouldn't be a bother..."

"He'll be a pleasure. And I see no reason you cannot stay too."

"Do you think--you being a widow...?"

"You are still my servant, are you not?" she asked, with a smile that belied her bereavement.

"It would be my pleasure to serve you in whatever way you might desire," I replied.

And more I saieth not.

Except one thing. Sometime during the night, while I was but half sleeping and half awake, I felt Sarah stir and rise, and heard the back door close gently. Thinking she had but gone to the privy, I lapsed back into contented sleep. When I next awoke, it was to the faint glimmering of golden light in the bedroom window, and a cascade of gold coins tinkling down on me, and Sarah standing above me, a naked goddess of wealth, pouring gold from a velvet bag, like manna from heaven.

"Great God in heaven--what is it?" I exclaimed.

"Gold," she answered. "My husband charged me to keep it for you."

As I picked up the pieces of eight and let them fall through my fingers, I saw Captain Kidd's mischievous grin and remembered what he'd said when I promised to look after Sarah. I wasn't sure at the time, but now I knew what he meant when he said, "I c'n promise ye, ye won't be sorry." To have Sarah and a fortune too…! Rest easy, Captain, it isn't too much a burden on me.

Two years later, in the fall of 1703, I was married. It was several months before I found Rebecca, living in a shack beside Beekman's swamp, sick with the pox. I moved her out into the countryside, to a hospice in Greenwich Village, hoping the fresh air might revive her. But the pox had too tight a grip on her and she died within a year. Yet, knowing her son was alive, and seeing him every week until she died, she told me it was the happiest time of her life. And sadly, it was.

John lost his mother and gained another just a few days later, when Sarah and I were married in the church her husband had helped build. John and the girls sat in Captain Kidd's pew while we exchanged vows in the company of our relieved friends and neighbors, who'd long been uneasy over the relationship of the widow Kidd and her resident servant.

After Sarah's third child was born, we decided we wanted to get out of New York (which was coming to resemble London more and more each year) and so we moved to New Jersey. Some would find it boring, but after my adventures with Captain Kidd, I am content in Jersey.

It would seem that my story has come to a happy end, despite a great deal of unhappiness along the way, and a great many tragic endings for others less fortunate than myself. But that's the way life is, isn't it? For a while we imagine ourselves the captain of our destiny, like Captain Kidd sailing down the Thames, until somebody claps his bare ass and you find yourself in the brig. If I've learned nothing else from my adventures, I've learned the value of humility. We are all, despite our illusions of grandeur, just crawling through life like millions of unimportant little bugs. Some, like Kidd, mistakenly believe the rich and powerful can aid them on their journey, when in truth we can only hope we're someplace else when God puts His foot down. I was lucky. I hope you are too.

And more I saieth not.

THE END

Made in United States
Orlando, FL
13 January 2023

28642954R10195